ACCEPTABLE LOSS

ANNE PERRY

ACCEPTABLE LOSS

A William Monk Novel

BALLANTINE BOOKS • NEW YORK

Published in the United States by Ballantine Books, an imprint of The Random House Publishing Group, a division of Random House, Inc., New York.

BALLANTINE and colophon are registered trademarks of Random House, Inc.

ISBN 978-0-345-51060-0

Printed in the United States of America

Book design by Karin Batten

To Lora Fountain

ACCEPTABLE LOSS

HESTER WAS HALF-ASLEEP when she heard the slight sound, as if someone were taking in a sharp breath and then letting out a soft, desperate gasp. Monk was motionless beside her, his hand loose on the pillow, his hair falling over his face.

It was not the first time in the last two weeks that Hester had heard Scuff crying in the night. It was a delicate relationship she had with the boy she and Monk had befriended. He had lived on the streets by the river and had largely provided for himself, which had made him wise beyond his age, and fiercely independent. He considered he was looking after Monk, who in Scuff's opinion lacked the knowledge and the fierce survival instincts required for his job as head of the Thames River Police at Wapping, in the heart of the London docks.

Until last month Scuff had come and gone as he'd pleased, spending only the occasional night at Monk's house in Paradise Place. However, since his kidnapping, and the atrocity on the boat at Execution Dock, he had come to live with them, going out only for short periods during the day, and tossing and turning at night, plagued by nightmares. He would not talk about them, and his pride would not let him admit to Hester that he was frightened of the dark, of closed doors, and, above all, of sleep.

Of course she knew why. Once the tight control he kept over himself in his waking hours slipped from him, he was back on the boat again, curled up on his side beneath the trapdoor to the bilges, nailed in with the half-rotted corpse of the missing boy, fighting the swirling water and the rats, the stench of it making him gag.

In his nightmares it did not seem to matter that he was now free, or that Jericho Phillips was dead; Scuff had seen the man's body himself, imprisoned in the iron cage in the river, his mouth gaping open as the rising tide trapped him, choking off his voice forever.

Hester heard the gasping sound again, and slipped out of bed. She pulled on a wrap, not so much for warmth in the late September night, but for modesty so as not to embarrass Scuff if he was awake. She crept across the room and along the passage. His bedroom door was open just wide enough for him to pass through. The gas lamp was on low, maintaining the fiction that she had forgotten and left it on, as she did every night. Neither of them ever mentioned this.

Scuff was lying tangled in the sheets, the blankets slipped halfway to the floor. He was curled up in just the same position as they had found him in when she and the rat-catcher, Sutton, had pried open the trapdoor.

Without debating with herself anymore, Hester went into the room and picked up the blankets, placing them over him and tucking them in lightly. Then she stood watching him. He whimpered again, and pulled at the sheet as if he were cold. She could see in the faint glow of the gaslight that he was still dreaming. His face was tight, eyes closed hard, jaw so clenched he must have been grinding his teeth. Every now and again his body moved, his hands coming up as if to reach for something.

How could she wake him without robbing him of his pride? He would never forgive her for treating him like a child. And yet his cheeks were smooth, his neck so slender and his shoulders so narrow that there was nothing of the man in him yet. He said he was eleven, but he looked about nine.

What lie would he not see through? She could not waken him without tacitly admitting that she had heard him crying in his dream. She turned and walked back to the door and went a little way along the passage. Then a better idea came to her. She tiptoed downstairs to the kitchen and poured a glass of milk. Then she took four cookies and put them on a plate. She went back upstairs, careful not to trip over her nightgown. Just before she reached his room, she deliberately banged the door of the linen cupboard. She knew it might waken Monk as well, but that could not be helped.

When she reached Scuff's room, he was lying in bed with the blankets up to his chin, fingers gripping them, eyes wide open.

"You awake too?" she said, as if mildly surprised. "So am I. I've got some milk and cookies. Would you like half?" She held up the plate.

He nodded. He could see there was only one glass, but the milk did not matter. It was the chance to be awake and not alone that he wanted.

She came in, leaving the door ajar, and sat on the edge of the bed. She put the glass on the table beside him and the plate on the blankets.

He picked up a biscuit and nibbled it, watching her. His eyes were wide and dark in the low lamplight, waiting for her to say something.

"I don't like being awake at this time of the night," she said, biting her lip a little. "I'm not really hungry; it just feels nice to eat something. Have the milk if you want it."

"I'll take 'alf," he said. Food was precious; he was always fair about it.

She smiled. "Good enough," she agreed, picking up a biscuit herself so he would feel comfortable eating.

He reached for the glass, holding it with both hands. He drank some, then looked at it to measure his share, drank a little more, then handed it to her. He sat very upright in the bed, his hair tousled and a rim of white on his upper lip.

She wanted to hold him, but she knew better. He might have wanted it too, but he would never have allowed such an admission. It would mean he was dependent, and he could not afford that. He had lived in the docks, scavenging for pieces of coal off the barges, brass screws, and other small valuable objects that had fallen off boats into the Thames mud. The low tide allowed boys like him—mudlarks—to survive. He had a mother somewhere, but perhaps she had too many younger children, and neither the time nor room to care for him. Or maybe she had a new husband who did not want another man's son in the house. Boys like himself had been his friends, sharing food, warmth, and one another's pain, comrades in survival.

"Have another biscuit," Hester offered.

"I've 'ad two," he pointed out. "That was 'alf."

"Yes, I know. I took more than I wanted," she replied. "I thought I was hungry, but now I'm just awake."

He looked at her carefully, deciding if she meant it, then took the last biscuit and ate it in three mouthfuls.

She smiled at him, and after a moment he smiled back.

"Are you sleepy?" she asked.

"No . . ."

"Nor am I." She hitched herself up a little so she could sit on the bed with her head against the headboard beside him, but still keeping a distance away. "Sometimes when I'm awake I read, but I haven't got a good book at the moment. The newspaper's full of all sorts of things I don't really want to know."

"Like wot?" he asked, twisting round so he was facing her a little more, settling in for a conversation.

She listed off a few social events she remembered, adding where they had been held and who had attended. Neither of them cared, but it was something to say. Presently she wandered off the subject and remembered past events, describing clothes and food, then behavior, wit, flirting, disasters, anything to keep him entertained. She even recalled the chaotic remembrance service where her friend Rose had been hopelessly and unintentionally drunk; she had climbed onto the stage and seized the violin from the very earnest young lady who had been playing it, and had then given her own rendition of several current music hall songs, growing bawdier with each.

Scuff giggled, trying to picture it in his mind. "Were it terrible?" he asked.

"Ghastly," Hester affirmed with relish. "She told them all the truth of what a fearful person the dead man had been, and why they had really come. It was awful then, but I laugh every time I think of it now."

"She were yer friend." He said the word slowly, tasting its value.

"Yes," she agreed.

"D'yer 'elp 'er?"

"As much as I could."

"Fig were my friend," he said very quietly. "I din't 'elp 'im. Nor the other neither."

"I know." She felt the lump, hard and painful, in her throat. Fig was one of the boys Jericho Phillips had murdered. "I'm sorry," she whispered.

"Yer can't 'elp it," he said reasonably. "Yer did yer best. No one can stop it." He moved an inch or two closer to her. "Tell me some more about Rose and the others."

She had seen survivor's guilt before. In her nursing in the Crimea she had heard soldiers cry out from the same nightmares and had seen them waken with the same shocked and helpless eyes, staring at the comfort around them, and feeling the horror inside.

She tried to think of something else to say to Scuff, happy things, anything to take away his memory of his own lost friends, adding a little more until she looked at him and saw his eyes closing. She lowered her voice, and then lowered it even more. He was so close to her now that he was touching her. She could feel the warmth of him through the sheet that separated them. A few minutes later he was asleep. Without being aware of it he had put his head against her shoulder. She stopped talking and lay still. It was a little cramped, but she did not move until morning, when she pretended to have been asleep also.

After a breakfast of hot porridge, toast, and marmalade, Monk sent Scuff out on an errand and turned to Hester.

"Nightmares again?" he asked.

"Sorry," she apologized. "I knew I'd probably waken you, but I couldn't leave him alone. I banged the door so—"

"You don't need to explain." He cut across her. The ghost of a smile softened the angular planes of his face for a moment, and then it was gone again. He looked grim, full of a pain he did not know how to deal with.

She knew he was remembering the terrible night on the river when Jericho Phillips had kidnapped Scuff to prevent Monk from completing the case against him, for which he would have assuredly hanged. Phillips had so very nearly succeeded. Had it not been for Sutton's little dog, Snoot, they would never have found the boy.

"He's still afraid," she said quietly. "He knows Phillips is dead—he saw the drowned body in the cage—but there are other people doing the same thing, other boats on the river that use boys for pornography and prostitution—boys just like him, his friends. People we can't help. I don't know what to say to him, because he's far too clever to believe comforting lies. And I don't want to lie to him anyway. Then he'd never trust me in anything. I wish he didn't care about them so much, and yet I'd hate it if he could feel safe only by never looking back. He thinks we can't help." She blinked hard. "William, parents ought to be able to help. That's part of what they are for. He sees us not even trying, just accepting defeat. He doesn't even understand why he feels so guilty, and thinks he's betraying them by being all right. He won't believe that we don't secretly think the same of him, whatever we say."

"I know." He took a deep breath and let it out slowly. "And that isn't the only problem."

She waited, her heart pounding. They had avoided saying it; all their time and emotion was concentrated on Scuff. But she had known it would have to come. Now she looked at the lines of strain in Monk's face, the shadows around his eyes, the lean, high cheekbones. There was a vulnerability there that only she understood.

She thought of Oliver Rathbone, who had been both Monk's friend and hers for so long, and beside whom they had fought desperate battles for justice, often at the risk of their reputations, even their lives. They had sat up for endless nights searching for answers, had faced victory and disaster together, horrors of grief, pity, and disillusion. Rathbone had once loved Hester, but she had chosen Monk. Then he had married Margaret Ballinger and found a happiness far better suited to his nature. Margaret could give him children, but more obvious than that, she was socially his equal. She was of a calmer, more judicious nature than Hester; she knew how to behave as Lady Rathbone, wife of the most gifted barrister in London, should.

Was it really conceivable that Margaret's father had been the power and the money behind Jericho Phillips's abominations? That is what Lord Justice Sullivan had claimed, right before his terrible suicide at Execution Dock. Hester longed for Monk to tell her that it was not true.

"You heard what Rathbone said about Arthur Ballinger and Phillips?" Monk said.

"Yes. Has he said anything more?"

"No. I suppose there's nothing legal, or he would have. He'd have no choice."

"You mean there's no proof, just Sullivan's word—and he's dead anyway?"

"Yes."

"But you believe it?" That also was not really a question.

"Of course I do," he said very softly. "Rathbone believes it, and do you think he would if there were any way in heaven or hell that he could avoid it?"

Monk lifted up his hand and touched Hester's cheek so softly, she felt the warmth of him more than the brush of his skin against hers.

"I have to know if Ballinger was involved, for Scuff, so at least he knows I'm trying," he continued. "And Rathbone has to know too, however much he would prefer not to."

"Are you going to speak to him?"

"I've been avoiding it, and so has he. He's been in court on another case for the last two weeks, but it's finished now and I can't put it off any longer."

"Are you sure he needs to know?" she pressed. "The pain of it would be intolerable, and he would have no choice but to do something about it."

"That's not like you," he said ruefully.

"To want to avoid someone else's pain?" She was momentarily indignant.

"To be evasive," he corrected her. "You are too good a nurse to want to put a bandage on something that you know needs surgery. If it's gangrene, you must take off the arm, or the patient will die. You taught me that."

"Am I being a coward?" She winced as she said the word. She knew that to a soldier, "coward" was the worst word in any language, worse even than "cheat" or "thief."

Monk leaned forward and kissed her, lingering only a moment. "You don't need courage if you aren't afraid," he answered. "It takes a little while to be certain you have no alternative. Scuff needs to know that we care enough for the truth itself, not just to rescue him and then turn away. I think Rathbone would want that too, whatever the cost."

"Whatever?" she questioned.

He hesitated. "Maybe not at any cost, but that doesn't change the reality of it."

HESTER WENT TO THE clinic that she had set up to treat and care for prostitutes and other street women who were sick or injured. It survived on charitable donations, and Margaret Rathbone was by far the most dedicated and the most able among those who sought and obtained such money. Margaret also spent a certain amount of time actually working there, cooking, cleaning, and practicing the little light nursing that she had learned from Hester. Of course she had done rather less of such work since her marriage, and no longer did nights. Still, Hester did not look forward to seeing her today and hoped it would be one of those times when Margaret was otherwise engaged.

She walked from Paradise Place down the hill to the ferry. The autumn wind was blustery, salt-smelling. From Wapping she took an omnibus westward toward Holborn. It was a long journey, but it was necessary that they live near Monk's work. His was a reasonably new position, back in the police again after years of being a private agent of inquiry, when he'd lurched from one case to another with no certainty of payment. For less than a year he had been head of the River Police in this area, which was a profoundly responsible position. There was no one in England with better skills in detection, or more courage and dedication—and, some might say, ruthlessness. But his art in managing men and placating his superiors in the political hierarchy was altogether another matter.

If the circumstances caused Hester a little more traveling, it was a small enough contribution to his success. Added to which, she really did like the house in Paradise Place, with its view over the infinitely changing water, not to mention the freedom from financial anxiety that a regular income gave them.

She walked briskly along Portpool Lane under the shadow of the Reid Brewery, and in at the door of the house that had once been part of a huge brothel. It was Oliver Rathbone who had helped her obtain the building, quite legally, but with considerable coercion of its previous owner, Squeaky Robinson. Squeaky had remained here, a partially reformed character. To begin with he had stayed because he had had nowhere else to go, but now he took a certain pride in the place, oozing self-righteousness at his newfound respectability.

Squeaky was in the entrance as she came in, his face gaunt, his stringy gray-white hair down to his collar as usual. He was wearing an ancient frock coat and today had on a faded silk cravat.

"We need more money," he said as soon as Hester was through the door. "I dunno how you expect me to do all these things on sixpence ha'penny!"

"You had fifty pounds just a week ago," she replied. She was so used to Squeaky's complaints that she would have worried if he had said that all was well.

"Mrs. Margaret says we're going to need new pans in the kitchen soon," he retaliated. "Lots of 'em. Big ones. Sometimes I think we're feeding half London."

"Lady Rathbone," Hester corrected him automatically. "And pans do wear out, Squeaky. They get to the point where they can't be mended anymore."

"Then, you tell her ladyship to come up with some money for 'em," he said waspishly.

"What happened to the fifty pounds?"

"Sheets and medicines," he replied instantly. "You can tell her now. She's through there." He jerked his head sideways, indicating the door to his left.

There was no point in putting it off. Not only would it look like cowardice, it would feel like it. As if obedient to his instruction, she went through into the next room.

Margaret Rathbone was standing near the central table with a pale blue notepad in her hand, and a pencil poised. She looked up as Hester came in. There was a moment's total silence between them, as if neither had expected to see the other, and yet both of them must have been preparing for this inevitable meeting. It was the first since Lord Justice Sullivan's suicide, and the accusations he had then made against Margaret's father—that he was the force behind the pornography—and the blackmail that had finally ruined the judge. There was no proof, just unforgettable words, and drowned bodies. Margaret would never admit the possibility, but Hester could not deny it. It left them no bridge to each other.

Margaret was not a beautiful woman, but her features were regular and her bearing unusually graceful. She had a dignity without arrogance—an unusual gift. Now she put the notepad down and looked unblinkingly at Hester. Her expression was guarded, as yet without warmth.

"I have the new sheets," she remarked. "Two dozen of them. They will more than make up for those we have to get rid of."

"The old ones will be good to tear up for bandages," Hester replied, walking farther into the room. "Thank you."

Margaret looked a little surprised, as if thanking her were inappropriate. "It was not my money," she observed.

"We would not have it if you had not persuaded someone to donate it," Hester pointed out. She made herself smile. "But as always, Squeaky is now complaining that the old pans cannot be mended anymore and we need new ones."

"Do we?"

Hester relaxed a little. "We will do. All I said was that we should start saving for them. I swear he wouldn't be happy if he didn't have something to be miserable about."

There was a polite tap on the door. Hester answered it, and Claudine Burroughs came in. She was a broad-hipped middle-aged woman with a face that had once been handsome, but time and unhappiness had taken away her bloom. She had discovered both her independence of spirit and a considerable purpose in life when she had volunteered to help in the clinic, mostly to irritate her unimaginative husband. She had defied his orders to cease her association with such a place, with more courage than she had known she possessed.

"Good morning, Mrs. Monk," she said cheerfully. "Morning, Lady Rathbone." Without waiting for a reply she launched into an account of the new patients who had been admitted since yesterday evening, and the progress of the more serious cases that had been there for some time. There were the usual fevers, stab wounds, a dislocated shoulder, sores, and infestations. The only thing less ordinary was an abscess, which Claudine reported triumphantly she had lanced, and which was now clean and should heal.

Margaret winced at the thought of the pain, not to mention the mess.

Hester applauded Claudine's medical confidence. They moved on to other housekeeping matters. Then they went to see the more serious cases, speaking only of business, and the morning passed quickly.

When Hester came downstairs to the entrance hall again, she found Oliver Rathbone waiting. She was startled to see him, off guard because she had been trying not to imagine what Monk would have said to him about Ballinger. Now a glance at Rathbone's face—sensitive, intelligent, faintly quizzical—and she knew that Monk had not spoken to him yet. She felt guilty, as if in knowing what was to come and not saying it, she were somehow deceiving him.

"Good morning, Oliver," she said with a slight smile. "If you are looking for Margaret, she is in the medicine room."

He raised his eyebrows. "Are you in a hurry?"

She could have kicked herself for dismissing him so quickly. She had not only been discourteous, she had made her unease obvious. Would apologizing make it worse?

"Are you all right, Hester?" he asked, taking a step toward her. "What about Scuff? How is he?"

Rathbone had been with them when they had searched so frantically for Scuff. He knew exactly how she'd felt. The horror of that day had touched him as nothing else had ever done in his life of prosecuting or defending some of the worst crimes in London. She saw the memory of it in his eyes now, and the gentleness. Stupidly the tears prickled in her own, and her throat was tight with the fear of what might come for him, if Sullivan had been telling the truth. She turned away so he could not read her face.

"He still has awful nightmares," she replied a little huskily. "I'm afraid it's going to take . . ." She hesitated. "Time."

"What will it take for him ever to be over it?" he asked.

"I don't know. Thinking it's over for his friends, other boys like him. Not lies."

He smiled very slightly. "He'd never believe you anyway, Hester. You're a terrible liar. Totally transparent."

She met his eyes with a flash of wit. "Or else I'm so good that you've never caught me?"

For an instant his face was blank with surprise, and then he laughed.

At that moment Margaret came in. Hester turned toward her and was struck with a sudden, quite unnecessary stab of guilt. She was relieved when Rathbone stepped around her, his face lighting with pleasure.

"Margaret! My big case is over. Have you time to join me for luncheon?"

"I'd be delighted," she replied without looking at Hester. "Especially if you can help me think of anyone further whom I can ask for money. We have new sheets, but soon we shall need pots and pans." She did not add that she was the only one raising funds, but it hung, unspoken, in the air.

Hester felt ashamed for her own failure to raise money, but Margaret's marriage to Rathbone gave her a position in society that Hester would never have. That fact was too obvious for either of them to need to say it. It was also unnecessary to add that Margaret's courtesy and natural good manners yielded far more reward than Hester's outspoken candor. People liked to feel that they were doing their Christian duty toward the less fortunate, but definitely not that they owed it in any way. And they certainly did not wish to hear the details of poverty or disease.

"Thank you," Hester said mildly, although it cost her an effort. "It would certainly be a great help."

Margaret smiled and took Rathbone's arm.

By THE MIDDLE OF the afternoon Hester had had little more for luncheon than a cold cheese sandwich and a cup of tea. She was helping one of the women finish the scrubbing when Rupert Cardew arrived. She was on her knees on the floor, a brush in her hand, a pail of soapy water beside her. She heard the footsteps and then saw the polished boots stop about a yard in front of her.

She sat back and looked up slowly. He was at least as tall as Monk, but fair where Monk was dark, and, on his recent visits to the clinic to add to their funding, so relaxed as to be casual. Monk, on the other hand, was always intensely alive, waiting to move.

"Sorry," Rupert apologized with a smile. "Didn't mean to catch you on your knees. But if you were praying for more money, then I'm here with the answer."

Hester climbed to her feet, declining his outstretched hand to assist her. Her plain blue skirt was wet where she had kneeled; and her white blouse, unadorned with lace, was rolled up above her elbows, and also wet in places. Her hair—not always her best feature—had been pinned back and adjusted several times as it had escaped, and was now completely shapeless.

"Good afternoon, Mr. Cardew." She could not call him "sir"—and she did not think he wished it—although she was perfectly aware of his father's title. Should she apologize for looking like a servant? Their friendship was recent, but she had liked him immediately, in spite of being aware that his beneficence toward the clinic sprang at least in part from a professional familiarity with some of its patients. His father, Lord Cardew, had sufficient wealth and position to make work unnecessary for his only surviving son. Rupert wasted his time, means, and talents with both charm and generosity, although lately he had lost some of his usual ease.

"I wasn't praying," she added, looking ruefully at her wet, rather red hands. "Perhaps I should have had more faith. Thank you." She took the considerable amount of money he held out. She did not count it, but there was clearly several hundred pounds in the bundle of Treasury notes he put in her hand.

"Debts of pleasure," he said with a wide smile. "Do you really have to do that yourself?" He eyed the floor and the bucket.

"Actually, it's quite satisfying," she told him. "Especially if you're in a temper. You can attack it, and then see the difference you have made."

"Next time I am in a temper, perhaps I'll try it," he promised with a smile. "You were an army nurse, weren't you?" he observed. "They should have set you at the enemy. You'd have frightened the wits out of them." He said it good-naturedly, as if in approval. "Would you like a cup of tea? I should have brought some cake."

"Bread and jam?" she offered. She could enjoy a few minutes' break and the light, superficial conversation with him. He reminded her of the young cavalry officers she had known in the Crimea: charming, funny, seemingly careless on the surface, and yet underneath it trying desperately not to think of tomorrow, or yesterday, and the friends they had lost, and would yet lose. However, as far as she knew, Rupert had no war to fight, no battle worth winning or losing.

"What kind of jam?" he asked, as if it mattered.

"Black currant," she replied. "Or possibly raspberry."

"Right." To her surprise he bent and picked up the bucket, carrying it away from himself a little so it did not soil his perfect trousers or splash his boots.

She was startled. She had never before seen him even acknowledge the necessity, never mind stoop to so lowly a task. She wondered what had made him think of it today. Certainly not any vulnerability in her. It had made no difference before.

He put the pail down at the scullery door. Emptying it could wait for someone else.

In the kitchen Hester pushed the kettle over onto the cooktop and started to cut bread. She offered to toast it, and then passed the fork over to him to hold in front of the open door of the stove.

They spoke easily of the clinic and some of the cases that had come in. Rupert had a quick compassion for the street women's pain, in spite of being one of those very willing to use their services.

With tea, toast, and jam on the table, conversation moved to other subjects with which there was no tension, no glaring contrasts: social gossip, places they had visited, exhibitions of art. He was interested in everything, and he listened as graciously as he spoke. Sometimes she forgot the great kitchen around her, the pots and pans, the stove, and in the next room the copper for boiling linen, and the laundry tubs, the scullery sinks, the racks of vegetables. She could have been at home as a young woman, fifteen years ago, before the war, before experience, passion, grief, or real happiness. There had been a kind of innocence to her life then; everything had been possible. Her parents had still been alive, and also her younger brother, who had been killed in the Crimea. The memories were both sweet and painful.

Deliberately she steered the subject back to the clinic. "We're very grateful for your gift. I had asked Lady Rathbone to see if she could raise some more money, but it is always difficult. We keep on asking, because there is so much needed all the time, but people do get tired of us." She smiled a trifle ruefully.

"Lady Rathbone. Is she the wife of Sir Oliver?" he asked with apparent interest, although it might merely have been the feigning required by good manners.

"Yes. Do you know them?"

"Only by repute." The idea seemed to amuse him. "Our paths don't cross, except perhaps at the theater, and I dare say he goes for reasons of business, and she, to be seen. I go because I enjoy it."

"Isn't that why you do most things?" she replied, and then wished she had not. It was too perceptive, too sharp.

He winced, but appeared unoffended. "You are about the only truly virtuous woman that I actually like," he said, as if surprised at it himself. "You haven't ever tried to redeem me, thank God."

"Good heavens!" She opened her eyes wide. "How remiss of me! Should I have, at least for appearances' sake?"

"If you told me you cared about appearances, I should not believe you," he answered, trying to be serious, and failing. "Although for some, there is nothing else." He was suddenly tense, muscles pulling in his neck. "Wasn't it Sir Oliver who defended Jericho Phillips and got him off?"

Hester felt a moment of chill, simply to be reminded of it. "Yes," she said with as little expression as she could.

"Don't look like that," he said gently. "The miserable devil got his just deserts in the end. He drowned—slowly—feeling the water creep up his body inch by inch as the tide came in. And he was terrified of drowning, phobic about it. Much worse for him than being hanged, which is supposed to be all over in a matter of seconds, so they say."

She stared at him, her mind racing.

He blushed, his fair skin coloring easily. "I'm sorry. I'm sure that's more detail than you wanted to know. I shouldn't have said that. Sometimes I speak too frankly to you. I apologize."

It was not the detail that had sent the icy chill creeping through her, for she knew all too well how Jericho Phillips had died. She had seen his dead face. It was the fact that Rupert Cardew knew of Phillips's terror of water. That meant that he had known Phillips himself. Why should that surprise her? Rupert had made no secret of the fact that he knew prostitutes and was prepared to pay for his pleasure. Perhaps that was more honest than seducing women and then leaving them, possibly with child. But Jericho Phillips had been a different matter—a blackmailer, a pornographer of children, of little boys as young as six or seven years.

Perhaps Rupert had known Phillips only casually, without realizing that he did? Was that one of the many scrapes from which Rupert's father had bailed him out? It should not surprise her. How easy it is when you like someone to be blind to the possibilities of ugliness in them, of weaknesses too deep to be passed over with tolerance.

What horror might be ahead for Margaret, if Sullivan had been telling the truth about Arthur Ballinger, and one day Margaret was forced to realize it? Margaret's loyalties would be torn apart, the whole fabric of love and belief threatened. Margaret was loyal to her father; of course she was, as Rupert was to his. And perhaps he had even more cause. His father had protected him, right or wrong. The cost to Lord Cardew must have been far more than money, and yet he had never failed.

Love does forgive, but can it forgive everything? Should it? Which loyalties came first—family, or belief in right and wrong?

What about her own father? That pain twisted deep into places she dared not look. Her father had died alone in England, betrayed and ashamed, while she had been out in the Crimea caring for strangers, ignorant to his plight. What loyalty was that?

"Hester?" Rupert's voice broke through her thoughts.

She looked up. She was glad that Rupert was just a friend, someone she was deeply grateful to but not tied to by blood, or love.

"You're right," she agreed. "It sounds as if fate were harsher to Phillips than the law would have been."

MONK WENT TO OLIVER Rathbone's office in the city late in the morning, and was informed courteously by his clerk that Sir Oliver had gone to luncheon. Monk duly returned at half past two, and was still obliged to wait. It might have been simpler to catch Rathbone with time to spare at his home in the evening, but Monk needed to speak with him when Margaret was not present.

At quarter to three Rathbone came back, entering with a smile on his face and the easy elegant manner he usually had when the taste of victory was still fresh on his tongue.

"Hello, Monk," he said with surprise. "Got another case for me already?" He came in and closed the door quietly. His pale gray suit was perfectly cut and fitted to his slender figure. The sunlight shone in through the long windows, catching the smoothness of his fair hair and the touches of gray at the temples.

"I hope I don't," Monk answered. "But I can't let this go by default."

"What are you talking about?" Rathbone sat down and crossed his legs. He appeared reasonably comfortable, even if in fact he was not. "You look as if you have just opened someone's bedroom door by mistake."

"I may have," Monk said wryly. The reference was meant only as an illustration, but it was too close to the truth.

Rathbone regarded him levelly, his face serious now. "It's not like you to be oblique. How bad is it?"

Monk hated what he had to say. Even now he was wondering if there were some last, desperate way to avoid it. "That night on Phillips's ship, after we found Scuff, and the rest of the boys, you told me that Margaret's father was behind it—"

"I told you that Sullivan said so. He told me while you were occupied with Phillips." Rathbone cut across him quickly. "Sullivan had no proof, and he's dead by his own hand now. Whatever he knew, or believed, is gone with him."

"The proof may be dead"—Monk did not move his eyes from Rathbone's—"but the question isn't. Someone is behind it. Phillips hadn't the money or the connections in society to run the boat and find the clients who were vulnerable, let alone blackmail them afterward."

"Could it have been Sullivan himself?" Rathbone suggested, and then looked away. Monk did not bother to answer—they both knew Sullivan had not had the nerve nor the intelligence it would have required. He'd been a man ruined by his appetite, and eventually killed by it. In the end, he'd been one more victim.

Rathbone looked up again. "All right, not Sullivan. But he could have implicated anyone, as long as it wasn't himself. There's nothing to act on, Monk. The man was desperate and pathetic. Now he's very horribly dead, and he took Phillips with him, which no man more richly deserved. There's nothing more I can do, or would. The boat has been broken up, the boys are free. Let the other victims nurse their wounds in peace." His face tightened in revulsion too deep to hide. "Pornography is cruel and obscene, but there's no way to prevent men looking at whatever they wish to, in their own homes. If you want a crusade, there are more fruitful causes."

"I want to stop Scuff's unhappiness," Monk replied. "And to do that I have to stop it from happening to other boys, the friends he's left behind."

"I'll help you—but within the law."

Monk rose to his feet. "I want whoever's behind it."

"Give me evidence, and I'll prosecute," Rathbone promised. "But I'm not indulging in a witch hunt. Don't you . . . or you'll regret it. Witch hunts get out of hand, and innocent people suffer. Leave it, Monk."

Monk said nothing. He shook Rathbone's hand and left.

CHAPTER

2

It was early morning, and Corney Reach was deserted. The heavy mist lent the river an eerie quality, as if the smooth, sullen face of it could have stretched to the horizon. It touched the skin and filled the nose with its clinging odor.

Here on this southern bank, the trees overhung the water, sometimes dipping so low they all but touched its surface. Within fifty yards they were shrouded, indistinct; a hundred yards, and they were no more than vague shapes, suggestions of outlines against the haze. The silence consumed everything except for the occasional whisper of the incoming tide over the stones, or through the tangled weeds close under the bank.

The corpse was motionless, facedown. Its coat and hair floated, wide, making it look bigger than it was. But even partly submerged, the blow to the back of the skull was visible. The current bumped the body gently against Monk's legs. He moved his weight slightly to avoid sinking in the mud.

"Want me to turn 'im over, sir?" Constable Coburn asked help-fully.

Monk shivered. The cold was inside him, not in the damp early autumn air. He hated looking at dead faces, even though this man might have been the victim of an accident. If it was an accident, he would resent having been called all the way up here, beyond the west-ern outskirts of the city. It would have been a waste of his time, and that of Orme, his sergeant, who was standing five or six yards away, also up to his knees in the river.

"Yes, please," Monk answered.

"Right, sir." Constable Coburn obediently leaned forward, ignor-ing the water soaking his uniform sleeves, and hauled the corpse over until it was floating on its back.

"Thank you," Monk acknowledged.

Orme moved closer, stirring up mud. He looked at Monk, then down at the body.

Monk studied the dead man's face. He seemed to be in his early thirties. He could not have been in the river long, because his features were barely distorted. There was just a slight bloating in the softer flesh, no damage from fish or other scavengers. His nose was sharp, a little bony, his mouth thin-lipped and wide, and his eyebrows pale. There seemed little color in his hair, but it would be easier to tell when it was dry.

Monk put out his hand and lifted one eyelid. The iris was blue, and the white was speckled with blood. He let it close again. "Any idea who he is?" he asked.

"Yes, sir." Coburn's face was shadowed with distaste. " 'E's Mickey Parfitt, sir, small-time piece o' dirt around 'ere. Inter fencin', pimpin', generally makin' a profit out of other folks' misery."

"You're certain?"

"No mistake, sir. See 'is right arm?"

Monk noticed nothing, but the jacket covered the man's right arm to the base of his fingers. Then he glanced at the left arm, and realized the right was at least three inches shorter. Monk gripped the arm and felt the wasted muscle. The left one was thin, but hard. In life it would have been strong, perhaps making up for the withered one.

"Who found him?" he asked.

" 'Orrie Jones, but 'e's only 'alf there," Coburn replied, tipping his head. "It were Tosh as called us. 'E worked fer Parfitt 'ere an' there. As much as 'e worked at all, that is. Nasty piece o' work, Tosh."

"Not a tosher?" Monk asked curiously, referring to the men who worked stretches of the sewers, fishing for valuables that had been washed down. They found all sorts of things, jewelry in particular. Given the right area, there were rich pickings to be had.

"Was, once, so 'e says," Coburn replied. "Got tired of it. Or maybe 'e lost 'is patch."

"What was 'Orrie Jones doing down by the riverbank so early?"

"That's a good question." Coburn pulled his mouth tight in an expression of disgust. " 'E says as 'e were takin' a breath of air before startin' 'is day's work."

"Do you think he killed Parfitt?" Monk said doubtfully.

"No. 'E's daft, but 'e's 'armless. But I reckon as 'e could a bin lookin' fer 'im."

"Any idea why? And why would he expect to find Parfitt down by the riverbank at five or six in the morning?"

Coburn bit his lip. "Good question, sir. 'Orrie did odd jobs fer Mickey, rowed 'im about, like, fetched an' carried fer 'im, ran errands. 'E must 'ave 'ad a good idea 'e was 'ere."

"A good idea that he was dead?" Monk suggested.

"Mebbe."

"And who killed him?"

Coburn shook his head. "Mebbe that too, but 'e wouldn't tell us."

"Then, we'd better find Mickey's friends, and enemies," Monk responded. "I suppose there's no hope it could be an accident?"

" 'Ope all you like, sir, but we don't often get so lucky that a piece o' vermin like Mickey 'as accidents."

Monk glanced up at Orme.

Orme frowned. He was a quiet, solid man, used to the river and to those who preyed on its business and its pleasures. "Wonder if the blow killed him, or if he drowned," he said thoughtfully. "An' what was he doing down here anyway? Was he alone? How far upstream did he go into the water?"

Monk was thinking of the blood in the dead man's eyes. The eyes did not look like those of someone who had drowned. He bent down and lifted one eyelid again, then the other. It was the same—stained with small hemorrhages. Carefully, using both hands, he pulled the jacket open and the collar of the wet shirt, exposing the thin neck.

Orme let out a sigh between his teeth.

"Oh, Gawd!" Coburn said hoarsely.

The throat was horribly swollen, but the thin line of a ligature was still unmistakable, biting deep into the flesh. Irregularly, every few inches, there were spreading bruises, as if whatever it was had knots in it that had further lacerated the flesh.

"There's no way that happened by accident," Monk said grimly. "I'm afraid we very definitely have a murder. Let's get him out of the water and ask the police surgeon to tell us what he can. And we'll speak to Mr. 'Orrie Jones, who so fortuitously found him. And Tosh. What's the rest of his name?" He looked at Coburn.

"Never heard it," Coburn said apologetically.

They waded ashore, Orme and Coburn dragging the body. Then the three of them lifted it awkwardly onto the bank, scrambling to keep a footing as the mud gave way beneath their feet. The last thing Monk wanted was to land spread-eagled in the water, soaked to the skin. It was bad enough that his shoes were sodden and his trouser legs were flapping coldly around his ankles.

They laid the body in the cart that Coburn had sent for, and then followed behind it in a grim troop across the fields to the roadway. Then they climbed up into it for the rest of the journey.

Monk was only slowly getting used to the tidal waters of the Thames, even this far upstream. Initially he had assumed that the body would have been carried down toward the sea, but just in time he prevented himself from saying so.

"How far do you think he was carried?" he asked Coburn. Ignorance of the local tide was acceptable. There were several factors involved: speed, currents, obstacles, as well as time.

"Depends where 'e went in," Coburn said, chewing his lip. He guided the horse to the right, down toward Chiswick. "Could a bin carried both ways, if nothing on the shore stopped 'im. 'Ard to tell."

"Many barges this far up?" Monk asked. He had seen only two all the time they had been there, and it was now midmorning.

"Not many," Coburn replied. "An' they usually stay as far out as they can. Nobody wants to get caught up on sandbanks, fallen logs, rubbish. Easier to find out what 'e were doin' in the water at all than try to reckon where 'e went in by where we found 'im."

The town was barely a mile away, and they arrived in clear sunshine. The streets were full of carts, drays, wagons of one sort or another, and the pavements were crowded with people. Several barges lay moored at the docks, loading and unloading.

The police surgeon had come from the city and took charge of what was left of Mickey Parfitt, promising a report in good time. He seemed to be waiting for a challenge, a demand for haste, but he did not get one. Monk already knew that Parfitt had been strangled and had taken a hard blow to the head first—there was no sense in hitting a man after he was dead. The weapon that had struck him could have been almost anything. What had strangled him was more interesting, but the shape of the bruises told him that. The surgeon would have to cut the ligature off to find out more.

"I want to see this Tosh," Monk said to Coburn as they left the morgue.

"Yes, sir. Thought yer would. Got 'im at the station. Unusually 'elpful, 'e is." Again the look of distaste twisted his mouth.

Monk made no reply but followed Coburn across the roadway and into the police station, where Tosh was sitting in the interview room, sipping a mug of tea and eating a large, sugary bun. He looked suitably sober, as befitted a man who had reported finding a corpse. However, Monk detected a certain sheen of satisfaction in his long face as he rose to his feet slowly, careful not to spill his tea.

"Morning, gentlemen," Tosh said in a remarkably well-modulated voice. He was a tall man, narrow-shouldered, with rather a long nose and decidedly frizzy hair, which stood out all over his head. "Sad business." He turned to Monk, recognizing authority immediately. "Tosh Wilkin. What can I do to 'elp you?"

Monk introduced himself.

"'Ow do yer do, Mr. Monk?" Tosh said soberly. "All the way up from Wapping, eh? You must take it all very serious."

"Murder is always serious, Mr. Wilkin."

"Murder, is it?" Tosh affected mild surprise. "'Ere was I 'oping 'e were just unfortunate, an' fell in by 'imself."

"Really? You didn't notice the ligature around his neck?"

Tosh affected innocence. "The what?"

"The knotted rope around his neck," Monk elaborated. He watched Tosh's eyes, his face, the long, scrupulously clean hands at his sides. Nothing gave him away.

"Can't say as I did," Tosh replied. "But, then, I didn't look more 'n to make sure 'Orrie wasn't 'avin' visions, like. Police business, either way. Don't do for ordinary folk to meddle. 'Don't touch' is my watchword. Just called Constable Coburn 'ere."

He hesitated, as if undecided about exactly how to go on. He looked only at Monk, avoiding the eyes of the other two. "Actually, Mr. Monk, to tell the truth, 'Orrie came to me early, about 'alf past six in the morning. I could 'ave brained 'im for waking me up. But 'e said 'e took Mickey out to 'is boat, about eleven o'clock or so, last night. Mickey told 'im to go back for 'im in about an hour. Well, when 'Orrie went, there were nobody there. No Mickey, no anyone. 'E said 'e 'ung around for a while, calling out, looking, but then 'e reckoned 'e must 'ave got it wrong, an' 'e went 'ome. But when Mickey wasn't there this morning, 'Orrie was scared something 'ad 'appened."

"At half past six?" Monk said with disbelief.

"That's it," Tosh agreed. "You see, I didn't believe 'im. I told 'im to get out an' leave me alone. Go back to bed like civilized folk, and don't be so stupid. An' off 'e went."

Monk waited impatiently.

"Then I got to worrying meself," Tosh continued, looking at Monk gravely. "So instead o' going back to sleep, I lay there for a while, then I got up and dressed, an' I was on me way down the path, just to check up, so to speak, when I saw 'Orrie come up at a run, all red-faced an' out o' breath."

Monk looked from Tosh to Constable Coburn, and back again.

"Where is this boat that 'Orrie took Mickey to last night?" he asked.

"Moves around," Coburn answered.

"Moored up between 'ere an' Barnes," Tosh said, and gestured upriver. "Which don't mean to say poor Mickey went into the river there. Tides can play funny games wi' things—floaters in particular."

"So 'Orrie took Parfitt to his boat shortly after eleven o'clock last night, and went to collect him an hour or so later, and he wasn't there?"

Tosh nodded his fuzzy head. "Yer got it. Given, o' course, that 'Orrie isn't always that exact with time."

"Is 'Orrie short for Horace?"

Tosh half hid a smile. " 'Orrible. When you've met 'im, you'll see why. 'E's not . . ." He tapped his forehead, and left the rest to Monk's imagination.

Monk remembered the corpse's withered arm. "I assume Mr. Parfitt was not able to row himself? Was this usually Mr. Jones's job?"

"Yes. 'E obeys well enough, but not much use for anything else."

"I see. And do you know for yourself that what he says is true, or do you just believe him?"

Tosh's eyes opened very wide with exaggerated surprise, sending a row of wrinkles up his forehead. "I believe 'im 'cos it makes sense, and 'e 'asn't the wit to lie. One of the benefits of employing idiots—they're not imaginative enough to tell a decent lie. And 'aven't the brains to remember it if they did."

Monk forbore from responding to that. "So after he had appealed to you, at about six-thirty in the morning," he continued, "you told him to go back to bed, but in fact 'Orrie actually continued to search for Mr. Parfitt along the riverbank?"

"Yes, that's right," Tosh confirmed.

"Remarkable that in so short a time he actually found him, don't you think?" Monk asked. "It's a big river, lots of weeds and obstructions, tides in and out, and traffic."

Tosh blinked. "'Adn't thought of it like that, but o' course you're right. Remarkable it is, sir."

"I think this would be a good time to meet this Mr. 'Orrible Jones," Monk observed.

"Oh, yes, sir." Tosh blinked and smiled, showing very white and curiously pointed teeth.

THEY FOUND 'ORRIE JONES sweeping the sawdust on the floor of a pub just off one of the alleys leading down to the riverfront. Coburn pointed him out, although there was no need. He was stout and of less than average height. He was an unusually ugly man. His brown hair grew at all angles from his head, rather like the spines of a hedgehog. His nose was broad, but it was his eyes that were his most unnerving feature.

"Mornin' 'Orrie," Coburn said cheerfully, stopping in front of him.

'Orrie grasped the broom handle, his knuckles white. One large, dark eye was fixed balefully on the constable; the other wandered toward the far corner. Monk had no idea whether 'Orrie could see him or not.

"Yer found 'oo done that ter Mickey?" 'Orrie demanded.

"Done what?" Monk inquired, wanting to know if 'Orrie was aware of the strangulation, before Coburn mentioned it.

"Pushed 'im in the water." 'Orrie shifted his gaze, or at least half of it.

"Could he swim?" Monk asked.

"Not with 'is 'ead stove in," 'Orrie replied. His face was so vacant, Monk was not sure if he felt anger, pity, or even disinterest. It set Monk at an unexpected disadvantage.

"It doesn't surprise you that he is dead?" Monk asked.

'Orrie's gaze wandered round the room. "Don't surprise me when nobody's dead," he replied.

Monk found himself irritated. It was a perfectly reasonable answer, and yet it sidestepped the real question. Was that intentional?

"How long did you look for him last night when you went back to the boat and discovered he had gone?" he persisted.

"Till I couldn't find 'im," 'Orrie said patiently. "Dunno 'ow long it were. In't no use looking after that."

Monk thought he saw 'Orrie smile, but decided to pretend he hadn't. "Were you late going back for him?" he said sharply.

This time it was 'Orrie who looked uncomfortable, shifting his weight awkwardly. "Yeah. I got 'eld up. Some fool wouldn't pay, an' we 'ad ter ask 'im a bit 'arder. Crumble'll tell yer."

Monk looked at Coburn.

"Crumble is one of Parfitt's pimps," Coburn replied.

'Orrie looked at him with disapproval. "Yer shouldn't say things like that, Mr. Coburn. Crumble just looks after things."

Coburn shrugged.

Monk did not pursue it. 'Orrie was probably telling the truth, and it was quite possible that none of them had a very clear idea of time. Monk would have to look further into the various sources of money to see whether 'Orrible Jones had any apparent motive either to kill Parfitt himself or to shield anyone else who had.

They questioned 'Orrie further, but he had nothing to add to the simple fact that he had rowed Mickey Parfitt out to his boat, which was moored upstream from the local island, Chiswick Eyot, shortly after eleven o'clock. He had waited until midnight to go back for him, and then had been delayed by trouble in one of the taverns, where a customer had refused to pay for several drinks. Monk had no doubt it was actually a brothel, but for the purpose of accounting for 'Orrie's time, it came to the same thing. When 'Orrie had rowed back just before one, Mickey Parfitt was nowhere to be seen. He said he had looked for him until he believed it was pointless, and then he had gone back home and gone to bed.

In the morning, when 'Orrie had called on Mickey and found he was still not around, he had been sufficiently concerned to go and waken Tosh. Tosh had told him to go back to bed, but instead 'Orrie had begun to search for Mickey. In little more than an hour, he had found the body.

Monk excused 'Orrie, for the time being, and went to find Crumble, who appeared to have no other name. He was in the cellar of the pub, moving kegs around with more ease than Monk would have expected from a man so small. He was less than five feet, with round eyes, and features so indistinct that they seemed about to blur into one another. His eyebrows were ragged, his nose shapeless—perhaps the bone had been broken too many times. He spoke with a soft, curiously high-pitched voice.

"Needed a little 'elp," he explained when they asked him about 'Orrie's delay in returning for Parfitt the previous night. "Weren't thinkin' o' the time. Can't let people get away without payin', or word'll get about, an' everyone'll be tryin' it. Mr. Parfitt's money."

Monk made a mental note to find out whose money it would be now, and perhaps also roughly how much of it there was. Constable Coburn would be well qualified to do that.

He went through the pattern of the evening once again, then thanked Crumble and left.

It was after six by the time Monk and Orme finally found themselves upstream toward Mortlake. They had borrowed a police boat and now rowed across from the north bank to the south. Finally they were approaching the large vessel moored close to the trees in a quiet, easily overlooked place, sheltered from the wake of passing barges and unseen from the road.

The north bank opposite was marshy and completely deserted—a place no one would be likely to wander. There were no paths in it, no place to tie a boat and no reason to.

They rowed across the bright water. The early evening sun was low on the western horizon, already filling the sky with color. It was not yet a year since Monk had taken this job, but even in that time the strength of his arms and chest had increased enormously. He hardly felt the pull of the oars, and he was so accustomed to working with Orme that they fell into rhythm without a word.

He knew that Parfitt had been murdered, most probably on this boat that lay motionless on the silent river ahead of them. Still, the movement, the creak of the oarlocks, the whisper of water passing, the faint drip from the oars, had a kind of timeless calm that eased the knots inside him. He found he was smiling.

They pulled up alongside the boat and shipped their oars. Orme stood and caught the rope ladder that lay over the surprisingly high side. They tied their own ropes to it, and then climbed up.

The boat was larger than it had looked from the shore. It was a good fifty feet long, and about twenty wide at its broadest point. Given the height of it, there would be two decks above the waterline, and perhaps another below, then the bilges. What did Mickey Parfitt use something this size for, moored away up here beyond the docks? Certainly not cargo. There were no masts for sails, and no towpaths on the shore.

Monk glanced at Orme.

Orme's face was turned away, but Monk saw the hard lines of his jaw, the muscles knotted, his shoulders tight.

"We'd better go below," Monk said quietly. They had brought crowbars in case it proved necessary to break open the hatches.

He wondered what had happened on this boat. Had someone crept aboard in the dark, rowing out just as they had, climbing on board silently, creeping soundlessly across the wooden planking and taking Mickey Parfitt by surprise? Or was it someone he had expected, someone he had assumed to be a friend, and then he had suddenly, horribly, found that he was wrong?

Orme was bending over the hatch.

"We'll have to break it," he said, frowning. "He must've been killed on deck."

"Or he never got this far," Monk replied.

Orme looked up at him. "You mean it could have nothing to do with this? Why would 'Orrie tell that story about bringing him here if he didn't? If he's got the guts to lie at all, surely he'd say he knew nothing about it?"

Monk took one of the crowbars and levered it into the lock in the hatch. "Maybe other people know he took Parfitt out. He might have been seen on the dockside."

"At eleven at night?" Orme said skeptically. He slid his own crowbar into place and leaned hard on it, but the heavy metal hasp of the lock did not budge.

Monk put his weight behind his crowbar too, working in unison with Orme.

On the fourth attempt the wood splintered. On the fifth it gave, tearing the other end of the lock off and pulling the screws out.

"What the hell has he got in here that's so valuable?" Orme said in amazement. "Smuggling? Brandy, tobacco? Must be a hell of a lot of it. Unless whoever killed him took it?"

Monk did not reply. He hoped that was what it was. "I think 'Orrie's afraid of Tosh, don't you?"

Orme straightened his back, pulling the hatch open. "You mean Tosh told him what to say? That would mean Tosh has a fair idea of what really happened."

The sky was darkening around them, the light draining out of the air. There was no sound but the faint ripple of the water.

"Or else he's protecting someone else," Monk suggested. He moved closer to the black square of the hatch. Only the new wood where the screws were torn out showed pale. "We'd better get down there while we can still see. We'll need a lantern below anyway."

They did not look at each other. They both knew what they were afraid of. The same memories crowded both their minds.

Orme struck a match. In the still air he did not have to shelter it; carrying it carefully, he started down the wooden steps into the bowels of the boat.

Monk followed. It was surprisingly easy, and he knew as he went down and his hand found the rail that this deck was designed for passengers, not cargo. A sense of foreboding closed in on him. Even the smell in the air was disturbingly familiar: the richness of cigar smoke, the overripe sweetness of good alcohol, but stale, mixed with the odor of human bodies.

Orme held the lantern high and shed its light onto the smooth painted walls of a wide cabin. It looked something like a floating withdrawing room. There were cupboards at one end, and a bench with a polished mahogany surface, a gleaming brass rail around the edges.

It brought back a memory of Jericho Phillips's boat so sharply that for an instant Monk felt his gorge rise and was afraid he was going to be sick. He strode across the carpeted floor to the door into the next cabin and jerked it open so hard it crashed against the wall and swung back on him.

Orme followed him with the light. Monk heard his breath expelled in a sigh. This cabin was similar, only larger, and at the far end there was a makeshift stage.

"Oh, Jesus!" Orme said, then apologized instantly. The horror in his voice made his words scarcely a blasphemy, more a cry for help, as if God could change the truth of what the sergeant knew.

Monk needed no explanation; it was his worst imagining come true again. This was another boat, just like Jericho Phillips's, where pornographic shows of children entertained those with a perverted addiction to such things, and with an addiction to the danger of watching it live. This was what Phillips would have done with Scuff, and Monk and Hester would never have found him. Even if they had, what of his heart and mind would have remained whole, let alone his body?

Were there boys here now, locked behind other doors, too afraid to make a sound?

Orme moved forward, and Monk put a hand on his arm. "Listen," he ordered. Orme was breathing hard, shaking a little. For all his years on the river, there were still times when the sight of pain tore through his control.

They both stood motionless, ears straining. The boat was well made. Even the joints in the wood did not creak with the faint movement of the water. The tide had turned and was coming in again.

"They must be here." Monk dropped his voice to a whisper. "They can't bring them out here for the show every time. Too many other boats—they'd be seen. And too many chances to escape. They're here somewhere." He could not even bring himself to say that they might all be dead.

"A mutiny?" Orme suggested with a lift of hope. "Maybe they killed him? One hit him with something, two others strangled him? That could be why the odd marks. Maybe it isn't a rope at all? Could be boys' shirts, all tied together." He turned to face Monk, his features ghostly in the lantern light. "They'd have gone. We'll never find them." All the emotion of his unspoken meaning was in his face.

"No point in even looking," Monk agreed. "Murder by persons unknown." He took a deep breath. "But we'd better make certain. There'll be rooms for them below, and a galley of some sort. They have to feed them."

Orme said nothing.

They found the ladder down and descended to the deck below. Immediately it was different. The heavier, more fetid air closed over them, and the lantern shone on darker walls only a couple of feet away. Monk felt the sweat break out on his skin, and then chill instantly. His heart was knocking in his chest.

Orme pushed at the first door, but it held fast. He lifted his foot and kicked it with all his weight. It burst in, and there was a cry from behind it. He held the lantern higher and the yellow light showed four small boys, thin, narrow-chested, half-naked, and cowering together in the corner.

Monk wiped his hand over his face, forcing himself to focus.

"It's all right," he said quietly. "Nobody's going to hurt you. Parfitt is dead. We're going to take you away from here." He stepped forward.

They all shrank farther back, flinching, though his hand was several feet away from the closest of them.

He stopped. What could he tell them that they could believe? They probably didn't know anything but this. Where was he going to send them, anyway? Back into the streets? Some orphanage, where they would be looked after? By whom? Perhaps Hester would know.

"I'm not going to hurt you," he repeated, feeling useless. They wouldn't believe him; they shouldn't. Perhaps they shouldn't believe anyone. "Are there more of you?"

One nodded slowly.

"We'll get you all, and then take you ashore." Where to? How many boats would they need? It was night already; what was he going to do with them? A dozen or more small boys: frightened, hungry, possibly ill, certainly hideously abused. Then he thought of Durban, his predecessor, and remembered his work with the Foundling Hospital. "We'll go where they'll look after you," he said more firmly. "Give you warm clothes, food, a clean bed to sleep in."

They looked at him as if they had no idea what he was saying.

It took Monk and Orme the rest of the night to find all of the fourteen boys and take them ashore, a boatload at a time, persuade them they were safe, and then get them to the nearest hospital that would accept them. Later the hospital would send them on to a proper institution specifically for foundlings. Technically, of course, they were too old for that, but Monk trusted in the charity of the matrons in charge.

DAWN WAS COMING UP, pale over the east and lighting the water, clean and chill, soft colors half bleached away, when Monk stood with Orme on the dock outside the Wapping station of the River Police. He was so tired, his bones ached. He realized that in the three weeks since Jericho Phillips's death he had slowly let go of at least part of the horror of it. Now it was back as though it had been only yesterday. It was the sweat and alcohol in the air, the claustrophobia belowdecks. But sharper and more real than anything else, filling his nose and throat, it was the smell of fear and death.

Mickey Parfitt was another Jericho Phillips, one that catered to an upriver clientele, away from the teeming closeness of the docks. Instead it was the quiet reaches of the river where deserted banks were marshy, mist-laden at morning and evening, and stretches of silver water were tree-lined. But in the night the same twisted brutality was enacted upon children. Probably the same blackmail of men addicted to their appetites, to the danger of illegal indulgence, the adrenaline pumping through their blood at the fear of being caught. It was the same obliviousness to what they were doing to others, perhaps because the others were children of the streets and docksides, already abandoned by circumstance.

Did Monk want to know who had killed Mickey Parfitt? Not really. It was a case in which he would be happier to fail. But could he simply not try? That was a different thing. Then he would be acting as both judge and jury. About Parfitt he was sure, but what about the murderer's next victim, and the one after that? Could Monk really set himself up to decide whose murder was acceptable and whose deserved trial and probably punishment? He had made too many mistakes in the past for such certainty. Or was that the coward's fear of responsibility? Leave it to someone else; then it can't be your fault.

"Where do we begin?" Orme said quietly as the light broadened in the sky.

A string of barges was coming slowly up the river, their wash barely disturbing the surface.

Monk glanced sideways once, seeing the anger and the grief in Orme's blunt face. They faced a long, slow journey barely begun, and Orme's trust mattered to Monk intensely.

"Find out more about him," he replied slowly, searching for the words. "Perhaps his death was justified, perhaps not. It could have been a rival. Who was behind him? Who put in the money—or took it out? Was he blackmailing people too?"

Orme nodded slowly. He looked quickly at Monk, then back again at the river.

"Have some breakfast first, and a little sleep. Get warm," Monk added with a slight smile.

3

Oliver Rathbone waited in the withdrawing room for Margaret to come downstairs. They were going to dine with her parents, and as usual, it was a somewhat formal affair. Her two sisters and their husbands would also be present.

He walked to the windows and stared out at the darkening garden. The September sun was warm on the last of the flowers in the herbaceous border: purples and golds, autumn colors. It was the richest season; soon even the leaves would flame. Berries would ripen. Blue wood smoke and early morning frosts were not far away. For him the glory of autumn always held an echo of sadness, a knowledge that beauty is a living thing, delicate, capable of injury, even of death.

This would be the first time he would dine with Arthur Ballinger since the drownings at Execution Dock. Rathbone was dreading it, yet of course it was inevitable. Ballinger was his father-in-law, and Margaret was unusually close to her family.

Sullivan had made it hideously clear that he blamed the man

behind the child-abuse racket for his downfall, from beginning to end, but he had offered no proof that it was Ballinger, so legally and morally there was nothing Rathbone could do about it. Sullivan's words had been no more than those of a desperate man, disgraced beyond recall.

Outside, a flock of starlings swirled up into the evening sky, and clouds drifted in from the south.

For Margaret's sake, Rathbone knew he must pretend. It would be difficult. He did not find family gatherings easy anyway. He was very close to his own father, but their dinners together had the quiet comfort of old friends, conversation about art and philosophy, law and literature, gentle amusement at the oddities of life and human nature. There were companionable silences while they ate bread and cheese, good pâté, drank a little red wine. Sometimes they had apple pie and cream by the fireside in the evening, and shared a joke or two.

The door opened and Margaret came in. She saw Rathbone standing and immediately apologized, assuming she had kept him waiting. She looked lovely in a gown of rich, soft green, the huge crinoline skirt bordered with a pattern of Greek keys in gold.

"I was early," he replied, finding it easier to smile than he had expected. "But I would have been happy to wait. You look wonderful. Is the gown new? Surely I couldn't have forgotten it?"

The stiffness disappeared from her back and became the grace he had first seen in her when he had been drawn to her sense of humor, and the innate dignity that was her loveliest gift.

Now he found his anxiety slipping away. They would negotiate the evening, whatever challenges it offered. It was a family occasion; the past and its unproved accusations should be left behind. To entertain them was unjust.

"Come." He offered her his arm. "The carriage will be at the door any moment." He smiled at her and saw the answering pleasure in her eyes.

THEY ARRIVED JUST AFTER Margaret's elder sister, Gwen, and her husband, Wilbert, and followed them into the long oak-paneled withdrawing room. Wilbert was thin, fair-haired, and rather earnest. Rathbone had never discovered exactly what occupation he followed, but apparently he had inherited money and was interested in politics. Gwen was only a year or two older than Margaret, and not unlike her to look at. She had the same high, smooth brow and soft hair; her features were prettier, but lacked a little of Margaret's individuality. Because of that, to him she was less attractive.

The eldest sister, Celia, was already present, sitting on the couch opposite her husband, George. She was the handsomest of the three. She had beautiful dark hair and eyes, but Rathbone noticed that she was beginning to thicken a little in the waist and was already more buxom than he cared for. The diamonds at her ears must have cost as much as a good pair of carriage horses, if not more.

Mrs. Ballinger let go the embrace of her middle daughter and came forward to welcome Margaret, the last of her daughters to achieve matrimony, but also the one who had done the best. Rathbone had not only money, but now a title, and he was very personable into the bargain.

"How lovely to see you again, Oliver," she said warmly. "I am so happy your commitments allowed you time for a little pleasure. Margaret, my dear, you look wonderful!" She kissed Margaret on both cheeks and offered her hand to Rathbone.

A moment later Ballinger himself was shaking Rathbone's hand with a firm grip. However, his eyes were guarded, offering no clues as to his inner thoughts. Had it always been like that, or was Rathbone noticing it now, because of Phillips's death and Sullivan's accusation?

They had barely time to exchange greetings and make a few polite inquiries as to health and recent social engagements, when dinner was announced and they went into the enormous and lavish dining room with its hot Indian-red walls and glittering chandeliers, its over-spilling bowls of fruit on the sideboard. The table, which could have comfortably seated sixteen, was superbly set with the best crystal and silver, cut-glass bowls of bonbons, and snow-white linen napkins folded like swans. In the center, there was one of the loveliest arrangements of flowers that Rathbone could remember seeing—late roses in crimson and apricot, and tawny bronze chrysanthemum heads. It was given additional character by two spires of something deep, rich purple.

"Mama-in-law," he said spontaneously, "this is quite amazing. I have never seen a more exquisite table anywhere."

She blushed with pleasure. "Thank you, Oliver. I believe even the best food is complemented by beauty to the eye." She glanced at her husband to see if he had heard the compliment, and when she saw that he had, her satisfaction doubled.

They took their places, and the first course was served—a delicate soup, quickly finished. It was followed by baked fish.

Celia made some trivial remark about a display of drawings she had seen, and her mother replied. Ballinger looked around them all, smiling. Gradually the conversation embraced each one of them in turn. There was laughter and compliments. Rathbone began to feel included.

Ballinger asked his opinion a number of times on various subjects. The fish was removed, and saddle of mutton was served with roasted and boiled vegetables, rich sauce, and garnishes. The men ate heartily, the women accepting less and eating a mouthful or two, and then resting before eating a little more. Conversation moved to more serious subjects: social issues and matters of reform.

Ballinger made a joke with quick, dry wit, and they all laughed. Rathbone told an anecdote. They applauded it, Ballinger leading, looking at them all to join in, which they did, as if given permission to be enthusiastic.

There was more wine, and then pudding was served, an excellent apple flan with thick cream, or treacle tart for those who preferred. Most of the men took both.

Rathbone looked across at Margaret and saw the flush in her cheeks, her eyes bright and soft. He realized with surprise and considerable pleasure not only that she was happy but that she was actually proud of him, not for his skills in argument or his professional reputation, but for his charm, which was so much more personal a thing. The warmth inside him had nothing to do with the dinner or the wine.

"They tried to get some curb on it through the House of Lords several years ago," he said in answer to a question of Wilbert's about industrial pollution in rivers, in particular the Thames.

"I remember that." George looked at Ballinger, then at Rathbone. "Narrowly defeated, if I'm right?"

Ballinger nodded, suddenly very sober. "Lord Cardew was one of the main backers of that, poor man."

"Hopeless cause," George said with a shake of his head. "Far too much power behind it. Richer than the Bank of England. Put all the filth there is into the rivers, and we're helpless to stop them."

"We did stop them," Ballinger said sharply, a ring of pride to his voice.

"But it failed," George pointed out.

"In Parliament, yes," Ballinger argued. "But there was a civil suit a few months after that, which they won on appeal a year later."

Rathbone was interested. Pollution was a subject he cared about increasingly as he realized the human misery it caused. But he knew the industrial might behind it and was surprised that an appeal could succeed.

"Really? How on earth did anyone manage that? It would come before the Court of Appeal, and with that sort of money at stake, most likely Lord Garslake himself would hear it." Garslake was Master of the Rolls, the head of all civil justice appeals. His leanings were well known, his financial interests less so.

Ballinger smiled. "He was persuaded to change his views," he said quietly.

"I'd like to know how." George was openly skeptical.

Ballinger looked at him with amusement. "I dare say you would, but it is not a public matter."

"Did Lord Cardew have something to do with it?" Mrs. Ballinger asked. "I know he felt deeply on the subject."

Ballinger patted her arm lightly. "My dear, you know better than to ask, as I know better than to tell you."

"You said 'poor man.' " Wilbert raised his eyebrows questioningly. "Why?"

Ballinger shook his head. "Oh, because his elder son died. Boating accident somewhere in the Mediterranean. Dreadful business."

His face was dark, as if the sorrow of it were still with him, in spite of the legal success.

Margaret's fingers rested gently on her father's. "Papa, you grieved for him at the time. I know it won't heal—perhaps such things never do—but you can't go on hurting for him. At least he still has one son living."

Ballinger raised his head a little and turned over his hand to clasp hers and hold it.

"You are quite right of course, my dear. But not everyone is as fortunate in their children as I am. You could not know, nor should you, but Charles Cardew was a magnificent young man: sober, honest, highly intelligent, with a great future in front of him. Rupert is in most ways his exact opposite. Handsomer, to his downfall." He stopped abruptly, as if feeling that he had said too much.

"Is it a downfall to be handsome?" Gwen asked curiously. "Was poor Charles plain, then?"

Ballinger looked at her with a smile. "You know nothing of such men, my dear. Rupert Cardew is a wastrel, a womanizer, flattering and deceiving even married women, whom one would imagine to have more judgment and more sense."

Margaret looked uncomfortable. She met Rathbone's eyes, and then deliberately avoided them.

"Perhaps his grief sent him a little mad?" Gwen suggested. "It can do so. Were they close?"

"I have no idea," Ballinger replied, regarding her with slight surprise. "I don't think so. And Rupert was wild and selfish long before Charles's death. It is generous of you to try to excuse him, but I'm afraid his behavior is far worse than you imagine."

Gwen would not let it go. "Really? Lots of young men drink a little too much, Papa. Most of us know that. We only pretend not to."

"We have to pretend a lot of things," Celia added. "It is very foolish to admit to everything you know. You can make life impossible for yourself."

"Really, Celia!" George remonstrated, no amusement in his face whatever.

Rathbone turned to Margaret and saw the humor in her eyes. It was a moment of understanding where words were unnecessary. He found himself looking forward to the journey home, when they would be alone in the carriage, and then even more so to arriving.

"I'm surprised if you haven't heard word, one place or another, Oliver." Ballinger lingered a moment before continuing. "Poor Cardew has had to bail Rupert out of more than one scandal that would have blackened the family name if he hadn't."

"I thought that was what you were referring to," Gwen said ruefully.

"I'm afraid Rupert Cardew went a great deal further than that," Ballinger told her. "He has an ungovernable temper when he is roused. He has beaten people very badly. It is only his father's intervention that has saved him from prison." His voice dropped. "And yet he loves the boy, as fathers do love their children, no matter what sins they commit." He looked at Margaret, then at Gwen, and finally at Celia.

He sat quite still, a large man, heavy-shouldered, powerful, his thick-featured face benign, until one tried to read the heavy-lidded eyes, as black as coal under their drooping lids.

No one spoke. There was an intensity of emotion at the table into which speech would have been intrusive, even clumsy.

Rathbone knew that Hester had been accepting considerable donations of money from Rupert for the financing of the clinic. Would she have taken them were she aware of his darker nature, so different from the sunny charm he presented to her?

Perhaps Ballinger's loyalty—one that could not be revealed—had also bound him to Lord Justice Sullivan. Ballinger's purchase of the obscene photographs that Claudine Burroughs had witnessed when she'd followed Arthur that night had not been for his own personal use but had been part of a last desperate attempt to rescue Sullivan from himself. That the attempt had failed was a grief Ballinger could reveal to no one at all. In that light, Arthur's sin was of a completely different weight. And Sullivan was dead. It was Sullivan's surviving family that Ballinger would be protecting. The thought eased the knots inside Rathbone, and suddenly he was smiling.

It was Mrs. Ballinger who resumed the conversation. Rathbone allowed the words to pass over him. He thought instead of Ballinger's love for his daughters, all of whom seemed to have brought him happiness.

Rathbone looked at Margaret now, leaning forward listening to George as if what he was saying interested her, though Rathbone knew that it did not. But she would never hurt George's feelings, for Celia's sake. The loyalty was deep, always to be trusted, relied on in hard times and easy. He found himself gazing at her, proud of her gentleness.

The last course was served, and then the ladies withdrew, leaving the gentlemen to pass the port and take a little cheese if they cared to.

IN THE WITHDRAWING ROOM the conversation was trivial again: small matters of gossip and amusement. Rathbone found it hard to join in, because he was not acquainted with most of the people they referred to, and it was even harder to laugh at the humor. The wit lacked the dryness that pleased him.

"You are quiet, Oliver," Mrs. Ballinger observed, turning from Celia to face him, her brow furrowed. "Does something trouble you? I hope it was nothing in the dinner."

"Of course it wasn't, my dear," Ballinger said quickly. "He is out of sorts because over the port and cheese I criticized his friend Monk, who is, I think, a far more dangerous man than Oliver wishes to accept. His loyalty does him credit, but I believe it is misplaced. It is not an uncommon trait to think well of our friends, in spite of evidence to the contrary." He smiled, a brief flash of teeth. "And it is in a way admirable, I suppose." He shrugged again, very slightly, merely a creasing of the fine fabric of his jacket. "But as he himself has just observed, in the law we cannot afford such emotional luxuries. We are the last refuge of those who desperately need no more and no less than justice."

"Bravo, Papa," Margaret said with a faint flush of pink across her cheeks. "How perfectly you balance the head and the heart. You are right, of course. We cannot favor loyalty over justice, or we betray not only those who trust in us, but ourselves as well." She looked at Rathbone, waiting for him to concede her father's point.

In that instant he realized how deep her loyalty was to her father, so deep that she did not even perceive that it was instinctive rather than a matter of reason. It made her side against Monk without hesitation. Was that what it came to—the loyalty of blood? Or was her devotion to her father stronger than any other love?

Did he feel any less for his own father?

She was waiting now, the question in her eyes. It was not really about the law. It was about Monk, and the long past they shared, the battles Margaret had not been part of, and it was perhaps also about Hester.

"My loyalty has always been to the truth," Rathbone replied, choosing his words with intense care. "But I believe that Monk's has also. On occasion he has been mistaken. So have I. He was slipshod in his prosecution of Jericho Phillips, and the man got off because I was more skilled, and more diligent. However, if you recall, Phillips was undoubtedly guilty, which means that Monk's judgment of the man's character was not at fault."

Ballinger rested his large square-ended fingers very gently on the leather arm of his chair. "That may be true, Oliver, but you have missed the point. Monk has no right to be judging Jericho Phillips, or anyone else. He is a collector of evidence to present before the court—no more than that."

"A sort of collector of moral refuse," George added smugly, glancing at Ballinger, and away again.

Celia smiled.

"Then, what are we?" Oliver said, hearing the cutting edge of his own voice. "Sorters of that same refuse? Personally I am quite happy if the police at least begin the process, and give me some sort of pattern, either to confirm or deny."

"Oh, really!" Wilbert protested.

Margaret looked unhappy, a mounting shadow in her eyes. Rathbone realized with surprise that she had not expected him to argue. In her opinion he should not have defended either Monk or himself. This quiet room was like thousands of other withdrawing rooms in London, but in subtle ways he felt alien in it. The painted walls were very similar to all the others—the heavily swagged curtains, the long windows onto the great garden, certainly the busy red and green carpet, even the brass fire irons in the hearth. It was the beliefs that were foreign to him, things as invisible and as necessary as the air.

"Perhaps we should speak of something else," Ballinger said, leaning a little farther back in his armchair and crossing his legs. "I had a most amusing evening last Thursday . . ."

For the best part of the next hour he regaled them with a detailed and amusing account of his journey across the river, with lurid descriptions of the ferryman and his interests. Apparently he had gone to visit an old friend named Harkness who lived in Mortlake.

When at last he finished, Celia began to laugh. "Really, Papa! You had me hanging on every word you said! I could see the wretched ferryman, bowlegs and all."

"You think I'm joking? To entertain you?" Ballinger asked.

"Of course," she rejoined. "And I thank you for it. You are superb, as always."

"Not at all." He turned to Rathbone. "Go to the ferry at Fulham and look for him. You'll find him there. Ask him about our conversation. I challenge you! Any of you!" He looked back at Wilbert, and then George.

"I believe you," Margaret stated, still smiling. "It explains why you go to dine with a bore like Mr. Harkness. It isn't the dinner at all; it's the ride!"

This time they all laughed.

THEY LEFT LATE, AFTER more wine, Belgian chocolates, and a last cup of tea.

"Thank you," Margaret said quietly as their carriage moved out into the traffic and she and Rathbone sat side by side in the back. The silk of her gown spread out and covered his knees, rustling slightly as she turned toward him. He could see her face in the flickering glow from the lamps of carriages moving in the opposite direction. She was smiling, her eyes soft.

For an instant he felt a complete belonging, a sweetness that ran right through him. He understood without effort exactly why Ballinger found his other sons-in-law irritating, why he had to bait them, and then in the end make them laugh. Whatever the trivial differences between all of them, there was an underlying loyalty that remained steadfast through the surface ruffles caused by a moment's annoyance or trivial misunderstandings. One did not have to like in order to belong. True loyalty was deeper than that, stronger, impervious to superficial emotions.

He put his hand out and took Margaret's where it lay on the silk of her skirt. It was warm, and her fingers closed over his with a sudden strength.

4

Monk began to look more deeply into the life of Mickey Parfitt, his friends and enemies, his patrons, and the men he had used and cheated, and whose appetites he had fed. And if Parfitt were truly like Jericho Phillips, then of course there would also be those he had blackmailed. But does a blackmailed man turn on the one who supplies his addiction? Only if he has reached the last shreds of despair and has nothing left to lose.

Perhaps Monk should see if any well-known man had committed suicide in the last few days, or had met with a death that was open to that interpretation.

Mickey Parfitt was not in himself a person of any importance. People were dying up and down the river every week. The River Police could spare only a couple of men to investigate a crime of such little effect on the city or its population. One petty criminal more or less did not stir fear or righteous outrage, not really even interest.

It was a still, hazy morning when Monk and Orme took a hansom from Wapping all the way out to Chiswick. They would have gone by water, but that would have meant following the twists and turns of the river, and rowing that distance would have been backbreaking work. They could certainly not have spared two more men for the task.

"Hardly know if I care," Orme said grimly as he sat staring straight ahead of him inside the cab. It was going to be a mild day, but he was dressed as always in a plain, dark jacket and trousers with a cap pulled over his brow.

Monk knew what was in his mind: the frightened, blank-eyed children he had seen on Phillips's boat, and that other boy's thin, broken body they had pulled out of the water. Monk didn't care himself if they caught Mickey's killer or not, and to Orme, of all people, he could not pretend that he did.

"Perhaps we won't find whoever did it," he said wryly.

Orme looked at him, weighing how seriously he meant it.

Monk shrugged. "Of course murder deserves to be punished, whoever the victim is. If we get close, we'll scare the wits out of him." That was not a joke. In the past many people had been frightened of Monk. It was not something he was entirely proud of. Some of them had been the men he worked with, who were younger, less able, less agile of mind, afraid of his cutting judgment. He'd been admired, but also feared.

But that had been before the accident that had robbed him of his memory, and when he had still been in the Metropolitan Police. Then, after he had been dismissed, he had worked for himself, solving crimes for those who'd employed him privately. It was only after Durban's death that he had been offered this position to lead the Thames Police on the river.

Durban had not possessed Monk's ruthless skill in hunting down the truth—few people did. But he had known how to lead men, how to earn their loyalty, draw out the best in them, even inspire a kind of love. Above all they had trusted him.

Monk had known him all too briefly. They had been friends. It was Durban, knowing he was dying, who had suggested that Monk take his place. Now Monk had to justify that honor placed on him.

He had to learn the art of leading men, starting with Orme, who had been Durban's closest ally.

"And we'll catch him if we can," he added, as if it were an unnecessary afterthought.

Orme smiled as if he understood beyond the words, and said nothing. He sat back a little in the seat and his shoulders relaxed.

At the small local police station in Chiswick they were greeted cautiously, and taken into a warm, poky office that smelled of strong tea and tobacco smoke. The walls were lined with shelves; the table was piled with papers.

Monk and Orme requested as much local knowledge as possible, and Monk asked the sergeant in charge a number of questions. Orme listened and took notes, writing rapidly and with surprising neatness.

"'E were a nasty piece o' work," the sergeant said, describing Mickey Parfitt. "Can't let murder go, but if we could, 'ooever done 'im in'd be my first pick not ter find, as it were." He sighed. "'Owever, seems we can't do that, or Gawd knows where it'd finish. We'll do all we can to 'elp yer find the poor sod 'oo did it." A look of amusement flashed across his broad face. "Mind, yer've got a lot ter choose from, an' that's the truth."

"What was he doing out there on the boat by himself?" Monk asked, perching on the edge of one of the rickety chairs. "Any ideas? If you could prove anything, you'd have had him locked up already, but whom do you suspect? And don't tell me there's too many to choose from."

The sergeant smiled widely, a warm, spontaneous gesture that lit his bony face. "Wouldn't think of it, sir. We're too far up the river for smuggling. There in't nobody up 'ere worth thievin' from, although I used ter wonder if 'e were fencin' stuff, so I made the chance to go out an' look, but I didn't see a thing."

"Lot of people coming and going?" Monk asked.

"Yeah. That's part o' why I thought 'e were fencin' stuff."

"What sort of people?" Monk found himself tense, waiting. He did not look at Orme, but he could feel Orme stiffen also.

"No women," the sergeant replied, shaking his head. "So if that's what ye're thinking, ye're wrong. If it was that simple, I'd 'ave stopped 'im meself. Always men, an' if yer looked close enough, well-to-do men at that. Gamblin's my thoughts. 'Igh stakes, life or death sort o' stuff. 'Ad one top 'isself almost a year ago. No doubt of it—did it 'isself. Shot through the 'ead." His amiable face twisted in an expression of pity. "Alone in a small boat, pretty little gun there with 'im. Pearl 'andled. S'pose 'e lost more 'n 'e could pay. Dunno wot gets into folk." A tiredness touched him, as if he had seen too much and it exhausted his pity.

Monk thought of the man alone in the boat, holding the gun in his hands, probably cold, almost certainly shaking. It had to do with honor, as the sergeant supposed, but not money—the dishonor of being exposed as a man who looked at obscene photographs, and used the degradation and abuse of little boys to satisfy his dark hunger. But Monk did not need to tell the sergeant that now.

"Who works for him?" he asked. "I know about 'Orrie Jones, and Tosh Wilkin and Crumble. What can you tell me about them?"

" 'Orrie's a bit simple," the sergeant replied. "But not as daft as 'e makes out. 'E can be sharp enough if it suits 'im. Crumble's a follower. Does as 'e's told. Tosh yer need to watch." He shook his head. " 'E's another bad 'un. Never bin able ter catch 'im in enough ter put 'im away." His face brightened. "Think 'e could've bin the one ter do Mickey?"

"I doubt it," Monk said with regret. "I think it was very much in Tosh's interest to keep Mickey alive and profitable, earning money for both of them."

"Was 'e an opulent receiver, then?" That was the term for someone who bought and sold high-quality stolen articles, such as jewelry, works of art, ivory, or gold.

"No," Monk replied with near certainty. "He was a pornographer, and probably a pimp of little boys, for a few select customers."

The sergeant blasphemed quietly, half under his breath. He did not apologize, so perhaps he was taking the Lord's name very much in earnest.

"Still willing to help us find whoever killed him?" Monk asked, a harsh smile twisting his mouth.

The sergeant looked straight at him, blue eyes steady. "O' course, sir, but I'm sorry to say, I don't think as I know anything as'd be of use to yer."

Monk laughed, a harsh, oblique pleasure in it. "What a shame. I'm sure you would have a list of ferrymen, boatbuilders, cabdrivers, shopkeepers near the water, the kind of person who might have seen something."

"Course, sir."

"Did Mickey often go out to his boat alone?"

"No idea, sir. 'Ard to say on a misty night 'oo goes where. That's the trouble with the river, but being River Police an' all, I expect you know that better than I do."

"Did Mickey own the boat?"

The sergeant looked startled. "Dunno. But I s'pose yer could find out."

"I intend to." Monk thanked him and went outside into the brightening morning air. The sharp light off the water shifted and glittered with the incoming tide. Barge sails showed rusty-red, canvases barely filled. A few leaves were beginning to turn color. Some even drifted down.

Already the street was busy. Carts rattled over the rough stones, and men shouted to one another as they loaded and unloaded sacks, barrels, lengths of timber.

"What d'you reckon he was out there for at that hour of night?" Orme asked quietly as they walked over the road to the water's edge. "Someone set him up?"

"Possibly," Monk conceded. "Hitting him over the head could be a crime of opportunity. The assailant could have used any piece of wood lying around, a broken oar, half a branch, anything. But who carries around a rope with knots in it?"

"Piece of rigging from a boat?" Orme questioned. "Always rope on boats, or in a boatyard."

"True," Monk agreed. "But did he carry it with him? Or did he kill Mickey somewhere else, then toss him into the water and let him drift? There aren't any boatyards upstream of where he was found—at

least not near his own boat, which is where we think he went in. I
suppose we could be wrong. But if the next boatyard is miles upriver,
why carry him back again? Just to confuse us?"

Orme pursed his lips. "Premeditated," he said with certainty.
"Somebody came meaning to kill him. Not surprising, considering his
occupation. What's surprising is that it didn't happen sooner."

"Maybe 'Orrie, Crumble, and Tosh looked after him?" Monk was
thinking aloud. "In which case either they were outwitted or they
turned on him and at least one of them sold him to his murderer."

Orme looked at him sideways, a rare amusement in his eyes, perhaps at the justice of the idea. Then, before Monk could be absolutely
certain of it, he looked away again. "I suppose we'd better look for
who that could be," he said expressionlessly.

They spent the morning speaking to the various men whose live-
lihood kept them on the river, or close to its banks: boatbuilders,
shipwrights, chandlers, breakers, suppliers of oars, sculls, and other
fittings for boats. They learned nothing that added to what they already knew.

They had a lunch of bread, cold ham, and chicken, and a glass of
ale each. Then Orme left to question the ferrymen. Monk went to
find 'Orrie Jones again, in the cellars of the public house, moving kegs
of ale.

"I told yer," 'Orrie said, his wandering eye veering wildly, the
other fixed on Monk. "I took 'im out ter the boat. Summink arter
eleven, it were. 'E tol' me ter come back fer 'im, but I were 'eld up, an'
I were late. When I got there, bit before one, 'e were gorn. I din't see
nobody else, an' I dunno 'oo killed 'im."

"What did he go out to the boat for?" Monk asked patiently. He
did not know why he was asking all this. It probably made no difference. He was doing it to convince himself that he was trying to find
the truth and to prove who had killed Parfitt.

'Orrie was staring at him incredulously, leaning a little against a
pile of kegs. " 'Ow do I know? Yer think I asked 'im?"

"Who else did you tell?" Monk persisted.

'Orrie looked indignant. "Nob'dy! Yer sayin' as I set 'im up?"

"Did you?" It was a possibility, a fight over the spoils?

"Course I didn't. Why'd I do a thing like that?" 'Orrie protested.

"For money," Monk replied. "Or because you were more scared of whoever paid you than you were of Mickey Parfitt."

'Orrie drew in his breath to argue, then let it out again, clearly having thought better of it. He looked sideways at Monk, for once both his eyes more or less in the same direction. "I din't tell no one, but Mickey went out there often, like. There were things that needed seein' ter, an' 'e din't trust no one else ter do it right."

"He didn't trust you?" Monk pressed, pretending surprise.

'Orrie's face tightened, sensible to the insult. It was clear from his furrowed expression that he was now taking a great deal more care before he answered. "Mebbe someb'dy were watchin'?" he suggested. " 'E were clever, were Mickey, but 'e got enemies. King o' that bit o' the river, 'e were."

"Who else did you see when you went back for him?" Monk asked.

This time 'Orrie weighed his answer for several moments. Monk waited with interest, studying 'Orrie's extraordinary face. Sometimes the lie a man chose could tell you more about him than the truth.

"There's always people on the water," 'Orrie started cautiously.

Monk smiled. "Of course. If there weren't, there'd be no business."

"Right." 'Orrie nodded slowly, still apparently watching Monk. "People wi' money," he added.

"So, what did Mickey Parfitt sell to them?" Monk asked him.

'Orrie looked totally blank, as if he had not understood.

" 'Orrible, what did Mickey Parfitt sell to these men with money?" Monk repeated carefully. "He made a very good living, or he couldn't have afforded a boat at all, never mind one with fittings like those in his boat."

"I dunno," 'Orrie said helplessly. "Yer suppose 'e told the likes o' me?"

"No, 'Orrie, I suppose you had enough sense to see for yourself!"

'Orrie shook his head. "Not me. I never bin on the boat. I took folk out an' I brung 'em back. I dunno wot they done. Gamblin', mebbe?" He looked hopeful.

Monk stared at him. With his swiveling eye it was impossible to tell if he was frightened, half-witted, or simply physically disadvantaged. Monk considered asking him what the boys were for, but perhaps it would be better to keep that question for later. Let 'Orrie wonder for a while where they had gone to. Or perhaps he really didn't know. It might have been Crumble, or even Tosh, who'd looked after them.

'Orrie smiled. "Ask Tosh. 'E'll know," he offered.

Monk thanked him and went in search of Tosh. It took him nearly an hour, and a great deal of questioning, but at last he found him in a cramped but surprisingly tidy office. There was a woodstove burning in one corner, in spite of the comparative warmth of the day. Instantly Monk knew what had happened, and cursed himself for his stupidity. He should have left someone following Tosh, and probably Crumble as well. Then they would have found the papers in time to save them. Tosh and Crumble might deny it, but Mickey was bound to have had certain things noted down: debts and IOUs, if nothing else.

Tosh looked up at Monk, his face calm, even affecting interest. "Found anything yet as ter 'oo killed poor Mickey?" he inquired politely. Today he had a yellow vest on, and he flicked a piece of ash off it carefully.

Monk stood still in the middle of the floor, three feet from Tosh and the stove, controlling his anger with difficulty. "Business rival or a dissatisfied customer," he replied. "Or one who couldn't take being blackmailed anymore. Like the poor sod who shot himself on the river last year."

Tosh's face tightened almost imperceptibly. "Dunno why 'e did that," he said smoothly. "Could a bin anything. Mebbe 'is wife ran orff. It 'appens."

"Rubbish!" Monk snapped at him. "Upper-class women with rich husbands don't run off with other men and create a scandal. They stay at home and take lovers on the side. They do it very discreetly, and everybody else pretends not to know. Leaves the husbands the latitude to do the same, should they wish to."

"Looks like you know 'em better 'n I do," Tosh replied with a slight sneer. "But, then, I s'pose I would, bein' police an' all. So you'd be best placed to guess why 'at poor bastard shot 'isself. Don't see as 'ow it 'as anything ter do wiv 'oo croaked Mickey. In fact, 'e's fer sure one 'o them 'oo didn't, seein' as e's dead 'isself."

Monk ignored the jibe. "Revenge?" he suggested. "One of the dead man's family coming after Mickey, maybe?"

"Only makes sense if Mickey'd killed 'im." Tosh was watching him very carefully now. "Which 'e didn't."

Monk smiled. "I thought you'd know about it."

A flicker of anger crossed Tosh's face. "I dunno nothing about it!"

"What did Mickey sell to his customers, Tosh? And don't tell me again that you don't know. You've just destroyed all the papers, except those that prove his ownership of the boat, so that you can keep it for yourself."

There was an ugly stain of color in Tosh's face now, but he didn't attempt to deny it. "Jus' burned a few private things. A man's a right ter that. In't you got no respect for the dead? Mickey were the victim of a murder! In't it your job ter be on 'is side?" He looked up, his eyes gleaming with bright, malicious innocence.

Monk looked back, equally blankly, wondering where the blackmailing photographs were. He glanced around the small room. There were cupboards and drawers on every wall, as if for an office of detailed business dealings. Here there would be just a record of debts and payments, dates, names, amounts. The pictures would have been far more carefully hidden, as Jericho Phillips's had been. Perhaps even Tosh didn't know that.

The thought of Phillips's pictures still made Monk's stomach lurch with rage and disgust so violent that he was nauseous with it, but he forced a smile. "Looking for the pictures, were you?"

Tosh was staring at him, studying his face. He must have considered lying, and decided against it. "Just wanted to find out 'oo owed 'im still. An' o' course 'oo 'e owed. Got ter pay the bills." He gave a tight, ugly smile.

"Of course," Monk agreed. "I imagine his partners will be after their share of the takings—present and future. Will you be keeping the business on, Tosh?"

This time Tosh was caught. " 'Ow do I know?" he answered irritably. "I jus' worked for 'im. In't none of it mine."

"No, of course not," Monk agreed, and saw the anger harden in Tosh's face. He would have liked it to have been his. He would be waiting now for the silent partner, whoever it was who had put in the money in the first place, to turn up and take the lion's share. Someone had backed Mickey Parfitt, just as someone had backed Jericho Phillips.

Sullivan had said that it was Ballinger who' been behind Phillips. Was that true, or the lie of a desperate man seeking a last revenge? But to what end if Ballinger was not actually involved? Because Ballinger had seen his weakness, and in some way used it?

And could Ballinger be behind both of them? Or was Monk only entertaining the idea because he was so desperate to believe he could end this hideous trade, at least here on the river he had taken for his own? And it was even more urgent to him to give Scuff the illusion of safety that would stop the nightmares and make him believe there really was someone who could protect him from the worst fears and atrocities of life.

And did Monk need, for himself, to be the one who saved Scuff? If so, that was his own weakness, and to pursue Ballinger for it was worse than unjust; it was vicious and irrational, the kind of obsession he most despised in others.

"Tell me about the night Mickey was killed," he said abruptly.

Tosh was startled, but after the initial surprise, his confidence returned, as if now Monk had moved away from the area of danger.

"I told yer already . . ." He repeated the detailed account of his movements exactly as he had said before, almost reciting it. Of course Monk would check, but—looking at Tosh's face—he was certain he would find it all well proved, perhaps as well as if Tosh had known he would need it to withstand investigation. A faint satisfaction gleamed behind his anger now.

"WHAT DO YOU THINK?" Monk said to Orme as they sat in the hansom on the way back toward Wapping. It was dusk, and they had done all they could for the day. Monk was tired; not his feet—he was used to walking—but in his mind. He felt as if Jericho Phillips were back and he, Monk, were retracing the pain of the old failure.

Did he secretly want Parfitt's murderer to escape, because he would like to kill all men like that himself? Especially if Parfitt had, like Phillips, been prepared to murder the boys who became trouble-some as they grew too mature to satisfy the tastes of their abusers? Could it even be one of them, escaped, returned, and now strong enough, who had killed Parfitt in revenge?

If it was, then Monk had no desire to catch him. Perhaps he would deliberately fail to, even at the cost of his own so fiercely nur-tured reputation.

He looked across at Orme beside him, trying to read his face in the flashes of lamplight from passing hansoms going the other way. It told him nothing, except that Orme was troubled also, which Monk already knew.

"Who put up the money for the boat in the first place?" Monk asked.

Orme pursed his lips. "And why'd he kill Parfitt? Getting above himself, d'you suppose? Stealing the profits?"

"Perhaps," Monk replied. "What did Crumble have to say?"

"Just what you'd expect," Orme said. "Lots of men coming and going, mostly well-dressed but keeping very quiet. Always after dark, and trying to look like they were just taking a ferry, or something like that." Orme's mouth was drawn tight, his lips a thin line in the re-flected lamplight. "It's Phillips all over again. Just this time somebody else got to him before we did."

"One of his clients? Victims of blackmail? One of his boys?" Monk tried to frame the ugliest thought in his mind, the one he did not want ever to look at. But Orme's own honesty was too all-inclusive for Monk to say anything less now without it being a deliberate evasion. It cost Monk an effort. He had never worked with others before whom he trusted. He had commanded, but not led. He was only lately beginning to appreciate the difference. "Or his backer needing to silence him?"

"Could be," Orme replied quietly. "Don't know how we'll find that out, let alone get evidence."

"No," Monk agreed. "Neither do I, yet."

WHEN MONK FINALLY REACHED home, it had long been dark. The glare of the city lights was reflected back from a low overcast sky, making the blackness of the river look like a tunnel through the sparks and gleams and the glittering smear of brightness all around.

He walked up the hill from the ferry landing at Princes Stairs, turned right on Union Road, then left into Paradise Place. He could hear the wind in the leaves of the trees over on Southwark Park, and somewhere a dog was barking.

He let himself in with his own key. Too often he was home long after Hester needed to be asleep, although she almost always waited up for him. This time she was sitting in the big chair in the front room, the gas lamp still burning. Her sewing had slipped from her hands and was in a heap on the floor. She was sound asleep.

He smiled and walked quietly over to her. How could he avoid startling her? He went back and closed the door with a loud snap of the latch.

She woke sharply, pulling herself upright. Then she saw him and smiled.

"I'm sorry," she apologized. "I must have drifted off." She was still blinking sleepily, but trying through the remnant of dreams to study his face.

"I'll get us a cup of tea," he said gently. This was home: comfortable, familiar, where he had been happier than he had thought possible. Here he was freer than anywhere else in the world, and yet also more bound, because it mattered so much; to lose it would be unbearable. It would have been easier to care less, to believe there was something else that could nourish his heart, if need be. But there wasn't, and he knew it.

"How's Scuff?" he asked over his shoulder.

"Fine," Hester answered, bending to pick up the fallen sewing and put it away. "I didn't tell him you found another boat. If he has to know, I'll tell him later." She came up behind him. "Are you hungry?"

"Yes." Suddenly he realized that he was. "Bread will do."

"Cold game pie?" she offered.

"Ah! Yes."

It was not until he was sitting down with pie and vegetables and a cup of tea that he realized she intended to draw from him all that he had learned so far.

"Not as much as the pie is worth," he said.

"What isn't?" She tried to look as if she did not know what he meant, but ended with a brief laugh at herself. "Is it another one like Phillips's?" she said softly.

"Yes. I'm sorry."

Between mouthfuls Monk told her what he knew so far, keeping his voice so low that he would hear any creak of Scuff's footsteps on the stairs.

She was very grave. "Could it be Arthur Ballinger?" she asked when he came to a stop. She knew of Sullivan's charge.

"Yes," he answered. "Not to have killed him, of course, but he could be the one backing the enterprise financially, and taking a share of the profits."

"Could you prove it?"

"Perhaps. I'll put Orme on to the accounts tomorrow, and see if he can trace the ownership of the boat back to someone. Although I'll be surprised if it's that easy."

She was sitting upright, her back stiff. The lamplight made her hair look fairer than it was, almost like a halo. "So why would Ballinger kill him, or have him killed? Do you think Phillips's death scared him and he was afraid you would pursue the issue until you found who was behind it?"

Monk considered the idea for several moments. Would he have taken Sullivan's word, unverified as it was, and continued to hunt for whoever had conceived the original idea, found the rich men ripe for the danger and the titillation of child pornography? Perhaps the threat of the double disgrace of child abuse and homosexuality was part of the excitement. These men had not considered the possibility that the very hand that tempted them, and then fed them, would in the end also administer the wounds that would bleed them dry. For that Monk had a shard of pity.

What he did not forgive was that they had not considered the wretched children who paid for men's entertainment with humiliation and pain, sometimes with their lives.

Yes, he knew now, here in the place of his own precious safety, that he did not want to catch whoever had killed Mickey Parfitt. The law would not recognize self-defense, because this murder had obviously not been done in hot blood. The knotted rope embedded in Parfitt's throat alone proved that. But morally that is what it was: getting rid of a predator who destroyed the young and the weak.

"William?" Hester prompted.

He looked up. "Yes, I suppose Ballinger might have been frightened by Phillips's death. Sooner or later I would have gone after whoever was behind Phillips. But if Parfitt hadn't been murdered, it might have been later."

The shadow of a smile touched her mouth. "How much later? A month? Two?"

He shrugged slightly.

She was very serious now. "Do you suppose Parfitt knew that, and got greedy, put on a little pressure, took advantage of what he thought was a vulnerability?"

It was possible. If Parfitt were the opportunist he seemed, then he might well have seized the chance to try to take over a far larger part of the business. It was something Monk could not evade, wherever it led him.

As if reading his thoughts, Hester asked the question he did not want to answer. "Could Sullivan have been telling the truth?"

"I don't know," he admitted, looking up and meeting her eyes. "I'd give a lot for it not to be, for Margaret's sake, and even more for Rathbone's."

"And Scuff?"

He frowned. "Is it better for him to let it all go, hoping he'll forget it, or to drag it out into the open and get rid of it, if we can? That means exposing it like a great new wound, for him to see and feel all over again."

"And all the other boys?" Her voice was measured.

"We can't heal the world," he replied. "There will always be those we can't do anything about. What we can touch is so small as to be almost invisible, compared with what we can't."

"It isn't how much you do; it's the question of whether doing anything or nothing is better for him."

"Is that what matters? What's right for Scuff?" he asked.

"Yes!" She breathed in and out, and looked away from his eyes. "No! Of course that's not all. But it's where I start. You didn't answer me. Which is better for Scuff?"

"I know he still has nightmares. I hear you get up in the night. I know he's probably about nine or ten, for all that he says he's eleven, and has been saying for nearly a year. In some ways he's far older than that. Fairy tales won't do for him. The only thing he'll believe is something close to the truth." He lowered his voice. "He doesn't have a very high opinion of my knowledge, or my common sense. He takes great pride in looking after me. But at least he thinks I don't ever lie to him. It's the only thing he knows for certain. I can't break that."

"I know." Hester was still chewing her lip. "You're right; to try to protect him from it is ridiculous. It's a sort of denial of his experience, as if we didn't believe him. That's the last thing he needs. I don't know how much he's a child and how much a man." She smiled, and he saw the hurt behind it. "And I don't think I really know very much about children anyway. I think he's afraid of being touched, in case he loses the independence he needs to keep in order to survive. Maybe one day . . ."

"You'll do it right," Monk said gently. "You're good with the difficult ones."

He looked at her sitting across the table from him in the lamp-lit kitchen, with its gleaming pans and familiar china on the dresser. Her eyelids were heavy, her hair falling out of its pins from her sleep in the chair, her plain blue dress vaguely reminiscent of her nursing days. But she was ready now to fight anyone and everyone to defend Scuff. With a thrill of surprise, Monk suddenly understood what beauty was really about.

"I'll find whoever killed Mickey Parfitt and put an end to the pornography boats, whoever is behind them. No matter who gets hurt by it," he promised.

"Even if it's Oliver?" she asked.

He hesitated only a moment. "Yes."

She smiled, and there was an intense gentleness in her eyes. "The man you used to be could do that, but are you sure you can now? Whoever's behind this won't go down easily. He'll take everyone with him that he can. Think of what he's already done, and you'll know that. It could be you, me"—her voice dropped—"Scuff, anyone. Are you prepared for that?"

This time he was silent for several moments before he answered.

"This first surrender would only be the beginning," he said. "If I back off now, I may spend the rest of my life giving in every time I could lose anything."

She leaned forward a little and put her hand over his. She nodded, but she did not speak.

THE FOLLOWING DAY MONK and Orme returned to Chiswick to begin following the money invested in Mickey's business and the financing of his boat. The only part of it that would be clear was the payment to the previous owner, and probably much of the maintenance costs and the occasional repair and improvement. Mickey must have handled a great deal of money at one time or another. At least some of it would have left traces.

Whoever had repaired the boat would also know where it had been.

"Think it'll help?" Orme said bleakly. They were standing on the bank of the river just above the Hammersmith Creek, the next bend eastward toward the city.

"Got a better idea?" Monk asked. "We know what 'Orrie, Crumble, and Tosh are going to tell us. Asking again won't make any difference."

The breeze was cool on their faces and smelled of mud and weeds. Orme stared across the water. "Tosh is a bad 'un," he replied. "But I can't see why he'd kill Mickey. He hasn't the skill to take his place, and he's not stupid enough to think he has. Crumble just does as he's told. Can't work out whether 'Orrie's as daft as he looks or not."

"Fear or money . . . ," Monk said thoughtfully. "Probably money, sooner or later. We have to find whatever records remain, and re-create as much as we can from other people. A lot of money passed through Parfitt's hands. He will have had to account to the man behind it all."

Orme winced. "One of his customers?"

"I hope so." Monk was surprised how intensely he meant that.

THEY SPENT THAT DAY and the following two searching for every trace of money or records that Parfitt might have kept, other than those Tosh had burned. They questioned ferrymen and bargemen, workers in every boatyard on either side of the river from Brentford to Hammersmith, every supplier of rope, paint, canvas, nails, or any other ships' goods or tools. They followed the course of the boat's mornings, its few trips up and down the river. The repairs, mooring fees, quantities of food, and alcohol made the nature of the business obvious. The income must have been very large indeed.

The pattern of it also showed where the boat had been most of the time, including where clients had been picked up, in Chiswick along the mall, and in such places of pleasure as the infamous Cremorne Gardens.

By daylight, Cremorne Gardens were a magnificent replacement of what Vauxhall Gardens had once been. There were long, smooth lawns shaded by elegant trees. There were flower beds, walks, colored lamps, grottoes, illuminated temples, conservatories, a platform with a thousand mirrors where an orchestra played. There were ballets performed, a marionette theater, even a circus. On the greater open spaces there were fireworks displays, and the place was famous for its balloon ascents.

By night it was also notorious for its lewd dancing, its drinking and assignations of all kinds, some consummated on the spot, as the bushes, narrower walks, and grottoes allowed. Other assignations, further outside the law, would happen elsewhere, less publicly.

"Who took 'em all out and back for their evening's entertainment from up here?" Orme asked, more of himself than of Monk.

"Probably 'Orrie or Crumble," Monk replied as they watched the light fade over the stretch of the river, flies dipping lazily on the water, fish making little rings of ripples as they broke the surface. "But if they say it was gambling, it would be difficult to prove otherwise."

"What were the children doing?" Orme said sarcastically. "Serving their brandy? D'you suppose they could tell us anything?" His voice cracked a little. "Some of them are only five or six years old. They don't even know what happened to them. They think they're being punished for something they did."

Monk looked at Orme's face in the evening light, blunt, almost bruised by this new realization about himself. Orme had served the law all his life, and now he doubted what they were doing.

A few days ago Monk had wondered if Orme had thought Monk was squeamish, too soft to do his job. Now he saw in Orme's averted face exactly the same pain he felt himself. But victims need justice, not pity. He thought of Scuff, and wondered if either was really any good. What they needed was for it not to have happened in the first place.

IT WAS FIRST THING the following morning when the police surgeon reported to Monk regarding the death of Mickey Parfitt. The surgeon was a dark man, thin-faced with a gallows humor. He found Monk in the Chiswick Police Station studying the records they had re-created regarding the finances of Parfitt's business.

"Morning," the surgeon said cheerfully, closing the door behind him firmly.

They had met several times before. "Good morning, Dr. Gordimer," Monk replied. "I assume you have something on Parfitt's death?"

"Came for the hospitality," Gordimer replied bleakly, staring around the small, chaotic office with its piles of books and papers balanced precariously on every available surface. Any misplaced addition would send at least one pile crashing. "This is better than the morgue—marginally. Well, warmer at least."

"I prefer the Dog and Duck," Monk said drily.

Gordimer grunted. "Do you normally make this much mess? Have you lost something? You'll probably lose it all at this rate."

"Have you got anything new about Parfitt? I already know he was hit over the head and then strangled."

"Ah, but what with?" Gordimer said with satisfaction.

"Rope? Twine? Something better?" Monk put down the paper he was reading and stared hopefully at the surgeon's sardonic face.

"Much better," Gordimer said with a smile. He fished into his pocket and brought out a length of cloth. It was filthy and blood-spotted, but very recognizably knotted at regular lengths.

Monk reached for it.

Gordimer moved it just beyond his grasp.

"What is it?" Monk said curiously. "Looks like a rag."

Gordimer nodded. "A very expensive silk rag, to be precise. From close and expert examination, I believe that when it is unknotted and carefully washed, even ironed, it will prove to be a gentleman's cravat. From the little I have learned, it is made of heavy silk, embroidered with gold leopards—three of them, one above the other, very like those on the queen's arms in the flag."

Monk's stomach lurched. "You're not—"

"No," Gordimer agreed drily. "I'm not. I said 'like.' There is nothing royal about this. Any gentleman of means—and, I would add, good taste—might acquire such a cravat."

"Expensive?"

"Very."

"It was what killed him?"

"I dug it out of his neck, man! What more do you want?"

"Can you take a photograph of it and have it attested to?" Monk asked. "Then we can undo it and wash it and see it more clearly. If we can find out who owned it, we shall be a great deal further forward."

"Probably," Gordimer agreed. "Very probably."

"Thank you," Monk said sincerely.

"My pleasure," Gordimer replied. "At least I think so. Not totally sure, nasty little swine like Parfitt."

Monk smiled at him, and said nothing.

———————

BUT FINDING THE OWNER of the cravat was easier to say than to do. Monk had not expected any help from Tosh, Crumble, or 'Orrie Jones, nor did he receive it. The best places to try after that were where customers of that wealth and fashion might be picked up for the boat, such as Cremorne Gardens. But there was no point in visiting during the day; the people he was looking for were those of the night.

He began just before dusk. The cravat itself was safely locked away as evidence—he could not risk being robbed of it. He had with him a very accurate drawing of it as it would have been had the valet just presented it to its owner to put on. It was even colored, very carefully, with paint, the little gold leopards standing out.

He went in to Cremorne Gardens through the great arched wrought-iron gates with the name in huge letters over the top. There were little knots of people standing around, arms waving expressively, and there was lots of laughter and the sound of music in the air.

He walked past them to begin with, looking for the more discreet business, not the idlers but the people who were familiar with the place and had come for a specific purpose. Those were the ones who might have the information he was looking for.

Everyone he saw was drinking, showing off, always with a roving eye looking for more and greater pleasure. When Monk demanded their attention, they were annoyed and disinclined to look at the drawing for more than a second or two before denying having seen such a cravat before.

Monk's temper began to fray. He was still not sure he wanted to find whoever had wrapped this beautiful piece of silk around Parfitt's neck and tightened it until he was dead. If the law had done it with an ordinary piece of hempen rope, they would have called it justice.

What he wanted was the man who'd put up the money to buy and furnish the boat, who befriended those with weaknesses. It was he who had brought men to that dark place on the river, where they could feel the excitement of danger, where the lazy blood suddenly pumped harder with horror, the scent of pain, and the knowledge that they were flirting with ruin. He had carefully photographed the obscenity. Then, when the blood was cold, clogging again in the veins with familiar safety, he would tell them that there was an indelible record of what they had done, and their own private dabbling in hell would cost them money—for the rest of their lives.

Monk followed a winding gravel pathway to a graceful pavilion under the trees, and stood watching men and women parade by, their faces garish for a moment under the lights. A short man with a black mustache linked arms with a girl half his age. Her ample flesh strained at her bodice. Her laughter sounded vaguely tinny, as if it were forced through her throat. Many of those women were paid for what they did.

Another couple strolled past; his hat was askew, her red skirts swaying. The men were buying pleasures they could not win at home. Perhaps they were clumsy, greedy, or inadequate? Perhaps the sanctity of the home prevented the passion they had been taught a lady did not enjoy? It was more likely that love of any kind was the last thing in their hearts. They might need pain, danger, or simply endless variety.

They were all around him, laughing too loudly, the women too brightly colored.

In all of it Monk could sense a pervasive loneliness, a compulsion, not an enjoyment.

He approached a man selling tickets to one of the dance floors.

"I want to be discreet," he said with a very slight smile. "There are gentlemen here who would rather not have it known that they take their pleasures in such a place. Or should I say, they perhaps prefer the darkness, if you understand me?"

"Yes, sir," the man said guardedly. "Can't say as I can do anything about that."

"Yes, you can. I am from the Thames River Police. I can come back here in uniform, with a lot of assistance, also in uniform, if you make that necessary. I'm hoping to find a little cooperation that will very quietly embarrass a few, rather than more publicly embarrass many."

"I see, sir," the man said quickly. "Which 'few' did you 'ave in mind? I'm sure as I can 'elp yer."

"I thought you might." Monk pulled out the drawing of the cravat. "Specifically, whoever wears a tie like this one."

The man regarded it with disinterest. Then something in it struck a chord of memory. Monk saw it in his face. The man flushed, weighing the chances of lying and getting away with it. He looked at Monk's eyes, and made his decision. "Looks like the young man wot comes with Mr. Bledsoe, sir. Not that I could say for sure, like."

"Describe him," Monk said curtly.

"Tall, fair 'air. 'Andsome. Full o' charm. But, then, them gents is. Born to it. I guess it comes on the silver spoon they got in their gobs."

"I imagine so. Tell me about Mr. Bledsoe. How do you know his name?"

"'Cos I 'eard 'im called by it, o' course! D'yer think I'm a bleedin' mind reader?"

Monk ignored the challenge. "What does he look like?" he asked curiously.

"Shorter. Dark 'air. Eyes a bit close tergether. Always wears a top 'at. S'pose it makes 'im a bit taller." He snickered at the idea. "Big 'ands. I noticed as 'e 'ad great big 'ands."

Monk thanked him and left.

It did not take him long the next day to look up the Bledsoe family, and make a few inquiries at police stations in Mayfair, Park Lane, and Kensington. He mentioned that a piece of jewelry had been lost and he wanted to return it to its owner discreetly. No one argued with him, and he had no conscience about lying.

He found the Honorable Alexander Bledsoe, who answered the description of the man in Cremorne Gardens with extraordinary accuracy. His well-cared-for but unusually large hands removed any doubt. He chose to see Monk without family or servants present.

"What can I do for you, Officer?" he said with carefully judged casualness.

"I'm looking for the gentleman who lost a rather fine silk cravat," Monk replied smoothly. "I believe he might be a friend of yours."

"Not that I know of." Bledsoe smiled slightly, his shoulders relaxed, and the uneasiness vanished. "But if anyone mentions it, I'll tell them it's been found. Leave it at the local station, there's a good fellow. Someone'll pick it up." He seemed to consider looking into his pocket for a coin. His hand moved, and then stopped. He turned as if to leave.

Monk pulled the picture of the cravat out of his pocket and held it up. "It's rather distinctive," he observed.

Bledsoe glanced at it and frowned. "What the hell is this?" he said sharply. "If you've found the thing, where is it?"

"At the police station, in safekeeping," Monk replied.

"Well, get the damn thing and bring it to me. I'll see that it's returned," Bledsoe said irritably.

"It's important that I return it to the right person. Do you know who that is, sir?" Monk persisted.

"Yes, I do!" Bledsoe snapped. "Now go and fetch it! Dammit, man, what's the matter with you?"

Monk folded the picture and replaced it in his pocket. "Whose is it, sir?"

Bledsoe glared at him. "Rupert Cardew's. At least it looks like one he wore. For God's sake, why are you making such a hell of a fuss about a damn cravat?"

Monk felt a void open up inside him. He knew how much Hester liked Rupert Cardew, and how he had helped the clinic. His generosity had enabled them to buy far more medicine than before, and so treat more people.

"Are you sure?" He was startled by the hoarseness in his voice.

"Yes, I am!" Bledsoe was losing his temper. "Now fetch it, and I'll give it back to him, or I'll see that you pay for your insolence."

"I'm sorry, sir. I can't return it to you in the foreseeable future, or to Mr. Cardew. It was used in a crime. It will be evidence when the case comes to court."

"What do you mean, a crime?" Bledsoe was taken aback, his skin losing its color, his stance suddenly changed.

"It was used to strangle a man," Monk told him with some satisfaction.

The blood rushed hot into Bledsoe's face. "You tricked me!" he accused him.

"I asked you if you knew whose it was. You answered me," Monk said icily. "Do you mean that had you known it was used in a crime, then you would have lied?"

"Damn you!" Bledsoe said between his teeth. "I shall deny it."

Monk looked at him, lifting his own lip in a suggestion of disdain. "If that is what your code of honor says you must do, sir, then you must follow your conscience. It is very noble of you."

Bledsoe looked startled. "Noble?"

"Yes, sir. Now that I know whose it is, it will be easy enough to prove. You will look something of a fool in court, and everything of a liar, but you will have been loyal to your friend. Good day, sir." He turned on his heel and strode away. He was furious, but far more than that, he was filled with misery. He desperately did not want the suspect to be someone he liked—worse, someone Hester liked.

Mickey Parfitt had been a monster. Any of his victims could have been tempted to destroy him, even if afterward they would have regretted either their rage or their loss of the fuel he'd supplied for their appetite. It simply had not occurred to Monk that Rupert Cardew, with his wealth, his privilege, and above all his charm, should have become entangled in such filth.

Why not? Dependency had nothing to do with position. It was about need.

Perhaps someone had stolen the cravat from him? Monk hoped so. It would not solve the crime, but then, perhaps that did not matter.

Over the next two days he traced Rupert Cardew to various prostitutes in the Chiswick area and farther south along the riverbank. The water and its people seemed to fascinate Rupert, as if there were both a vitality and a danger in its moods, its sleeping surface, so often smooth, reflecting the light and hiding its own heart.

He found other witnesses who had seen Rupert, who knew his tastes, women he had used from time to time. It was not difficult to follow the trail of the money he had gambled and lost, the debts he had paid only with his father's help.

Eventually there was no reasonable doubt left. Monk took Orme with him and went to the magnificent house in Chelsea where Rupert

Cardew still lived with his father. He chose to go early in the morning on purpose, so there was little chance either Lord Cardew or Rupert would be out.

The butler admitted him. Perhaps he should have gone to the back door, but that was something he had always refused to do, even when he had been a junior officer in the Metropolitan Police. Now, as commander of the Thames River Police he did not even think of it.

"I require to speak to Mr. Rupert Cardew regarding a most serious matter," he said gravely as he was shown to the morning room to await Rupert's convenience.

The interior of the house was magnificent, in the manner of one that has been lived in by the same family for generations. Little was new. The large hallway had a marble-flagged floor, worn uneven by the passage of feet over generations. The wooden banister sweeping down from the gallery above was darkened in places by the constant touch of hands. There was a carved chest with animals on it, which had been carefully mended.

In the morning room the carpet was beautiful, but the sun of countless summers had muted the colors. The leather on the chairs was scuffed in places. At another time he would have loved the room. Today it hurt, fueling his anger against Mickey Parfitt and all that he'd soiled with his manipulation of weakness.

He told the footman that he would wait until Mr. Cardew had had his breakfast, and asked to see the valet. He felt deceitful to show the picture of the cravat to a servant first, trading on his innocence, but in the end it was less cruel than placing him in the position where he could lie, and would feel obliged to do so.

When it was identified, Monk waited until Rupert came into the morning room. He looked as easy and charming as when Monk had met him at the clinic in Portpool Lane.

"Morning, Monk," he said with a smile. Then he stopped. "God, man, you look dreadful! Nothing wrong with Mrs. Monk, I hope?" For a moment fear flickered in his face, as if it mattered to him.

Monk felt the deceit scorch inside him. He pulled the picture out of his pocket again and held it up.

"Your valet says that this is yours. It's pretty distinctive."

Rupert frowned. "It's a piece of paper! Did you find my cravat?"

"If this is yours, yes. Is it?" Monk insisted.

Rupert looked at him with complete incomprehension. "Why on earth does it matter? Yes, it's mine. Why?"

Monk had a moment's doubt. Had Cardew no idea what he had done? Was Parfitt so worthless that he really didn't think killing him mattered?

As if reciting something pointless, Monk told him, "It was used to murder someone called Mickey Parfitt. We found his body in the water at—" He stopped.

Rupert was ashen. Suddenly the meaning of it was clear to him.

"And you think I did it?" He had trouble articulating the words. He swayed a little, put out his hand to grasp something, but there was nothing there.

"Yes, Mr. Cardew, I do think so," Monk said quietly. "I wish I didn't. I wish I could believe he died of natural causes, but that is impossible. He was strangled with your cravat."

"I . . ." Rupert made a jerky little movement with his hand, his eyes never leaving Monk's face. "Is there any point in my denying it?"

"It's not my decision," Monk told him. "I might choose to believe you, whatever the facts say. But you knew him, you patronized his appalling boat. He blackmailed most of his clients. It was only a case of which one broke first."

"I didn't kill him," Rupert said quietly, his face scarlet. "I paid."

"And lent someone your cravat to kill him with?"

"It was stolen. Or . . . or I lost it. I don't know." Rupert's expression said he did not expect to be believed.

Monk wished Rupert would stop. It was hopeless. "Please don't make it worse than it is," he said.

"Have you told my father?"

"No. You may, if you prefer. But don't—"

"Run away?" Rupert asked with a flash of agonizing humor. "I won't. Please wait here. I shall return in a few minutes."

He kept his word. Ten minutes later he was in a hansom, sitting silently between Monk and Orme.

5

Rᴀᴛʜʙᴏɴᴇ ꜰᴇʟᴛ ᴀ ᴛᴏᴜᴄʜ of chill in the pit of his stomach when his clerk told him Monk was in the waiting room, looking tired and rather drawn.

"Send him in," Rathbone replied. He wanted to get it over with. He would find it hard to give his full attention to a client, with his imagination racing as to what it was that Monk had discovered. The fact that he had come to Rathbone at all made it inescapable that it had to do with Mickey Parfitt's murder and the boat on which he'd practiced his particularly filthy trade.

Rathbone had tried to put from his mind Sullivan's words blaming Arthur Ballinger for his downfall—first the temptation, then the corruption. Had his mind been deranged, and he had blamed Ballinger because he could not accept his own responsibility for what he had become? There had never been anything but words, perhaps hysterical—no facts, not even any details Sullivan could not have invented himself.

Monk came in through the door and closed it behind him. The clerk was right: he looked tired and miserable, almost defeated. The iron fist inside Rathbone's stomach clenched tighter. He waited.

"I found out who killed Mickey Parfitt," Monk said quietly. "The proof seems pretty conclusive. I thought you'd like to know."

"I would!" Rathbone snapped. "So damned well tell me! Don't stand there like an undertaker with toothache—tell me!"

A smile flickered across Monk's face and disappeared. "Rupert Cardew."

Rathbone was stunned. He had difficulty believing it. Certainly Rupert was a little dissolute, but surely not more than many young men with too much money and too many privileges. How on earth could he have become so degraded so young?

And yet even as a kind of sorrow washed over Rathbone, so did a relief. It was ridiculous to think that Arthur Ballinger could really have been involved with pornography, blackmail, and murder. If Claudine Burroughs had been correct and it really was Ballinger she had seen in the alley outside the shop with the photographs, then Ballinger must have been helping a friend, acting in his capacity of solicitor for some poor devil in over his head. Possibly he had even been attempting to pay off the blackmail by stealing the photographs with which the friend was being coerced. Yes, of course. A simple explanation; as soon as Rathbone thought of it, he wondered why it had taken him so long.

"I'm very sorry," he said, meeting Monk's eyes and seeing the sadness in them. For Hester, no doubt. Cardew had given much to the clinic, and she was not only grateful, but she liked him. How typical of Hester to befriend the troubled, someone others would shun when they knew.

Until she knew also; then she too would shun him. Many things she would forgive, but she would never countenance a man who abused and murdered children—vulnerable children, cold, hungry, and alone, like Scuff.

Monk stood very straight; he always did, with a kind of grace that was almost an arrogance. Except that, knowing him as well as he did, Rathbone understood that most of it was defense, his armor of belief in himself, the more rigid since his loss of memory had left him uniquely vulnerable.

Now it would be Hester whose pain Monk was preparing for. There would be no way he could comfort her, or ease the disillusion. Rupert Cardew must be like the young officers she had known in the Crimea, the ones she had seen wounded, dying, still struggling to keep some kind of dignity. She had been helpless then to save most of them, and she could do nothing for Rupert now.

Monk gave a slight shrug. "I thought you would want to know." He did not add anything about Ballinger, or Margaret, but it did not need to be said between them. Neither of them would ever forget that night on Jericho Phillips's boat—the horror and the fear that Scuff was already dead and they were too late, the stench of the dead rats in the bilges as they pulled him out, small and very white, his body shaking. Nor would they forget the corpses at Execution Dock.

"You are sure it was him?" Rathbone asked. He was surprised how normal his voice sounded.

"The bastard was strangled with his cravat," Monk told him. "The surgeon cut it out of Parfitt's neck where the flesh had swollen over it. The design is unusual—dark blue with gold leopards on it, in threes."

Rathbone felt the knots ease in his stomach even more. It was proof. He was filled with shame that someone else's despair should be such a relief to him. He knew now with certainty that he had been afraid that Ballinger was somehow involved; as the fear slipped away, he understood the power of it, and was almost giddy at the release.

"Yes," he said. "You are right, that does seem conclusive. I'm very sorry. Lord Cardew will be devastated. Poor man."

Monk said nothing. His face was still pale, and there was a bleakness in his eyes. He nodded slowly, gave Rathbone a slight smile in acknowledgment, then turned on his heel and left.

Rathbone heard him outside declining the clerk's offer of a cup of tea.

With the door closed again, Rathbone sat down behind his desk and found himself shaking with an overwhelming sense of having escaped a danger he had been bracing himself against until his body had ached with the strain of it. He had failed to pursue the possibility of Ballinger's guilt because of the irredeemable pain it would have caused Margaret were her father to be implicated. She loved her father unconditionally, with the same love that she must have borne for him in childhood, and Rathbone admired her for it.

It was the first time he had ever avoided seeking the truth, and he was ashamed. Fate had allowed him to escape facing the possible reality, and it was an undeserved gift.

This evening he would take Margaret to the dinner party for which they had already accepted an invitation. He would make it a celebration, a time of happiness she would remember. He allowed himself to think of that until the clerk told him the first client of the day had arrived.

THE DINNER PARTY WAS magnificent. Rathbone had recently given Margaret a beautiful necklace of garnets and river pearls, with earrings and a bracelet to match. It was a bit extravagant, but exactly the kind of rich yet discreet setting she most liked. This evening she wore them with a gown of deep wine-red silk. It was fuller-skirted than she usually chose and perhaps even a little lower at the bosom. The jewels gleamed against her pale, flawless skin, and with a faint flush of happiness in her cheeks she was lovelier than he had ever seen her before.

They swept into the main reception room with a rustle of silk and to polite words of welcome. There were nearly a score of people present. The men were in elegant black, women in a blaze of colors, from the youngest in gleaming pastels to older doyennes of the aristocracy in burgundies, midnight blues, plums, and rich browns. Diamonds glinted with suppressed fire; ropes of pearls glowed on bare skin. There was soft laughter, the clink of glass, slight movement, like a wind through a field of flowers.

Margaret held Rathbone's arm a little more tightly. He could smell the warmth of her perfume, sweet and indefinable.

"Ah! Sir Oliver—Lady Rathbone! How delightful to see you." The welcome was repeated again and again. He knew them all and didn't need to rack his memory for a name, a position, or an achievement. He replied easily, shared a joke or an item of news, a comment on the latest book or exhibition of art.

It was not until they went in to dinner that he realized there was an odd number of them, something no hostess in England would ever allow intentionally.

"What is it?" Margaret whispered, seeing his puzzlement.

"There are nineteen of us," he replied, speaking almost under his breath.

"Something must have happened," she said with certainty. "Someone is ill." She looked around casually, trying to conceal the fact. "It's a man," she said finally. "There are ten women here."

Then suddenly the answer was obvious, as was the reason no one had mentioned it. The missing man was Lord Cardew.

Considering who had been invited, Rathbone was certain that when the ladies had retired after dinner, the gentlemen would be discussing over port and cigars the vexed question of industrial pollution. He remembered Ballinger saying it was a subject Lord Cardew had been involved in for years. Rathbone wondered if it had been Cardew who had somehow prevailed upon Lord Justice Garslake to change his mind, and thus the ruling of the Court of Appeal on the case.

He felt a sinking sensation of misery inside himself, and guilt that he was here with his happiness unclouded. It was in no way his fault that Rupert Cardew had murdered Parfitt. It was Rathbone's relief that shamed him, and the fact that he had been prepared to look the other way when discomfort threatened his own happiness. Perhaps Lord Cardew had done that for years—refused to see what Rupert really was, face the truth and at least attempt to do something about it. In that, then, they would be the same, except that Rathbone had not had to pay anything for it.

"Oliver?" Margaret's voice interrupted his thoughts.

He dismissed them immediately, forcing himself to think only of the moment, and of her.

"Yes," he lied. "Someone must have been taken ill. Let us hope it is slight and he will soon be better." He put his hand over hers briefly, then moved forward, smiling, and took his place at the table.

No one mentioned Cardew, or any other subject that could cloud the enjoyment of the occasion. Rathbone was happy to see Margaret so forgetting her earlier shyness that she laughed openly, making amusing and sometimes even slightly barbed responses to the opinions with which she disagreed. More than once a ripple of laughter swept around the table, a flash of appreciation for her wit.

Rathbone was proud of her.

He thought of Hester—her quick tongue, the passion that made her outrageous at times, her fury at incompetence and the pride that covered deceit, the pity that made her crusade so inappropriately, caring too little for the consequences. He would always find her exciting, but he had once mistaken that for love and imagined he would be happy with her. Thank heaven she had refused him. At a dinner party like this, he would always have been waiting for her to say something disastrous, something so candid it could never be forgotten, much less ignored.

He looked across the table now at Margaret, her face serious as she answered the man to her left, talking about the enormous power of industry and the complexity of profit and responsibility. There was nothing dismissive in his attitude. He was not in the slightest humoring her as he explained how such giants could not be fought against.

Rathbone smiled. And then, as if sensing his gaze on her, Margaret looked up, and her eyes were warm, bright, full of happiness.

That sweet mood of intimacy lasted all through the carriage ride home, and became more intense as they dismissed the servants for the night and went upstairs alone. Suddenly passion was easy and without hesitation. There was no moment of reassurance necessary, no asking. To have spoken at all would have been to doubt the gift of such happiness.

But the next morning in Rathbone's office, his peace of mind and heart was shattered.

"Lord Cardew is here to see you, Sir Oliver," the clerk said gravely. "I told him that I would have to consult you, but I took the liberty of asking Lady Lavinia Stock if she would consult you at another time.

The matter is trivial, and she was quite agreeable to postponing her appointment."

Rathbone stared at him, horrified. The man was an excellent clerk, and had given too many years' loyal service for Rathbone to dispense with him, but this was nonetheless a liberty.

The clerk had a slight flush in his cheeks, but he met Rathbone's eyes without blinking.

"Knowing you as I do, sir, I felt certain that you would offer him at least the kindness of listening to him, even should you not wish to take the case—or not feel it is one you are able to handle."

Rathbone drew in his breath to give a swift retort, and realized with a mild amusement that the man had very neatly boxed him in. He would never admit that he was not able to handle a case, nor on the other hand could he refuse to listen to Cardew in what must be the most appalling state of distress of his life.

"You had better show him in, since you have clearly made up your mind that I should take the case," he said drily.

The clerk bowed. "It is not for me to decide which cases you take, Sir Oliver. I will show Lord Cardew in immediately. Shall I make tea, or perhaps in the circumstances you would prefer something a little stronger? Perhaps the brandy?"

"Tea will be excellent, thank you. I shall need to be very sober indeed to help in this matter. And . . ."

"Yes, Sir Oliver?"

"We shall have words about this later."

"Yes, sir. I'll bring the tea as soon as it is brewed."

He returned a moment later and opened the door for Lord Cardew. He was in his early sixties, although today he looked twenty years more. His skin was drained of all color, and dry like old parchment. He stood straight, shoulders squared, but he moved as if his whole body were filled with pain.

Anything as banal as "Good morning" seemed ridiculous. There could be nothing good in it for this man. Rathbone thanked the clerk and excused him, then gestured to the big leather chair opposite the desk, for Cardew to sit down.

"I am aware of what has happened," Rathbone said quickly, to spare Cardew the pain of telling him. "At least the rudiments."

Cardew looked startled.

"Commander Monk has long been a friend of mine," Rathbone explained.

"He tells you of all his cases?" Cardew asked with disbelief.

"Not at all, sir. But this one distressed him more than most, because of its connection to the Jericho Phillips case a very short while ago."

Cardew looked like an old man too stubborn to admit defeat. Rathbone had seen other men like that, for whom surrender was too alien to be considered. They were bewildered, carrying on from force of habit and inability to think of any alternative.

"Why should he be distressed?" Cardew asked. "He is doing his job. In his place I would assume my son to be guilty. Such evidence as they have indicates it to be so. That creature was undoubtedly killed with Rupert's cravat. Even I could not argue against it. The thing is distinctive. I know. I gave it to him. Apparently they cut it off the wretched man's neck."

"Did Rupert confess that he did it?" Rathbone asked.

A flush spread up Cardew's cheeks, and he lowered his eyes. Cowardice was a sin neither his nature nor his upbringing could forgive. A gentleman did not make excuses, he did not complain, and above all he did not lie to escape the consequences of his acts.

"No, he did not," he said, so quietly that Rathbone barely heard him.

Rathbone considered any words of comfort he could offer, and all were inadequate, trite, or the very lies that Cardew so despised.

"What is it you would like me to do?" Rathbone said gently.

Cardew looked up. "Do you know what Parfitt was?"

"I know at least something of it." Memory assailed Rathbone like a wave of nausea. "I know what Jericho Phillips was. I was there on his boat. I saw his corpse at Execution Dock, and I could look at it without regret. He died obscenely, but I could feel only relief that he was gone. I'm not proud of that. Indeed, it is something I prefer not to recall."

"Then, you will understand why I have no pity for Mickey Parfitt," Cardew replied. "Is there not some plea of mitigation you can make for the man who killed him—if only to save him from the gallows?" He said the last word as if sticking a knife into himself.

"I can try," Rathbone said reluctantly. How often had this man pleaded with someone for leniency toward the son who had let him down with such anguish? Did he never grow tired of it? Did he wonder now whether, if he had made Rupert pay for his errors earlier, pay the full price then when they'd been so much less, might Rupert have learned the lesson, and this would not now be happening? Did he go on, exhausted as he was, because he understood that his gentleness before had been only an evasion of the inevitable? That in that space between, it had grown until now the price would be his life?

Cardew leaned forward, his face tense, his eyes fixed on Rathbone's. "He won't tell me what happened. I was able to see him only briefly before they took him away. But if he killed Parfitt, then perhaps it was in self-defense. Or the defense of someone else. Is that mitigation in the law?"

"If it was to save the life of someone else who was in immediate danger of being killed, then it is certainly more than mitigation," Rathbone answered. "If it can be proved beyond a reasonable doubt, it is justification. But I'm afraid that might be very difficult to convince a jury of now, when Rupert has been arrested, since an innocent man would have said so at the time."

Cardew winced. "Of course. Yet I cannot believe that Rupert would kill him without the most terrible compulsion to do so. He has a temper, but he is not a fool." He swallowed hard, as if he had an obstruction in his throat. "And in spite of his immorality in other directions, he has a sense of honor, in his own way. Killing a man in cold blood, even a man like Parfitt, would not be . . . acceptable. It is a coward's way." Unconsciously his shoulders squared a little as he said this, as though facing some threat himself.

Rathbone smiled slightly, but utterly without pleasure. "I have some difficulty in deciding for myself what 'cold blood' really is."

At that moment the clerk knocked on the door and, with Rathbone's permission, came in with the tray, of tea in a silver pot, a silver

cream jug and sugar bowl, and silver tongs and teaspoons. The porcelain was plain, delicate, and ornamented only by a small blue crown.
In spite of Rathbone's refusal, the clerk had also brought a bottle of
Napoleon brandy, and set it on the sideboard. He poured the tea,
then excused himself and withdrew.

"How civilized," Cardew said with a desperate edge to his voice.
"How intensely British. We sit here with tea in German porcelain
cups, with French brandy if we need the fire of it, and we talk about
murder, justice, and hanging. We would sit exactly like this, with the
same tone of voice, if we were speaking of the weather."

"Because we have to use our intelligence, not our emotions,"
Rathbone answered. "The self-indulgence of feelings will not help
your son."

"Self-indulgence," Cardew said with the first touch of bitterness
that Rathbone had heard in him. "Rupert's sin, which I never curbed
in him. I saw it, and I let it pass, as if he would grow out of it. Why is
it we still see our sons as children who can be excused, given time and
love and patience, even when they are grown men and need to know
better? The world will make no such excuses for them, and it is deceit
that we do. Unspoken, of course, but a deceit nevertheless."

"Because we love day by day, inch by inch," Rathbone replied.
"We don't notice the passing of time and the dangers that we should
have prevented, or at least should have warned of. But none of that
will help us now." He looked steadily at Cardew. "You obviously are
familiar with Parfitt's name and reputation. How do you come to
know that, sir?"

Cardew was startled, then deeply uncomfortable.

Rathbone had a nightmarish thought that perhaps Cardew himself had once been tempted to such pastimes as Parfitt had provided,
and then he dismissed it as ridiculous and repulsive. Nevertheless, the
question required an answer, and he waited for it.

Cardew avoided his eyes again. "Rupert has caused me a certain
embarrassment most of his adult life, let us say the last fifteen years,
since he was eighteen. Often I have known in what ways because
I . . . I helped him when necessary." It was an evasion of the ugliness

of the truth, and they were both embarrassingly aware of it. Even now Cardew could not bring himself to be literal.

Rathbone was not enlightened by euphemisms. "Lord Cardew," he said grimly, "I cannot do anything useful for your son if I don't know what I am fighting against. What trouble? He paid for prostitution—unflattering, but not unusual. Certainly not a crime for which any gentleman is punished by the law, especially a man who is not married and therefore does not owe a sexual loyalty to anyone. It is not worth mentioning—and is far better than seducing a young woman of virtue and with expectation of marriage. That is a moral offense of some weight, but still not punishable by law."

Cardew's face was ashen, his shoulders so tight that in places they strained the fabric of his jacket, but he said nothing.

"Force would be a different matter," Rathbone continued. "Rape is a crime, no matter who the victim is, although society would bother little if the woman were of questionable virtue anyway. Unless there were a great deal of violence involved. Is that the case?"

"Rupert has a temper," Cardew said almost under his breath, his voice cracking with emotional tension, "but so far as I am aware, his quarrels were always with other men."

"Violent?" Rathbone pressed.

Cardew hesitated. "Yes . . . sometimes. I don't know what they were about. I preferred not to."

"But they were not justified?"

"Justified? How can beating a man nearly senseless be justified?"

"Self-defense . . . or defense of someone else weaker, already injured, or in some other way helpless."

"I wish I could believe it was as excusable as that."

"Is that all—just fighting?"

"Is that not enough?" Cardew said miserably. "The use of prostitutes, drunkenness, brawling until you injure a man for the rest of his life? Good God, Rathbone, Rupert was brought up as a gentleman. He is heir to all I have, the privileges and the responsibilities. How can I ever allow him to marry a decent woman? I couldn't do that to another man's daughter."

Rathbone had seen scores of men sit in this chair in his quiet office, so racked with fear and pain that it filled the room like a charge of electricity. But none deeper than this, perhaps the worse because Cardew's pain was not for himself but for someone he loved. Had Rupert any idea of the hell he was inflicting? If he could even imagine it, then he was close to inexcusable.

Rathbone thought of Arthur Ballinger, and how loyal his children were, especially Margaret. To torture him like this would have been unthinkable.

How worthless Rupert Cardew was in comparison. What utter selfishness governed him?

Rathbone thought of his own father. Their friendship was perhaps the most precious thing in his life because it was the bedrock on which all else rested. He could not remember a time when Henry Rathbone had not been there to advise, to share a problem, to encourage, and at times to praise.

Would he and Margaret have sons one day, and would he be as good a father?

What had Lord Cardew done, or omitted to do, that had led to this tragedy? Bought his son's love with a leniency that in the end corroded both of them? Averted the pain of confrontation, the loneliness of the turning away, even if only fleetingly? Rathbone understood it so easily, but as he looked at Cardew's haunted face, he could also imagine the price.

Was that the guilt that Cardew felt, that somehow he should have prevented this? A word, a silence, a decision carried through, and it might all have been different?

There was nothing left to do now but try to help.

"Why would Rupert kill Mickey Parfitt?" Rathbone asked. "There must be some connection. It wasn't a crime of rage. Mickey was hit on the head; then, when he was at least dazed, possibly unconscious, he was deliberately strangled with a cravat, which was knotted, to be more effective with pressure on the throat, the windpipe, the veins of the neck. That is not impulse of fury or hot temper. And I don't see how it could possibly be self-defense." He found it hard to keep his eyes on Cardew's face, but he owed it to the man at least to look at him while he said such things.

Cardew sat motionless.

"No one happens by chance to find his best cravat in his pocket, handily knotted so as to be a more effective weapon," Rathbone continued. "He carried it with him for the purpose of killing someone. It is not a weapon of self-defense. The bough of a tree might be perhaps, but if he had already struck him senseless with it, and if escape from his own danger were the purpose, he would have left then. But he remained, took off his cravat, knotted it, and then strangled the unconscious man lying at his feet. Not to mention then dropping him into the river."

Cardew winced each time Rathbone spoke. "Parfitt was an abomination," Cardew said with loathing. "The most degraded of human beings, scarcely fit to walk upright. He preyed upon the weaknesses of others, indulging them until his victims became almost as depraved as he was. Then he blackmailed them. And if you think that was the depth to which he sank, think of the children he used to do this. They were blameless, and they suffered the most, and without escape. Any man who killed him has done a service, as a doctor who has rid us of a filthy disease." He took a deep breath. "And don't bother to tell me that that does not justify murder. I am perfectly aware of it. I need help, Sir Oliver, not a sermon on the sanctity of all human life."

Rathbone smiled bleakly. "I have no intention of offering you one, Lord Cardew. I totally agree with you. And believe me, if it is I who stand in court before a judge and jury to plead Rupert's case, I will draw such a portrait of Mickey Parfitt that they will see him for what he was. But I will need more than his depravity to justify his death. The jury will require to know why Rupert in particular, of all his victims, was the one who actually killed him. I must tell it from his point of view, in particulars, not generalities. They must walk in his shoes, feel his fear, outrage, whatever it was that drove him to such an act. The prosecutor will be clever and articulate also, and will defend Parfitt's right to live as he would that of any of us."

"Of course. I understand. We cannot allow any one of us to be the unappointed judge and executioner of another. The simple answer is that I don't know why Rupert killed him. I didn't have the chance to ask him. And to tell you the truth, I am not sure whether he would tell me . . ." He struggled for a moment to find words for what he could hardly bear to say.

Rathbone put an end to it, as one would put an animal out of its pain. "Of course," he said, cutting across him, "it is often easier to speak to someone whose opinion does not touch your emotions. It happens to many of the people I see in my office. With your permission, I shall go to the prison and speak to Rupert immediately." He rose to his feet. "I think we should address this as soon as possible. I will see that he is being reasonably treated, and that he has all that he is permitted for his comfort. I will speak to you as soon as I have something of value to say." He held out his hand.

Cardew rose to his feet slowly. It seemed to cost him some effort, but when he clasped Rathbone's hand, it was with surprising power. A drowning man, reaching for help amid the overwhelming waves.

By early afternoon Rathbone was in the entrance of Newgate Prison. The huge iron doors closed behind him, and a sour-faced warden beckoned him along the narrow corridors toward the cell where he would be permitted to interview Rupert Cardew. His footsteps sounded hard on the floor, but the echo died almost immediately, as if the stone of the walls suffocated it. The place was a curious mixture of life and death. Rathbone was acutely conscious of emotional pain, of fear, remorse, the dread of physical extinction and what might lie beyond in the nightmares of the soul. And yet the place stifled life. There was no energy, nothing could breathe here, nothing could grow or have will.

The warden walked ahead of him without ever turning to ascertain if he was following. But, then, who would wish to wander alone in this maze of corridors, all the same and all leading nowhere?

The man stopped, took a key from the chain at his belt, and unlocked the iron door, swinging it open with a squeal of unoiled hinges.

"Thank you," Rathbone said curtly, walking past him. "I'll knock when I'm ready to leave."

The man acknowledged with a silent nod and slammed the door shut. The sound of the lock going home on the outside was as loud as the clang of iron on stone had been.

The cell was bare except for two wooden chairs and a small table, which was scarred and dented. One leg was shorter than the other three, so that when Rathbone touched it, the table wobbled before settling back to its place.

Rupert Cardew stood in the center of the small space. He was wearing the shirt and trousers in which he must have been arrested, and he was crumpled and unshaven. However, he held himself upright and met Rathbone's eyes without wavering.

"I'm here at your father's request," Rathbone began. He was used to meeting accused men or women in circumstances like these, but it never grew any easier. For almost all of the major cases he dealt with, it was the person's first time in prison, and the sheer shock of it caused either numbness or a panic that was close to hysteria. All too often, the shadow of the hangman's noose darkened all reason and hope. Even the innocent were terrified. There was no trust in the judgment of the law when it was your own life in the balance.

Rupert nodded. He found it difficult to speak, and when he forced the words out, his tone was uneven.

"I knew he would . . . help. I . . . I'm not sure what you can do. The evidence seems to be . . . to be . . ." He breathed in and out deeply. "If I were Monk, I would believe as he does. The cravat is mine—no argument."

Rathbone heard the nervousness in his voice, the tension. He put his hand out and pulled the chair nearest him away from the table. He waved at the other. "Sit down, Mr. Cardew. I need you to tell me as much as you can, from the beginning. It might be simpler if I ask you questions."

Rupert obeyed, unintentionally scraping the chair legs on the floor. He sat down awkwardly, but his hands on the table were strong and lean, and Rathbone saw with respect that they did not tremble.

"You do not question that it was your cravat?" Rathbone asked.

"No," Rupert said wryly. "I don't imagine there are many like that. My father gave it to me. I expect he had it made. His tailor would swear to it."

"I see." He was not surprised, but it might have been an advantage if the point could have been argued. "What time did you leave home that evening?"

"I expected you to ask me that. Early. It was a lovely evening." He gave a twisted grimace, not quite a smile, as if the bitter humor of it were momentarily overwhelming. "I walked down by the river for an hour or more. I lost track of time. . . ."

Rathbone held up his hand to stop him. "Down by the river where? You don't live anywhere near Chiswick."

"Of course not. Who the devil lives in Chiswick? But I didn't want to wander along the Embankment and run into half a dozen people I know who would want to talk politics, or gossip. I took a boat up the river, and I've racked my brain to recall anyone I knew who saw me. But the whole charm of going up on the water is the peace of it, the very fact that you don't meet anyone you know. I'm sorry." He shrugged very slightly, with barely a movement of his shoulders.

"You didn't row yourself!" Rathbone observed.

"Well, actually, I did."

"You hired a boat? From whom? They'll have a record of it."

"No. I have my own. At least, I share it with a fellow I know. But he's in Italy at the moment. No use, is it!"

"No," Rathbone agreed. "Where did you go—exactly?"

"Chiswick. I tied it up at one of the mooring posts up there opposite the Chiswick Eyot. Then I went along the Mall and had a drink at the pub off Black Lion Lane. I spoke to a few lads I know, but I doubt they'd remember it. Just stupid remarks about the weather, that sort of thing."

"Then what?"

Rupert looked down at his hands on the table. "Then I went and visited a woman I know—a girl."

"Is that a euphemism for a prostitute?" Rathbone inquired.

A dull color marked Rupert's cheeks. "Yes."

"Her name?"

"Hattie Benson."

"You know her? Other than in the carnal sense?"

Rupert looked up quickly. "Yes. But I don't imagine her word is going to help a lot. I still had my cravat then. I remember taking it off, so it must have been before Parfitt was killed with it. Unless someone killed him with another silk cravat, exactly like mine. That's a bit of a stretch, isn't it?" There was a flicker of hope in his voice, but he killed it himself, before Rathbone had the chance.

"Yes. I'm afraid it is," Rathbone replied. "Where did you go after you left Miss Benson?"

"I don't know. I was pretty drunk. I fell asleep somewhere, I don't remember where. When I woke up, it was dark, and I felt like hell. I went over to the horse trough, stuck my head into the water, sobered up a bit, and then rowed home." He looked at Rathbone, waiting for the condemnation he expected.

"The prosecution won't be able to make a case unless they can prove that you knew Mickey Parfitt, and had some reason to want him dead," Rathbone told him. "Tell me of all your dealings with him, and don't lie to me. If they catch you out even once, it will be sufficient to shatter any credibility you might have with the jury."

Rupert stared at him, the skin tight across his cheeks, his mouth drawn into a line of pain.

"It is too late for discretion," Rathbone warned him. "I shall not tell anyone anything you can afford for me to hide. Particularly I shall not tell your father. He will suffer quite enough in spite of all I can do."

Rupert looked as if Rathbone had struck him and bruised his face deeper than the flesh.

"I did not kill Parfitt," he said clearly.

Rathbone continued exactly as if he had not spoken. "What was your connection with him? When and where did you first meet? If any of this is verifiable, I'd like to know that too."

Rupert looked down at the scarred tabletop. "I met him just over two years ago. I was out with a group of friends, at Black Lion Lane again. We were all pretty high and bored. Somebody began telling tall stories about women they'd had, not just in London, but Paris, somebody said Berlin, and someone else said Madrid. The stories got taller and taller, most of them lies, I expect." He took a deep breath. "Then someone said he knew of a place a lot more daring than anything mentioned so far. He said danger was the thing that really made your heart beat, and the blood—" He stopped. He was looking at Rathbone's exquisite suit, his crisp, clean shirt.

"I can imagine," Rathbone said drily. "You don't have to fill in the details of what he described. The risk of ruin was the ultimate temptation."

"Yes," Rupert said very quietly. "I can't believe now that I was so stupid!"

"It was a boat on the river?"

"You know what it was."

"I still need you to tell me."

Rupert winced. "I went out, with the others. I suppose there were half a dozen of us, something like that. The boat was moored up on the other side of the Chiswick Eyot. Quite a row. With the cooler air I was close to sober when we got there. At first it looked like another brothel, except on a boat. We were made welcome, given some of the best brandy I've ever had. Then . . . then there was a kind of performance, very explicit . . . men and little boys. Some of them were not more than five or six years old." His voice cracked, and his face was scarlet.

Rathbone waited.

"It . . . it was a form of club. There were . . . initiation rites. We had to . . . take part . . . and be photographed. It was a dare—the ultimate risk . . . in which you could lose everything. We all did it." His voice sank to a whisper. "I didn't have the courage to refuse. Afterward I scrambled up the gangway and vomited over the side into the river. I wanted to leave, but there was no way, other than jumping into the water and hoping to survive." He gulped. "If I'd been worth anything, I'd have done that. Wading out of the river covered in mud and sodden to the skin on the streets of Chiswick would have been better than the hell that followed."

Rathbone could imagine it more easily than he wished. There

had been some days at university when he himself had been less than sober, less than discreet. He would greatly prefer that his father did not know about those days, even if he might guess. His excesses had never been of this magnitude, but the hot burn of shame was just as real.

"Please go on," he said more gently.

"I staggered back toward the gangway downstairs again, and one of Parfitt's men came up behind me. We collided, and somehow the next thing I knew I was falling downward, thumping and bashing myself against the walls, until I landed at the bottom. I can remember faces peering at me in a sort of haze, and I felt dreadful. Then I must have passed out, because the next thing I knew I was lying on a bed in one of the cabins, and Mickey Parfitt himself was looking at me, sneering.

" 'Shouldn't drink so much, Mr. Cardew,' he said with satisfaction oozing out of him. 'Fell downstairs, you did. But had your bit of fun first.' At the time I didn't remember the staged show with the little boys, or the photograph, so I didn't feel anything much. He gave me a stiff jolt of brandy and helped me to my feet. I went back over the river with my friends—what a damn stupid word for them!" For a moment bitterness flashed across his face.

Rathbone felt himself sympathizing and, to his amazement, also believing him. "Then what happened?" he asked, although he knew.

Rupert looked down again. "About a week later Parfitt sent a letter to my home, inviting me to join them on the boat again. I burned the letter."

"But he wrote again?"

"Yes. I ignored it the second time. Burned it without opening it, actually. The third time he sent a letter to my father. I recognized the writing. I burned the one to my father, but I read the one to me. He said that I had entered into a contract with him, and there was a photograph to prove it. Whether I went to the boat again or not, I still owed him the money."

"Blackmail." Rathbone nodded. It was cleverer than he had thought, much harder to prove in court. How could he show that there had been no "gentleman's agreement"? Such things were often unwritten, especially regarding something like gambling, or the services of a prostitute. No one put those "agreements" in writing.

Rupert nodded. "I realized it only then. God, I was so stupid!" His voice was heavy with self-disgust.

"Did you pay?"

Rupert's face tightened. "With that photograph? Of course I did. I meant to buy myself a little time, and then think what to do. I knew if I didn't do something, the bastard would have me paying for the rest of my life."

Rathbone looked at him, searching his eyes. He saw desperation, profound embarrassment, even shame, but curiously, no awareness of having just admitted to the perfect motive for murder. Was that because he felt himself justified? And if he did, could Rathbone disagree with him? If ever a man deserved to be gotten rid of, it was Mickey Parfitt. Thinking of him, it was as if Jericho Phillips had risen from the dead.

"Well, you're rid of him now," he said with asperity.

"Hardly," Rupert said bitterly. "He'll take me down to the grave with him. It almost makes me wish I had killed him!"

"Didn't you?"

Rupert's head jerked up, his eyes hot. "No, I didn't!"

Rathbone was used to denial. Almost everyone claimed either that they did not do it at all or that, if they did, it was either an accident or the victim deserved it. And yet he was on the brink of believing Rupert Cardew, which was totally unreasonable. Every scrap of evidence pointed to him.

"Then, who did?" he said grimly. "With your cravat?"

"I don't know. Whoever found it, I suppose."

Rathbone opened his eyes wide. "They chanced on your cravat, lying wherever it was, and thought, 'Ah, I know what I'll do with this. I'll tie a few knots in it, and then I'll strangle someone. What about Mickey Parfitt? We'd all be better off without him.' "

Rupert flushed hotly. "I don't know who killed him, or why. There could be a dozen reasons, and fifty men with one at least as good as mine. I only know that I didn't. I've never been so drunk that I couldn't remember what I'd done—just not always where, or with whom." He gave a slight shrug, and a flicker of humor lit his eyes for an instant, then vanished.

Rathbone's mind raced. Was it conceivable that Rupert really was innocent, at least of the murder? A reasonable doubt would prevent his conviction, but not remove from people's minds the belief that he was guilty. Some might praise him for it, but the stain would still be indelible. The only good answer would be to prove someone else's guilt.

"What do you know about Parfitt?" he asked. "Apart from what you have told me. Where did he come from? Who are his partners in the boat? He didn't find the money to buy it in the first place without help. Who was it? Who else shares the profit? Who are his other clients whom he might have pushed over the edge into ruin? And did he blackmail only for money, or for favors also?"

"Favors?" Rupert blinked. "You mean—"

"Political favors," Rathbone corrected him. "Or worse, perhaps, judicial favors?"

"Judicial . . . ?" Rupert began, and then stopped as understanding swept over him. "God, I never thought of that. Would he really?"

"I don't know. But you see the possibilities?"

Rupert was pale now. Was he thinking of his father, and the power he had in the House of Lords, the influence on members who fought for reform? If Rupert's own reputation were in the balance, what might Cardew have been coerced into doing to save him?

"What made you think of that?" he asked. "Do you know something?" There was fear in his voice now, no anger left.

"No," Rathbone said truthfully. "But that is what Jericho Phillips did, and it seems an obvious thing."

"Phillips?" Rupert asked.

"Yes."

"Then Parfitt would too. He learned all his skills from Phillips. He started by working for him, downriver from Chiswick, nearer Westminster and that way."

"You're sure?"

"Yes."

"Then, you know more about him than the one visit you're telling me about."

Rupert paled. "Look . . . I went three times, and I'm ashamed of it. The first time, it wasn't so bad. Or the second. Young men, but we all know that kind of thing goes on. A bit of gambling, and a hell of a lot to drink. If I'd had any sense, I'd have known that wasn't all there was to it, but I didn't think. I . . . I wanted to stay in with the friends I had. I haven't been back, ever."

Against all his experiences of frightened men lying when accused, Rathbone believed him. But at the same time, it robbed him of a defense that he could hope to succeed with, or at least use to mitigate the sentence sufficiently to avoid the rope. He shrank from telling Rupert this now. He could not work with him paralyzed with fear. He had to have as much of the truth as possible in order to defend against the evidence the Crown would bring. Mickey Parfitt's death was not a cause célèbre, but Rupert Cardew in the dock most certainly would be.

"Do you know who has been?" Rathbone asked.

Rupert was stunned. "I can't tell you the names of my friends who were there! For God's sake, that would be a despicable thing to do."

"Even if one of them murdered Mickey Parfitt?"

"Betray them all because one of them might have killed him? Is that what you would do, Sir Oliver?" Suddenly the challenge was sharp and very personal.

Rathbone admired him for it. "You want me to answer that truthfully?" he asked.

"Yes, I do. Would you?"

"No, Mr. Cardew. But, then, my friends don't frequent places like that, so far as I know. But I wouldn't know, because I don't. I've seen what men like Phillips and Parfitt do to children, and I'd be happy if the law allowed anyone who wished to get rid of them all. But if we permit people to make their own decisions as to who should live and who should die, it would be a license to murder at will. We can always find excuses when we want them. All of which you know as well as I do."

"I still can't tell you the names of the men I know who went to that boat."

"Not yet. When you know more of what Parfitt did, and how he used his power, you may change your mind." Rathbone rose to his feet.

"Will you represent me?" Rupert asked, standing also. His knuckles were clenched, and he had to brace himself to keep his body from shaking.

"Yes," Rathbone replied without hesitation, surprising himself by the firmness of his decision, as if no other answer had occurred to him.

BUT NONE OF IT seemed so easy to explain to Margaret that evening in their own quiet dining room, with the faint aroma of apple wood burning in the fire and the gaslights soft.

"Rupert Cardew?" she said with amazement. "How awful for his father. The poor man must be devastated." Her face was bleak with pity.

"Yes. I wish I could offer him more hope," Rathbone agreed. They were at the dining room table. The air was warm outside, and the long curtains still weren't drawn, letting in the sweet smells of earth and leaves as the garden faded with the year. There were golden chrysanthemums and purple asters in bloom. The summer flowers were cut down, but it was too early for the leaves to turn. There was no rich perfume of wood smoke or bonfires yet.

"There's nothing you can do, Oliver," she said gently. "Just don't shun him when he comes back into society again. So many people do, because they don't know what to say, and it's easier to say nothing than face other people's pain."

"If he's found guilty, they'll hang him," he replied. "There won't be any 'coming back.' "

Her eyes widened with surprise. "For goodness' sake, I meant Lord Cardew, not Rupert! Of course they'll hang him. There's no other possible answer."

He looked at her and saw no trace of indecision in her face, and only a remnant of the pity she had felt for Lord Cardew, nothing fresh for Rupert.

"Parfitt tried to blackmail him," he said, reaching absentmindedly for the salt, and then, realizing that he had already used it, putting it down again. "It would have gone on forever."

"Of course it would. Until his father refused to pay," she said drily, returning her attention to her meal. They had an excellent cook, both imaginative and skilled, but tonight Rathbone barely tasted his food.

"You haven't asked me if I believe he did it," he pointed out, and then realized how critical he sounded.

Margaret put her fork down. "Do you doubt it?"

"There must always be room for doubt—"

"Don't be pedantic, Oliver," she interrupted him. "I know that, legally. I mean do you, personally, doubt it?"

"Yes, I do. He denies it, and I believe he may be speaking the truth. He is hardly the only one to wish Parfitt dead."

"There is all the difference in the world between wishing some-one dead and making it so," she said reasonably. "How much differ-ence is there between a man who will pay others to torture and abuse small boys for his gratification, and one who will kill the provider of such abomination rather than continue to pay for it?"

He heard the anger in her voice, and the revulsion. He would not have expected anything less. He felt it himself. And yet he also un-derstood Rupert's horror when he realized what his blindness and stu-pidity had led him into. Was he naïve to believe that Rupert might actually be innocent of the murder of Parfitt? Was he acting on ex-actly the kind of emotional loyalty, devoid of reason, that he saw in Margaret's family? Lord Cardew reminded him of his own father, and his pity was instinctive and immediate.

"I've agreed to defend him," he said aloud.

Margaret froze.

Now he was compelled to justify himself. "Everyone deserves a defense, Margaret, the benefit of doubt until guilt is proved."

"Of course he needs to be defended," she agreed, her eyes bright and angry. "But not by you. You are the finest barrister in London, maybe in the whole of England. Your very presence will draw atten-tion to the case and make people believe there is something to be said for the whole repulsive business. Whatever you argue on the niceties of the law, the vast majority of people will believe you are doing it because of his father's title and money, not because you have any real belief in his innocence."

"No one will who knows me," he said with a touch of chill. Her accusation hurt. It caught him by surprise that she should think it.

"Most people don't know you," she said reasonably, but there was a pucker between her brows. "They will simply leap to the easiest conclusion."

"And I should cater to them?" he inquired.

"You are exaggerating," she answered coolly. "I didn't suggest that you follow every whim of public opinion, merely that you do not need to defend every criminal, no matter how base their crime, just to prove that the law must be honored. Let someone else defend Rupert Cardew."

"You mean so that we may hang him and then go home and still sleep well?"

"Yes, I suppose I do mean that." Now it was a definite retaliation. "If you are going to hang anyone at all, then Rupert Cardew deserves it. The use of children in prostitution and pornography is bestial. Anyone who had a part in that, of any sort, deserves the rope." She leaned forward over her plate, the food now entirely forgotten. "And don't tell me he didn't actively participate. That is irrelevant, Oliver, and you know it. He knew, and he did nothing about it. He could have called the police, made the whole thing public, but instead he chose to kill Parfitt, in order to spare his own embarrassment, and that of his friends who are little better. You can't defend him, because it is indefensible."

He was stunned into silence.

"I suppose Lord Cardew asked you to," she went on. "And you were too softhearted to refuse him. Of course the poor man believes his son is innocent. What else could he bear to believe?"

"Perhaps he is right?" he said softly, placing his knife and fork on the plate. His food was half-eaten, but he no longer wanted it.

"Nonsense," she answered. "And Cook will be offended if you don't eat at least most of that."

"Tell her I'm ill. In fact, I'll tell her myself." Rathbone rose to his feet. The thought of remaining at the table in a bitter silence was so unpleasant, he would rather retreat into work. Any excuse would do. "As you have pointed out, it will be exceedingly difficult to present any believable defense. And if I don't make a reasonable show of it, I will not only let Rupert Cardew down, and his father, I will damage my own reputation. I cannot afford to do that." He turned at the door. "Don't wait up for me. I shall probably be a long time."

Margaret opened her mouth to speak, and then changed her mind. He would never know whether it would have been an apology or not. He chose to think that it would. But even so, the laughter, the intimacy, of the previous evening seemed an age ago, hard even to recall to the inner mind, where treasures are stored.

CHAPTER

6

HESTER FELT AWKWARD STANDING on the steps of Lord Cardew's
beautiful house in Cheyne Walk at ten o'clock the following morning. It was a bright, windy day, and the river was choppy as the tide
came in. Pleasure boats were bobbing up and down, people clutching
hats, ribbons flying. The russet-colored sails of a barge billowed out,
the hull listing over.

She had brought news of death before, and of maiming, burning,
disfigurement. There was never an easy way to deal with grief, nothing to say that could make it any different. If there was healing with
time, then it came from within.

It was difficult to speak with someone whose only living child was
accused of something as hideous as this. If he had killed someone in a
fight or, more cold-bloodedly, in revenge, it would have been bad
enough. But to be tied in the mind with a man as fearful as Mickey
Parfitt, to have known him, used his services, and said nothing—that
left a stain that would be indelible.

And yet it seemed unacceptably cruel to ignore the father's pain as if it were of no importance, or an embarrassment one would rather avoid.

The door was opened by a butler whose expression was guarded, his eyes already showing the strain.

"Good morning, madam. May I help you?"

"Good morning." She produced her card. "Mr. Rupert Cardew has been extremely generous to me and to the clinic for the poor that I run. It seems an appropriate time to offer Lord Cardew any service I can perform for him." She smiled very slightly, sufficient only to show goodwill.

The stiffness in the butler's face eased. "Certainly, madam. If you care to come inside, I will inform his lordship that you are here."

She dropped her card onto the small silver tray, then followed the butler through the hall with its carved mantel and exquisitely wrought plaster ceiling and cornices. He left her in the firelit morning room with its faded carpets and the seascapes on the walls, the numerous bookcases, the spines lettered in gold, but of odd sizes. She knew at a glance that they were bought to read, not for show.

The butler excused himself, closing the door. In other circum-stances Hester might have looked at the titles of the books. It was always interesting to know what other people read, but she could not keep her mind on anything at the moment. Even in the silence, she kept imagining footsteps in the hall; her mind raced to find words that would sound anything but futile.

She paced from the bookcase to the window and back again. She was staring at the garden when the door finally opened, catching her by surprise.

"I apologize for keeping you waiting, Mrs. Monk," Lord Cardew said quietly, closing the door behind him.

"It is gracious of you to see me at all," she answered. "I would not have been surprised had you declined. Especially since, now that I am here, I hardly know what to say that makes any sense—only that if I can be of service to you, then I wish to be."

Cardew looked exhausted. His skin was papery, as if there were no blood in the flesh beneath it. But it was the emptiness in his eyes that she found the most painful. There was a kind of shapeless panic in them, a despair too big for him to handle.

"Thank you, but I have no idea what anyone can do," he replied. "But your kindness is a small light in a very large darkness." He was a slender man, but he must once have been elegant, supple, like a military man. He reminded her of the soldiers she had known in the past. The whole Crimean War seemed to belong to another age now. He also made her think of her own father, perhaps only because he also had looked older than he was, as if the weight of failure were crushing him.

She had not been at home when her father had most needed her. He had died alone while she was nursing strangers in Sevastopol. He had trusted where he should not have; a man with every appearance of honor had deceived him totally. Her father was one of many so betrayed, but the debts he could not meet had broken his spirit. He had believed that taking his own life was the only course left him.

That too, Hester had not been at home to prevent, or to aid her mother's grief. What she could have done had never been spoken of; it was simply her absence at the time of need that wounded.

"We can find out what really happened," she said impulsively. "It can't be as simple as it seems. Either it was someone else altogether who killed Parfitt, and Rupert doesn't know who, or he does know but he is defending them because he believes that is the right thing to do. Or possibly he did kill Parfitt, but for a reason that would make it understandable." She waited for Cardew to answer.

He struggled with an emotion so sharp, the pain of it was visible in his face. "My dear Mrs. Monk, for all the help you give to the poor women who come to you in their distress, you can have no idea what kind of world men like Parfitt inhabit. I cannot be responsible for your stumbling into such abomination, even by accident. But your kindness is most touching. Your compassion is—"

"Pointless," she interrupted him gently, "if you will not permit me to be what help I can. I have been a nurse on the battlefield. I walked among the dead and the dying after Balaklava. I was in the hospital in Sevastopol, with the rats, the hunger, and the disease. I have nursed in a fever hospital in the slums here in London, and I have waited in a locked house for the bubonic plague to run its course. Please don't tell me what I can or cannot do for a friend who is clearly in trouble."

He had no idea how to answer her. She was an example of all the compassion he idealized in women, and at the same time she broke the only mold with which he was familiar.

She seized the chance to continue. "I know at least something of what they did on such boats, Lord Cardew. I was there when they arrested Jericho Phillips, and he escaped, and then was murdered also. If Mickey Parfitt was of the same nature, there is much to argue in defense of anyone who rid the world of him. But to defend Rupert before a court, we need to know the truth. You are quite right in supposing such a creature is well beyond the knowledge of most people fit to sit on a jury."

"Surely the police—," he began.

"It is not their job to find mitigating circumstances, only to prove what happened. Did Rupert tell you what that was? I imagine he may not have wished to."

"It is a little late to spare my feelings," Cardew said drily, the ghost of a smile in his eyes. "He said he did not kill Parfitt. I would give everything I have to be able to believe him, but . . ." He looked away from her, then back again, his eyes slowly filling with tears. "But his past choices make that impossible. I'm sorry, Mrs. Monk, but I do not see how you can help. I would prefer that you did not risk any danger to yourself, either in person or in the form of the distress such knowledge would cause you. The things one sees, one cannot afterward forget."

She gave him a tiny smile, an echo of the one he had given her. "I will not do anything against my will, Lord Cardew. Thank you for your kindness in receiving me."

SHE RETURNED HOME DEEP in thought, weighing Lord Cardew's words. He longed to believe in Rupert's innocence, and yet could not. Perhaps it was his fear that prevented him, like the vertigo that draws one to the edge of a precipice, and would have one plunge over it, simply to be free from the terror.

But according to Monk's description of the knotted cravat, the crime had not been committed in fear or panic. It takes more than a few seconds to tie half a dozen tight knots in a silk cravat. Who would create such a weapon, thereby ruining a beautiful garment, unless they intended to use it? No argument of self-defense would stand against that kind of reasoning, unless Rupert were held prisoner somewhere, with time unobserved, and with his hands free to do such a thing.

She had offered to help, remembering only his kindness, his wit, the unostentatious generosity with which he'd given so much money. But how well did she really know him? All kinds of people could be charming. It required imagination, understanding, the ability to know what pleases others, and perhaps a certain sense of humor, an ease of wit. It did not need honesty or the will to place others before oneself. And as she looked back now, picturing him in her mind, she also remembered an anxiety in him, a sudden avoidance of her eyes, which she had taken for embarrassment at being in a place like the clinic. But perhaps it had been shame at the memory of his own acts, uglier than anything those women had endured.

What she could not tell Lord Cardew was that, for her own reasons, she needed to know the truth of what had happened to Mickey Parfitt. If some victim such as Rupert had killed him, then his trade was over. But if it were a rival, or even the man who had staked him the original price of the boat, then as soon as Parfitt's murder was solved, and the hue and cry had died down, the whole hideous business would begin again exactly as before. The only difference would be the men running it for the giant behind the scenes, and probably another site to moor the boat. She needed to know it was over, for Scuff's sake. The dreams would not leave him until he had seen more than Jericho Phillips dead, or Mickey Parfitt.

Was Rupert Cardew no more than another victim, one who'd struck back and would die for it?

When she reached home, she found Scuff in the kitchen eating a thick slice of bread spread with butter and piled with jam. He stopped chewing when he saw her, his mouth full, the bread held tightly in both his hands.

She tried to hide a smile. At last he was feeling sufficiently at home to take something to eat when he wanted it. She must watch to make certain it did not extend to more than bread—for example, the cold pie put aside for tonight's supper.

"Good idea," she said casually. "I'll have a piece too. Would you like a cup of tea with it? I would." She walked past him to fill the kettle and put it on the cooktop.

He swallowed. She heard the gulp.

"Yeah," he said casually. "Shall I cut it for yer?"

"Yes, please. But I'll have a little less jam, if you don't mind." She did not turn to watch him do it, but concentrated on the task of making tea.

"Where yer bin?" he asked, elaborately unconcerned. She heard the sawing of the knife on the crust of the bread.

She knew he was thinking about Mickey Parfitt. Monk had told him elements of the truth; the details did not matter.

"To see Lord Cardew," she replied, putting the blue and white teapot on the edge of the stove to warm. "I'm afraid I let my feelings run away with me, and I offered to help him do something for Rupert." Now she turned to look at him, needing to know how he felt about it. She saw a wince of fear in his face, then the immediate hiding of it. Was he afraid for her, of losing the new, precious safety he had?

" 'Ow could we 'elp 'im, if 'e done Mickey Parfitt?" he asked, his eyes fixed on hers. "They'll 'ang 'im, never mind as Parfitt should a bin chucked in the river the day 'e were born."

"Well, there must have been lots of people who would like to see Parfitt dead," Hester began. "It is just possible it wasn't Rupert who actually killed him. But even if he did do it, there might have been something that made it not as bad as straight murder."

"Like wot?" Scuff was balancing the bread in his hands, ready to cut more when he was free to concentrate on it.

"I'm not quite sure," she admitted. "Self-defense is one. And sometimes it's an accident, maybe a real accident, or maybe you're partly to blame because you were being very careless, not so much that you didn't mean to kill anyone so much as you just didn't care."

He looked at her, biting his lips anxiously. " 'E could a done that? I mean, killed 'im by accident, like?"

"No," she said honestly. "I don't think so. Actually, his father said that he claimed he didn't do it at all. And lots of people must have hated Parfitt."

"D'yer believe 'im, then?"

"I don't know. His father said he has behaved pretty badly in the past, but not as badly as that. I need to know more about him, perhaps things his father doesn't know about because Rupert was too ashamed to say. I'll be out for quite a while, I think."

" 'Oo are ye gonna ask, then? Other toffs, an' the like? Will 'is friends tell yer? I wouldn't tell on a friend, specially not to a copper's wife." Then he realized that was silly. " 'Ceptin' I don't s'pose you'll tell 'em 'oo yer are."

She smiled, taking the now steaming kettle off the stove and warming the teapot before putting the leaves in. "Of course not. I'm going to the clinic first to ask a few questions of the women we've got in at the moment. There, at least, I have something of an advantage. Then tomorrow I'll move a little farther afield."

He nodded. "Yer think as mebbe 'e done a good thing, killin' Mickey Parfitt, an' all?"

"I wouldn't push it quite that far," she said cautiously. "But not totally bad."

"Ye're right." Scuff nodded again, more vehemently. "We gotter chip in. Yer gonna make that tea? It's steamin' its 'ead off. An' there's more jam."

When Hester arrived at the clinic, she began by going over the books with Squeaky Robinson.

"We're doing well," he said with considerable satisfaction. He pointed to the place on the page where the final tally was. Even his lugubrious nature could not but be pleased by it. "And we don't need much," he added. "Just new plates as they got broke. We've got sheets, even spare nightshirts, towels. Got medicines—laudanum, quinine, brandy, all sorts."

Hester avoided his eyes. "I know. It's excellent."

"What are you going to do, then?" he asked.

She thought of pretending that she did not know what he meant. "Use it wisely," she replied.

"Yeah, you better," he agreed. "In't no more where that come from. Poor bastard's gonna hang, by all accounts. 'Less, of course, someone does something about it?"

"What did you have in mind, Squeaky?" Then immediately she regretted asking. Whatever he had was probably illegal. He had not lost his connections in the criminal underworld, nor had his nature changed, only his loyalties. He had not needed to go looking for Claudine Burroughs when she had gone on the wild adventure that had ended with her seeing a man she thought was Arthur Ballinger, in the alley outside a shop that sold pornography, but he had done so out of loyalty to Claudine. Because Ballinger had been looking at a picture so obscene it had horrified her, she had fled into the deeper alleys, finally to become totally exhausted and lost. Only Squeaky's perseverance had saved her.

He had never been a hero before. He loved it.

"Well?" Hester pressed him.

"D'you reckon Cardew was framed?" he asked, his eyes narrowing.

"I don't know," she said frankly. "There are certainly plenty of other people who might have wanted Parfitt dead."

"Yeah," Squeaky agreed. "Thing is, how come Parfitt didn't know that? What kind of an idiot stands alone on the deck of a boat and lets a man get on board he knows hates him? I wouldn't! And believe me, if you've got a nice little business in the flesh trade, you know who your rivals are. You're prepared. You keep folks around you as you can trust, to take care of your back, like." He was watching her, waiting to see her reaction.

"Yes, I suppose you would. So he must have been attacked by someone he thought was safe."

"Yeah. Like someone what had come to pay him money for something they'd want more of in another little while. You don't bite the hand that feeds you."

She let out her breath slowly. "Unless you have a temper you can't control and you don't think very far ahead. And also you are used to having someone else clean up behind you so you get out of paying the consequences. I think I had better find out a lot more about Rupert Cardew, if I can."

"And help him," Squeaky confirmed. "I don't mind dealing in women what wants to be in the business anyway, but kids is another thing. And blackmail's bad for business. Charge a fair price, and when it's paid, you're square, I say."

She gave him a weary look.

He shrugged. "Fair's fair," he retorted. "You save Mr. Cardew for any reason you like. I say save him because Mickey Parfitt needed putting away anyhow. He gives the business a bad name, and 'cos Mr. Cardew was very generous to us. We could get used to living this way. Does a lot of good to them that can't get nobody else to help them."

"Very pious, Squeaky," Hester said.

"Thank you," he replied. It had indeed been a compliment, rather than sarcasm, but there was a gleam in his eye that was definitely understanding, and might even have been humor.

There was a brief knock on the door, and before Hester could reply, it opened and Margaret Rathbone came in. She was dressed in very smart deep green, but there was little color in her face, and her eyes were cold.

"Good morning, Hester. Am I interrupting?"

"Not at all," Hester assured her. "I was about to leave." She felt more awkward than she could explain to herself, as if she were being devious in intending to help Rupert Cardew as much as was possible. Why? It had nothing to do with Margaret's father, except that in her mind she still at least half believed that he had some interest in the boat, even if only to find the vulnerable men who would participate.

"I wouldn't consider buying any more new crockery than necessary," Margaret continued. "I'm afraid our source of funds has been radically reduced." There was a look in her face that might have been pity, but Hester felt it was distaste.

"I am aware of that," she responded as expressionlessly as she could manage, but there was still a touch of asperity in her voice. "But it is only an accusation so far. It has yet to be proved."

Margaret's brows rose. "Surely you don't think Mr. Monk is mistaken?" She too was trying to keep the irony from her tone, and like Hester was not entirely successful.

"I don't think he is mistaken," Hester retorted. "But I am aware, as he is, that it is always a possibility. Evidence can be interpreted more than one way. New facts emerge. Sometimes what people say proves to be untrue."

Margaret gave a tight little smile. "I'm sorry, Hester, but you are deluding yourself. I understand that you found Rupert charming, but I'm afraid he is a thoroughly dissolute young man. If you could see him as he really is, I cannot believe that you would have such pity for him. It belongs far more to his victims."

"Like Mickey Parfitt?" Hester snapped back. "I cannot agree with you." She turned briefly to Squeaky Robinson. "However, Lady Rathbone is quite correct about the funds. In the meantime we shall spend only as necessary, and then with due caution." She swept past Margaret on the way out, without inquiring whether it was she or Squeaky whom Margaret had come to see, disliking herself for her anger, and unable to control it.

She went first to the kitchen for a mug of tea, then back upstairs into the first room along the corridor. In it was Phoebe Weller, a woman somewhere between twenty-five and thirty-five, with lovely auburn hair, a lush body, and a face disfigured by the scars of pox.

"How are you, Phoebe?" Hester said conversationally.

Phoebe was lying back in the bed, her eyes half closed, a tiny smile on her face. She was not in a half coma, as a casual observer might have thought, but was half-asleep, dreaming that she might always sleep alone, in a clean bed, and need do nothing hard or dangerous to assure the next cup of hot tea or slice of bread and jam.

She woke up when she heard Hester saying her name. "Oh . . . I don't think as I'm well yet," she whispered.

"Probably not," Hester agreed, tongue in cheek. "Would a fresh cup of tea help?"

Phoebe opened her eyes and sat up smartly, ignoring the bruised leg and wrenched ankle and the heavily dressed wound on her leg that had brought her here. "Ye're right, an' all, so 'elp me, it would."

Hester passed it to her, and she took the tea with both hands.

Hester sat down in the chair next to the bed and made herself comfortable, smoothing her gray skirts, as if she meant to stay.

"I'm gonna get better!" Phoebe said. "I just need another few days."

"I'm sure you are," Hester agreed amiably. "You've worked in one or two different places, haven't you?"

"Yeah . . ." The answer was guarded.

"In some of the posh areas, Chelsea way, and farther up the river?"

"Yeah . . ."

"Ever heard anything about Rupert Cardew, Lord Cardew's son? I need to know, Phoebe, and I need the truth."

Phoebe stared at her.

"Just a friendly warning," Hester went on. "I don't care what the truth is, good or bad, but if you lie to me and I catch you, next time someone beats you, you'll be in the street, and the cabs'll run over you before I stretch out a hand to help. Do you understand? The truth is what I need."

Phoebe considered it, clearly weighing one possibility against the other.

Hester waited.

"Wot d'yer wanna know?" Phoebe said at last.

"Do you know girls who've slept with him, for money?"

"Course, fer money," Phoebe said patiently. "Don't matter if 'e's 'andsome as the devil 'isself, an' kind, an' makes yer laugh, a girl's still ter eat, and there's yer protectors wot needs their share."

"Do you know anyone who slept with Rupert Cardew?"

"Yeah! Told yer! Dunnit meself, couple o' times."

Hester squashed the flicker of revulsion. It was stupid. What had she imagined Rupert had done that he knew the street women so well, even cared enough to give money to someone helping them?

"What is his character like?" she said.

"Cripes! Yer in't thinkin' o'—"

"No, I'm not," Hester assured her tartly. "But if I were?"

"Yer in't!"

"I told you. But why not?"

"'Cos 'e's funny, makes yer laugh till yer burst yer stays, an' 'e in't never mean about payin', but 'e's got a temper like a cornered rat, 'e 'as."

"Did he hit you?" Hester felt cold, and there was a churning in the pit of her stomach.

Phoebe opened her eyes wide. "Me? No! But 'e beat the shit out o' Joe Biggins fer crossin' 'im up. Not only 'im. Spoiled, I reckon. In't used ter bein' told no by anyone, an' din't take it kindly. I 'eard say 'e near killed some bleedin' pimp wot got on the wrong side of 'im. Dunno wot about. Beat one other poor sod once, jus' another bleedin' punter wot got up 'is nose. Paid 'im a lot o' money not ter make a fuss."

"Why? Do you know?"

Phoebe shrugged pale, smooth shoulders. "No. Could a bin anythin'. 'Eard it were bad. 'Alf killed the stupid sod. Broke 'is arms an' 'is face, an' cracked 'is 'ead. Told yer, 'e's got a temper like yer wouldn't credit someone wot acts the gentleman most o' the time. Treats yer right, like yer worth summink. Please an' thank yer. On the other 'and, never takes less than his money's worth neither! 'Ealthy as an 'orse." She gave a shrug and a smile, woman to woman.

Hester nodded, trying to keep her expression one of mild interest, no more. There were things she would prefer not to have known. It was peculiarly embarrassing. "Does he drink a lot?"

"Pretty fair. Seen worse."

"Do you know other girls he's . . . been with?"

"Dozen or so. Wot's this about? Wot's 'e done?"

"He's accused of killing someone."

"If it's a pimp, then I reckon as they're probably right. Never growed up, that one. Loses 'is 'ead an' smashes things, like a child wot no one ever walloped when they should 'ave. My pa'd 'ave tanned me backside till I ate standin' up fer a week if I carried on like 'e does sometimes. Sorry, miss, but yer wanted the truth, an' that's it."

"He used lots of different women? Why, do you think? Why not stick to the same ones?"

"Bored, I s'pec. Some o' them toffs bore easy."

"Ever like little girls, really young?"

"Wot?" Phoebe looked horrified. "Not as I knows of. Perhaps go fer older, 'e would. More experience. Filthy temper, like I said, but 'e could be kind too. Wouldn't do nothin' filthy with little girls, like. Never took advantage o' no one new or scared, far as I know. An' yer get to 'ear who ter be careful of. We got ter take care o' each other."

"And boys?"

"Wot yer mean, 'boys'? Jeez!" She looked genuinely shocked. "Yer never sayin' 'e's doin' it wi' boys. 'Ell, not 'im! It's against the law, but that don't stop them as want ter—girls or boys. But not 'im."

"Are you sure?"

"Course I'm sure! Jeez!"

Hester thanked her, and went to ask several other patients for their opinions also. Then, armed with names, she went to other street corners where she found old patients who knew her name and reputation, and were willing to speak to her.

Most had never heard of Rupert Cardew, but those who had bore out what Phoebe had said: funny, honest, at times kind, but with an uncontrollable temper, for which he seemed to take no responsibility. They believed him perfectly capable of killing in a rage, but no one had heard even a murmur that his taste ran to anything except women: well-endowed ones rather than thin, and certainly not childlike. He appreciated laughter, a little spirit, and most definitely good conversation. All of that she reluctantly recognized in them, and thus she could not help but believe them.

She went home late in the evening, tired and hungry, her feet sore. She had a whole lot more information, but she was not sure that she was really any wiser. Rupert could certainly have killed someone in a rage; in fact he was very fortunate that he had not already done so. But the more she learned of him, the less he seemed to have any reason to kill Mickey Parfitt in particular. Lord Cardew had paid his son's debts when they must have outgrown his allowance. Time and time again he had rescued Rupert from the consequences of his self-indulgence and lack of discipline. Surely Parfitt, of all people, he would have paid off?

Or had there been some quarrel between Rupert and Parfitt that was deeper than blackmail money? Parfitt made his living from por-

nography and blackmail; he would know just how far to push before
he drove any of his victims to despair. And after Jericho Phillips's
death, wouldn't he have been even more careful, erring on the side of
caution rather than ruthlessness? A blackmail victim driven to either
murder or suicide is of no use.

Monk was quiet and sunk in his own thoughts over their late supper. He mentioned only that he was still trying to examine the trade
on the boat and see if there were any other witnesses who would be
useful. Under Orme's supervision, the Foundling Hospital matron
had spoken to the boys from the boat, but they were too frightened
and bewildered to say anything of use, and she had very quickly drawn
the interviews to a close. The matron understood what was in the
balance, but her first care was to the children she had there, not future victims. White-faced and holding a child in her arms, she had
told Orme to leave.

He had understood and had gone out silently, sick with grief.

Now Hester cleared away the dishes and said nothing. Scuff
looked from one to the other of them, troubled, but he asked no questions. He went upstairs to bed early.

MONK HAD ALREADY GONE the next morning by the time Hester
served breakfast for Scuff and herself. She had made porridge because
she knew he liked it, and it kept him from being hungry, well up to
midday.

"Did 'e do it, then?" he asked when his bowl was empty and he
was ready for the toast, jam, and tea. His face was earnest. His eyes
searched hers, trying to understand, looking for something to stop the
fear growing inside him.

She hung up the striped dish towel she had been drying the dishes
with and came back to the table. She sat down and poured herself a
cup of tea.

"You know, I'm still not sure," she said honestly. "It's very difficult
to be certain that you know all the things you need to in order to be
right."

Scuff nodded slowly, as if he understood, but she could see from the trouble in his eyes that he didn't.

"Wot's Mr. Monk doin'? Why's 'e all angry?" His voice dropped. "Did I do summink?"

"No," Hester said, keeping her voice level with difficulty, trying to swallow back the emotion. "We're all upset because we like Rupert, and we don't want him to have done it, but we can't help thinking that he did."

"Oh!" His face cleared only slightly. "Would yer still like 'im, even if it turns out ye're right, an' 'e did?"

"Yes, of course we would. You don't stop caring about people because they make mistakes. But that wouldn't save him from the law."

"They'll 'ang 'im?"

"Probably." The idea was so horrible, she found her throat tight and the tears stinging hard behind her eyes. She tried to force the picture out of her head, and failed.

Scuff took a deep breath. "Then we'd better do summink, eh?" he said, his eyes steady on her face.

"Yes. I'd intended to start this morning."

He stuffed the rest of his toast into his mouth and stood up.

She started to say that he shouldn't come because it could be dangerous, and because he really couldn't help. Then she knew that both were wrong. Instead she took the last swallow of her tea and stood up as well. He needed to be part of this.

She already knew all she could learn of Rupert, and none of it helped. Now she needed to know more of Mickey Parfitt, the business in general and his part in it in particular. Her first instinct was to protect Scuff from the details of such a trade. Then she remembered with misery that he was already more familiar with them than she was. The only question was how much reminding him of them might increase his nightmares.

Or would he ever get over them if he always looked the other way? Might they even grow larger and larger, fed by her belief that they were too terrible to be faced?

"Where are we gonna begin?" he asked, standing by the front door.

"That's the problem," Hester admitted. "There are a lot of 'maybes' and not much certainty. It might be useful to speak to Rupert's friends, but I doubt they would say anything to me if it made them look bad, which most of it would."

Scuff's face was creased up with disgust.

"We can try other prostitutes," she suggested. "There may have been talk that we could follow up, but I think that could take a long time. Squeaky Robinson gave me a few names we can begin with."

Scuff looked at her guardedly. "Wot kind o' people?"

"People who owe Squeaky a favor or two. And I know some like that myself—a couple of brothel-keepers, an abortionist, an apothecary."

"I could go an' ask Mr. Crow? If yer like?" he offered.

"We could go and ask," she corrected him. "I think that's an excellent idea. But do you know where to find him?"

"Course I do, but it in't no decent place fer a lady ter come." Now he looked worried.

"Scuff," she said seriously, "I'll make a bargain with you . . ."

He stared at her dubiously.

"I'll look out for you, but not look after you, if you do the same for me." She held out her hand to shake on it.

He considered for a moment or two, then gripped it in his small, thin fingers and shook. "Deal," he confirmed.

They went straight from Paradise Place to Princes Stairs and took the ferry across to Wapping, past the police station that Monk commanded. Then they turned west along the High Street, at Scuff's direction, toward the Pool of London and the biggest docks.

They did not talk. Scuff seemed to be watching and listening. His jacket was buttoned right up to his chin, and his cap was jammed hard onto his head. He had on new boots, his first that were actually a pair. Hester was sunk in her own contemplation of what she needed to learn and how much she could ask without endangering both of them. Pornography and prostitution were vast trades, and there was a great deal of money to be made in either of them. And of course there was a corresponding danger from the law. Not only profit but survival depended on knowing what not to say, and particularly who not to say it to.

It took them most of the morning amid the noise and traffic, the wagons and cranes and piles of cargo and timber, before they eventually found Crow in a tenement building on Jacob Street. It was just inland from St. Saviour's Wharf, on the south side of the river.

Crow was a lanky man in his midthirties, with coal-black hair, which he wore thick, swept back off his high forehead, and long enough for it to sit on his collar at the back. He had a lugubrious face until he smiled—a broad, flashing grin showing excellent teeth.

They had only just caught him. He was coming down the steps with his black gladstone bag in his hands. He was dressed in a shabby frock coat and black trousers barely adequate to cover his long legs. He was clearly delighted to see Scuff, and his eyes went to him first, before he greeted Hester.

"Hello, Mrs. Monk! What are you doing in these parts? Trouble?"

"Of course," she replied, holding out her hand.

He spread his own lean fingers and looked at them in distaste. "I'm filthy," he said, shaking his head. His glance went to Scuff again, as if to reassure himself as to his well-being. Crow had dropped every other business to help search for Scuff when the boy had been kidnapped by Jericho Phillips.

Hester dropped her hand, smiling back at him. "You heard about the murder of Mickey Parfitt?" she asked, falling in step beside him as they walked back along the narrow street toward the river, stepping carefully to avoid the gutter.

"Of course," Crow acknowledged. "No ill will, Mrs. Monk, but I hope you don't find the poor sod that did for him. If you've come to ask me to help you, sorry but I'm too busy. You'd be surprised the number of sick people there are around here." He looked up at the dense tenement buildings to the left and right of them, grimed with smoke and constantly dripping water from the eaves.

She glanced at him. His face was set in hard lines, the easy smile vanished. She had known him off and on since Monk's first case on the river, nearly a year ago now, but she realized she had seen only the thinnest surface of his character. He was a man who never spoke of his background, but he had had a good deal of medical training and used it to help those on the edge of the law—animal or human—or in the iron grip of poverty. He took his payment in whatever form was offered—a debt in hand, if necessary, and kindness in return when it was needed.

She had no idea what had happened to prevent him from gaining his qualifications and practicing as a full doctor. His speech was not from the dockland area, but she could not place it. He cared for Scuff, and that was all that mattered. One knew far less about most people than one imagined. Parents, place and date of birth, education, all told less of the heart than a few actions under pressure when the cost was high.

"I'm afraid we already have a very good idea who it was." She answered his challenge while watching her step as she picked her way over broken cobbles. "I'm trying to find a reason to cast doubt on his guilt, or if not that, then at least to show that he doesn't deserve the rope."

Crow was surprised. "You want him to get off?"

Hester would not have put it quite so bluntly, and she drew in her breath to deny it. Then she saw Scuff looking at her and realized that perhaps Crow was right, that that was what she wanted. It was difficult to answer the question honestly with Scuff between them, grasping every word.

"I want the trade finished, wiped out," she said. "To do that I need to break the man behind it—the one with the money. I'd rather not sacrifice Rupert Cardew in the process."

Crow's eyes widened incredulously. "Would you like the crown jewels at the same time, maybe, just as a nice finish?" He skirted around a pile of refuse, and a rat scuttled away.

"Not particularly," Hester answered, keeping her face perfectly straight. "I haven't sufficient use for them. One would have to walk terribly upright to keep a crown from falling off. I don't think I could do that."

Scuff was puzzled.

"She's joking," Crow told him, putting his hand on the boy's shoulder. "At least I hope she is."

"Half," Hester conceded. Then she smiled. "I might be able to, but if I dropped anything, somebody else would have to pick it up for me."

"If you were wearing a crown, I expect they'd feel obliged," Crow answered.

Scuff laughed, but the fear of being lost again, separated from her, was tight underneath, as sharp as a knife point.

They all walked in silence for a couple of hundred yards past more boxes, barrels, and piles of wood. Finally they reached the steps to the ferry to the north bank. The tide was turning and the water was choppy. Strings of lighters were making their way upriver laden with coal, timber, and round wooden barrels lashed together. A coastal barge passed by, sails full-set, billowing out. The light was bright on the water, and the wind caught the edges of the waves, whipping up a fine spray.

"I want to know the details the police won't be able to find," Hester told Crow after they were ashore on the north bank. "Any whispers." She did not really know what she was asking for. The facts said that Rupert was guilty. But might a jury be persuaded to ask for leniency? Or when they heard what bestiality Parfitt sold, might they believe that any man who'd become involved, no matter how ignorant he'd been initially, was little better than Parfitt himself?

Or was it just that she liked Rupert, and for Scuff's sake she was desperate to find the man behind Parfitt's business, so she could prevent him from starting up again with someone new? Scuff needed to see them succeed, to believe it really could happen, and that he was a part of it.

"Crow . . .", she began. "Do you think it could be something as simple as a business rivalry? Parfitt must have earned a lot of money from that boat. If someone else took over his trade and his clients, they'd make just as much, wouldn't they? Perhaps what I really need to know is how the business was run. Who profits from his death, in a business way? Never mind the blackmail or the moral side of it. Let's look at the money."

He nodded very slowly, his smile widening. "Give me a couple of days." He tilted his head a little to one side. "I suppose you want the details, rather than just my conclusions?"

"Yes, please. My conclusions might be different."

He did not answer that, but a brief flash of amusement lit his eyes. "It'll be ugly," he warned.

"Of course it will. Thank you."

There was really nothing more to be added now, and she thanked Crow and left.

"Where we goin' now?" Scuff asked, keeping up with her by adding an extra skip into his step now and then. "We in't just leavin' it to 'im, are we?"

"No," Hester answered decisively. "We are going to see if someone else with an interest in the boat's profits might have been there the night Parfitt was killed."

" 'Ow're we gonna do that?"

"Well, if it is one of the people I think it might be, he will have to have come up the river from his home. If I can find someone who saw him, it would be a start."

She had not told Scuff anything about what Sullivan had said of Arthur Ballinger, and she assumed Monk hadn't either. If there was really anything behind it, ignorance would be the safest shield for him.

"Like a cabby?"

"I think I'll begin with the ferryman. Cabbies don't see a lot of people's faces, especially after dark."

"Course!" Scuff said eagerly. "Yer sittin' in a boat, an' the ferryman's gotta see yer, eh? So if 'e don't wanna be seen an' 'ave folks remember 'im, 'e'd row up the river 'isself. Or if 'e couldn't, then 'e'd cross where 'e'd least likely be noticed a 'ole lot."

"Definitely," she agreed. "Let's try the ferrymen in Chiswick first."

It took them well into the afternoon to get from the eastern end, nearer the sea and the great wharfs and docks, right across the city by omnibus to the statelier, greener western edge, and then beyond that again into the lush countryside, and over the river to the southern bank. There was no omnibus across Barn Elms Park to the little township of Barnes itself and finally to the High Street right on the water's edge. They were both tired and thirsty, and had sore feet, by the time they stopped at the White Hart Inn, but Scuff never complained.

Hester wondered if his silence was in any way because he was thinking about this utterly different place—green, well kept, almost sparkling in the bright, hard light off the water. On the surface, it seemed a world away from the dark river edge where Jericho Phillips had kept his boat. There the tide carried in and out the detritus of the port, the broken pieces of driftwood, some half-submerged, bits of cloth and rope, food refuse and sewage. There was the noise of the city even at night, the clip of hooves on the cobbles, shouts, laughter, the rattle of wheels, and of course always the lights—streetlamps, carriage lamps—unless the mist rolled in and blotted them out. Then there were the mournful booms of the foghorns.

Here the river was narrower. There were shipbuilding yards on the northern bank farther down. The shops were open, busy; occasional carts went by; people called out; but it was all smaller, and there was no smell of industrial chimney smoke, salt and fish, no cry of gulls. A single barge drifted upriver, sails barely arced in the breeze.

Scuff could not help staring around him at the women in clean, pale dresses, walking and laughing as if they had nothing else to do.

Hester and Scuff ate first, a very late luncheon of cold game pie, vegetables, and—as a special treat—a very light shandy.

Scuff finished his glass and put it down, licking his lips and looking at her hopefully.

"When you're older," she replied.

" 'Ow long do I 'ave ter get older?" he asked.

"You'll be doing it all the time."

"Afore I can 'ave another one o' these?" He was not about to let it go.

"About three months." She had difficulty not smiling. "But you may have another piece of pie, if you wish? Or plum pie, if you prefer?"

He decided to press his luck. He frowned at her. " 'Ow about both?"

She thought of the errand they were on, and what had driven them to it. "Good idea," she agreed. "I might do the same."

When there was nothing at all left on either plate, she paid the bill. Scuff thanked her gravely, and then hiccuped. They walked down to the river and started looking for ferries, fishermen, anybody who hung around the water's edge talking, pottering with boats or tackle, generally observing the afternoon slip by.

It was more than two hours, pleasant but unprofitable, before they found the bowlegged ferryman who said he had carried a gentleman from the city over late on the night before the morning Mickey Parfitt's body was found in Corney Reach.

"Aw, I dunno 'is name, lady," the ferryman said dubiously. "Never ask folks's names—got no reason ter, 'ave I? Don' ask where they're goin' neither. 'Tain't none o' my business. Jus' be civil, talk a little ter pass the time, like, an' get 'im ter the other side safe an' dry. I recall, though, as this gent were a real toff, knowed all kinds o' things."

Hester felt the grip tighten in the pit of her stomach, and suddenly the possibility of profound tragedy was real. "Truly? How old would you say he was?"

The man bent his head a little to one side and looked at her, then at Scuff, then back at her again. "Why yer wanna know, missus? 'E done yer wrong some'ow?"

She knew what he was thinking, and she played on it without a moment's shame. "I don't know, unless I know if it was he," she answered, keeping the amusement out of her eyes deliberately. She wanted to laugh. Then she thought of all the women of whom it would be true, and the amusement vanished. A knot of shame pulled tight inside her for her callousness.

"Don't think so, love," he said sadly, biting his lower lip. "This feller'd be a bit too old fer you."

"Too old?" she said with surprise. She gulped. It could not be Rupert. He was not much more than thirty, younger than she. "Are you sure?" She was fishing for time, trying to think of an excuse for asking him to describe the man in more detail.

The ferryman sucked in his cheeks and then blew them out again. "Mebbe I shouldn't a said that. Still an 'andsome enough figure of a man."

"Fair hair?" Hester asked, thinking of Rupert standing in the sun in the doorway of the clinic. "Slender, but quite tall?"

"No," the ferryman said decisively. "Sorry, love. 'E'd a bin sixty, like as not, dark 'air, near black, close as I could tell in the lamplight, like. But a big man, 'e were, an' not tall, as yer might say. More like most."

Considering that the ferryman was unusually short, Hester wondered what he considered was average. However, it might only insult him to ask, and apart from anything else, she needed his help.

"Did he come back again later?" she asked, changing the subject. She felt awkward, now that she had established that it was not the mythical deserting husband she had suggested. Then a new idea occurred to her. "You see, I'm afraid it could have been my father. He has a terrible temper, and . . ." She left the rest unsaid, a suggestion in the air. "He wasn't . . . hurt, was he?"

"Yer do pick 'em, don't yer?" The ferryman shrugged. "But 'e were fine. Bit scruffed up, like 'e 'ad a bit of a tussle, but right as rain in 'isself. Walked down the bank an' leaped inter his boat. Don't you worry about 'im. Don't know about the young feller with the fair 'air. I never see'd 'im."

"Perhaps he wasn't here." She said it with an upsurge of relief. She knew it was foolish even as she welcomed it. It meant nothing, only one difficulty avoided of a hundred.

"Wot does it mean?" Scuff asked as they thanked the man and walked away along the path. "Is it good?"

"I'm not sure," Hester replied. That at least was true. "It certainly wasn't Rupert. Even in the pitch dark you couldn't mistake him for sixty. And if this man were scruffed up, he would have been in a fight, which, from the sound of it, he won."

"Like chokin' Mickey Parfitt and sending 'im over the side?"

"Yes, something like that," she agreed.

He shivered. "Was there other people in the boat?"

"Not that evening, apparently, except for the boys, locked in belowdecks."

He hesitated. "Where are they now?"

Hester heard the strain in his voice, saw the memory bright and terrible in his eyes.

"They're all safe," she told him unwaveringly. "Looked after and clean and fed."

It was a moment or two before he was satisfied enough to believe her. Gradually the stiffness eased out of his back and shoulders. "So 'oo were it, then? Were it the man 'oo killed Mickey Parfitt?"

"Quite possibly."

" 'Ow do we find out 'oo 'e is?"

"I have an idea about that. Right now we are going home."

"We in't gonna look fer 'im?" He was shivering very slightly, trying to stand so straight that it didn't show. He pulled his coat tighter deliberately, although it was not any colder.

"I need to ask William a few questions before that. I don't think I will get two chances to speak to him about this, so I need to do it properly the first time."

" 'E in't gonna let yer," Scuff warned. "I wouldn't, if I was 'im."

"I dare say not." She did not bother to hide her smile. "Which is why I won't ask him, and neither will you."

"I might."

She looked at him. It wasn't a threat. He was afraid for her. She saw it in his eyes, like a hard, twisting pain. He had found some kind of safety for the first time in his life, and it was threatened already. He was used to loss. Although this was too deep for him to handle alone, he was too used to loneliness to be able to share, too vulnerable even to acknowledge it.

"I'll come wif yer," he said, watching her face, waiting for her to refuse him.

"Thank you," she accepted. It was rash. Perhaps it would cost them both. "If William is angry later, I'll tell him you came only to make sure I was safe.

He smiled and pushed his hands deeper into his pockets. "Right," he agreed, overwhelmed with relief.

WHAT HESTER ACTUALLY WANTED to know from Monk was what he had been told about where Arthur Ballinger had been on the night of Parfitt's death. The ferryman's description fitted him extraordinarily well—although, of course, it also fitted several thousand other men closely enough. She hated even thinking that it might've been Ballinger, because of how it would hurt Rathbone, and of course Margaret, but for Scuff's sake, whoever was behind the boats run by men like Phillips and Parfitt, he had to be stopped, and to be hanged for murder was as good as being imprisoned for the kidnapping and abuse of children. Blackmail she doubted could ever be proved, because no one would admit to being a victim. That was part of the blackmailer's skill.

"Why?" Monk said immediately.

They were standing side by side with the French doors ajar in the calm late evening, the smell of earth and damp leaves in the air. Dusk had fallen, and there was little sound outside in the small garden except for the wind through the leaves, and once or twice the hoot of an owl flying low. The sky was totally clear, the last light on the river below like the sheen on a pewter plate. Up here the noise of boats was inaudible, no shouts, no foghorns. A single barge with a lateen sail moved upriver as silently as a ghost.

"Why?" Monk repeated, watching her.

Hester had never intended to deceive him, just to keep her own counsel a little. "Because I was speaking to Crow this morning, in case he can help."

"Help whom?" he asked softly. "Rupert Cardew? I can't blame him for killing Mickey Parfitt, but the law won't excuse him, Hester, no matter how vile Parfitt was. Not unless it was self-defense. And honestly, that's unbelievable. Can you imagine a man like Parfitt standing by while Cardew took off his cravat and put half a dozen knots in it, then looped it around Parfitt's throat and pulled it tight?"

"Didn't he hit him over the head first?" she argued. "If Parfitt were unconscious, he wouldn't be able to stop him. Rupert might . . ." She stopped. It was exactly the argument Monk was making. "Yes, I see," she admitted. "If he was unconscious, then he was no danger to Rupert, or anyone else."

"Precisely. You can't help him, Hester." There was sorrow in his voice, and defeat, and in his eyes a bitter humor. She knew he was remembering with irony their crossing swords with Rathbone when he had defended Jericho Phillips in court, and they had been so sure of victory, taking it for granted because they'd been convinced of his total moral guilt.

She wanted to argue, but every reason that struggled to the surface of her mind was pointless when she tried to put it into words. It all ended the same way: She didn't want Rupert to be guilty. She liked him, and was grateful for his support of the clinic. She was desperately sorry for his father. She knew perfectly well that Rupert was not the power nor the money behind Parfitt's business, and she wanted to destroy the man who was. She was trying to force the evidence to fit her own needs, which was not only dishonest, it was in the end also pointless.

"No, I suppose not," she conceded.

He reached out his hand and took hers gently. There was nothing to add.

SINCE SCUFF'S RESCUE FROM Phillips's boat—hurt, frightened, and very weak—he had made a point of going out during most days, as soon as he was well enough, just to prove that he was still independent and quite able to look after himself. Both Monk and Hester were careful to make no remark on it.

It was the evening of the third day after Hester had met with Crow that Scuff came in well before supper, sniffing appreciatively at the kitchen door as the aroma of a hot pie baking greeted him and he saw Hester take down the skillet and set it on the top of the stove.

"Crow got summink for yer," he said cheerfully. "Said ter tell yer 'e'll meet yer at the riverside opposite the Chiswick Eyot termorrer at midday, wi' wot yer asked fer. Cheapest'd be if we got the train ter 'Ammersmith, an' then an 'ansom ter the 'Ammersmith Bridge, an' along that way. I know where it is." He inhaled deeply. "'S that apple pie?"

Hester and Scuff were at the appointed place a quarter of an hour early the following day, standing watching the boats on the river.

There was a movement Hester caught almost at the corner of her vision, and she turned to see Crow's lanky figure striding along the quayside, his coat flapping, his black hair flying in the wind.

She started toward him.

He glanced at Scuff as she reached him, but he was still standing a few paces away, staring upriver.

"Is it something he shouldn't know?" Hester asked quickly. "I can send him off on an errand. He insisted on coming. He's . . . looking after me." Surely she did not need to explain that to Crow?

"It's an even worse business than I thought," he said quietly. "But I don't know what good that'll do your friend. If I'd known what that bastard did to little boys, I'd have killed him myself, and not as nicely as a quick blow on the head." His face was hard, lips tight. "I'd have practiced a spot of surgery he wouldn't have approved of, and made damn sure he saw and felt every bit of it. He'd have watched himself bleed to death." He looked at Scuff, and as Scuff turned and saw him, the rage was wiped from Crow's eyes. He made himself smile back, the wide grin that was so characteristic of him.

"You got summink for us?" Scuff asked expectantly, crossing over to them.

"Of course," Crow replied. "D'you think I'd come all the way up here to the end of the world if I hadn't? It's this way." And without any further explanation he led them along the road, ships and taverns on one side, the steep drop to the river on the other.

After about a hundred yards he crossed the street, dodging the few carts there were, and went into the narrow entrance of a lane running inland between shops and houses. Then he led them past a stretch of open green, and into a small alley off Chiswick Field. He knocked on the door of one of the houses, then, after a slight hesitation, knocked again with exactly the same pattern.

It was opened immediately by a girl of about nineteen or twenty. She was plump with very fair skin, completely without blemishes, and hair so pale as to be almost white in the dark hallway. She saw Crow, and her face tightened with fear, but she made no attempt to close the door again.

Crow gave his huge smile, all shining teeth, and pushed the door wider so it almost touched the wall behind it.

"Hello, Hattie," he said cheerfully. "Good time to call, is it? I brought someone to see you." Without looking back he beckoned to Hester and Scuff to follow him in.

Scuff closed the door and trailed behind, looking from one side to the other, almost treading on Hester's heels.

Hattie took them to a narrow kitchen, where a small fire kept a cooktop hot and a pump in the corner dripped water into a tin bowl.

"Wot yer want?" she said, gulping with tension. She had wide, light blue eyes, and she kept them on Crow as if there were no one else in the room.

"Tell Mrs. Monk what you told me about Rupert Cardew," Crow replied. His voice was gentle, almost coaxing, but there was a quality of power in it that belied his easy expression.

Hattie gulped. Hester saw that her hands were shaking. "I took it," she said, not to Hester as directed, but still to Crow.

"You took what, Hattie?" he pressed.

She put her white hand up to her throat. " 'Is tie. 'E 'ad it orff any'ow, an' when 'e weren't lookin', I 'id it. 'E were stupid drunk, an' 'e never noticed 'e'd gone wifout it."

"His cravat. What color was it, Hattie?"

"Blue, wi' little yeller animals on it." She made a faint squiggle in the air with her finger.

"Why did you take it?"

"I dunno."

"Yes, you do. Was it Mickey Parfitt who told you to?"

"No! It . . ." She gulped again. " It were the night before 'e were found in the river."

"Who did you take it from, Hattie?"

"Mr. Cardew. I told you."

"And who for? Who did you give it to?"

She shook her head, and her body stiffened until her muscles seemed to lock. "No . . . I dunno who got it. I in't sayin' nothin'! It's more 'n me life's worth."

Crow turned to Hester. "I can't get any more out of her than that. I'm sorry."

Hester looked at the girl again. Perhaps it would place her life in jeopardy. That was not difficult to believe. "It doesn't matter," she said quietly. "All that is important is that Rupert didn't have it, so he couldn't have been the one who knotted it and put it around Mickey Parfitt's neck. Thank you. That makes all the difference." She smiled back at Crow, and felt her smile grow wider and wider on her face. Of course she would have to press Hattie later as to whom she had given the cravat to, but it might be possible to find out through someone else. There would be others around who would have seen a stranger— or any visitor, for that matter. For the moment the relief that Rupert was not guilty was all she needed.

The identities of the murderer of Mickey Parfitt and the man behind the pornographic business on the boats were next, a piece at a time. She smiled across at Hattie and thanked her again.

7

MONK WENT ACROSS THE river on the early morning ferry. It was a cool, quiet day, barely a ripple on the water in the slack tide. Swathes of mist half veiled the ships at anchor. Strings of barges seemed to appear out of nowhere.

He had been collecting the evidence against Rupert Cardew to present when he came to trial. It was a miserable job, and in truth he had little more taste for it than Hester had. But the more he learned, the easier it became to see Rupert as a spoiled young man whose louche style of life and ungoverned temper had finally caught up with him. In Mickey Parfitt he had met the one problem his father could not solve for him. No amount of money would have been sufficient to stop the blackmail that had clearly worked so well.

The only inconsistency was that Parfitt was a professional at extortion. He had been thirty-seven years old, and had survived for the last ten of these by profiting one way or another from other men's weaknesses. There had been at least one suicide among his victims, possibly more, but no one had ever attacked him before. It seemed he had judged very precisely where to draw the line in his bloodsucking, or his threats. A dead victim is bad for business, and he never forgot that—at least not until recently.

Was that a weakness in the case, or simply a fact yet to be explained? Rathbone had not merely beaten Monk in the trial of Jericho Phillips, he had humiliated him, and later—when she had testified—Hester as well. He had done it with the knowledge of how to hurt that only a friend possesses.

Monk still felt a tide of anger burn up in him when he remembered it. Perhaps it hurt him more on her behalf than it had Hester herself. They had never spoken of it, as if it were a wound still too painful to touch.

This time Monk would make sure that Rupert Cardew was guilty, and that he had proved it beyond any doubt, reasonable or not; or else Monk would find the man who was guilty, and prove that.

Of course what he wanted, far more than the poor devil who'd killed Mickey Parfitt, was the man who had set him up in business, and had found his clientele among those whose weakness for the excitement of the forbidden, the illegal, and the obscene he had fed and exploited. Monk would find and prove that, whoever it was, even if it were Arthur Ballinger himself, as Sullivan had claimed. Indeed, even were it Lord Cardew—anyone, without exception.

The ferry reached the far side. Monk paid the fare and climbed the slippery steps up to the dock.

He was reluctant to prosecute Rupert Cardew, but there was no possible way to avoid it. What grieved him most was that the whole thing was so utterly pointless. He would never have taken off his distinctive silk cravat, deliberately knotted it, and then strangled an unconscious man. It seemed such an unnecessary thing to do—and, Monk realized, one that would give him no emotional satisfaction. There was no bodily contact, no release of the pent-up violence. There was something cold-blooded about it. But that was the only part he did not understand. The passion to destroy Parfitt he understood perfectly.

He reached the top of the steps as the sun came through the haze and made the dew on the stone momentarily bright. He walked quickly toward the road.

Had Rupert really been naïve enough to think that would end the trade? Was he so spoiled, so cosseted from reality, that he believed a man like Parfitt was the power behind the business, the one who found the vulnerable patrons and then judged exactly how far to bleed each one?

But it was the man behind Parfitt that Monk wanted, and that was what he had in mind an hour later when he called to see Oliver Rathbone. After a short wait, he was shown into Rathbone's neat and elegant room.

"Good morning, Monk," Rathbone said with some surprise. "A new case?" He indicated the chair opposite his desk for Monk to sit down.

"Thank you." Monk accepted, leaning back as if he were relaxed, crossing his legs. "The same case."

Rathbone smiled, sitting also and hitching his trouser to stop it from creasing as he crossed his legs, and he too leaned back. "Since we are on opposite sides, this should prove interesting. What can I do for you?"

"Perhaps save Cardew from the rope."

Rathbone's smile vanished, a look of pain in his eyes. Monk saw it and understood. Monk was glad it was not his skill or judgment on which rested the weight of the saving or losing of a man's life.

"I'm sorry," Monk apologized. It was probably inappropriate, but for a moment they were not adversaries. They felt the same pity, and revulsion, at the thought of hanging. "I have no wish to prosecute him at all," he went on. "When I first found Parfitt's body, I considered not even looking for whoever killed him, after I'd seen the boat and the boys kept there. But when the cravat turned up, I had no choice."

Rathbone's face was bleak. "I know that. What is it you want, Monk?"

"The man behind it. Don't you?"

"Of course. But I have no idea who that is." He met Monk's eyes directly, without a flicker. Was he remembering the night when Sullivan had killed Phillips so hideously, and then himself, after he had said that the man behind it all was Arthur Ballinger? Why had he pointed to Ballinger? Had it been anger, ignorance, madness, while the balance of his mind turned? Had it been revenge for something quite different? Or the truth?

Rathbone could not afford to think that the man was Margaret's father. The price of that would be devastating, yet nor could he afford to ignore it. Monk did not want to do this either, but he also could not look away, for Cardew, and, more important to him, for Scuff.

"No . . ." Monk said slowly. "But if the right pressure were put upon Cardew, then he might give enough information for us to find out."

"Why should he?" Rathbone asked, his voice tight and careful. "Surely by doing that he would automatically be admitting to the most powerful motive for killing Parfitt. I know that you believe you can prove that he did kill Parfitt, but he swears he did not."

"And you believe him?" Monk said. "Actually, there is no point in your assuming that, even if you are right. It is what the jury believes that matters. If he will give us a record of every payment he made to Parfitt, dates and amounts, we might be able to trace it through Parfitt's books. If it comes out in the open in court, it could shake other things loose."

"And hang Cardew for certain," Rathbone said quietly. "His own society will never forgive him for frequenting a boat like that, whether he killed the bastard who ran it or not." His mouth pulled into a delicately bitter smile. "Apart from anything else, it would betray the fact that men of his social and financial class were the chief clients, and enablers of creatures like Parfitt. And while that is true, making it public is another thing altogether."

"I know that," Monk conceded. "But his revulsion when he learned the real nature of the business, but was still bled dry, will earn him some sympathy. That is your job, not protecting the reputations of others like him. I know no evidence that his story on that account is anything but the truth."

Rathbone put his elbows on the desk, and his fingertips very gently together. "You are offering me life in prison in exchange for full admission, with details you can prove, of his visit to the boat, the nature of what went on there, and his payment of blackmail money to Parfitt? And all this is in the hope that it will somehow lead you to the man behind it?"

There was no point in arguing the shadings of meaning. "Yes."

"I'll ask him, but I'm not sure if I can recommend it is in his interest. God, what a mess!"

Monk did not answer him.

MONK WORKED ON THE river the rest of the day. There had been a large theft of spices from an East Indiaman in the Pool of London, and it took him until nearly midnight to trace the goods and arrest at least half the men involved in the crime. By quarter to one, a new moon in a mackerel sky made the river ghostly. Ships were riding at anchor, sails furled, like a gently stirring lace fretwork against the light, beautiful and totally without color. There was only a faint murmur of water and the sharp smell of salt in the air.

Monk stepped off the ferry at Princes Stairs and walked slowly up the hill to home.

Hester had left the light on in the parlor, but it was only when he stepped in to turn the gas off that he saw she was curled up in the large armchair, sound asleep.

His first thought was clear. She'd been waiting for him, or she would have been in bed. Was Scuff ill? No, of course not. If he were, she would have been with him. He remembered how many nights she had spent in the chair beside Scuff's bed when he had been injured hunting the assassin in the sewers.

He bent down and spoke her name softly, not to startle her.

"Hester."

She opened her eyes and sat up, smiling, pushing her hair back off her face where it had fallen out of its pins. "He didn't do it," she said with intense pleasure.

Monk was confused and too tired to think. "Who didn't?"

"Rupert Cardew." She stood up, so close to him that he could feel the warmth of her and smell her skin and her hair, clean cotton and, very faintly, soap. "I'm sorry," she went on. "I know that leaves the case open and you have to go back and start again. But I'm just so glad it wasn't Rupert."

"He told you that?" he asked. "I'm surprised they let you in to see him. Did his father take you?"

A look of disgust flickered across her face. "William, for heaven's sake! I'm not a complete simpleton. No, I haven't been to see him, nor would I expect him to say anything different." She smoothed her skirts without much effect; they were creased beyond any help but a flat iron. "With help from Crow, I found a prostitute Rupert visited earlier that day, and she admits that she stole his cravat and gave it to someone else, but she's terrified to say who. But if Rupert didn't have it, then he couldn't have used it to strangle Mickey Parfitt, and that's the only real evidence against him. All the rest just bears that up. He never denied having been on the boat, or having been blackmailed for it. But so have many other people."

She had just broken his case against Cardew. He should have been disconcerted, even angry, but instead he felt an absurd sense of relief.

She saw it in his eyes and put her arms around his neck, pulling his head down gently and kissing him.

MONK WOKE LATE, AND Hester was already up. It was a moment or two before he remembered what Hester had told him about the cravat. When it came back, he leaped out of bed, washed, shaved, and dressed as fast as he could. He had a new idea forming in his mind, and he had to draw the pieces of it together, prove them one by one.

He ate the most perfunctory breakfast, and left the house with only a brief word to Scuff and a quick moment of meeting Hester's eyes, touching her cheek, and then going out of the door.

As he crossed the river again, in the rhythmic movement of the ferry, his mind was absorbed in what this new revelation meant. He had no doubt of what Hester had said, but later he would go and see this young woman and make certain that she had not been influenced to swear she'd taken the cravat. Her testimony might have to stand

up in court. Was it conceivable that Lord Cardew had hired someone
to find her and had possibly even paid her to come up with such a lie?
He did not believe it, but it was necessary that he be thorough. If they
ever found anyone else to accuse, that person would no doubt hire a
barrister to defend him who was something like as clever as Oliver
Rathbone. The question would be asked.

But Monk would put it off until he had explored other possibilities. Orme had gone over Parfitt's financial records, such as they were,
and had found nothing to suggest that Parfitt had withheld any of the
proceeds from the man who had given him the boat. If he had, then
it was well hidden, and certainly not spent on his own pleasure. He
lived no more comfortably than could be accounted for by the obvious takings of the boat's trade, without the blackmail. Whoever was
behind it had had no apparent motive to get rid of Parfitt. He would
only have to be replaced with someone just like him.

Did he already have someone in mind? A friend, a relative, a
creditor to whom he owed some favor?

That was the man Monk wanted to catch so intensely that he
could taste it like a bitter flavor in his mouth. Was it Ballinger? Or
was it even possible that Ballinger was another victim, like Sullivan
had been, except turned to recruit more victims, perhaps as the price
of his own survival? A dangerous tactic. Ballinger was not a man
whose flaws one could manipulate.

Before anything else, Monk needed to know as much as possible
of the facts. Where had Ballinger been on the night of Parfitt's death?

Hester had told him of the ferryman rowing a man resembling
Ballinger across the river and then later bringing him back. It would
not be difficult to ascertain if it had been Ballinger. If he had been
visiting a friend, he would have no occasion to deny it.

"CERTAINLY," BALLINGER SAID WITH a smile when Monk visited him in his offices in the city. "Bertie Harkness." He sat at ease
behind a large desk. The room was unostentatiously comfortable.
Bookcases lined two walls, filled in a disorderly manner with dark
leather-bound volumes, clearly there for use, not ornament. There

were old hunting prints on the walls, personal mementoes on sills, a portrait of his wife in a silver frame, a bronze bust of Julius Caesar, a pair of pearl-handled opera glasses.

"Known each other for years," Ballinger continued. "In fact, far longer than I care to remember. I drop by for a late supper and a little conversation every now and again." He looked puzzled. "Why does this concern you, Inspector? I find it impossible to believe that you suspect Harkness of anything." His eyebrows rose. "Or is it me you suspect?" He said it with faint amusement, but his eyes were unnervingly direct.

Monk made himself look surprised. "Of what? You might have some sympathy with whoever killed Mickey Parfitt. Many people might have, myself included. But I don't think you would lie to protect him." He gave a slight shrug. "Unless he were a member of your own family, for example. But I have no reason whatever to suspect that."

Ballinger still appeared puzzled. Monk looked at his hands on the leather inlaid surface of the desk. They were motionless, deliberately held still.

Monk smiled. "I have an idea as to the time you crossed the river, by ferry . . ." He saw a very faint smile lift the corners of Ballinger's mouth, and in that instant Monk knew that in spite of Ballinger's affectation to the contrary, he was not surprised. "Naturally, we questioned anyone that we knew would be in the area," Monk went on almost expressionlessly. "Such as ferrymen. It is always possible that any witness might have seen something that would later have meaning for them."

"I did not see Rupert Cardew," Ballinger replied, studying Monk's face. "At least not so far as I know. I observed a few other people on the river; some of them looked to be young men, no doubt about private pleasures. I could not responsibly identify any of them. I'm sorry."

"Even so," Monk persisted. "If you could tell me the time, as closely as you know it, and exactly what you did see, it might help."

Ballinger hesitated, as if still puzzled as to its importance.

"Even if it merely confirms someone else's story," Monk added. "Or proves it false."

"I couldn't identify anyone," Ballinger said, and gave a slight gesture of helplessness. "Apart from the ferryman, of course, Stanley Willington."

"Of course," Monk agreed. "But if you saw one person, or two, it could help. Or if you saw no one, at a time someone claimed to be there . . ." He allowed it to hang in the air, self-explanatory.

"Yes . . . I see. Let me think." Ballinger's eyes never left Monk's, as if it were a kind of duel to which neither of them would admit. "I took a hansom as far as Chiswick. I think I arrived there about nine. There were still a number of people around, although it was dark. I saw them as figures on the quayside, talking, laughing. I smelled smoke—cigars. I recall that. It is a highly recognizable aroma. And it suggests gentlemen."

Monk nodded. It was a clever observation, and he acknowledged it.

"I waited about ten minutes for a ferry. I preferred to have Stanley. He entertains me." The description was good, and it matched Willington's own account, as no doubt Ballinger knew it would.

Ballinger continued. All of it was in accordance with what Monk already knew, but it served the purpose he intended. He would check on it, not only with the men on the river, all the way up to Mortlake, a distance of nearly a mile and a half, but with Bertie Harkness, whose address Ballinger also offered.

"Thank you," Monk said when he was finished and standing by the door. "It may help us catch someone in a lie."

"I admit, I don't see the purpose," Ballinger replied. "Was I misinformed that you have evidence sufficient to bring Rupert Cardew to trial?"

Monk smiled, perhaps a little wolfishly, memory harsh in his mind. "He is defended by Oliver Rathbone," he replied, "so I need every scrap of evidence I can find. There must be no surprises, no loopholes. I'm sure you understand."

Ballinger inhaled deeply, then let out a sigh, and smiled back. "Of course," he agreed, not bothering to conceal the pleasure in his eyes.

—————

MONK SPENT ANOTHER COMPLETE day checking on all the accounts he had from 'Orrie Jones, Crumble, Tosh, and various other people on the river who had serviced the boat, before he finally called on Bertram Harkness.

Harkness was a portly man in his early sixties, roughly Ballinger's own age. He had a military bearing, although he professed no retired rank and made no mention of service. His hair was short and graying, as was his bristling mustache.

He received Monk in the study of his house, a room lined with books, drawings, and a curious mixture of exotic seashells and miniature bronzes of guns, mostly Napoleonic cannons.

"I don't know what you think I can tell you," he said rather abruptly. "I was reasonably near the river that night, but I saw nothing and heard nothing. I had a late supper with Arthur Ballinger, whom I have known for years. Since our school days, actually. He often drops by. Been a bit out of it since my injury. Took a bad fall from my horse." He tapped his right thigh. "Good of Ballinger. Keeps me up with the news I can't get from the papers, you know?"

"I see. Yes, it must be pleasant to hear a little deeper insight than is printed for the general public," Monk agreed.

"Damned right. So, what on earth is it you want from me, young man? Ballinger came up by river. Pleasant way to travel on an autumn evening. But for God's sake, if he'd seen something of this wretched murder, don't you think he'd have told you?" There was challenge in his voice, and the slightly aggressive cock of his head.

"Yes, sir," Monk said politely, increasingly aware that Harkness's temper was thin. "He has already told me precisely what he saw. But it is the timing that matters, and he is not certain about it. I thought you might be able to help in that."

Harkness appeared mollified. "Ah! Bad business. Sorry for Cardew, poor devil. Lost his eldest son, and spoiled the younger. Happens. Easy mistake. Now he's going to pay for it up to the hilt. Both sons gone. Family name ruined. Damned grief, children. I'd have the bastard horse-whipped, if they weren't going to hang him anyway."

"The time, Mr. Harkness," Monk reminded him. "It would help a great deal if you could tell me enough for me to know precisely when Mr. Ballinger was on the river, both coming here and going home again."

"Doesn't the damn ferryman know?"

"No, sir."

"Well, I didn't look at the clock," he said brusquely. "We sat down to supper about ten, as I recall. Talked for an hour or so afterward. Dare say he left at midnight. Whatever he says, that'll be the truth." Harkness regarded Monk with disfavor. "Good sportsman, Ballinger. Always admire that, you know? No, I don't suppose you do." He looked Monk up and down. "Don't look like a damn policeman, I'll give you that."

Monk swallowed his temper with considerable difficulty. " 'Good sportsman'?" he inquired.

"That's what I said. Good God, man, isn't that simple enough for you? Damn good at the oars. And wrestling. Strong, you see?"

"Yes, sir." Monk breathed out slowly. There it was, the sudden gift in all the other irrelevant evidence. The idea burned hot and bright in his mind. "Thank you, Mr. Harkness."

Harkness shrugged. "I like to be fair," he replied, standing a little straighter.

Monk forbore from making any reply to that, although one rested on his tongue. He thanked Harkness again and allowed the butler to show him out into the blustery darkness of the street, with the damp smell of the river in the air.

He took nearly half an hour to find a ferryman willing to row him back from Mortlake to Chiswick, and he timed how long it took. While he was sitting in the boat he considered what Harkness had told him, and went over in his mind all the times and details that he had been able to confirm.

Of course none of the times was exact. The only way to check them was against what other people had said. 'Orrie had taken Parfitt over to the boat where it was moored upriver, just short of Corney Reach, and had left him there, after quarter past eleven. For what purpose, he had said he did not know.

'Orrie was supposed to have gone back for him within the hour, but had been held up, and when he had done so, at about ten to one, Parfitt had not been there.

Crumble had verified 'Orrie's departure and return on both journeys. Tosh had backed him up, giving his own movements—not difficult since he and Crumble had been together most of the time.

Ballinger had boarded the ferry at approximately ten past nine, and had been rowed all the way up past the Eyot, along Corney Reach, right to Mortlake, where Harkness swore to his arrival, and later his departure. The ferryman affirmed having collected him again at half past midnight, and reached Chiswick at one in the morning, more or less.

Whereas Rupert Cardew had been drunk and unaccounted for for most of the evening after he had left Hattie Benson, who said she had stolen his cravat and given it to someone she refused to name. Fear? Or had she been paid to say this, and her fear was for the consequences of lying?

Parfitt's body had been found almost halfway along Corney Reach, upriver from where his boat had been moored. The questions burned in Monk's mind. How far had it drifted—or been dragged? Where had he actually been killed? Was it necessarily on the boat? Could he have had 'Orrie take him to the boat, and then left it again in some kind of dinghy from the boat itself? Or could someone else have come by water, and he had gone with them?

Monk needed answers to all of these questions.

Had Mickey's murderer taken him away and dropped his body overboard higher up, for it to drift downstream, misleading them all? The more Monk thought of that, the more it seemed to make sense. He could have been approaching the whole crime from the wrong direction from the beginning. It had looked like a murder of desperation, committed by a man angry and afraid of exposure, or bled dry by blackmail and facing exposure. But perhaps it had been more carefully planned than that, and by a far cooler head—not a crime of passion but a business decision.

Could Parfitt have been rebelling against his backer, his greed jeopardizing the whole project? Or had he been skimming to keep a higher percentage of the profit for himself?

Which brought Monk back to the question he both dreaded and most wanted to answer—could Ballinger himself have killed Parfitt? Or was that thought ridiculous?

He went over the times of every movement again, carefully. If everyone were telling the truth—Tosh, 'Orrie Jones, Crumble, the ferryman, Harkness, Hattie Benson, even Rupert Cardew—then it would have been possible for Ballinger, a strong rower, according to Harkness, to have taken Harkness's own boat from its moorings and met Parfitt somewhere along the river out of sight. He could have killed him and put his body in the water, then rowed back to moor the boat again, and taken the ferry back to Chiswick, exactly as he had said. It was tight, but still possible. The thought churned in his stomach—heavy, sick, and impossible to get rid of.

How honest was his own thinking in this? Did he want the answer so desperately that he would settle for anything except defeat?

What he needed was proof that Ballinger had known Parfitt, and, if possible, Jericho Phillips as well. That would take a long and very careful retracing of all the evidence, examining it, looking for a completely different pattern from before. He must start straightaway, as soon as he had seen this Hattie Benson and had verified for himself her evidence regarding the cravat.

HE FOUND HER BY the middle of the following morning, sitting in the kitchen of her small, shared house in Chiswick. She looked tired and puffy-eyed, but even with a torn wrap around her nightgown and her hair tousled and falling out of its pins, there was a beauty in her flawless skin and the naïveté of her face.

"I in't done nothin'," she said before Monk even sat down on the rickety-backed chair at the other side of the table from her.

He smiled bleakly. "I don't want to prosecute you, Miss Benson. I believe you can help me."

She rolled her eyes. "Oh, yeah? This time o' the mornin', an' all. Yer should be ashamed o' yerself. Wot'd yer wife say, then, eh?"

"You can ask her, if you meet her again," he replied with a rueful smile. "I would like you to tell me what you told her about taking Rupert Cardew's dark blue cravat with the leopards on it."

Hattie stared at him, her mouth open.

"She came here with a man called Crow, I believe," Monk continued. "You told them what happened the afternoon before Mickey Parfitt's body was discovered in the river. I need you to tell me again, with rather more detail."

She froze. "I can't!"

"Yes, you can," he insisted. "Unless, of course, you were lying." How could he persuade her to tell him, and be sure it was the truth? Perhaps she had been merely a witness at the time she had spoken to Hester and Crow, but now she realized what danger she would be in if she told the police that Cardew was innocent. She might only now be grasping the fact that they would begin to investigate the case all over again, going back to people she knew, and who knew her.

"Hattie." He leaned forward a little across the table, forcing himself to speak gently. "I don't want to charge you with stealing the cravat, whether it was to keep for yourself, to sell, or to give it to someone else. I certainly don't think it likely that you strangled Mickey Parfitt with it, although it isn't impossible." He let the suggestion hang in the air.

"Yer mad, you are!" she said in horror. " 'Ow in Gawd's name d'yer think I could strangle a man like Mickey? 'E may a bin skinny as a broomstick, but 'e were strong! 'E'd a bashed me 'ead in."

"He was violent?" he asked.

"O' course 'e were violent, yer stupid sod!" she shouted at him. "Beat the shit out o' anyone wot crossed 'im."

"Like who?"

"Yer thinkin' they killed 'im? I tell you, an' yer don't think they're gonna come arter me?"

"You could have killed Mickey," he went on thoughtfully. "Someone hit him hard on the back of the head, probably with a piece of fallen branch from a tree. Then, when he was unconscious, they strangled him. It doesn't take a lot of strength to do that."

"Well, I didn't! I 'ad customers all night, till past two in the mornin'. Then I were knackered," she said defiantly.

"Names would help me to believe you."

"Oh, yeah! I'm gonna be in great shape fer me business if I give yer a list o' toffs wot come 'ere fer a bit o' fun, aren't I? Do wonders fer me reputation, that would!"

"I expect I can find them from somebody else." He said it lightly, as if it were an easy thing to do. "I can ask one of the pubs along the mall who was there that evening."

Her face went even paler, her skin as white as milk. "Please, mister, yer'll ruin me! If I lose all me customers, I in't got nothin' else I can do! An' I owe money. They'll come arter me!" She leaned toward him, and he could feel the warmth of her, a faint smell of perfume and sweat. "If I tell yer I took the cravat that afternoon, then yer'll know it wasn't Mr. Cardew as killed Mickey, an' then yer'll start all over again wi' Tosh, an' 'e'll skin me alive for bringin' trouble on 'im. 'E'll beat the 'ell out o' me, an' then I won't be able ter work."

"You're right," Monk said gently. "That would be unfair."

She took a deep, shaky breath and made an attempt at a smile.

"Better to let Rupert Cardew hang," he said quietly. "Who do you suppose did kill Mickey?"

Her hands were gripped so tight, there were white ridges on her knuckles.

"I dunno," she whispered.

"He'll need to come back and make sure you don't tell anyone," he pointed out. "Rupert will remember that you took his cravat. He'll say so, in court, even if no one believes him. I dare say the prosecution will call you to give evidence, just to deny it. Close off all escape for him, as it were."

"Jesus! Ye're a bastard!" she said huskily. "Worse than Tosh, yer are."

"No, I'm not, Hattie." He shook his head, although he felt a sharp stab of truth in what she said. "I want you to tell me the truth, then I'll keep you safe."

"Yeah?" she said contemptuously. "An' 'ow are yer gonna do that, then? Buy a nice little room somewhere where they'll never find me, will yer? An' food an' summink ter do, then?"

The answer was instant in his mind. "Yes, actually, that's exactly what I'll do. But to do it, I need the truth, preferably with some way you can prove it."

She blinked, hope flickering in her eyes. "Like 'ow?"

"Describe the cravat to me."

"Eh? It were just a dark blue tie, that sort o' shape." She made a picture in the air. "Silk," she added.

"How long?"

Again she gestured, holding her hands just under three feet apart.

"Go on," he prompted. "What else?"

"It's narrer in the middle an' wide at both ends," she said. "One end bigger than the other . . . longer, like."

"Was it plain or patterned?"

"Patterned. Yer know that, fer Gawd's sake! It 'ad little yeller animals on it, three at a time. Cats, or summink."

"How?"

"One on top o' the other. Three of 'em."

"Thank you, Hattie. I believe you. Now go and pack some clothes into a bag, get dressed, and I will take you to a safe place."

She remained sitting down. "Where?"

"In the city, Portpool Lane. You will be safe there. You will be fed and have your own room. You'll work for it, at whatever Mrs. Monk tells you to do." He saw the look on her face. "It used to be a brothel," he said with a broad smile. "It's a clinic for sick women, and injured ones."

She swore at him, colorfully and with profound feeling, but she did as he told her.

They took a hansom from the Chiswick mall all the way into the city. It was a long and expensive ride, but Monk felt it was more than warranted by the circumstances. He did not wish her to be seen with him; in fact, he could not afford it. It would be so easy for anyone to make a few inquiries and find the clinic. Perhaps he should warn Squeaky Robinson to keep a close eye on Hattie and see that she did not show herself in the rooms where casual patients came for treatment or help, at least until the case had come to trial and she had testified. After that, her safety could be reconsidered.

As the wheels rumbled over the streets, he engaged her in conversation, as much in order to take her mind off her present situation as in the expectation of learning anything more. Either way, he failed.

"Yer gotta keep 'im from findin' me," she said, hugging her arms around her body and sitting forward on the seat. " 'E'll do me, 'e will."

"Who?" he asked.

"Tosh, o' course!" she answered angrily. "I in't scared o' Crumble. 'E couldn't squash a fly. Feared of 'is own shadder, an' fearder still o' Tosh."

"What about 'Orrie Jones?"

"I dunno. Sometimes I think 'e's 'alf-witted, other times I in't so sure. But 'e wouldn't do nuffink 'less Tosh told 'im ter, wotever 'e thought fer 'isself."

"Did you ever hear the name of Jericho Phillips?"

"No. 'Oo's 'e?"

"He's dead now, but he used to run a boat like Mickey's, but down the river."

"An' now Mickey's dead, eh?" she said thoughtfully. "Could Mr. Cardew a killed 'im?"

"No. We know who killed Phillips. The man who did it killed himself also."

She gave a little grunt.

"Why did you think it was the same person?" he asked. "Do you think Mickey and Phillips knew each other?"

"Dunno. Mickey din't work for 'isself. 'E come from Chiswick, same like the rest of us. 'E never 'ad money ter get a boat. Someone else staked 'im. Mebbe it were the same person."

"Rupert Cardew?"

"Don't be daft!" she retorted. "Why'd 'e have me steal 'is necktie ter make it look like 'e killed Mickey if 'e were behind it all? It's someone wi' twice the brains 'e 'as."

"More than Mickey, or Tosh?"

"They got cunning; it in't the same."

He did not argue. Deliberately he guided the conversation to other, more pleasant subjects, and finally they arrived at Portpool

Lane. He took her inside, introduced her to Squeaky Robinson, and then to Claudine Burroughs, explaining the need to keep her safe.

"She can help me," Claudine said decisively. "I won't let her out of my sight."

Monk thanked her, wondering wryly how Hattie would take to that. It might well be the best care she had ever known.

IN THE MORNING MONK went to see Rathbone and told him that he had now found evidence that made it extremely unlikely that Rupert Cardew was responsible for the death of Mickey Parfitt.

Rathbone was startled. "And the cravat? Was it not his?" he asked, as if unable to believe in the release from the responsibility of an impossible task.

"Yes, it was his," Monk replied, sitting down in the chair opposite Rathbone's desk without being invited. "A prostitute stole it from him that afternoon and gave it to someone she is too afraid to name. But I believe her. She can describe it far too precisely for her to have only seen it around his neck. She had seen it undone, felt it, and knew it was silk. She admitted to taking it."

Rathbone drew in his breath as if to speak, then changed his mind.

Monk smiled, sitting back a little in the chair. "Did Lord Cardew pay her to say this?" He said aloud what he knew was in Rathbone's mind. "You could always ask him."

"Where is she?" Rathbone did not bother to express his opinion of that remark.

"I would prefer not to tell you," Monk replied. "For your safety as well as hers."

Rathbone's eyes widened for a moment, then his face was expressionless again. "Now what will you do about it?" he asked. "Are you happy to mark the case as 'unsolved' and move on? Does anyone really want to know who killed Parfitt?"

"Lord Cardew might," Monk observed. "A shadow hangs over his son as long as we don't know. But whether he does or not, I do. Not because I give a damn about Parfitt, but I need to find out who was behind him, Oliver." He did not look away. He knew exactly what Rathbone was thinking, remembering, and what the weight of it would be if Monk were right.

For several seconds they stared at each other, then Monk rose to his feet. "I'm sorry," he said very quietly, little more than a whisper. "I can't let it go."

Rathbone did not reply.

Monk let himself out, passing the clerk in the entrance lobby, and thanking him.

In spite of the sun, the air outside felt cold.

MONK SPENT THE NEXT two days questioning everybody who had anything to do with Mickey Parfitt, or who might have seen anyone on the river or the dockside at either Chiswick or Mortlake the night of Parfitt's death. 'Orrie, Crumble, and Tosh repeated their stories almost word for word, and he could not shake them. Nothing was changed. It was still possible that Ballinger could physically have killed Parfitt, but without a motive, without proof that they knew each other, it was nothing more than an idea.

Monk was pacing the path by the side of the river along Corney Reach when he ran into the fisherman.

"Don't walk up be'ind a man like that!" the fisherman spat. "I could a taken yer eye out wi' me rod, yer great fool! Where d'yer grow up, then? In the middle of a desert?" He was a skinny little man with a long nose and a lantern jaw. The cap pulled forward over his eyes hid whatever hair he had left.

Monk apologized, which was received with ill grace. He was about to move on when, out of sheer habit, he asked the question. "Do you spend a lot of time here?"

The man squinted at him. "Course I do, yer daft sod. I live up there." He jerked his head back toward the lane leading out of the town into the fields.

"Do you have a boat?"

"Yeah, but it in't fer 'ire. I don't want some great lummox crashing about in it who don't know one end from the other."

"I grew up in boats," Monk said testily. The fact that he had only the briefest flashes of memory about that time was none of the man's affair. "I'm looking for witnesses, not to go rowing myself."

"Witnesses ter wot? I in't seen nothing. In't even seen a bleedin' fish terday."

"Not today. The day before Mickey Parfitt's body was pulled out of the river."

The man narrowed his eyes. "Seen, like wot?"

"People coming and going, other than the ferrymen. Anyone you know behaving differently from usual. Anyone in a hurry, frightened, quarreling, running away."

The man shook his head.

"Jeez! Yer don't want much, do yer? All I saw were Tosh racin' up ter Mickey on the dockside, yellin' at 'im ter wait. Then 'e pulls a piece o' paper out of 'is pocket an' gives it to 'im. Mickey reads it, swears summink 'orrible, grabs a pencil from Tosh, an' writes summink on it, then 'e gives it back to 'im. Arter that 'e calls the ferryman and tells 'im 'e's changed 'is mind. 'E rushes away lookin' all excited, an' far as I know, nobody gone after 'im, nobody 'it 'im nor strangled 'im nor threw 'im in the river."

Monk felt a sharp flicker of excitement stir inside him. "But Mickey changed his mind about where he was going?" he urged.

"I jus' said that, yer damn fool! In't yer listenin'?" the man snapped.

"What time was this, roughly?"

"About 'alf past ten."

"Thank you. I'm most obliged. What is your name, if I need to speak to you again?" He nearly added, in case he needed him to testify, then thought better of it. He would send Orme for him, and allow no choice.

"'Orace Butterworth," the man replied grimly. "Now get out of it. Yer frightenin' the fish."

Monk considered carefully how to make the best use of this delicate piece of information. Was this the message that had taken

Mickey out to the boat, and then upriver toward Mortlake to meet his death? Who was it from? What had he believed he was going for? It must have been urgent, to take him back out again at that hour.

Tosh would be very unlikely to tell Monk. Nor would he tell him who the messenger was or where he'd come from. It would too easily implicate him in being party to the murder that had followed. He would simply deny it all, say that Butterworth was wrong, probably made it all up. A good lawyer would demolish the story in minutes.

He must build a chain of evidence. Who was the weakest link? 'Orrie Jones. That was where to begin.

He found 'Orrie in a boatyard patiently sanding a piece of wood. There were other men around, all sawing, planing, chiseling, carefully fitting planks, easing tongues into grooves. The ground was covered with sawdust, and it was in the air with the smell of wood and sap, and there was the constant, irregular sound of friction, banging, and someone whistling half under his breath.

Lower down, closer to the water's edge, one old man with tattooed arms was caulking the sides of a boat, his feet now and then shifting as the water seeped up through the shingle and soaked his boots.

They were sheltered from the breeze. The tide slurped on the stone of the slipway. There was a smell of river mud and wet wood.

'Orrie looked up and saw Monk approaching, and his face took on a look of infinite weariness.

"You again," he sighed. "In't it enough yer 'ang the poor bastard, yer gotta 'it every nail inter 'is coffin as well?"

"Have to be sure it fits, 'Orrie, just like those pieces you're putting together."

"So wot is it now, then?" 'Orrie's good eye swiveled around.

"When did Mickey ask you to row him out to the boat?"

"I dunno!"

"Yes, you do. Think!"

'Orrie met his eyes and gave him that rare focused look of total clarity. "Why? What does it matter now? Don't make no difference to 'oo killed 'im."

"You tell the defense lawyer that, 'Orrie. If you can't answer, he'll pick your life apart detail by detail, and—"

"I dunno when 'e decided ter go out ter the boat!" 'Orrie protested angrily. "But 'e din't ask me until a bit before eleven. I know 'cos I jus' started a pint, an' I 'ad ter put it down."

"At the pub?"

"O' course at the pub! D'yer think I were pullin' it out o' the river?"

"I don't care where you got it. Why did Mickey decide so late? Were you at his beck and call anytime?"

'Orrie stiffened. "No, I weren't! I weren't 'is bleedin' servant. Summink came up."

Monk nodded, trying to curb his impatience and look encouraging. "An appointment, unexpectedly?"

"Right!"

"And he thought it was important enough to go? Not so convenient for him either. Was he angry? Or afraid?"

"No, 'e weren't. 'E were 'appy."

"Why?"

'Orrie drew in his breath, looked at Monk, weighed up his best advantage, and decided to answer. "Well, it don't matter now. The poor sod's dead, eh? 'E thought as it were a good chance o' new business. But don't waste yer breath askin' me wot, 'cos I dunno."

"Of course you don't. Did he come for you personally, or did he send you a note?" He made his tone deliberately insulting. "Maybe someone read it for you?"

"I read it meself!" 'Orrie snapped. "Jus' 'cos I got a walleye don't mean I'm stupid."

"Really? What did you do with the note?"

"I kept it 'o course. Never know when yer gonna need paper for summink."

'Orrie fished in his trouser pocket and slammed a grimy piece of paper onto the wood he was working with. He glared at Monk.

Monk picked up the paper and saw written in an untidy but obviously educated script:

Excellent new opportunity for business. Meet you on the
boat, midnight. Be there, or I'll give it to Jackie.

And underneath was a further note scrawled in a completely different hand:

Meet me at the dock, 11 o'clock. Don't be late. Mickey.

Monk looked at the paper a few moments longer, feeling the tex-
ture of it between his fingers. It was good paper, pale blue and smooth,
torn from a larger sheet.

He turned it over and saw on the other side what had apparently
been part of a longer letter, or a list. This one was written in ink, but
the words were harder to decipher, as if it were another language,
perhaps Latin, although, with only half of some of the words, it was
hard to tell. The letters were well formed, the script disciplined. He
wondered where it came from.

"Thank you, 'Orrie," Monk said in a whisper, letting his breath
out slowly. "That is just about perfect."

THE CHARGES HAD BEEN withdrawn against Rupert Cardew, and he was released from custody.

Once again the case was open.

Monk stood in the station at Wapping with the note 'Orrie had given him in his hand. It was strong evidence, but against whom? The pencil had smudged until it was only just legible, and the dirt and finger marks on that paper made it impossible to place. It could have been written by anyone.

Monk was not even certain if it was the man behind the blackmail, except who else would Parfitt have turned out for at that time of night? Anyone else he would simply have told to come at a more convenient hour. Who else but someone he knew, and trusted, would he have met alone, at night on the boat?

"Has to be," Orme agreed. "But we aren't going to tie it to anyone, with the note in that state. All it proves is that someone baited him to go there. And we know it was premeditated anyway, and with

Cardew's cravat." Orme picked up the paper, turning it over in his hands. "Any idea where it came from?" he asked, squinting a little as he tried to read it, then looking up slightly at Monk.

"No," Monk said honestly.

"Ballinger?" Orme said.

"Could be. Parfitt knew who it was from, or he wouldn't have gone. Obviously he knew him well enough that no signature was necessary."

Orme's face was grim in the yellow glare of the lamplight. Outside, the wind was rising, and it was beginning to rain. It was going to be a choppy crossing on the ferry.

"Has to be the man behind the blackmail," Orme said quietly. "We have to get it right this time."

Monk felt a faint heat in his face, a remembrance of shame. Orme had never referred to it, but Monk had let them both down with his carelessness in the Jericho Phillips case. He had underestimated Rathbone's skill and his dedication to the processes of the law. After all his years dealing with crime, he had still been naïve because his emotions had been so intensely involved. He must not ever make that mistake again. Rathbone was his friend, and he would feel a desperate pity for him if Ballinger were guilty, but Monk must not for an instant forget that if that were so, then Rathbone would be the enemy, and would fight with every art and skill he had to defend Arthur. He would for any client—that was his duty. But for Margaret's father, he would go to the very edge of the abyss. Perhaps even further. Wouldn't Monk himself, for Hester?

Orme shook his head. "We've got nothing except coincidence," he said warningly. "Lot of possibles that won't carry any weight with a jury. Maybe wouldn't even get us to court."

"I know," Monk told him.

"Ballinger's a highly respectable man," Orme went on. "One of their own, so to speak. A solicitor. His wife and daughters'll be in the gallery, all looking sweet and supportive, and like they believe every word he says. What we've got are out of the gutter, and look like it. 'Orrible Jones, with his eyes all over the place, like a horse that's been spooked. Crumble, all quiet and sneaky. Tosh Wilkin, who's a villain if ever I saw one. Hattie Benson, who's a prostitute, an' scared stiff. Looks like she's lying, even when she isn't."

"All right!" Monk said sharply. "I know! We haven't got enough."

"We've got the ferryman, Stanley Willington, but he just bears out what Ballinger says himself. Picked him up at Chiswick, took him over the river, and brought him back again. And of course he has Mr. Harkness swearing to his being in Mortlake all the time between. It's all very tidy, and hard to shake. He had time to row down as far as the boat, then back again, and catch a hansom to where Willington picked him up. And we know from Harkness that he was a strong rower, but will Harkness say that on the stand, when he understands what that means?"

"Probably not," Monk conceded. He took the piece of paper from where Orme had left it on the desk. "We need to make enough sense of this, for certain. The man who killed Mickey Parfitt wrote this to lure him to his death. God knows, no man better deserved it."

"I know." Orme gave him a tight smile, understanding in his eyes, and a surprising gentleness. "We've still got to find him."

MONK WENT BACK TO Chiswick to learn more about the boat and its patrons. It was late October, more than a month since Mickey Parfitt's body had been found floating at Corney Reach. The air was much colder. The last echoes of summer were completely gone, and the leaves were falling. It had stopped raining, but there was a smell of damp in the air, and occasionally a drift of wood smoke from bonfires. The late flowers were richly bronze and purple, heavier, darker than the blue and gold of spring. The few stubble fields he passed were brazen, almost barbaric in their beauty, vividly and unmistakably waning.

It had always been Monk's favorite season. He had flashes of memory sometimes of the great barren hills of Northumberland, where he knew he'd been born, so different from the lush easiness of the south. The earth there seemed to be all bones, no flesh, the skies unending. He would go back one day soon and see if it was still as beautiful, or if it was only the familiarity then that had made it seem so.

Now he had to follow the dirt and violence of Mickey Parfitt's life and all the people he had known, used, cheated, and betrayed.

It was time to face the details of what had happened on the boat. Monk had been putting it off, perhaps as much for himself as for them, but he must speak to the boys himself, gently, persistently, ruthlessly. He must have the hospital matron there as a witness, so nothing rested on him alone, but this time he could not allow her to intervene. He realized how deeply he had been dreading it, why he had sent Orme instead of going himself, telling himself that Orme had children and would be better at it.

It took him two days of gentle, endlessly repeated questions, and it hurt more profoundly than he had imagined. The matron looked at him as if he had been a criminal himself, but she did not stop him more than two or three times. His assumption about Crumble had been correct: cook, companion, laundryman, gang master for cleaning chores, and jailer. Sometimes, here and there, abuser as well. The boys' pale, blurred, and frightened faces reflected more misery than anger. They were too young to understand that it could all have been wildly and beautifully different. They might well have known hunger, cold, and exhaustion, but without the added horror. They could have had safety in sleep, been touched only in tenderness, or in the occasional, well-earned chastening. They could have been spared all their lives from the obscenity of degraded human appetite, from the sight of men who despised others because they despised themselves.

Now, having questioned the boys, it was Monk who had dreams he could not bear. He woke in the night, his body aching and drenched in a sweat, tears on his face. He lay in the dark, staring up at the faint shadow patterns on the ceiling as the wind moved in the trees outside. He wanted to waken Hester, even if he did not tell her why, just so he would not be alone with what was in his mind. Even if he just touched her, felt the warmth of her . . .

But she would hurt for him. She would need him to explain it, at least a little, and how could he do that? If he gave it words, it would re-create the reality in his mind—the white faces, the frightened eyes, the small bodies shivering with memory, self-loathing, and the terror of new pain.

And she would think of Scuff. She would wonder about all the other children, and that was a burden, selfish of him to share just to lighten it a fraction for himself.

Could he tell her without weeping? Perhaps not. She could not heal his sense of horror for him. He would keep it closed inside him. She would always know it was there, because she had seen Phillips's boat, but she did not need to hear it again and see it through his eyes. Memory was a necessary tool in life; sometimes it was a blessed thing, and sometimes it was a curse.

If he even got up, he would disturb her. He might pretend there was nothing wrong, but his need, his pain, would creep through. She would unravel it all.

He turned over, as if he were half-asleep, and lay on his other side. He would go back to sleep in some time, and, if he were lucky, the dreams would be different.

HE WOKE EXHAUSTED THE following morning, his eyes gritty and his head aching. Hester did not even ask him how he was. She looked at him, her face bleak and tender, and words would have been superfluous anyway.

She got up and went to the kitchen, raked out the ashes, and lit the stove, banking it up to get hot quickly. It was early, and she did not waken Scuff. Today was Sunday. They could stay here together, perhaps even go to church, like a regular family. Scuff liked that because everyone could see them together, see that he belonged.

She gave Monk piping hot tea and fresh toast with his favorite jam, then sat opposite him at the table. There was no sound in the kitchen, and the only light was from the gas bracket on the wall casting a yellow glow, shadows everywhere.

When he had said nothing for several minutes, she prompted him.

"Do you really want to find who killed Parfitt?" she asked quietly, pushing the toast across the table toward him.

"Yes, of course I do!" he said vehemently, then looked at her face. He knew he had to be more honest; even a half lie to her built a barrier he could not live with. "No, not entirely. Parfitt was vile, and if it was one of his victims, I'd be happy to let him go. If it was one of the boys, or even two or three of them, I don't even know if I'll arrest them. Even if I could prove which ones, I might not try to."

She said nothing.

He took the toast and buttered it.

"But if it's the man behind the whole trade, probably behind Phillips as well, then yes, I want to find him. And I want to hang him."

Monk fished the note out of his inside pocket where he carried it, carefully, in an envelope. It was both a talisman and a weight dragging him down. He took the note out of the envelope and put it on the table between them, well away from the jam or the teapot. "This was written by a literate person, adult. It's a strong hand, used to writing."

She looked at him, then down at the torn piece of paper. She picked it up and read it. "But you have no idea who wrote it?"

"No. It's good-quality paper and perfectly ordinary pencil. The envelope's mine."

She turned the note over in her hands. The silence seemed to stretch until he could hear the ticking of the clock on the mantel over the stove. Her shoulders were stiff; a tiny muscle clenched in her jaw was flickering.

"Hester?" His voice was quiet and yet filled the room.

She looked up at him. "The words are Latin. They're medicines. This is part of a list of things we order regularly for the clinic."

He stared at her. This was the last thing he had expected her to say.

"You recognize the handwriting?" he asked.

"Claudine's," she said. "But she could have given the list to several people."

"Margaret," he replied. "Isn't she the one who keeps the money, and buys such things?"

"Yes. But so does Squeaky, sometimes." Her voice was tight, full of grief.

He reached across the table and put his hand over hers. He knew what she was afraid of. Squeaky had kept a brothel when they'd first met him. He had seemed on the surface to have reformed his ways, under duress, perhaps, but still quite genuinely. He had even taken a kind of pleasure in his respectability. Had it all been an act to cover an even darker side? Had they been too blinded by hope and wish to look at him more closely? How big a descent was it from running a brothel for women to investing in pornography with boys?

Monk felt a little sick. He knew how much Hester had believed in all the people in the clinic, considered them friends, colleagues, people she trusted with a common passion.

"I have to ask him," he said. "I can't—"

"No," she cut across his words. "I will. I won't let him dupe me, I promise."

"Hester . . ."

She stood up. "I will. Now—today."

"It's Sunday."

"I know."

He looked at her stiff, straight back, the way she walked, the very careful manner in which she picked up the plates and put them into the basin to wash, deliberately, as if in a moment's absence of mind she might grip them so hard she would break one.

Perhaps he should let her speak to Squeaky. Then she would not feel so powerless, so incapable.

"I'll wait outside," he told her.

She was standing at the basin, and she turned to give him a swift look, something close to a smile. "I've got to leave bread out for Scuff, and butter and jam. I'll waken him, and then I'm ready."

SQUEAKY LOOKED UP FROM his ledger as Hester came into his room and closed the door behind her.

"You look as if you lost sixpence and found nothing," he said dourly. "Her ladyship giving you difficulties?"

"No, not at the moment," she replied. She took the envelope out of her pocket, and then the list as well. She put them both on the table in front of him, but kept her finger on the list, leaning forward a little so her weight was on her hand.

There was not a flicker in his face.

"It's torn," he observed. "In't no use like that. What're you giving it to me for? Get Claudine ter make it out again."

"Is it Claudine's hand?" she asked.

"Course it is! You gone blind or summink?" He squinted up at her. "You look sick. What's wrong?" Now he was anxious, even concerned for her.

She turned the paper over.

He frowned, looking at it, reading it. "What in hell's that?" he demanded. "It means summink, or you wouldn't be looking at it with a face on you like a burst boot. Who's supposed to go . . . Oh, jeez!"

The usual trace of color vanished from his sallow face. "It's to do with that bleeding murder, isn't it? You can't think Claudine had anything to do with it? That's just stupid. You've taken leave of your wits if you think she'd even know about things like that. You think she went up there and done in Mickey Parfitt? With Cardew's necktie, and all? You think he left it behind here, and she—"

"No, Squeaky, I don't. But did you?" Even as she said it, she thought of Hattie Benson safe downstairs in the laundry, with Claudine apparently looking after her, and Squeaky supposed to keep everyone else from going down and seeing her.

His face was full of conflicting emotions: anger, hurt, fear, and also a kind of gentleness. "No, I didn't. I s'pose I had that coming, for my past life, and if I'd've known what Parfitt was, I might have. I'd also have more sense than to write him a note on paper from here!"

"Is it from here?" Hester asked.

He looked at it again. "No. We don't spend that sort of money on paper. Even the ledger isn't that good. But just 'cos it's quality don't mean Claudine had anything to do with it. She may be an odd old article, but when you get to know her, she's solid. She's got guts, and she don't never tell no lies. You can't think that of her. It's wrong."

"I didn't," she admitted.

He winced. "You thought I did it." It was a statement. "Well, I could have. He needed doing, best at the end of a rope. And I wouldn't help you catch whoever did do it. But it weren't me."

She believed him.

"Thank you," she said quietly. "Tomorrow I'll ask Claudine if she remembers writing this, and what she did with it."

"Don't you let her feel you think as she done it!" he warned. "It'd hurt her something terrible, and she don't deserve that."

In spite of herself, Hester smiled. She could remember very clearly how Claudine and Squeaky had hated each other in the beginning. She had thought him obscene, both physically and morally. He had seen her as arrogant, useless, and cold, a middle-aged woman sterile of mind and devoid of passions. It had been her crazy pursuit of Phillips's pornographic photographs, at fearful risk to herself, that had finally changed his mind. And it was his effective, if rather quixotic, rescue of her that had changed her mind about him.

"I won't," she promised.

HESTER WAS IN EARLY on Monday morning, but a brief and businesslike meeting with Margaret in the pantry delayed her meeting with Claudine.

"We are rather short of laundry supplies," Margaret warned. "I have just been down there and cautioned them to be a little less generous in their use. We cannot afford to replace them at this rate."

"Thank you," Hester said briefly. "Is there anything else?"

Margaret hesitated, seemingly on the edge of saying something more, then changed her mind and went out of the room. Hester heard her footsteps on the wooden floor, brisk and purposeful.

She found Claudine in the medicine room and showed her the paper, holding out only the side with the list on it.

Claudine frowned, then looked up and met Hester's eyes. "What happened to it? I wrote it out for Margaret, and she got me all those things. That list is several weeks old."

Hester felt bruised, suddenly tired. "How many weeks?"

"I don't know. Four, maybe five. Why? It hardly matters," Claudine replied.

"You're sure you gave it to Margaret?" Hester insisted.

"Yes, of course I am."

"She actually got all those things for you?"

"Yes. If she hadn't, I would have written it out again. But I didn't have to. What is this about, Hester? Is something missing?"

"No. Nothing at all. It doesn't have to do with the clinic."

"I don't understand." Claudine looked thoroughly puzzled.

Hester shook her head a little. "You don't want to," she said gently. "It's the message on the other side that's important, not this. What happened to the list after she brought you the items on it?"

"I've no idea. I didn't see it again after I gave it to her."

"You didn't check off the items against it?" Hester suggested.

"I had the receipts from the apothecary. Those are all I need for the ledger."

"Are you quite sure you didn't ever see the list again?"

"Not until now. Why?"

"Thank you." Hester gave her a tiny smile, almost more of a grimace, and went out of the room, closing the door softly.

She gave the list back to Monk.

He waited.

"It's Claudine's list for Margaret to shop from," she told him. "Margaret never gave it back, because Claudine took the prices from the apothecary's receipts." She swallowed hard. "I wish it weren't."

"I know," he murmured. "I'm sorry. I can't leave it. If it's Ballinger, I must still find him, not for Parfitt's sake but because of the children."

She nodded. "Oliver will defend him. He can't refuse." She watched Monk's face. "We'll have to have irrefutable proof."

RUPERT CARDEW CLOSED THE door of the morning room behind him and stared at Monk. He still looked tired, as if the shock of arrest had not completely left him, even though he was now free. However, he was composed and courteous, and, as always, beautifully dressed.

"What can I do for you, Mr. Monk?" he asked.

Monk felt churlish, and it put him at a disadvantage.

"I apologize. What I have to ask you is extremely unpleasant, but this is a case I cannot afford to leave."

Rupert looked surprised. "Really? You care so much that Parfitt is dead?"

"On the contrary. If that were all, I would be delighted to turn my time to something more important," Monk admitted. "But I want to find the man behind the blackmail."

Rupert smiled very slightly, not in amusement but in self-criticism. "Are you going to warn me that I am still vulnerable? I assure you, I know that."

"I assumed you were aware of it, Mr. Cardew," Monk told him. "That is not why I came."

"Oh?" Rupert looked surprised, but not worried.

"I need to know a great deal more from you than you have told me so far," Monk replied. "I'm sorry." He meant the apology more than Cardew would understand, or believe.

"I don't know anything more," Rupert said simply. "I really have no idea who killed Parfitt. For God's sake, man, don't you think I'd have told you already if I did?"

"Of course, if you had realized, or thought for a moment that I would believe you. I think it was Arthur Ballinger who did it; if not personally, then by using one of Parfitt's own men." He saw Cardew start with surprise, and ignored it. "But I have to prove it beyond any doubt," he continued. "If Ballinger is charged, he will be defended by Oliver Rathbone, and I know from experience that Rathbone could get even Jericho Phillips off. How hard do you imagine he is going to fight for his father-in-law?"

Rupert's mouth tightened, and the corners went down. "I see. But I still don't know anything."

"You know about the trade," Monk said grimly.

Rupert blushed. "I don't know about his side of it."

"I didn't expect you to. I can deduce a good deal of that. I need to know his clients, how the blackmail was paid, the sort of amounts, and exactly what the performances were like and who attended."

Rupert went white.

Monk ignored that also. "And I need to know about the suicide a few months ago. What led up to it?"

"I can't tell you that!" Rupert was appalled. "That would be a . . . betrayal."

"I knew you would see it that way," Monk said quietly. "Yes. You would, in a sense, be betraying the other men who used the abuse of children for their entertainment."

He saw Rupert wince, the shame filling his face. He had expected it. It hurt Monk to have to be so blunt, but it changed nothing. "Whereas if you don't tell me, you will be betraying the children on that boat—and all those like them. And if you think carefully and with absolute honesty, you'll realize you will be betraying your father, and perhaps the better part of yourself."

Rupert shook his head slowly. "You don't know what you're asking . . ."

"Really?" Monk raised his eyebrows. "Do you think your social class are the only people who feel loyalty toward their friends, or to those to whom they are bound by promises of conspiracy, and hiding their shame? You are ashamed of it, aren't you?"

A flame of anger lit Rupert's eyes. "Yes, of course I am! You . . ." He struggled for words, and could not find them.

"And you think embarrassment and an apology are enough to make the balance even again?"

"No, I don't! I'll regret it the rest of my life!" Rupert was shouting now. "But I can't undo it."

"Remorse is excellent," Monk said levelly. "But it isn't enough. Nor is money. If you want any kind of redemption, then you must help me stop at least some of it from happening again."

"How many times do I have to tell you? I don't know who killed Parfitt!" Rupert said desperately. "It may well have been Ballinger, but I don't know anything to help you prove it. I didn't see him, and I wouldn't recognize him if I had. I don't even remember half that evening, except as a nightmare. Telling you the names of my friends who went there isn't going to do anything except embarrass them and make me a social outcast."

"That's the price," Monk replied. "And is their friendship worth that much to you?"

"Don't be such a damn fool!" Rupert's voice was high and angry again, touched with fear. "Everyone will despise me for ratting on friends, not just the men concerned, and their families, and their friends."

Monk felt the resolve harden in him, like a cold, gray stone in his gut. "Then, tell me about the 'performances.'" He accentuated the word. "Where did you meet? Did you all go to Chiswick separately, or together? Shared a hansom, perhaps? You wouldn't go in your own carriages—they might be recognized—or want your coachman to know, for that matter."

"Separately, mostly," Rupert answered grimly. "What has that to do with Ballinger, or anything else?"

Monk ignored the question. "How do you get from the shore to Parfitt's boat?"

"Someone rowed us. Either that revolting little man with the walleye—"

"'Orrible Jones?"

"If you say so. Or the other. Why?"

Monk ignored that question too. "By agreement? How did you know he wasn't just a ferryman? How did he know who you were, and that you wanted to go to that boat and not just to the other shore? How did he know you were one of Parfitt's clients? You could even have been police."

"It's not illegal," Rupert said miserably.

"Just immoral?" Monk asked sarcastically. "That's why you do it up there in Chiswick, miles from home, and at night on the river?"

Rupert glared at him. "I didn't say I was proud of it, just that it isn't anything to do with the police."

"Actually, torturing and imprisoning children is illegal," Monk told him.

"We didn't do . . . that . . . to anyone!"

"You just watched other people do it!" Monk's disgust made his voice shake, his throat straining with the force of his emotions. "And homosexuality is illegal too."

Rupert's face was scarlet.

"Apart from the question of legality, Mr. Cardew," Monk went on ruthlessly, "would you like to be forced to have anal intercourse with another man, for the entertainment of a crowd of drunken lechers? Did that happen to you when you were six or seven years old, and you screamed, and bled, and that's why—"

"Stop it!" Rupert shouted, his voice cracking. "All right! I understand. It was bestial, and I shall pay for it in shame for the rest of my life!"

"And you will also tell me who else was there," Monk said. "Every man whose face you recognized. I can't arrest them for it, but I can question them for information. I'm going to hang the creature behind this, and I'm going to use every perverted bastard I can find to do it."

"You're going to talk to them?" Rupert whispered, horrified.

"If I have to. And you are going to tell me step by step what happened, every filthy act, every scream, every injury and humiliation, every terrified and weeping child that was tortured for your amusement. I'll have nightmares too, maybe for the rest of my life, but I'm going to paint such a picture that your friends will never doubt that I know what happened, as well as if I'd been there too." He drew in his breath. He was shaking, and his body was covered with sweat.

"And the jury will know exactly what those men were paying to hide. Perhaps they'll wake up terrified as well, and they'll be as passionate as I am in helping to get rid of at least some of the obscene trade. You'll help me willingly or unwillingly, Mr. Cardew. I imagine, for your father's sake, if nothing else, you would prefer to do it here and now, in private, while it is still a voluntary thing, and perhaps partially redeem yourself. Believe me, if you don't and I have to force you in front of a jury, it will be a lot worse."

Rupert stared at him, defeat in his eyes and a depth of misery that for an instant almost weakened Monk's resolve. Then Monk thought of Scuff, the trust that was just beginning between them, and the moment of indecision vanished.

"Now," he prompted. "Detail by detail. Make me feel as if I am there."

Rupert began haltingly, still standing motionless in the quiet morning room with its sun-faded carpet and old books. His voice was low and strained. Frequently he stopped, and Monk had to prompt him to go on. He hated doing it; he felt as if he were beating an animal. And he knew he would feel unclean afterward, tarnished with cruelty. But he did not stop until Rupert had told him every detail of the entire hideous business. His face was mottled and stained with tears. Perhaps he would never forget this either, and not ever be the same as he had been before.

"And the man it broke?" Monk persisted. "The one who took his own life, shot himself alone in the small boat."

"Tadley . . ." Rupert whispered. "He couldn't pay."

"Did Parfitt drive him that far on purpose? An example to others of what happens if you don't honor your debts?"

"It wasn't a debt!" Rupert snapped back at him. "It was extortion. I told you . . . I didn't know about it until afterward. Not that I could have paid it for him if I had."

"So, what was it, a misjudgment of Parfitt's? Is suicide good for business, or bad?"

Rupert shot him a look of utter loathing. It stung Monk more than he would have expected, perhaps because he knew the loathing was fair.

"It is a salutary reminder to pay on time instead of letting the payments mount up," Rupert replied coldly. "And it is bad for business. But, then, murder is worse."

"Tell me about Tadley," Monk instructed.

"He was a family man, but unhappy, lonely, I think. I don't know that he particularly cared for boys. I had the feeling he wanted to experience some kind of excitement, some danger, a sense of being completely alive. I know that sounds—"

"No," Monk cut across him. "It sounds like many people whose lives are suffocated by tedium, duty. Trying so hard to live up to what other people have expected of them that they become imprisoned inside it. Without dreams, you die."

Rupert stared at him. "I'm sorry," he said quietly. "I misjudged you. I thought—"

"I know." Monk smiled bleakly. "You thought I had no devils inside, no idea of what they are even. You're wrong."

Rupert nodded, almost close to a smile.

Monk bit his lip. "Now tell me the names of the other men who went to the boat."

Rupert stared at him, but the anger had gone from his face. "Please," Monk added.

Rupert gave him a list, and Monk wrote it in his notebook.

"Thank you," Monk said when it was finished. "I'll get him this time." Perhaps it was a dangerous thing to say, almost a promise, but he risked saying it, and committing himself. It felt good.

MONK DECIDED TO RETRACE Ballinger's footsteps on the night of Parfitt's death. He should duplicate all the conditions as closely as possible.

The first part of his journey did not really matter. It was the return that counted. Nevertheless he went to the street outside Ballinger's house, at the time in the evening when Ballinger said he had left.

Of course one thing he could not duplicate was the daylight. In September it would have been dusk later, and the weather would have been milder. But he did not think that would substantially alter the time. If anything, Ballinger would have found it easier, and therefore faster.

Monk caught a hansom without more than a few minutes' wait, and settled himself for the long journey to Chiswick. It was tedious, and his mind wandered over all he had learned so far, juggling the pieces to try to make a picture that would hold against the assaults of doubt and reason. It was still all too tenuous, too full of other possible explanations.

He reached Chiswick cold and irritable, his legs cramped from sitting still. He paid the cabby and walked down across the street onto the dockside. It was fully dark now, with a gusty wind blowing off the water. This far upriver it did not smell of salt, but rather of weed and mud.

The clouds raced past, and for a few moments the moon showed, about half full, gleaming briefly on the water. There was a ferry twenty yards away. A couple of young men were sitting in it, and the sound of their laughter, happy and more than a little drunk, drifted across the distance between them.

Monk waited until they docked, then walked down and asked the ferryman to take him across. At the far side he thanked the man, paid, and walked up to the road to look for a hansom. That took rather longer, but even so he was in Mortlake by the time Ballinger had said he'd arrived at Harkness's house.

Now he had more than two hours to wait until Harkness had said Ballinger had left. He spent it walking along the waterfront with a lantern, looking at the boats pulled up in slipways, at the moorings, judging how long it would take to get any of them waterborne, and how wet he might get doing it.

He looked ahead and saw the sign for the Bull's Head swinging gently in the wind, creaking a little. He decided to go in and have a sandwich and a pint of ale.

Monk asked the landlord casually about hiring boats just to row a bit up and down the water, not really fishing, just being by himself and forgetting the city and its life and its noise. The man seemed to find that odd, but he told Monk of half a dozen different people who might be happy to oblige him.

Monk thanked him and left. He found one light, fast boat he could hire for a couple of shillings, and promised to return it before morning. If they thought he was eccentric, no one said so.

He walked back up toward Harkness's house and reached it a few moments before the earliest he could leave and still be following Ballinger's path. He stared around. There was no one in sight, but he had not expected anyone. A witness would have been a stroke of luck too far!

Some moments later he walked briskly back downriver toward the Bull's Head. The wind was sharper from the west and carrying the smell of rain with it. He imagined the marshes and the fields beyond, damp earth turned by the plow. Past that, woods with heavy leaves falling, berries turning red, the pungency of wood smoke, crows in high nests for the winter.

He found the boat he had hired, and after only a few moments' fumbling, he got it down the slip and into the water. He reached for the oars, fit them into the oarlocks, and pulled away from the shore out into the stream.

After a few more strokes he settled to row down the river to Corney Reach. Tonight, the tide was against him. It had turned while he was in the Bull's Head and was now coming in. He must check what it had been on the night of Parfitt's death. It would make a difference, but perhaps little enough—unless high or low water had occurred during the time Ballinger had actually killed Parfitt, which was unlikely. But it was a detail to be sure of, so absolutely nothing caught him by surprise. Anyway, since he had to row back up to Mortlake, the tide would be with him one way, and against him the other.

It was a pleasant sensation to feel the power of the boat sliding through the water. It was silent here apart from the bow wave's whisper, and the rattle of the oarlocks as the oars turned. Now and then a small night bird called from the trees along the shore. Once, far in the distance, a dog barked.

He saw the dark hull of Parfitt's boat before he expected to. He had lost all sense of time. He pulled over to it and rested on his oars. He imagined himself going up on deck. How long would it take to climb the ropes up the sides? An estimate?

But Rathbone would ask him. It would destroy the validity of the whole experiment if he had to admit that he had not actually done it. Damn!

He bent to the oar again and pulled the boat closer. What if there were no ropes there anymore? Then he would have to do the whole thing over again, when the ropes had been replaced.

He was right up to the boat now. He could see almost nothing. There was one riding light, simply to avoid the boat being struck in the dark. 'Orrie must have been keeping it burning. It shed no more than a glimmer onto the deck, and nothing at all on the steep sides.

Monk put out his hand and met wooden boards, overlapping. Carefully he pulled himself along, the boat moving jerkily under him. It was three yards before he found the ropes and tied the boat's painter to one of them. Awkwardly, skinning his knuckles, he climbed up and hauled himself onto the deck.

He stood there for several moments, trying to judge how long it would take to strike someone, then loop the cravat around their neck and tighten it until they choked to death, then finally put them over the side, into a boat or straight into the water. He mimicked hurling overboard the branch that had been used to strike Parfitt as well, and remembered that it might have been even more difficult climbing up with that slung over his back. He would have to allow for that.

But since Parfitt had been expecting Ballinger, perhaps he had let down a rope ladder. There was one inside the boat; there would have to be for the guests to climb aboard in their expensive clothes and boots. No one would be amused by falling into the water, and most certainly no one would want to be soaked, chilled, and smelling of river mud all night.

He must also check that Ballinger had no injury or muscular disability that would make it impossible for him to climb. Rathbone could, and would, nicely catch him out if that were so. He smiled grimly, imagining describing all this to the jury, and then having Rathbone produce some doctor who would swear that Ballinger couldn't lift his arms above his shoulders.

He heard an owl hoot on the farther bank, and a small animal slipped into the water with only the faintest sound. He saw the ripple of its movement more than he heard it.

It was time to go back over the side and row back to Mortlake, then find a hansom back to the far side of the Chiswick crossing.

When he finally stood on the dockside, waiting for the ferry back, it was less than five minutes later than Ballinger had done so, as the ferryman had confirmed for him, on the night of Parfitt's murder.

Monk had a ridiculous sense of exhilaration for the small victory that it was. He had proved that it was possible, that's all. But he had not proved that it was so.

THE NEXT DAY HE went to see Winchester, the lawyer certain to prosecute the case against Ballinger, were it to be brought to court.

"Ah! So you're Monk." He was a tall man, maybe an inch or so taller than Monk himself, broad-shouldered with a mane of straight black hair liberally threaded with gray. He had a somewhat hawkish face with a long nose and intensely dark eyes. The most remarkable aspect of him was the humor in his features, the readiness for wit, which seemed to be always just beneath the surface.

"Winchester," he introduced himself. "Sit down." He gestured toward a well-worn, comfortable-looking leather chair. He himself half sat on the edge of the desk.

"Tell me your evidence," he invited.

Monk detailed it meticulously, and only what he could prove.

"Good," Winchester said, pursing his lips. "I can see that you're remembering the last time you faced Oliver Rathbone, and got mauled." He said it without apology, a rueful amusement in his eyes. "We need to do better this time."

"I intend to," Monk assured him. He told him detail by detail how he had copied Ballinger's trip up to Mortlake, exactly as he had sworn to, leaving time to kill Parfitt, and then back again.

Winchester did not laugh, but his eyes betrayed that inside he was highly amused.

"Ballinger was an excellent oarsman in his youth," Monk went on. "But of course you will need to find testimony that he is still perfectly capable of rowing the distances now, and of climbing up the rope ladder at the side of Parfitt's boat."

"Thank you," Winchester said wryly. "I had thought of that."

Monk did not apologize.

"And I have a great deal of evidence as to exactly what trade Parfitt carried on," Monk added. He recounted that as well, hating the words, even more the pictures they conjured in his mind.

Now all the light was gone from Winchester's face, and he looked almost bruised. His anger was palpable. "I'll call whoever I believe may help the case," he said grimly. "I cannot promise to spare anyone. I hope you haven't made any guarantees, because I will not keep them."

"I haven't."

"Not to your wife? Or Margaret Rathbone?"

"Not to anyone."

"Cardew? Are you prepared to crucify Cardew, if it's unavoidable?"

Wordlessly Monk passed him a copy of the list of names Rupert had given him, including Tadley, with a note of his suicide.

Winchester read it, his mouth pulled tight and crooked with revulsion. "Thank you. That cannot have been easy."

"I don't intend to spare anyone either," Monk told him.

"For the love of heaven, take good care of Hattie Benson!" Winchester said grimly. "She is the one thing preventing them from blaming it all on Cardew. The only question I have to ask you is, are you
certain in your own mind that it was Ballinger? Could it not have
been a business rivalry—pure greed on the part of Tosh Wilkin, for
example? He's a particularly nasty piece of work. All Rathbone has to
do is raise a reasonable doubt."

Monk realized that Winchester was watching him extremely
closely. Memory rose up in him, hot and powerful, of having lost the
trial against Jericho Phillips, and how ashamed he had been, how
naked he had felt as the entire courtroom had stared at him and his
failure, his mistakes.

"No, I'm not certain," he said. "I believe it was Ballinger, because
Sullivan said so before he died. It had to be someone of Ballinger's
social standing to see the weakness of men like Sullivan, pander to it,
and feed it until it was out of control, and then blackmail them for it.
Tosh Wilkin hasn't the imagination or the connections to do that.
And if he were the one taking the blackmail money, I don't believe he
would have the self-control not to spend it. And that he hasn't done."

"But could he have killed Parfitt, on Ballinger's instructions?"
Winchester insisted.

"He could have. I don't believe Ballinger, a master at blackmail,
would give such power over himself into the hands of a man like
Tosh, who would certainly use it."

Winchester's long fingers touched the list that Monk had given
him. "What about someone on this list? They would have much to
gain if Parfitt were dead. The end of paying blackmail has been motive for more than one murder. The jury wouldn't have much difficulty believing that. Reasonable doubt—more than reasonable."

"You don't bite the hand that feeds your addiction," Monk replied. "Then you have to find a new supplier, and where would you do
that? And why?"

Winchester nodded slowly. "You'd better be right, Monk. And don't imagine Ballinger won't fight you in every way he can think of. He won't go down easily. Rathbone will fight for him, and you don't need me to tell you he's a very clever man, and far more ruthless than his charming manner would lead you to believe."

"I know."

"Yes, of course you do. But don't allow yourself to forget it simply because you believe Ballinger is guilty and therefore you are fighting a just cause."

Monk looked steadily at Winchester's curious long-nosed face, with its subtle wit, and wondered if Ballinger had already started to fight, and whether Winchester knew it.

"It will be personal," Winchester warned. "Your reputation—perhaps your wife's?"

Monk felt his muscles clench. "I know."

"Are you prepared for it? He may call her to the stand, with reference to Rupert Cardew."

"Yes. She will be prepared this time."

Winchester offered his hand. "Then, we'll get him, Mr. Monk. Deo volente."

Monk rose to his feet. "Yes—God willing," he echoed, and took Winchester's outstretched hand.

WINCHESTER'S MENTION OF HATTIE Benson sent Monk straight to the clinic at Portpool Lane, just to assure himself that she was still safe and well, and that her courage had not failed her.

He was met in the outer hallway by a grim-looking Squeaky Robinson.

"She isn't here," Squeaky said flatly.

Monk's stomach lurched, and he found it hard to catch his breath. "What happened? Where is she?"

"No need to look like I hit you," Squeaky said reproachfully. "She's gone to help buy some more surgical stuff. Dunno where, 'cos she had to look for it. Heard of some doctor what was selling old stuff."

"I'm not looking for Hester!" Monk said, almost choking in relief. "I want the young woman I brought here a week or so back. Where is she?"

Squeaky looked Monk up and down, from his shiny leather boots to his elegant coat wet on the shoulders, and then he sighed. "Down in the laundry washing sheets like she should be. I ain't bringing her up here, 'cos I'm told not to, so you'd better go down there and find her!" Thus dismissing Monk, he sat down to study his figures again.

Monk thanked him, a trifle sarcastically, and went along the narrow passage and down a couple of flights of steps, through the kitchen, and into the laundry beyond. A lean, dark young woman with freckles was poking a wooden pole into the huge copper, moving the sheets around. The pot was belching steam, and the air was thick with it.

"Where's Hattie?" Monk asked.

"Dunno," the young woman replied without turning away from the task.

Monk took a pace toward her and spoke more sharply. "That won't do! If you want to stay here and be looked after, you'll tell me where she is!"

She stopped poking and let the long pole slip onto the floor. She turned and looked at him indignantly, her hair damp, streaked onto her face, her skin pink. "I dunno where she is, an' yer can call me everything you want, an' I still dunno. She were s'posed ter be 'ere, 'cos it were 'er turn ter 'elp, an' she in't! So you go an' bleedin' find 'er!"

Monk turned on his heel and strode out of the room, taking the steps up again two at a time. Back in the scullery he found a young woman with a red face, peeling potatoes. He could smell the sharp astringency of onions, and there were strings of them hanging from the ceiling beams.

"Have you seen Hattie Benson?" he demanded.

She turned to look at him, startled by his voice. "No, I in't seen 'er since—I dunno—yesterday. Yer tried the laundry? That's where she is most times."

"Yes, I have. Where else?" He controlled his rising fear with difficulty. His heart was pounding, his breath ragged already. He was being absurd; she was probably making beds, or rolling bandages, or any of a dozen other tasks.

The woman shrugged. "I dunno."

Without bothering to press her, since she was clearly useless, he left the scullery and tried the medicine storage room, the linen closets, and then all the bedrooms one by one. He went from the far end of the three old houses joined together by a warren of passages and interlocking rooms, which had once been Squeaky Robinson's brothel and was now the clinic. Nowhere did he find Hattie Benson, or anyone who had seen her in the last three hours, now three and a half, nearly four. The fear inside him was close to panic.

Hester was not here, nor was Margaret. And he was not sure if he would have asked Margaret, even if she were. He did the next best thing after that and looked for Claudine.

He found her in the medicine room. She was becoming quite proficient in nursing. Hester had said she was intelligent and, more important, deeply interested. Her long, unhappy marriage had eroded her self-belief to an almost crippling level. Curiously, it was her adventure where she had finally seen Arthur Ballinger outside the shops selling pornographic photographs, and from which Squeaky Robinson had eventually rescued her, that had liberated her from that.

Now she stood carefully measuring what was left in the various jars and bottles, and writing it down in a notebook. She was standing straight, and there was a slight smile on her face. She turned as she heard Monk's footsteps stop. It needed only a glance at his face for her to realize his distress.

"What's happened?" she asked immediately, putting down the bottle she was holding and closing the notebook. "What is it?"

"Hattie Benson's gone," Monk replied. "I've been from one end of the building to the other, and asked everybody. No one has seen her since about nine this morning."

Claudine did not reply for several moments, but it was not because she was dumbfounded. She was clearly calculating what to do next.

"We must think," she said. "She knew not to go anywhere outside. She would not have run errands for anyone, even a few yards.

She was quite clever enough to be frightened. There are no doors to the outside here where a stranger could come in unseen. Have you spoken to Squeaky?"

"Yes. He didn't see her leave, and he's been at the front all morning, at least since she was last seen," he replied. "I've got—"

"I know," she agreed calmly, her voice reassuring.

He looked at her pleasant face. It was far from beautiful, but full of strength and—at this moment—a quiet courage.

"Then, she went out at the back," he said more steadily. "That means she did it deliberately. She tricked someone into leaving her alone. Why? What on earth would make her do that? Did someone here threaten her? Who have you had in since she came?"

"An old woman upstairs with a fever," Claudine replied. "She's delirious and probably dying. And a young woman with a stab wound and a broken collarbone. All others were just in and out."

He stared at her.

"One of us?" she said with a catch in her voice. She seemed about to add something else, then changed her mind.

He knew from her face that she was thinking of Margaret, and trying to deny it to herself. He was thinking the same. There had to be some more complex explanation, but just at the moment it did not matter.

"I've got to see if I can find her," Monk said, although he had no idea where to begin. Should he even tell Hester? There was nothing she could do, except run into danger herself.

"Where will you look?" Claudine asked him.

"I don't know. If she was alone, or escaped from whoever she went with, she'll probably go back to the places she knows. All I can do is ask."

"Can I help?"

"No . . . thank you. Just . . . don't tell Hester . . . yet."

"I won't have to," Claudine said grimly. "She'll know."

Monk left without adding anything more. Once outside in Portpool Lane he walked as rapidly as he could, not even aware of the rain. He would like to have run but it was pointless, and he needed his strength. He could not stop until he found Hattie.

He asked questions of street peddlers, a seller of matches, another with bootlaces, one with hot chocolate and ham sandwiches. The sandwich man had seen a young woman with pale skin and very fair hair, in company with a woman a little older, brown-haired, going down Leather Lane toward High Holborn, at almost half past nine. They had been on foot, and hurrying.

It was confusing. Was that Hattie or not? With a woman? Who? It was the best lead he had. Standing in the traffic, people passing him by, the rattle of wheels and clip of hooves on the road, the spray of dirty water from the gutters soaking his legs, he was overwhelmed with the uselessness of it. It might have been Hattie, or equally easily it might not. And she could have been going anywhere in London.

There was no point in waiting here. He might as well see if any-one else had seen them. He could think as he walked. He might real-ize something that had eluded him so far.

But he did not, and in the late afternoon as it was growing dusk, he knew nothing more than half a dozen sightings, which might have been Hattie or any other fair-haired young woman. He decided to take a hansom and go out to Chiswick. At least there she was known, and any sighting would be real. It was just possible she had become homesick and gone back to the one place where she had friends, and which was familiar to her. She might feel safer there, even if in fact she was not.

The ride seemed interminable. Every dark street looked like every other. Lamps were lit, glaring eyes in the increasing gloom. Every-thing was full of shadows. The moving carriage lamps were yellow, and there was the hiss of wheels on the wet cobbles even though the rain had stopped.

Finally Monk reached the Chiswick mall on the edge of the river opposite the Eyot. He leaped out of the hansom, paid the driver, and strode over toward the lights moving down by the stretch of mud and stones left by the low tide. He could hear voices. If it was the police, he would ask for their help.

As he reached the steps, his stomach was churning, his breath tight in his chest, throat aching.

One of the men held his lantern higher, and Monk could see that there were four of them, grim, wet, feet and ankles caked with river mud. There was a woman's body on the stones, and the yellow light shone on her face, and on the pale blond hair that was almost silver.

Monk knew it was Hattie, even before he was close enough to see her features.

9

Rᴀᴛʜʙᴏɴᴇ ᴡᴀs ᴀᴛ ʜɪs parents-in-law's for dinner again when the butler announced that a Mr. Monk had called to see Mr. Ballinger and was waiting for him in the morning room.

"What an inconvenient time to call!" Mrs. Ballinger said stiffly, her eyes wide. She looked at the butler. "Tell him to wait. In fact, better than that, tell him to come back tomorrow morning, at a reasonable hour." She turned to Rathbone. "I'm sorry, Oliver. I know he is a friend of yours, more or less, but this is too much. The man has no breeding at all."

The butler had not moved.

"What is it, Withers?" Ballinger said tartly. "Tell Monk, if he wants to wait, I'll see him when I've had dinner. And when the evening is over and my visitors have gone home."

The butler, acutely embarrassed, moved from one foot to the other, his face a dull pink.

Rathbone stood up. "I'll go and see what he wants," he offered, going toward the door as he spoke.

"For heaven's sake, Oliver, let the man wait!" George snapped. "You're not his lackey to go jumping up and down after him simply because he arrives at the door."

Rathbone felt Margaret's eyes on him as he left, but he did not turn back. He realized, as he closed the drawing room door behind him and walked across the wide hall with its sweeping staircase, that he was afraid. He knew Monk too well to imagine that he had called at this hour without a very compelling reason.

Rathbone had seen the pride and the pain in Monk when Rathbone had beaten him in court over Jericho Phillips. He knew Monk would not let that happen again.

He opened the morning room door and came face-to-face with him.

"Why are you here?" Rathbone asked, closing the door behind him and remaining standing in front of it.

"I'm sorry," Monk apologized. "I thought this better than at his place of business. This affords him a less public exhibition, at least for the time being."

"What the devil are you talking about?" Rathbone demanded, although he felt a hollow fear that he knew.

"And you are here also," Monk continued. "Your clerk said that you would be. Perhaps it is as well."

"Monk!" Rathbone kept his voice level with difficulty.

Monk straightened up and put his shoulders back, altering his weight from the easier stance he had held before. "I have new evidence that is compelling. I have come to arrest Arthur Ballinger for the murder of Michael Parfitt," he replied.

"Don't be ridiculous!" Rathbone said sharply. It was like a bad dream spiraling out of control. "Ballinger was at Bertram Harkness's house. You know that, and if you don't, I certainly do."

"I know," Monk said calmly. "It is not far from where Parfitt was found, and the movement of the tide can account for the difference. Don't make this any harder than it has to be—"

"I'll make it as hard as I can!" Rathbone heard his own voice rising, losing control. "You can't come in here to the man's own house and accuse him, just because of what Sullivan said. He was desperate and on the brink of suicide. You know that as well as I do."

"Oliver—," Monk began.

Rathbone thought of Margaret in the quiet family withdrawing room across the hall, just beyond the closed doors. He must protect her from this. With an effort he lowered his voice.

"Think of it, Monk. Even if you were right and Ballinger had some involvement with Phillips, and even with Parfitt, why on earth would he kill Parfitt? From what Sullivan said, supposing he were sane, and right about the facts—which we don't know—Ballinger would have had every reason to keep him alive! He would be a source of considerable income for him."

Monk made no move to go round him. His face was grim, eyes hard and steady, but there was an emotion in them that Rathbone found chilling.

Rathbone tried again. "He might have been acting for a client," he protested. "After all, he is a solicitor. Perhaps he was trying to get Parfitt to stop blackmailing someone. Had you considered that?"

There was a flicker of uncertainty in Monk's face, there and then gone again. "Yes, it occurred to me," he answered. "But if that is the case, then the charge would be accomplice to murder or, at best, accessory before and after the fact. He lured Parfitt to the boat, and he was in the immediate vicinity. So far we can't place anyone else there. Don't make a scene. It will only be harder for the family. I'm quite willing to have him come with me of his own volition, without anyone else knowing the seriousness of it."

Rathbone was still prepared to argue, but the door opened behind him, and George came into the room.

"What on earth is going on? Can't you deal with this, Oliver?" he asked angrily.

Rathbone felt his own temper rise. He wanted to snap back at someone, and held himself in check with difficulty.

"It would be better if you asked Papa-in-law to come out here."

George stared at Monk. "Look, I don't know what you think you want . . . Inspector . . . or whatever you are, but this is not the time to arrive at a gentleman's home, delaying dinner and making a vulgar scene—"

"For God's sake, George, just go and fetch him!" Rathbone snarled, his voice thick with anger. "If it were as simple as that, don't you think I'd have dealt with it?"

George's temper flared in instant response. "How the devil do I know what you'd do? He's a friend of yours."

The drawing room door opened wider, sending a stream of brighter light into the hallway. Margaret crossed to the entrance of the morning room, the silk of her gown gleaming, her face tight with anxiety. "What is it, Oliver?"

"Nothing!" George told her sharply.

"Please ask your father to come out," Oliver contradicted him.

She hesitated.

It was Monk who moved forward now. "Please, Lady Rathbone, ask your father to come out. It will be less distressing for your mother and sisters if we can discuss this matter privately."

She looked at Rathbone, and then, as he nodded, she turned and went back into the drawing room. George followed her. A moment later Ballinger came out, but he left the door ajar behind him. The room was silent, as if everyone within it was listening.

"Well, what the hell do you want?" he asked Monk. "You had better have a very good explanation for bursting in here like this."

Rathbone walked quickly to the drawing room door and closed it, then returned.

"I have," Monk said quietly. "I have a warrant for your arrest on the charge of murdering Michael Parfitt—"

"What?" Ballinger was aghast. "The wretched little pimp who was drowned in Chiswick? That's absurd! You've really exceeded yourself, Monk. You've let your hunger for revenge addle your brain. I'll have your job for this."

"I advise you to say nothing!" Rathbone cut in desperately, trying to prevent it from getting even worse.

Ballinger's face was red, ugly with anger. He swiveled to face Rathbone, then seemed to recall his composure and very deliberately forced himself to relax, lower his shoulders, and breathe out.

"That was not a threat," he said to Monk. "You are an incompetent fool, jumped up beyond your ability, but I mean you no harm. I will do everything according to the law."

"Of course you will," Monk agreed with a flash of humor so brief it was barely visible. "You are far too wise to add assault of a police officer to the situation."

"Are you intending to take me into custody, at this hour of the night?" Ballinger's tone was tinged with disbelief.

"I imagined you would prefer it in the dark," Monk responded. "But I can come back to your office in daylight, if you would rather. And if you should not be there, I can send police to look for you."

"God almighty, man!" Ballinger swore. "Your reputation will never recover from this!"

Monk did not answer. He looked for a moment at Rathbone, then turned and went out to the front door, waiting there for Ballinger to follow.

When the door closed behind them, Rathbone went at once to Margaret. She was white-faced, her eyes hollow. The muscles in her neck and shoulders suddenly looked as hard as cords, as if she might snap.

"You must get this stopped, Oliver." Her voice shook. "Tonight! Before anyone knows. I'll tell Mama and the others that Monk needed help with something. I won't have to think what, because I'll just say that he didn't tell us. You must—"

"Margaret." He put his hands on her shoulders lightly and felt how rigid they were. "Monk would not have come here if he didn't believe that—"

She pulled away from him, eyes blazing. "Are you saying he's right?"

"No, of course I'm not." His answer was instant, and not wholly honest. He took a deep gulp of air. "I'm saying that he must think he has some evidence, or he wouldn't dare come here and make such a claim."

"Then, prove him wrong! He's made some idiotic mistake, because he wants Rupert Cardew to be innocent."

"That's unfair. Monk has never . . ." He knew before he finished the sentence that it had been a mistake to defend him.

Her eyebrows rose. "Been wrong?"

"Of course he's been wrong. I was going to say 'deliberately unfair.' I will find out from him exactly what he thinks he has, and then I will figure out the best and most complete way to disprove it."

"Tonight!" she insisted. "Papa can't possibly spend the night in prison. It's—it's appalling. You know it is!"

"Margaret, there's nothing I can do tonight."

"That's why he did it, is it? He arrested Papa at this time of night so you couldn't do anything about it. If he'd done it in the daytime, you could have gotten him out! Oliver, you have to show them what a personal vengeance this is. Papa said Monk was an erratic and spiteful man, but I couldn't believe him, out of loyalty to you. But Papa was right. Monk can't ever forgive him for taking on Jericho Phillips and getting you to defend him. You made him and Hester look bad in court, made fools of them, and he's having his revenge now—on both of you!"

"Margaret!" His voice was sharp, peremptory. "Stop it! Yes, Monk lost in court the first time with Phillips, and I'm not proud of my part in that. But I did what the law requires, what justice demands. Monk knew that and understood it."

Margaret's eyes were brilliant with tears, but they were tears of shock and anger, and fear of a horror she could not grapple. "Oliver?"

"Listen to me!" he said grimly. "Monk wants to get that filthy trade off the river—and it is filthy; it's far worse than anything you've heard of in Portpool Lane. Some of those children are not more than five or six years old." He ignored the wince of pain that twisted her mouth. "Perhaps he is a little overzealous, but we need someone with a passion to destroy it, someone who cares enough to risk getting dirty or hurting themselves. This time he's made a mistake, but he's only going where he thinks the evidence is taking him."

She blinked hard, and the tears spilled onto her cheeks. "You'll act for Papa. You must. You'll—"

"Only if he wants me to. That has to be his choice. He may prefer someone else."

"Of course he won't!" She was indignant, but beneath the anger he saw the rising, desperate fear. "You have to help, Oliver. Or are you saying that your friendship with Monk makes you—"

He said the only thing he could. "He is your father, Margaret. Of course I will act for him, as long as it is what he wishes. But be prepared for him to prefer someone else, perhaps because I am too close." He did not add that Ballinger himself might distrust him because of his friendship with Monk.

A little of the fear slipped away from her. "Of course," she said quietly. "I'm sorry. I . . . it is so unjust! It's like a nightmare, one of those dreams when everything you love changes in front of you. You go to pick something up, and it turns into something else . . . something horrible. A cup of tea turns into a dish of maggots—or a person you've known all your life changes into an animal, a horrid one . . ." Now the tears slid down her cheeks and she could not control them.

Hesitantly he reached his arms out and touched her, then drew her closer to him and held her. He was not sure if she would resist, but her panic was only momentary. After a second of realization, she leaned against him and let him hold her tighter, more completely.

"I must go and tell the rest of the family," he murmured. "They will be distressed, and we must assure them that we will do everything necessary to get this all dealt with as quickly and as discreetly as possible."

"Yes." She pulled away from him reluctantly. "Of course."

He took a deep breath, and walked away from her and into the withdrawing room. He closed the door behind him and faced them. The women were sitting upright, tense, staring at him. The men were all standing.

"What the devil's going on, Oliver?" George demanded. "Where is Papa-in-law?"

Rathbone faced Mrs. Ballinger. "I'm sorry, Mama-in-law, but he has had to go with the police for the time being. Tomorrow morning I shall—"

"Tomorrow!" George interrupted angrily. "You mean you're just going to go home to bed and leave him in a police cell? What the—"

Mrs. Ballinger looked from one to the other of them, her face flushed and unhappy.

Celia took a step toward George, then changed her mind and moved to her mother instead.

"Be quiet!" Rathbone snapped at George, his voice hard-edged and loud. He turned again to Mrs. Ballinger. "There is nothing anyone can do tonight. There are no judges or magistrates available at this hour. But he is an innocent man, and of some substance; they will treat him reasonably. They know there'll be hell to pay if they do anything else."

George snorted. "Trust your friend to choose this time for precisely that reason. The man's despicable."

"Wilbert!" Gwen accused. "Why do you just stand there like a piece of furniture? Do something!"

"There's nothing to do," he retorted. "Oliver's right. There's no one to appeal to at this time of night."

"As I said," George glared at him, "that's Monk for you." He turned to Rathbone as if it were his fault.

Rathbone felt his face burn. "Would you rather he'd come during the day and arrested Papa-in-law in his offices, in front of his staff, and possibly his clients?"

The tide of color rushed up George's face.

"What will you do tomorrow, Oliver?" Celia asked. "There has to be some mistake. What is he accused of? And where's Margaret? She must be desperately upset. She was always the closest to Papa."

"That's not true," Gwen said instantly.

"Oh, hold your tongue!" Celia snapped. "We have to stop quarreling among ourselves and think what to do. What is it about, Oliver?"

Rathbone tried to smile, as if he were confident, but he knew it was sickly on his lips. "It is in connection with the murder of an extremely unpleasant man named Mickey Parfitt. He was strangled and thrown into the river, up beyond Chiswick."

"Chiswick?" Mrs. Ballinger said in disbelief. "Why does Mr. Monk imagine Arthur would have anything to do with it? That's absurd!"

"He was on the river that night," Rathbone replied. "He crossed at Chiswick, if you recall. He went to see Bertie Harkness. He told us about it over dinner."

"This is farcical," George interrupted again. "Surely Harkness can tell the police where he was? Monk deserves to be punished for this. It's totally incompetent. The man has a personal—"

"Oh, do be quiet!" Wilbert said impatiently. "You're talking about the police. He isn't some nincompoop running around doing whatever he likes. Anyway, why should he have anything personal against Papa-in-law? He doesn't even know him."

George's heavy eyebrows shot up. "Are you suggesting there is something in this? That Papa-in-law had something to do with this wretched man's murder?"

"Don't be stupid! Of course I'm not. It probably has to do with a client. He could be acting for someone who does."

"Oh, really!" Mrs. Ballinger protested.

"Mama-in-law," Rathbone seized the chance Wilbert had given him, "if he could act for Jericho Phillips, he could act for anyone. I'll go to the River Police first thing in the morning and find out from Monk himself exactly what evidence they have, and what they have made of it. And of course I'll see Papa-in-law and find out if he wishes me to act for him. Then we'll sort it all out."

"With an apology," George added.

Mrs. Ballinger looked at both of them, blinking, her face composed with an obvious effort. "Thank you, Oliver. I think it would be best if we all retired now. How is Margaret?"

"As brave as you all are," Rathbone replied, hoping it would remain true. He had been aware even as he spoke that he had promised more than he was certain he could fulfill.

RATHBONE WAS AT THE police station on the river's edge the next morning as Monk came up the steps from the ferry. It was not yet eight o'clock. The October light was bleak and pale on the water,

washing the color out of it. The wind smelled salty with the incoming
tide. Gulls were circling low, screaming as they scented fish, diving
now and then in the wake of a two-masted schooner moving upstream. To the north and south there were forests of masts all criss-
crossing, moving slightly on the uneasiness of the water. Long strings
of barges and lighters were threading their way through the ships at
anchor, carrying loads inland, or to Limehouse, the Isle of Dogs,
Greenwich, or even the estuary and the coast.

Monk reached the top of the steps and smiled very slightly when
he saw Rathbone. Neither of them said anything. Perhaps the understanding was already there. Rathbone could see in Monk's face, in his
eyes, the knowledge of the complexity, the mixed emotions he felt,
the embarrassment, the struggle of loyalties.

They walked almost in step across the dockside to the police station steps, then into the building. Monk said good morning to the
men who had obviously been on duty overnight. He checked that
there was nothing urgent that required his attention, then led the
way to his office and closed the door.

"Are you representing him?" Monk asked.

"Not yet, because I haven't seen him, but I expect I will."

Monk hesitated a moment before he asked, "Are you sure that's
wise?"

"If he wants me, I have no choice," Rathbone replied, and was
startled to hear the bitterness in his voice. He felt trapped, and was
ashamed that he did. If he'd totally believed in Ballinger's innocence,
if he'd trusted him as he wished to, then he would have been eager,
burning with the urgency to begin.

Monk looked away, not meeting his eyes anymore, and Rathbone
had the brief thought that it was because he did not wish to intrude;
he did not want Rathbone to see how much he understood.

"What do you have?" Rathbone said aloud. "Circumstantial evidence—a letter, which has yet to be proved genuine, yet to be dated,
and yet to be proved relevant. What else? We already know that Ballinger was on the river near Chiswick. He said as much himself at the
time. You say this prostitute wouldn't tell you who she gave the cravat
to, so you can't connect it to Ballinger. Isn't it far more reasonable to

suppose she gave it to someone she knew? And why would Ballinger kill a wretched creature like Parfitt? You can't produce a single person who can show that the two men ever even met each other." He stopped abruptly. He was talking to Monk as if he, Rathbone, were new at this and had no confidence in himself. He knew better. This is why a good lawyer did not instantly represent family: emotions got in the way right from the start.

Arthur Ballinger was not his father. How different it would have been if it had been Henry Rathbone. He would have known passionately and completely that he was innocent.

But, then, Monk would have known it too.

"I'm not supposing personal enmity," Monk replied, his voice level and quiet. "I have Ballinger at the time, extremely near the place, and a note, which only he could have written, inviting Parfitt to be in his boat to meet with him, for a business venture profitable to Parfitt."

"Such as what?" Rathbone retorted. "You have no proof of anything. Not even a suggestion."

"We know what Parfitt's business was, Oliver. You saw Phillips's boat; you know perfectly well what they do. If you want me to, I can describe Parfitt's boat as well, and the children we found there."

Rathbone felt his control slipping away from him. "You have no evidence that Ballinger was involved," he pointed out. "Absolutely nothing, or you'd have prosecuted him for it already. I know how desperately you want to catch whoever's behind the trade."

"Don't you?"

"Yes, of course I do! But not enough to risk prosecuting the wrong person. Just because Sullivan accused Ballinger, that doesn't make him guilty. Perhaps Ballinger was trying to rescue Sullivan from his own foolishness, and he failed. Sullivan might have blamed everybody but himself. We've both seen that before."

"I don't know why Ballinger would kill Parfitt," Monk said, still keeping his voice level and under tight control. "I don't have to know. All the prosecution has to show is that he had the opportunity, he could have had the means, and that he was the one who told Parfitt to be in the boat at that time, for a meeting. If Parfitt hadn't known him and believed there was a business connection, he wouldn't have gone."

Rathbone had no argument, except that there must be something more, some evidence undiscovered so far that would change the entire picture.

"I'm sorry," Monk added. "I'll go on investigating it, but largely to find the links between them and to destroy the trade. I wish the trail hadn't led to Ballinger, but it did. If you can get him to confess, it might at least spare his family some of the shame."

Rathbone felt bruised, stunned, as if he had taken a heavy blow and it had left him dizzy. "There has to be another answer."

"I hope so." Monk smiled bleakly. "It would be very nice to think it could be someone neither of us cares a damn about. But wishing doesn't make it so."

Rathbone could think of nothing more to say. He thanked Monk and excused himself.

He was in the outside office on his way to the dockside again when he almost bumped into a tall, thin man with white side whiskers and intense blue eyes. He was dressed in an expensive and very well-cut suit. Rathbone knew him by sight, and on this occasion would have avoided him if he could have.

"Morning, Commander Birkenshaw," he said briefly, and continued walking.

But Birkenshaw was not to be avoided. He came across the few yards between them and followed Rathbone outside into the brisk, fresh air on the dock.

"Thought you'd be here early," he said, matching his stride to Rathbone's. "Wretched business. I was hoping we could get it all untangled before it comes to anything. You've known Monk for many years, haven't you?"

"Yes. Eight or nine, I think," Rathbone replied reluctantly.

Birkenshaw was Monk's superior, and he was clearly very unhappy. His face was pinched with anxiety, and he kept his voice low, even though there was no one within earshot in the bright, sharp morning. The noise of the wind and water would have made overhearing unlikely anyway.

"Would you say you know him well?"

There was no evading an answer. "Yes. We've worked together on many cases."

"Clever," Birkenshaw conceded. "But reliable? I know Durban thought highly of him. He recommended him for the post when he knew he himself was dying. But he hadn't known Monk all that long; just the one case. I've heard from others since then that Monk's a bit erratic. Farnham, my predecessor, was uncertain as to his integrity, if it came to a difficult decision and Monk was personally convinced of someone's guilt."

"Then, it's as well that you are now in command, and not Farnham," Rathbone said tartly, and immediately regretted it. He saw the surprise in Birkenshaw's face, and then the irritation. It was not the answer he had been seeking.

"I don't think you fully appreciate the difficulty of the situation, Sir Oliver," Birkenshaw said patiently. "Murder is a desperately serious charge, and Monk has brought it against a man of means, position, and spotless reputation."

"I know. He is my father-in-law."

"I'm sorry. Of course. It must be appalling for you, and unspeakable for your wife. All the more will you wish to see that we are not acting precipitately. If Monk has made a mistake, however sincerely, then we will have damaged an innocent man's reputation and put his family through needless pain."

"It is good of you to be so concerned—," Rathbone began.

"Dammit, man!" Birkenshaw exploded. "I am concerned for the honor and ability of the River Police to carry out their job! If we prosecute a man of high profile unjustly, and the case is shown to have been flawed from the beginning, and brought by a man consumed with a personal vengeance, or even a preoccupation with one crime, then our reputation is damaged and our work crippled. It is my responsibility to see that that does not happen."

In spite of wishing not to, Rathbone could see that Birkenshaw was right. But if Birkenshaw overruled Monk, then Monk would no longer be able to command his men's loyalty or respect, and he would have to resign. That also was unfair, and Rathbone could not be party to it.

"Of course it is," he said as calmly as he could. "And if you have some proof that Monk has acted for personal motives, without just cause, then you must override him and withdraw the charges, with apology. If you do that, you will also have to dismiss him from office."

"I . . ." Birkenshaw shook his head, trying to deny the idea as he would shoo away some troublesome insect. "That's far too . . . extreme."

"No, it isn't," Rathbone contradicted him. "You will have made public your lack of confidence in him, and his men will no longer have sufficient confidence in him either. Very possibly Ballinger will want some compensation. I could not represent him in that, but he would have no difficulty in finding someone else willing to, particularly someone who had another client at some time prosecuted by Monk. If you weigh it carefully, Commander Birkenshaw, I think you will find that the River Police will suffer even more. You will have to go to trial, and Arthur Ballinger will either be cleared . . . or be hanged."

"Rathbone—," Birkenshaw started.

"I have said all I can," Rathbone replied, and with a brief nod, he turned on his heel and walked as rapidly as he could toward the High Street. With luck, he could catch a hansom cab from there westward back into the city.

But even though he was extraordinarily fortunate and found one within five minutes, he felt awful sitting in it, bowling along at a brisk pace, wheels rattling over the road toward familiar streets. He had been loyal to Monk, and to his own conscience, but had he in a way betrayed Margaret? He would not tell her of this conversation, and that in itself answered his doubts. It was not confidential. He knew before he even considered it that she would feel he had not acted in her father's best interest. And perhaps that was true.

Of course Rathbone could make an argument that Ballinger was definitely innocent, and should have his chance to prove it so no one could ever imagine that there had been pressure to withdraw the charge. That might appear a trifle like the Scottish verdict of "not proven," particularly if no one else was ever successfully brought to trial for Parfitt's death.

If it were his own father, what would Rathbone's decision be? It might well be to go ahead and prove his innocence. But then he might also be afraid that some lie, some misread evidence, some quirk of the law, would allow an injustice to happen. There were only three short weeks between conviction and hanging. That was no time at all in which to reverse a verdict, or even raise sufficient doubt to stay an execution.

Now he must prepare to face Ballinger himself—something he was dreading. He realized how little he really knew the man. He did not even know whether Ballinger would be frightened, angry, humble, accusatory, or even so shocked as to be almost numb and unable to think of how to defend himself.

Rathbone leaned sideways and peered out of the cab to the streets, looking to see where he was. He recognized St. Margaret's Arch. They were just coming into Eastcheap. They would probably go up King William Street, then bear left along Poultry and Cheapside to Newgate. Perhaps there would be a traffic jam and he would be granted a little more time in which to compose himself and think what he would say.

Ten minutes later the cab lurched to a stop. He sighed with relief, but that lasted only moments. All too soon he was on the pavement again in the sun, crossing the road, and then on the steps of Newgate Prison, his thoughts still whirling and uncertain.

He was granted access to Ballinger almost immediately, although he had been more than willing to wait. They met in a small cell with a stone floor and plain wooden furniture sufficient only to seat both of them, rather uncomfortably, with a battered wooden table on which to place books or papers, should they wish. It was not the same room in which he had seen Rupert Cardew, but the differences were negligible.

Ballinger looked rumpled and angry, but not as embarrassingly out of control as some people did when faced with sudden and appalling misfortune. He was shaved, and his hair was tidy. There was no sign in his face of hysteria, and his eyes looked no more puffy than was natural from a night with little or no sleep.

"Good morning, Oliver," he said without preamble. "Before you waste time on it, they are treating me perfectly well, and I have all I require in the way of such comforts as I am permitted. Margaret sent my valet with everything. You cannot yet begin to appreciate what a fine woman she is. If you are blessed with such daughters, you will be a most fortunate man. Now, will you act for me in this . . . this farce? I want to get it explained and discussed as soon as possible, before half the world knows about it." He smiled grimly, with only an echo of humor. "Perhaps I will have more understanding of my clients' fears in the future, and more sympathy."

"Of course I will act for you, if you are sure it is what you wish," Rathbone replied. "But have you considered the wisdom of having a member of the family in such a position? There are—"

Ballinger waved his hand sharply, dismissing the objections. "You are the finest lawyer in London, Oliver, perhaps in England. And I have no doubt whatever that you will fight for me harder than anyone else would, in spite of your past friendship with William Monk. You are my son-in-law, part of my family. I am well aware that we should not have favorite children, but Margaret is still mine. She always has been. There is a loyalty and a gentleness in her that is beyond even that of my other daughters. You will do everything that is humanly possible."

Ballinger shook his head. "Not that it should be necessary. The whole charge is a tissue of coincidences piled upon one another because Monk has little idea of a solicitor's responsibilities to his clients. He is also emotionally involved on a personal level through his wife and the little mudlark she has become attached to because the poor woman apparently cannot have children of her own."

Rathbone felt a stab of guilt so acute, it was hard to believe it was not an old physical injury torn open again. At the trial of Jericho Phillips he had ridiculed Hester when she had given testimony against Phillips, painting her as a childless woman who had half adopted a street urchin to fill her own loneliness, and implying that her judgment had become warped because of it. The jury had believed him and had discounted her testimony. He had not spoken of it since with Hester, and he did not know if she had entirely forgiven him for such a betrayal. He had not forgiven himself.

"We need to answer evidence." Rathbone controlled his emotion with difficulty. He owed his loyalty to Ballinger, who was his client and, if the case actually came to trial, would be fighting for his life. He was Margaret's father, which made him a part of Rathbone's life that could never be turned away from or forgotten.

"Of course," Ballinger agreed. "What evidence is it that Monk thinks he has? I cannot imagine."

"A note, written by you, inviting Parfitt to meet you on his boat, handed over to him in front of witnesses an hour or two before his death. When Parfitt read it, he immediately sent for 'Orrie Jones to row him out."

The color drained out of Ballinger's face, leaving him ashen. For a moment he seemed unable to speak. It might have been shock, disbelief, but Rathbone had a terrible fear that it was guilt.

"That's . . . impossible!" he said at last. "Who says so? Monk?"

"Yes. And he must have such a letter, or he would not dare claim to, even if you think him immoral enough to try."

"Then, it's a forgery," Ballinger said immediately. "For God's sake, Oliver, why on earth would I have business with a creature like Parfitt?"

"To buy him off for a client," Rathbone answered. He was sinking into a morass of nightmare, and yet strangely his mind was going on quite reasonably, as if he were something apart, almost a bystander watching this desperate, highly civilized discussion of murder and betrayal.

Ballinger hesitated, weighing his answer.

Rathbone watched him, feeling the sweat trickle down his body in fear that Ballinger was going to admit that it was his own blackmail he'd been dealing with. After his years of criminal prosecution and defense, nothing ought to have surprised Rathbone, but he could not believe that Arthur Ballinger could have become involved with Parfitt's vicious pornography.

Why not? Did he believe Ballinger was so moral? So happy in his present life? Or so careful? What did Rathbone think of him, not as his son-in-law, the husband of his admittedly favorite daughter, but as his lawyer, bound by duty to see the truth, because only by knowing it could he best defend him?

Rathbone realized again how very little he knew the man except in his role of successful husband and father. Alone, what was he like? What were his dreams, his fears, his pleasures? Who was he without the mask? Rathbone had no idea.

Ballinger was staring at him, still trying to decide how to answer.

"Were you acting for a client?" Rathbone repeated.

Ballinger appeared to have reached a decision. "No. I spent the evening with Bertie Harkness. Then I returned as I had come, cross-ing the river again at Chiswick. I may have passed Parfitt's wretched boat, but I neither saw nor heard anything untoward, which the fer-ryman will tell you. My time is accounted for. And if I had paid Parfitt on some client's behalf, I would have had more sense than to do it secretly and alone with such a man." He breathed in deeply. "For God's sake, Oliver, think about it! Would you go creeping around boats alone at night, in order to conduct a perfectly legal piece of business for a client, however desperate or foolish that client had been? And would you go alone?"

"No," Rathbone said without hesitation. It all sounded very rea-sonable, but it was not a defense. "We will have to have far more than a mere denial."

Ballinger managed a tight, bleak smile. "They have to prove that I was there, that I was in possession of Rupert Cardew's cravat, and that I had a compelling reason to kill Parfitt. They can do none of those things, because none of them is true. I was on the river, crossing it from the south side, on my way home. I was in a ferry, and the fer-ryman will vouch for it. From there I took a hansom straight home. No one can prove differently, because that's the truth."

"And you are sure you didn't have any dealings with Parfitt?" Rathbone pressed.

"For heaven's sake, what dealings would I have?" Ballinger pro-tested. "From what you say, the man's unspeakable!"

"You were prepared to act for Jericho Phillips," Rathbone pointed out. "And for Sullivan, who was using the filthy trade, and paying Phillips blackmail money. The prosecution would not find it difficult to suggest you did the same for Parfitt or, on the other hand, for one of his victims."

Ballinger swallowed. There was still no color in his face, and he looked cornered and embarrassed. "I acted for Sullivan because the man was desperate."

Rathbone could no longer put it off without very deliberately lying, both to Ballinger and to himself. He had pretended that he did not need an answer, and it lay like poison inside him.

"Sullivan told me that you were the one who introduced him to the pornography, and that you were behind Phillips financially."

Ballinger stared at him.

Seconds ticked by.

Ballinger gulped. "He told you that?" he said incredulously.

"Yes."

"And you said nothing . . . until now?"

"I chose to believe it was the hysterical accusation of a man whose mind was turned by despair, and who was about to take his own life."

"And so it was." Ballinger took an enormous breath, and the sweat beaded on his face, although the cell was cold. "My God, that makes sense of Monk's insane behavior. You spoke to him, didn't you!" That was a statement, not a question, close to the edge of blame.

Rathbone found himself off balance. He almost started to make excuses for himself.

"Are you telling me that you were not involved with Sullivan's behavior?" he said, measuring his words very deliberately.

Arthur Ballinger hesitated. He glanced down at his hands, strong and heavy on the table, then met Rathbone's eyes. "Sullivan black-mailed me into representing him," he said quietly. "Not for anything I did, but for Cardew. Helping him was his price for keeping Cardew out of it."

Rathbone was so amazed that for a moment he could think of nothing to say.

Ballinger stared at him, waiting.

"Cardew?" Rathbone said at length. "You were prepared to get involved with that sordid mess, to save Cardew?"

Ballinger's face softened, his shoulders eased a little bit, and he almost smiled. "I've admired him immensely, for a long time."

"He was involved with Phillips, and you admired him?" Rathbone's voice carried his disgust, and his disbelief.

"Rupert Cardew was involved with Phillips, for God's sake! I admired his father!" Ballinger said witheringly. "And I was desperately sorry for him. You haven't children yet, Oliver. You have no idea how you can love your child, regardless of how they behave, or what wretched things they do. You still care, you still forgive, and you can never abandon them, or stop hoping they will somehow change and be at least something of what you want for them."

Rathbone was totally confused. Was it possible?

Ballinger leaned forward across the table. "I did all I could to save Sullivan, for his own sake. I should not have been surprised that he took his own life, but I regret to say I did not see it beforehand, or I might have stopped him. Or perhaps not. He was a man with nothing left, and death was the only answer remaining. Thank God that at least he took with him the evidence that would have ruined Rupert Cardew as well."

"Took with him?" Rathbone echoed.

"I meant into oblivion," Ballinger elaborated. "I don't suppose he had it literally . . . in his pockets. It was his one half-decent act, poor devil."

"But he blamed you."

"So you say. Half-decent, but not entirely." He reached out his hand toward Rathbone. "But I will not say this in court, Oliver. I must clear my name without destroying Cardew. Possibly no one can save Rupert, but leave his father out of it."

"How is his father involved?" Rathbone found the words difficult to say. He knew of Lord Cardew only by repute, for his crusade against industrial pollution. The man had apparently found some means to change Lord Justice Garslake's mind, heaven knew how! Oliver himself had had only one highly emotional meeting with him, over the danger against Rupert, but he could not imagine Lord Cardew having anything to do with Parfitt or Phillips, unless he were tricked into it. Monk would have no interest in that.

"You don't need to know," Ballinger said softly. "Leave the man a little dignity, Oliver. And if you can, leave his name out of the court proceedings. You can defend me from this without mentioning Phillips, or Sullivan, or any of the others who were dragged down by him. I did not kill Parfitt, nor do I know who did, or specifically why. The man was human filth and must have had scores of enemies. If you can't find the one who killed him, at least oblige the jury to know what type of person that would be. Don't ruin Cardew in the process . . . please."

Rathbone felt as if certainty had crumbled in his hands. He was holding a dozen shards, none of which fitted together to make a comprehensible whole.

"Perhaps you can do it without destroying anyone else," Ballinger went on. "But if you can't save Monk from himself, then you must follow the law, and your own sense of right and wrong. You did not do this to him; he did it to himself."

"I'll do everything I can," Rathbone said gravely. "As it stands at the moment, I will be able to challenge the prosecutor on just about every point. But of course I shall not stop working until the case is thrown out."

Ballinger smiled. "Thank you. I knew you would."

It was the evening before Arthur Ballinger's trial began. Rathbone sat in his armchair before a fire not really necessary yet but vaguely comforting. Margaret sat opposite him playing at a piece of needlework, and unpicking as much of it as she sewed.

"Who will they call first?" she asked, looking at him intently, her face strained. Tiny lines around her eyes were visible in the light shining sideways from the gas bracket at her left. He had never noticed them in the daylight. He felt an intense pity for her, and longed to be able to give her some comfort, but promises that could not be kept were worse than none at all. After they were broken, she would never be able to trust him again, and he could not rob her of that.

"Oliver!" she prompted. "Who will they call first?"

"Probably Monk," he replied.

"Why? He didn't find that wretched man's body. Why not the policeman who did?"

"Maybe they'll call him, but it's rather tedious and adds nothing to the case. It's a dangerous thing to bore a jury."

"For heaven's sake! It's not an entertainment!" she said savagely. "The jury is there to do the most important job of their lives, not to be amused."

Rathbone tried not to let any emotion sharpen his voice.

"They are ordinary people, Margaret. They are frightened of making a mistake, awed that the responsibility is theirs for a decision they have had no training to reach. A man's life hangs in the balance, and they know it. They will find it difficult to concentrate, almost impossible to remember everything, and if either Winchester or I allow their minds to wander from what we are saying, they will forget half of it. Winchester is no fool, believe me. He will not repeat anything that is irrelevant."

"What do you mean, irrelevant?" she demanded. "How can the truth be irrelevant? It is somebody's life . . . Are they stupid?" Her voice was growing higher, less within the tight effort of control that she had kept up with difficulty since her father's arrest.

He leaned forward a little. "The description of the river where they found Parfitt is not important enough for the jury to hear it from both the local policeman and Monk," he explained. "It has nothing to do with who Parfitt was, or who killed him. They don't need it twice. They will cease to listen, and that matters."

"What will Monk say?" she persisted. "He'll shade everything because he hates Papa. He's never forgiven him for choosing you to defend Jericho Phillips. Men like Monk can't bear to be beaten. What are you going to do to show the jury that it's personal, that he wanted Papa to be guilty for his own reasons?"

Rathbone saw the anger in her face, and the fear. It was as if some part of her were facing an ordeal from which she might never recover. He ached to be able to reach out to her and simply hold her, to feel that intensity of closeness where pain can be shared. But she was too tightly knotted within herself to allow it, as if he were also the enemy.

"Margaret, Monk wants to end the abominable trade in child pornography, not persecute any one person. If he wanted revenge over Phillips, for heaven's sake, don't you think he got it at Execution Dock?"

She stared at him. "You don't believe me, do you? You're siding with Monk!"

He swallowed back the exasperation that filled him. "I am trying to defend your father. Personal attacks on the police are not going to accomplish that, unless Monk makes a mistake. If he does, I will take him apart for it, friend or not."

"Will you?" she said doubtfully.

That was unfair, and at any other time he would have told her so. "You know I will," he said gently. "Didn't I do that, to both Monk and Hester, to defend Jericho Phillips? And I despised the man. How much more so would I do it to defend your father?"

"You know he's innocent, don't you?" Now she was really afraid, shivering where she sat on the sofa only a couple of feet away from him. What could he possibly say? He did not know that Ballinger was innocent. Of the murder of Parfitt, he probably was, because why on earth would he do such a senseless and unnecessary thing? But of any involvement with those who used the boats and the wretched children on them, no, he was not certain of Ballinger's innocence at all.

"Oliver!" She was trembling now so intensely, he would have thought the room ice cold if he had not felt the heat of the fire scorching his legs.

"I know he didn't kill Parfitt," he answered her. "Of course I do. I'm afraid he might have gone further than he would like to have in defense of some of Parfitt's victims. I'm not absolutely certain that he doesn't know who did kill him, and he might be protecting them."

"Why? Why on earth would he defend a man who . . . who murdered—Oh." Her voice dropped. "You mean they might be his professional client? Yes, of course. He would go to trial and endure all the pain and the blame to protect a victim of Parfitt's blackmail, all because he had given his word." She stopped shivering, and the fabric that was stretched tight across her shoulders eased a little.

It was not what Rathbone had meant at all. He had been thinking of something far less noble, but now he had not the heart, or perhaps the courage, to deny it. He looked at her soft eyes, and her sudden reassurance, and the words died before he spoke them.

"It's possible. I need to be prepared for surprises."

"Wouldn't he trust you?" she pressed. "After all, you are his lawyer, and what he tells you is in confidence."

"Of course it is," he agreed with an attempt at a smile. "Even from you, my dear."

"Oh!" She searched his eyes, trying to read in them what he might be unable to tell her.

"What about this Winchester?" she said at length. "What is he like?"

"Very clever," he replied. "Rather personable. He is deceptively charming, and at times amusing, but underneath it he has a very sharp mind indeed."

"You're frightening me!" she snapped. "You sound as if you're saying he could win."

"Of course he could win," he answered her. "And if I forget it for even a moment, then I open the door for him to do just that." He took a deep breath and tried to calm his voice and make it gentle. "Margaret, they have a case. If they didn't, we wouldn't be going to court tomorrow. If I could have had it dismissed, don't you think I would have?"

"Yes! Yes, I know. But it's ridiculous! My father? How can anyone who knows him ever imagine that he would be . . . paddling about in the river murdering some . . . pornographer?"

Rathbone reached across and touched her hand, and she grasped hold of him. She clung so tightly, she pinched his flesh, but he did not pull away, and forced himself not to wince.

"Precisely because they do not know him," he replied. "It is my job to show the jury that he is exactly what he looks to be and claims to be—a respectable husband and father, a good solicitor, who, in the course of his professional duties, has had clients both good and bad, just as I have myself. He has done his best to help all of them, without making personal judgments as to their worthiness—which is what the law requires, and justice demands."

She tried to blink back the tears that filled her eyes, but they spilled down her cheeks. "You're right, Oliver, and I love you for it. I'm sorry. I'm just so frightened that somehow it will go wrong. I have no belief in justice. If it were real, he wouldn't even be facing trial at all. And I'm sorry, but I think Monk is ruthless, and I don't even trust Hester anymore. I think she'll do anything for him, even lie if she has to, to stop him from looking bad—again. He can't afford to make another terrible mistake, or he'll lose his job."

"You truly think she would lie for him?" he asked.

"For goodness' sake, Oliver! She loves him," she responded with exasperation. "She's loyal! She's his wife."

"Is that loyalty?" he said very softly.

She looked puzzled. "What do you mean? Of course it is."

"I don't believe it is loyal to help someone do something that is wrong, something that could end in another person's death. You would be helping them to commit a sin they would regret and pay for, for the rest of their lives. Would you want that? I wouldn't."

She looked confused.

"If you loved them?" he pressed.

"I . . . I don't know. I would want to defend them. Wouldn't you?" Now she was frowning. "Perhaps if I loved them enough, I wouldn't even think that they could be wrong. Not as wrong as that."

"And would you sacrifice your own judgment?"

"I don't know. But that isn't going to happen." She shook her head fractionally. "I'm not married to William Monk; I'm married to you. I can't grieve over Hester's problems. That's up to her."

Rathbone had a sharp flash of memory, so vivid that it seemed Hester was in front of him now, her face as intense as Margaret's, but angry, vulnerable, passionately concerned for the problems of someone else, needing to find an answer for them, unable to rest or sleep until she had. She had frightened him, and excited him. And he had loved her for that.

He lowered his eyes away from Margaret's gaze. He did not want to see into her emotions, in case it left an emptiness in him. And he did not want her to see into his.

He let go of her hands and stood up. "I'm going back into my study. I need to read it all one last time. Try to sleep. I'll see you in the morning." It was a lie. He did not need to, or intend to, read it all again. He simply wanted to be alone, where he also could rest. For all his attempts to comfort Margaret, he was a good deal more anxious than he wished her to know.

THE COURTROOM WAS PACKED, and people were turned away even before the preliminaries of the trial commenced. By the time the first witness was called, the atmosphere was like that before an electric storm. Rathbone was not surprised. He had expected it, because the prospect of a respectable lawyer charged with murdering a seedy riverside pimp in particularly squalid circumstances had driven the more lurid journalists to speculate up to the legal limit, and beyond, in what it was permissible to print. Even thought he had expected the crowd, he dreaded the pain he would see in Margaret's face. He had considered asking her not to come but had known that she would see it as an invitation to cowardice—worse than that, to betrayal.

Winchester called Monk first, as Rathbone had expected.

Monk climbed the spiral steps up to the witness stand high above the body of the court, and stood there elegantly, as always. He looked assured. Only Rathbone, who knew him so well, could see the tension in his body, the uncharacteristic complete stillness as he waited for Winchester to begin.

Winchester's first questions were simple, a matter of identifying Monk so the jury knew exactly who he was, and his seniority, then establishing time and place, and who had called Monk to the scene, for what reason.

"You were standing on the riverbank in the early morning mist," Winchester said.

"Actually, in the water," Monk corrected him.

"Shallow?"

"Over the knees, and muddy." Monk gave a slight wince at the memory of it.

"And no doubt cold," Winchester added.

"Yes."

"And the reason the local police had sent for you?"

"The body of a man, fully clothed, floating in the water. They turned him over to identify him, which was actually fairly easy in spite of a degree of water damage, because he had a withered arm."

"Withered?" Winchester questioned.

"His right arm was shorter than the left, and the muscle was badly wasted. It looked as if it was almost unusable."

"Whose was this body?"

"A local man called Mickey Parfitt."

"Did he appear to have drowned?" Winchester sounded no more than curious, his voice mild. "Do they call you for every drowning?"

"No," Monk replied. "There was a nasty injury to the back of his head, slightly to the right of the crown. And we discovered there was a tight ligature buried in the swollen flesh of his throat."

"Ligature? As in something long and thin tied around his throat and pulled so tight as to strangle him?"

"Yes."

"Did you notice what it was that had done this?"

"Not at that time. We only really looked at it later."

"Later?"

"When the police surgeon cut it off and brought it to me."

Winchester raised his hand in a slight gesture, as if to prevent Monk from saying anything more. "We will come to that later. At that time, Mr. Monk, standing in the water in the early morning light, did you believe that Mr. Parfitt had come to his death from natural causes?"

"I believed it extremely unlikely."

"An accident?"

"I could not think of any that would meet such evidence."

"So it was murder?"

"I thought so, yes."

"What did you do then, Mr. Monk?"

Monk described hauling the body out of the water, heavy and dripping with mud, then carrying it up to the cart, and finally back to Chiswick, leaving it in the morgue for the police surgeon to perform a postmortem.

"Then what, Mr. Monk?" Winchester looked relaxed, comfortable. Rathbone knew him by reputation, but he had not faced him across a courtroom before, and he could not read his mood. He seemed deceptively bland, almost casual, as if he imagined this case would require only half his attention.

"I started to make inquiries as to the nature and business of Mr. Parfitt, and why anyone might have wished to kill him," Monk replied.

"Routine?" Winchester said quickly.

"Yes."

"Then, unless Sir Oliver wishes to go into detail . . ." He swiveled a little to glance at Rathbone, his face sharp with inquiry, but it was rhetorical. He looked back at Monk. "I would be quite happy not to bore the gentlemen of the jury with every step of the way. What did you discover? For example, what was Mr. Parfitt's occupation, as far as you could ascertain, and please be careful to keep precisely to the facts."

Monk smiled bleakly. He knew that for all Winchester's casual air, he was as tightly coiled as Rathbone, concentrating just as intensely on every word, every nuance.

"The police told me that Mr. Parfitt owned a boat, which he kept at various different locations; at that time it was moored farther up Corney Reach, something like halfway between Chiswick and Mortlake. I went to the boat, taking Sergeant Orme with me."

"The local man?"

"No, my own sergeant from the station at Wapping."

"Why was that, Mr. Monk? Would not the local man have been of more assistance, given his knowledge of the area, the tides, and possibly of Mr. Parfitt himself?"

"He was still speaking with Mr. Parfitt's associates, and we found his local knowledge to be more advantageous in that undertaking."

"I see. We will hear from him later. My lord, I shall call Mr. Jones, Mr. Wilkin, and Mr. Crumble in due course. I think it would be simpler for the court to hear all Mr. Monk's evidence in one piece, even if it does disturb the narrative a little, if it so please your lordship?"

The judge nodded and made a small, impatient gesture with his hand.

Winchester inclined his head slightly to convey his thanks.

"Did you board this boat, Mr. Monk?" he asked.

Rathbone realized that he was sitting with his muscles clenched, and deliberately forced himself to relax them one by one. He could not look up at the dock to his left, where fifteen feet above him Arthur Ballinger was sitting immobile, staring down at them. If he did, he would draw the jury's attention, and he might regret that later. Even one fleeting expression that looked like arrogance or indifference could be interpreted as guilt, however little it actually meant. Better that they watch Monk.

"Yes," Monk answered. "We boarded it with very little difficulty. It was just a matter of coming alongside, tying our boat, and climbing up the ropes. The main hatch was locked, so we broke it open and went down the steps—"

"You mean the ladder?" Winchester interrupted. "Would you describe it for us, please?"

Rathbone hated this, but he must keep it from showing in his face. The jury would watch him too. From the way in which Winchester had asked the question, and the horror in Monk's face, it was clear that the answer to the question mattered.

Monk was standing stiffly, his hands now on the railing in front of him, holding on to it as if for balance. His face was pale, eyes hard, lips drawn back a little. From his manner he was in some pain that he could barely control.

"The boat was about fifty feet long, as near as I could judge," he began quietly. "I did not measure it. There appeared to be three decks including the open deck on top. This later proved to be the case. There was one mast, and a wheelhouse. We went down the first hatch, which was wide and gave easy access. The way down was not a ladder. It was strong and comfortable steps, which led into a large room fitted out rather like the bar of a gentleman's club. We found alcohol in the cupboards, and several dozens of glasses."

Rathbone saw the jury staring at Monk, puzzled as to why this very ordinary-sounding account was of any importance at all, let alone should stir the emotions of horror that were so clearly in Monk's face and his voice, even in the attitude of his body.

Rathbone felt his stomach twist. He knew exactly what Monk was doing.

"Please continue," Winchester prompted, his voice grave. He was an unconsciously elegant man with his height, good shoulders, and unusually handsome hair.

"The other half of that deck was a second room roughly the same size," Monk went on. "But it was arranged rather like a theatre, with a stage at the far end—just a bare platform, and lights."

"A curtain?" Winchester asked. "Room for musical players?"

Monk winced. "No curtain, no music."

Winchester nodded.

The judge grew more impatient. "Mr. Winchester, is this leading somewhere?"

"Yes, my lord, I am afraid it is. Mr. Monk?"

"We went down to the deck below that." Monk's voice dropped and he spoke more rapidly, as if he wanted to get it over with. "There were several small cabins, no more than cubicles, each big enough to hold a bed. In the room at the back we found a locked door, which we forced open. Inside the space were four small boys, aged from four to seven years old . . ."

There was a gasp from the body of the courtroom. A woman in a brown dress and bonnet gave a cry and instantly put her hand over her mouth to stifle it.

One of the jurors let out his breath in a low sigh.

"They were white-faced, crouched together"—Monk's voice cracked—"and terrified. We had to convince them that we did not intend to hurt them. They were cold, starved, and half-naked."

Winchester glanced at the judge and frowned at Monk, as though he would ask Monk if he was exaggerating. Then after several seconds of meeting Monk's eyes, he rubbed his hand over his own face and shook his head.

"I see. What did you do then, Mr. Monk?"

"Made every arrangement I could to get the children evacuated, fed, clothed, and safe for the night," Monk replied. "There were fourteen in all. We got in touch with a foundling hospital that would take them until they could be identified and, if they had homes, returned to them."

"Where did they come from?" Winchester asked, making no attempt to hide his own distress.

If you had dropped a pin in the room, the sound of it would have been heard.

"Up and down the river," Monk said. "Orphans, unwanted children, ones whose own parents couldn't feed them."

Winchester shivered. "When did they get to this boat? What were they doing there?"

"They were found and picked up at different times. They were used to participate in various sexual acts with older boys or men, for the entertainment of Mr. Parfitt's clients. These acts were—"

Rathbone rose to his feet.

The judge looked at him. "Yes, Sir Oliver. I was wondering when you would object to this. Mr. Winchester, how does Mr. Monk know all this? Surely it was not apparent to the naked eye when he broke into the lower deck of this boat? And you have not yet shown any proof that it was indeed Mr. Parfitt's boat. It could have been anyone's."

"My lord, I was going to ask what any of this appalling story has to do with Mr. Ballinger," Rathbone responded.

"Mr. Winchester?" The judge raised his eyebrows.

Winchester smiled. "I admit, my lord, I was attempting to show for members of the jury what a particularly repulsive character the victim was, before Sir Oliver would do it for me, as I fear he will, so that we may all appreciate that he is likely to have had a great number of enemies, and very few friends indeed."

There was a sigh of relief in the public gallery and a few faint titters of laughter. Even the jurors seemed to relax a little in their high-backed seats in the double jury row on the opposite side of the floor.

Rathbone could do nothing but concede the point.

The judge looked at Monk. "I hope you are not going to describe these acts, Commander Monk? If you intend to, I shall have to clear the court, at least of all ladies present."

"I did not see them performed, my lord," Monk said stiffly. "If I had been present, they would not have been. I was going to say that they were photographed, and the resulting pictures used to blackmail the wealthier men taking part."

The judge frowned. "I was not aware that it was possible to photograph people who are moving, Mr. Monk? Does it not take between five and ten seconds exposure, even with the very latest equipment?"

"Yes, my lord," Monk replied. "These pictures were posed for, deliberately. It was part of the initiation ceremony into the club. An added element of risk that, for these men, heightened their pleasure, and their sense of comradeship."

"Did you know this at the time?"

"No, my lord, but because of previous experiences on another very similar boat farther down the river, I suspected much of it." He looked at the judge coldly, his face hard and hurt.

"I see." The judge turned from Monk to Winchester. "I shall expect you to prove every step of this, Mr. Winchester, beyond reasonable doubt."

"Yes, my lord. I shall leave the jury with no doubt at all. I wish that none of this were so." He turned to the jury. "I apologize, gentlemen. This will be distressing to all of you, but for the sake of justice, I cannot spare your feelings. I . . ." He spread his hands helplessly.

Rathbone knew exactly what Winchester was doing, and there was no way Rathbone could prevent it. He had expected Winchester to be clever, but had hoped he would be sure enough of his case to be careless now and then, and take one or two things for granted, where Rathbone could trip him. So far he was treading almost softly, and it made the details all the more terrible. There was nothing for Rathbone to attack, nothing hysterical, nothing unnecessary. To question it would seem desperate, the first sign that he himself was not sure of his case.

He could not turn to look for her in the gallery, but he knew that Margaret would be watching him, waiting in an agony of tension for him to do something, anything but sit there helplessly. Rathbone was allowing Winchester to go on and on as if he, Rathbone, were tongue-tied. How could Rathbone explain to her, and her mother, that to make useless attacks weakened himself, not Winchester?

He should put her out of his mind; all else must be forgotten, except the defense. The battle was everything.

Monk was talking again in a low, shaking voice, describing the photographs he had seen.

Winchester held a packet in his hand. "My lord, if you believe it necessary, they can be shown to the gentlemen of the jury, just so they are without doubt that what Mr. Monk says is indeed quite a mild description of the terrible truth."

The judge leaned forward and held out his hand.

Winchester walked across the floor and gave him the packet. His lordship opened it and looked.

Rathbone had not actually seen the pictures, but looking at the judge's face was perhaps more powerful a flame to the imagination, a pain sharper than the actuality could have been, because it was a living thing in his mind, a monstrosity that changed and that he could never control.

Damn Winchester!

He looked across at the jury and saw their expressions. One man was white, his eyes blinking fiercely, not knowing where to look. Another kept rubbing his face with his hands, as if embarrassed. One man coughed, then blew his nose hard. Others were looking around the room, staring at the judge, fidgeting, breathing rapidly.

"Sir Oliver!" the judge said sharply, as if he had said it before and Rathbone had not heard him.

Rathbone rose to his feet. "Yes, my lord?"

"Are you content that the jury does not need to look at this . . . material?"

Rathbone knew he must answer immediately. He must be right. Had the suggestion, the emotional charge in the room, made the pictures seem worse than they really were? Perhaps the reality would be an anticlimax.

"If I may see them, my lord? And I presume Mr. Winchester will demonstrate to us how he knows beyond doubt that they we taken on the boat belonging to the victim."

"Naturally."

The judge's face tightened, but he beckoned the usher over and gave him the packet to pass to Rathbone.

Rathbone took it and looked at the first two pictures. They were pathetic and obscene beyond anything he had expected, but what had not even occurred to him was the worst of all: He recognized the man in the second one with a shock that brought the sweat out on his body, burning and then cold. Should the jury see it? Would it work in their favor, raise a reasonable doubt as to Ballinger's guilt, because surely a man who would do this to a child, for pleasure, would stoop to anything at all, even murder?

But the man in the photo was a public figure. How would the jurors respond to having their illusions so terribly crushed, torn apart, soiled forever? Rathbone could not know.

"Sir Oliver?" The judge's voice cut across his racing thoughts.

"I feel . . ." He had to stop and clear his throat. "I feel, my lord, that because of the men also depicted here, and the ruin it would bring upon them, and their families, that that is a separate issue, and not one I wish to pursue—at least not here. I would ask only that your lordship would inform the jury that, hideous as they are, none of them, in any way whatsoever, involve Mr. Ballinger."

The judge nodded slowly, and turned to the jury. "That indeed is so, gentlemen. And, no doubt, Sir Oliver will reaffirm that when he questions Mr. Monk. Please proceed, Mr. Winchester. I think you have more than adequately established for the jury that Mr. Parfitt was occupied in a trade vile beyond the imagination of a sane man. Although that fact seems to some to serve the defense rather more than the prosecution."

Winchester smiled ruefully, as though he had been caught out. "Perhaps I have not served my own interests as well as I hoped." He gave a very slight shrug. "I am obliged to go where the facts lead me." He looked up at Monk.

"Where did you find these photographs, Mr. Monk? Indeed, how do you know they have anything to do with Mr. Parfitt? Is he shown in any of them?"

"No. It is possible he was behind the camera," Monk replied. "We found that on the boat, but not immediately. It was very carefully concealed in what looked like a piece of nautical equipment."

"Would these men be likely to know that they were being photographed?" Winchester asked.

"Not unless they were told," Monk answered.

"Where did you find the photographs that you have shown us?"

"With the equipment."

"I see. And do they depict the inside of the boat you saw?"

"Yes."

"To your knowledge, Mr. Monk, was Mickey Parfitt alone in this ghastly trade?"

"No," Monk replied, his mouth tight. "He had at least three men we have been able to question, who worked quite openly for him, but of course there may be many others that we have not found."

"Really? What brings you to that conclusion, Mr. Monk?" Winchester continued to look innocent.

Rathbone felt himself stiffen in his seat. This was what Winchester had been leading up to, and Monk even more so. Rathbone had to make an intense effort to look unconcerned. Any anxiety, confusion, or surprise they saw could be read as guilt.

The silence of strain in the room was palpable.

"The photographs," Monk replied to Winchester.

"But you said you thought Parfitt took them himself?" Winchester sounded surprised.

"Probably," Monk conceded. "But not merely for his own pleasure."

"He sold them?" Winchester asked with a gesture of distaste. "I suppose there must be a market for such . . ." He searched for a word acceptable in court that would describe what he felt, and did not find it.

Monk smiled sourly. "Undoubtedly," he agreed. "But the market that would pay most highly, again and again, is the men who are shown in the pictures." There was rage in his voice, almost choking him, but looking up at him across the space of the open floor, Rathbone saw a pity in him also, and it took him by surprise.

"Oh." Winchester bit his lips. "Of course. How dull-witted of me.

Blackmail. And have you some reason to suppose that Parfitt did not commit the blackmail himself?"

"Parfitt came from a poor family of manual laborers and petty thieves on the riverside," Monk answered. "He was uneducated and lived by his wits. According to those who knew him, he had neither good looks nor charm, and was not particularly eloquent. His skills were his cunning and his encyclopedic knowledge of human weakness and depravity. How could he find the victims for such blackmail? It is hardly his social circle, and one cannot advertise the goods he had for sale."

Winchester looked as if he had been suddenly enlightened. His eyes widened. Then he smiled at his own attempt at playacting. He looked at the jury as if to apologize to them. Several of them smiled back at him.

"Of course," he said mildly. "There has to be a man of more sophistication, higher social connections, and possibly money to have provided him with this boat, and obviously excellent photographic equipment, in the first place."

"Yes."

Rathbone considered objecting, but a look at the jurors' faces, and he knew he would earn only their contempt. He would seem to be making ridiculous objections by which to try to distract them, which would only lend more credence to what Winchester was saying. And if he was honest, Rathbone himself believed there was someone behind Parfitt, pretty much as Monk and Winchester assumed.

"But you do not know who he is?" Winchester pursued.

"I believe that I do," Monk contradicted him. "But the proof is what I came here to present."

The jurors looked stunned. There was a buzz of excitement in the public gallery, rustles of movement and indrawn breath.

Winchester himself played it for all it was worth.

"Are you suggesting, Mr. Monk, that it was this . . . this investor who murdered Mickey Parfitt? Why, for heaven's sake? Was the boat not making him a fortune?"

Rathbone stood up at last. "My lord, this is the wildest speculation!"

"It is indeed," the judge answered tartly. "Mr. Winchester, you know better than this!"

"I apologize, my lord," Winchester said humbly. "I'm sorry."

It was only at that moment that Rathbone realized that Winchester had had nothing more to add anyway. Rathbone's intervention had saved him from the jury's realizing it.

"Have you anything else pertinent to say, Mr. Winchester?" the judge asked with evident impatience. "For example, something tangible, such as either of the weapons used in the attack of Mr. Parfitt, or a timetable of his movements? Or for that matter, a witness to anything at all? You have so far only a handful of obscene and repulsive photographs and a web of speculation, none of which you have connected to the accused."

Winchester looked suitably chastened and once again addressed Monk. "Sir, his lordship has excellent points, and has graciously reminded me that I have yet to mention the weapons used to take the life of this repulsive man. Did you seek them, and did you find them?"

"I did not find the weapon with which his head was struck," Monk replied. "It is difficult to know what that would have been, but any strong length of branch from a tree would have served, or a broken plank of wood, or an oar. There were many such lying on the bank, or floating in the water."

Winchester looked faintly disconcerted, but he did not interrupt.

"However, we did find the weapon with which he was strangled," Monk continued. "It was a dark blue cravat with an unusual pattern on it of leopards, very small and in threes, one above the other, in gold. It was made of silk, and there were six very tight knots in it, at slightly irregular distances matching the bruises perfectly."

Winchester allowed the jury a few moments to absorb this information. "Really! And where did you find the cravat, Mr. Monk?"

"The police surgeon cut it from around Parfitt's neck," Monk answered.

There was a sigh of breath and a buzz of movement around the court.

"And did you trace its owner?" Winchester asked.

"Yes, sir. It belonged to a Mr. Rupert Cardew . . ." Monk could not continue because of the uproar.

When the judge had regained control, Winchester thanked him and invited Monk to proceed.

"Mr. Cardew said that the item had been stolen from him the previous afternoon, and we later found evidence that that was indeed so."

"Did this evidence implicate Arthur Ballinger?"

"No, sir."

"So what did, Mr. Monk? So far, as I'm sure Sir Oliver would be quick to point out, there is nothing in the course of your investigation to suggest his name to you, much less to imply his guilt in the matter at all!"

"A short handwritten note inviting Parfitt to meet the accused at the boat, on the evening of his death," Monk replied.

Again there were gasps and cries in the body of the court, and it was several moments before the judge managed to restore order.

"And where did you find this extraordinary document?" Winchester inquired.

"Written above another note given to me, presumably without appreciating its importance, by Mr. Jones, one of Mr. Parfitt's employees," Monk told him. "Parfitt wrote down the time he wanted Jones to ferry him to his boat."

"Indeed. And was this note signed by the accused?"

"No. It was written on the back of a piece of paper, on the front of which was a list of medicines to be purchased for the use of patients in the Portpool Lane Clinic."

Winchester's black eyebrows shot up. "Good heavens! Are you certain?"

"Yes. We took it to the clinic and asked those who work there to identify it."

"Just a moment! What made you consider the possibility that it had anything to do with them, Mr. Monk?"

"I asked my wife, who is a nurse there, if she recognized the items on the list. She did. She also knew who had written the list and when, because of the writing and what was listed."

The silence in the courtroom was so thick, someone wheezing in the back row was momentarily audible.

Thoughts raced through Rathbone's mind as to what he could ask Monk, how he could tear this apart. And, looking at Monk's face, he knew that he was already prepared, even waiting. Was it possible that this time he really was sure?

"She wrote this list?" Winchester asked skeptically. "And you did not immediately recognize her hand, Mr. Monk? That strains credulity."

"No, she didn't write it," Monk replied with the vestige of a smile. "It was written by Mrs. Claudine Burroughs, a woman of good society who gives her time to helping the sick and the poor. I did not recognize her hand because I am not familiar with it, but my wife did."

"I see. And how did you deduce from this recognition that the subsequent note on the same piece of paper was written by Mr. Ballinger?"

"Because Mrs. Burroughs said she gave the list to Lady Rathbone to purchase the—"

There was another explosion of sound in the courtroom.

The judge banged his gavel and commanded silence, on pain of people's forcible removal from the room.

Rathbone felt the heat sear up his face until he could hardly breathe. He did not dare look at Margaret, or her family, although he knew exactly to the inch how far he would have to turn his head to do so.

"To purchase the medicines from the apothecary," Monk continued. "Which Lady Rathbone did, for she gave the receipts to Mrs. Burroughs but did not return the original list. It seems reasonable, even inevitable, to assume that she discarded it where Mr. Ballinger, her father, found it and tore off a piece to use for this note to Parfitt, not knowing that what was on the back was so distinctive."

"I see," Winchester said gravely. "And did you subsequently ask Mr. Ballinger to account for his whereabouts that evening?"

"Yes, sir," Monk replied. "He never pretended that he was not in the area, but he did say that he was in Mortlake, some short distance up the river from Corney Reach, where the body was found. He was in the company of a friend, which the friend verified. However, it is possible, if you are a strong rower, to take a boat from Mortlake to Corney Reach and come back again, then catch a hansom at the south side of the river to the ferry where Mr. Ballinger originally crossed, all in the time that he stated and his friend confirmed."

"Really?" Winchester affected surprise. "Are you sure?"

"Yes, sir. I did it myself, at the same time of the evening."

"Remarkable. Thank you, Commander Monk." Winchester turned to Rathbone with a smile.

Rathbone rose to his feet with a very slight tremble in his hands. He had just realized an astounding possibility. Neither Monk nor Winchester had mentioned Hattie Benson, either by name or occupation. Was that to spare Lord Cardew's feelings? Or had she withdrawn her testimony, refusing now to take the stand? Without her, Rupert was still a prime suspect.

Could he discredit this wretched note somehow? Suggest it had a different date, a different meaning? Even that it had originally been addressed to someone else?

He needed time.

"It is late, my lord," he said with exaggerated courtesy. "I have several questions to ask Mr. Monk, of fundamental importance to the whole case—things that may lead us in an extremely different direction. I would prefer, out of respect to yourself and the jury, to begin this when there is the opportunity to carry the matter to its conclusion."

The judge pulled out a magnificent gold pocket watch and regarded it soberly. "I hope your substance will equal your words, Sir Oliver? Very well. We shall adjourn until tomorrow morning."

Rathbone spent a miserable hour with Ballinger.

"I've no idea who wrote the damn note!" Ballinger said furiously. "The Burroughs woman is lying, or is forgetful. Margaret would have given it back to her with the medicines from the apothecary, and she left it lying around. Anyone could have found it and used it. What about Robinson, the old whoremonger who runs the place for them? That's the obvious answer. Use your brains, Oliver! Go for them. Go for him! He'll never make a credible witness. Tear him apart."

Rathbone said nothing. He disliked the idea, but it was reasonable, and perhaps the only course he had.

"I did not kill that filthy little man!" Ballinger's voice was raised, brittle with anger and fear. "For God's sake, do your job!"

MARGARET WAS ALREADY AT home when Rathbone arrived.

"How is he?" she said as soon as Rathbone was through the door, even before he had given his coat to the butler.

"Full of courage," he said gently, kissing her cheek. There was no point in telling her anything else.

She pulled away from him so she could see his face, as if from studying it she could better tell if he was merely trying to comfort her.

He looked at her steadily, lying superbly.

Finally she smiled, her face catching some of its old calm and the loveliness that had first drawn him to her.

"He's brave," she said simply. "And of course he is innocent. He knows you can get this ridiculous charge thrown out. After this, Oliver, you cannot remain such close friends with Monk." She looked at him gravely. "He has not the honor or the integrity you thought. I know that disillusion is terribly painful, but pretending it does not exist helps nothing. It doesn't change the truth. I'm so sorry." She smiled slightly, a warm little gesture. "Actually I'm sorry for myself too, because I admired Hester so much, and I shall lose her friendship over this as well. I doubt it will be practicable for me to remain at the clinic."

He was taken aback. "Margaret, all he's done is answer Winchester's questions, and he has no choice in the matter."

The warmth vanished from her eyes. "How can you say that? He was the one who went after Papa in the first place. We wouldn't even be answering the charge at all if he had simply followed the evidence to Rupert Cardew."

Suddenly he was cold. His whole fabric of certainty was tearing apart. He had drawn in his breath to say that Hattie could prove Cardew innocent, but he realized it was only her word that did, and Margaret would argue that Monk had coerced her. Rathbone knew that Monk was a man of passions and convictions, brave enough and perhaps ruthless enough to follow whatever he believed to be right.

What if Monk were tragically wrong? What if it had been Cardew all along, and Monk had simply refused to believe it? It is so easy to believe what we need to. He had been wrong before; everyone has.

Margaret was talking again.

"Consider it, Oliver. Think honestly. You know that Monk is convinced Papa had something to do with Jericho Phillips, because as Jericho's solicitor, Papa convinced you to represent Phillips. Monk doesn't understand that that is what lawyers do! I think he has never really forgiven you for defending Phillips in court. He doesn't like to be beaten." She took a step closer to him. "Poor people with little education can be very proud, very stiff, unable to accept criticism, let alone defeat, especially from a friend. He admires you and he can't bear to be wrong in your eyes. It's an ugly trait of character, a weakness, but it is not so rare."

Was she right? Monk was prickly, but a bit less so since his marriage to Hester. However, victory still mattered intensely to him. Rathbone could see in his mind's eye Monk's rage when Rathbone had beaten him in court over Phillips. Was this his revenge, even if Monk had not been aware of it himself? Was this the old Monk reasserting himself, the man who had been so feared before his accident and the loss of memory had made him so vulnerable?

He looked at Margaret. The gentleness was back in her face.

"I plan to take him through all the evidence tomorrow. I'll show the jury just how preposterous it is," he promised. "We will not be able to protect Rupert." He took a deep breath. "I wish he were not Lord Cardew's son. Poor man."

She touched his arm with her fingers, and he felt the warmth of it briefly. "You can't do anything about that, my dear. The exposure of the law is cruel. There is nothing we can do but bear it with dignity, and loyalty to one another."

She smiled and turned. "Dinner will be ready soon. You must be hungry. I worry about you sometimes when you are in a big trial like this. Do you look after yourself?"

Rathbone followed her, comforted, until another thought came to him. It struck him so hard, it was as if he had fallen and bruised himself almost to numbness, knowing the pain would follow. What if Monk were so desperate to stop the pornographic trade on the river that he was prepared to hang Ballinger for the death of Parfitt, not because he believed Ballinger was guilty of it, but because he knew he was the man behind the trade, and behind Phillips? One reason was as good as the other; in fact, perhaps he saw the death of Parfitt as the lesser sin?

Maybe the actual killer of Parfitt was some petty thief or extortioner, like Tosh Wilkin, or even one of Parfitt's victims? Even Rupert Cardew himself? But Monk chose to overlook that rather than ruin the real killer for ridding the world of a man they were all grateful to see dead—and Monk used the circumstances to frame Ballinger, because he was the architect of the greater crime?

Was Monk capable of such twisted thought?

Even as the question formed in his mind, Rathbone was tempted to think the same way. If Ballinger were behind it—untraceable, uncatchable, simply going to walk away and begin again—would not Rathbone also have been tempted to let him pay the price for the secondary crime?

Who had killed Parfitt? 'Orrie? Tosh Wilkin? Any one of his wretched victims first led into fornication, then abuse, then blackmail? It was a soft path to hell, one shallow step at a time, invited—not driven, not chased, but led.

Rupert Cardew?

Margaret turned, aware that Rathbone was not immediately behind her.

He moved more quickly and caught up with her. It was warm in the drawing room, comfortable to the body, and familiar to the mind. It was not cold yet outside, but the fire gave an added pleasure. It should have allowed him to relax, think of something other than the anxieties and the dangers of tomorrow, but it did not. He wanted to go to bed and pretend to be asleep. He needed to be alone, away from her fears and her loyalties. But if he did, he would have to explain it to her, and that would make it worse.

The effort of finding small conversation now was unbearable, but he knew that she needed him, needed to draw on his strength to calm the mounting fear inside her, and he must do that. That it was difficult was irrelevant.

IN THE MORNING THE courtroom was packed. Once again there were people lining up outside, angry to be turned away.

When Rathbone stood up to begin his cross-examination of Monk, the tension in the air was palpable. Winchester was silent, appearing at a glance to be at ease, but the constant slight movement of his head, the flexing of his fingers, betrayed him.

Everyone was waiting, all eyes on Rathbone.

He walked out into the middle of the floor and looked up at the witness stand.

"Mr. Monk, let us discuss this curious note that Mr. Jones found in his pocket and gave to you. As I recall, you said he had been given it so as not to forget the time Mr. Parfitt was to go to keep his appointment on his boat."

"That is what Mr. Jones told me," Monk agreed.

"And you traced it back, with the help of your wife, to the clinic on Portpool Lane where she works, helping sick women in the area?"

"Yes."

"Did you trace it any further than that? By which I mean did you ask Lady Rathbone where she had left it after she'd purchased the items and given them to Mrs. Burroughs?"

"She didn't give the list back," Monk replied. "There was no need. All the items that were bought had the apothecary's receipts."

"So the note could have ended up anywhere," Rathbone pointed out. "In the possession of Mrs. Burroughs, on a table somewhere, in the rubbish basket, on the apothecary's counter, or even in the possession of Mr. Robinson, the man who keeps the financial accounts for the clinic?"

Monk's face became suddenly bleak, his body stiffer where he stood in the witness box. As Rathbone met his eyes, he saw that Monk knew exactly what he was going to say next.

Rathbone smiled very slightly. "Mr. Monk, what was Mr. Robinson's occupation before he kept the finances of the clinic?"

Monk's face was almost expressionless. "He ran the same premises as a brothel, which you know perfectly well. It was you who perceived his skill at bookkeeping and the use he could be if he remained."

"Indeed," Rathbone conceded, his smile a little wider. "He had many acquaintances in the district, and an excellent knowledge of where to buy things at a good price. And since the patients are largely prostitutes, he would be familiar with their associates, their lives and habits. He would be hard to deceive. However, unfortunate as it may be, is it possible that Mr. Robinson could have reverted to his original profession and be involved with the trade in prostitution on the river?"

Monk hesitated. Rathbone had caught him exactly as he'd meant to. To say it was not possible would be ridiculous and would leave Rathbone the way open to make Monk seem absurdly naïve.

"Of course it's possible," Monk said harshly. "It is possible almost anyone could invest in such a trade. By its very nature, it is well hidden."

"Naturally," Rathbone agreed. "No one is likely to admit to such a vile thing. Would it be true to say that you have been looking, with some diligence, for this mysterious investor for some time?"

"Yes."

"Might you have failed to find him precisely because he has been under your nose the whole time?"

There was a ripple of laughter around the courtroom, tense, a trifle high-pitched as nerves were stretched in both horror and excitement.

Monk smiled wolfishly, with no pleasure. "The deepest sin is too often right under the noses of good people," he replied. "It remains hidden precisely because good people cannot imagine that those they trust could do such things. Perhaps I am so blinded. On the other hand, perhaps you are?"

Winchester put his hand over his face to hide his expression.

George rose to his feet in the gallery, and was sharply pulled back by Wilbert.

A sigh of horror, stifled laughter, and apprehension swept around the gallery.

A juror had a fit of coughing and could not find his handkerchief. Someone lent him one.

Rathbone had a choice, and he had to make it instantly. He could either attempt to defend himself—and there was no defense; Monk's shot had been deadly—or he could retreat with dignity. He chose the latter. It had the virtue of grace.

"Indeed," he said with an inclination of his head. "But considering the comparative history of your bookkeeper and my client, my assumption is more reasonable than yours."

"My bookkeeper is not in the dock," Monk pointed out.

"Not yet," Rathbone agreed, now smiling also.

The judge glanced at Winchester, but Winchester made no objection. He was enjoying the battle.

Rathbone took a deep breath and steadied himself. "The point at issue, Mr. Monk, is whether this note could have fallen into the hands of Mr. Robinson even more easily than into the hands of Mr. Ballinger, who, after all, has never even visited the clinic."

"That depends upon whether Lady Rathbone left the list at the clinic, or at her home, or her parents' home," Monk replied. "Since the accused is her father, and she is your wife, her testimony has to be compromised. Or it is possible that she simply does not remember."

Now Rathbone really had nowhere to turn, except to abandon that line of question. He started again.

"Mr. Monk, you said in your testimony yesterday that you discounted Mr. Rupert Cardew as a suspect in the murder of Mickey Parfitt. This was in spite of the fact that it appears to be absolutely undeniable that his cravat, which he was seen wearing earlier in the day, was the ligature used to strangle Parfitt. You gave as your reason for this a witness who swore that this highly individual cravat had been stolen from Mr. Cardew late in the afternoon of the same day. I am sure the jury wonders, as I do, how a man can have a cravat stolen from around his neck, and we wait eagerly for Mr. Winchester to call this person, so that we may hear."

Rathbone could see the sudden misery in Monk's face, in spite of his attempt to disguise it. The previous moment's triumph had vanished. He stiffened a little and his shoulders altered almost indefinably, pulling the fabric of his excellent jacket a little more taut. Did the court see it also? Winchester would, surely?

Monk did not speak.

Winchester did not rise to his feet and ask if there was a question in all this preamble. That in itself was indicative of danger, complexity, something hidden.

"How did you find this witness, Mr. Monk?" Rathbone went on.

"At the time, we suspected Mr. Rupert Cardew of having killed Parfitt," Monk replied levelly. His voice sounded emotionless, belying the tension in his body. "That was from having found the cravat, and having identified it as being his. In following his actions on the day Parfitt died, we learned where he had been, and of the loss of the cravat."

"And exactly how did you find out that it was Rupert Cardew's?" Rathbone affected innocence, even admiration.

"There was a reasonable assumption that it belonged to someone who knew Parfitt," Monk replied. "Since it was clearly expensive, that suggested one of his wealthier patrons. Such people do not fall within Parfitt's social circle, nor could he seek them out. It is far more likely that his reputation spread by word of mouth, and by suggestion from his patrons. Since we could not go to them—"

Rathbone interrupted, "Because you do not know who they are?"

"Exactly," Monk was forced to agree. "Therefore we started at the type of place where word of mouth would spread, or gentlemen with such tastes might be easily found."

"Which is?"

"Cremorne Gardens, among others."

There was a flicker of recognition in the faces of the jurors, and a rustle of indrawn breath in the gallery. The reputation of the place was known to many.

"What led you to Cremorne Gardens?" Rathbone asked.

"Common sense," Monk replied with a quiver of his lips that might almost have been a smile. "It is a natural place to seek clients for a trade such as Parfitt's."

Rathbone nodded with satisfaction. "I imagine so. And did you find Mr. Cardew there?"

"No, I found someone who could identify the cravat," Monk answered him.

"And shall we hear their testimony?"

"If Mr. Winchester wishes it, although I can see no reason. Mr. Cardew does not deny that it is his, nor does he deny that it was stolen from him that afternoon. The police surgeon will confirm that he took it from around Parfitt's throat."

"And this elusive witness, whose name I have not yet been told—Curiously enough, Mr. Winchester has not spoken of him, or her. Are you aware of why that is, Mr. Monk?"

Monk breathed in deeply. "He will not be calling Miss Benson." His voice was quiet, rough-edged. Even the judge leaned forward to hear him.

Rathbone affected amazement, but his pulse was racing, his mind suddenly filled with excitement.

"Indeed? This Miss Benson would appear to be key to your case, Mr. Monk? If you do not call her, you leave speculation in the minds of the jury either that she does not exist or that, if she did testify, she would not say what you wish her to. Can you explain such a decision to the court?" He made a slight, elegant gesture with his hand to include the rest of the room.

Monk was pale. "Yes, I can. Fearing for her safety, I had Miss Benson moved from her lodgings in Chiswick into the clinic in Portpool Lane. I believed she would be safe there. However, she chose to leave without telling anyone where she was going. I assume that she was afraid."

"Ah, yes—the clinic where the dubious Mr. Robinson keeps the books. Are you saying that you now do not know where she is?"

"Yes." There was something tight and strained in Monk's face, a pain that possibly only Rathbone knew him well enough to recognize.

The look that passed over Monk's face troubled Rathbone, but he did not know why. He had the feeling that he had missed something. "Then, we must draw our own conclusions, both as to why Miss Benson came up with her original story and why she now has taken flight and refuses to come forward and repeat it to us. Thank you, Mr. Monk. I do not believe I have anything further to ask you."

Monk moved to leave the stand.

"Oh! Just one more thing!" Rathbone said.

Monk stopped and turned back, his face bleak.

"Will Mr. Winchester be calling Mr. Cardew to explain this . . . theft? I have no notice that he will be a witness."

"I don't know. Quite possibly."

Rathbone inclined his head, satisfied. He waved dismissal graciously and returned to his seat.

Winchester rose and called Mr. Horrible Jones to the stand.

The judge frowned. "Is that his lawful name, Mr. Winchester?"

"It appears to be the only one he knows, my lord," Winchester responded.

"Very well. I suppose we have no choice. Proceed."

'Orrie climbed awkwardly up the winding steps to the stand and stood clutching the rail as if the whole edifice were swaying like a ship at sea. One eye swiveled dangerously; the other looked with grave apprehension at the jury, who either stared back at him or painfully avoided his gaze.

He was sworn in, and Winchester asked him with considerable courtesy to state his occupation and describe his relationship with Mickey Parfitt. When that was answered, Winchester asked him about finding Mickey's body with Tosh Wilkin, calling the police, and later the arrival of Monk and Orme.

It was all very predictable, and there was nothing for Rathbone to object to, and nothing for him to add.

Winchester obtained an account from 'Orrie of the entire evening of Parfitt's death, complete with reasonably accurate times. 'Orrie had an extensive knowledge of tides, and that was included, as well as the skills of rowing and general management of all river craft.

The jury's attention might have been lost, were it not for 'Orrie's remarkable appearance and the occasional wry observation that Winchester put in, which made people laugh.

"Thank you, Mr. Jones," he said at length. "You have given us an excellent account." He invited Rathbone to question the witness.

Rathbone looked up at 'Orrie. "So you were deeply involved in Parfitt's affairs? He relied on you for much, especially personally. You rowed him when he was on the river. Was that necessary because of his withered arm?"

"Yes, sir," 'Orrie replied, his tone indicating his contempt for such a foolish question.

"Was it always you, or did other people row him also?"

'Orrie looked indignant, grasping on to the rail till his knuckles gleamed.

"It were always me. Wot for'd 'e want anyone else?"

"No reason at all," Rathbone assured him. He did not care what 'Orrie thought, but he was aware already of antagonizing the jury. Winchester had been scrupulous in avoiding any mention of Parfitt's occupation, as if 'Orrie could have been unaware of it. If Rathbone raised it now, he would prejudice the jury against 'Orrie, and therefore his testimony.

"Mr. Jones, in the course of your assistance to Mr. Parfitt, did you ever meet Mr. Arthur Ballinger?"

"No, I didn't," 'Orrie said vigorously.

"Or hear his name mentioned?" Rathbone suggested. "Perhaps Mr. Parfitt might have had other meetings with him?"

"No, I didn't!"

"Did you ever hear any of your colleagues speak of him?"

"No! 'Ow many times do I 'ave ter tell yer? I in't got nothin' ter do wif 'im at all!" 'Orrie said indignantly.

"I quite believe you, Mr. Jones," Rathbone assured him. "I am certain your path and Mr. Ballinger's never crossed, as neither did Mr. Parfitt's. Thank you."

Winchester next called the police surgeon, who testified to all the more lurid details of the corpse, the injuries, exactly what had caused Parfitt's death and how it was most likely that it had been accomplished, including the surgeon's removal of the cravat imbedded in the swollen flesh.

"Struck on the head with a blunt instrument, such as a log of wood, a piece of a branch?" Winchester repeated.

"Yes."

"And then when he was lying there unconscious, his killer looped Mr. Cardew's silk cravat around his neck—"

"After having tied the knots in it," the surgeon corrected him.

Winchester looked as if he had been caught in an error, although Rathbone knew that he had done it on purpose. "Of course. I apologize. After having tied the knots, either then or earlier, the assailant looped the cravat around Mr. Parfitt's neck and then tightened it until he choked to death."

"Yes."

"Why the knots, sir?"

"To exert a greater pressure on the windpipe, I assume," the surgeon replied. "It would be much more effective."

"But take time?"

"Not if you did it in advance."

"Of course. Then hardly a crime of impulse, would you say?"

"Impossible. Vandalism to do that to a good piece of silk."

Winchester nodded. "A premeditated act. Thank you, sir."

There was nothing Rathbone could do except not call more attention to the doctor's testimony by going over it again. He declined to cross-examine.

AFTER LUNCHEON WINCHESTER CALLED Stanley Willington, the ferryman who had taken Ballinger from Chiswick to the Lonsdale Road on the south shore and then back again at about twelve-thirty in the morning. All the times were exactly as Ballinger had told Rathbone, and there was nothing to add, nothing to doubt.

Winchester then called Bertram Harkness, who was a very different proposition. He was both nervous and angry. He clearly wanted very much to account for Ballinger's time in such a way as to make it clear that he could not possibly have killed Parfitt, and yet he was not aware of what the ferryman had said, since being a later witness, he had not been permitted in court at that time.

He blustered. He did not like Winchester, and Winchester was clever enough to play on it. He was charming, even amusing in a mild way, as if to give them all a respite from the seriousness of the crime. Some people in the audience even laughed, although possibly more out of nervous relief than humor.

Harkness was furious. "You find this amusing, sir?" he demanded, his face scarlet. "You drag a good man here, blacken his name in front of all and sundry, accuse him of murder, and by implication God knows what else. Then you stand around in your elegant suit . . . and make jokes! You are a nincompoop, sir! An irresponsible nincompoop!"

Winchester looked startled, then embarrassed.

Rathbone swore under his breath. It was Harkness who looked ridiculous, not Winchester. The crowd in the gallery was already on Winchester's side; now they were all but rising to defend him.

"I apologize if I have hurt your feelings, Mr. Harkness," Winchester said gently. "Perhaps you would explain to me again exactly what happened, and the lie of the land around the area in which you live, so the jury may have that uppermost in their minds, and not some frivolous remark of mine."

But Harkness had lost the thread of the story he had been trying to concoct, somewhere between the truth as he guessed it and a later and longer version that would protect Ballinger.

"I understand your predicament," Winchester said softly. "You would have had no idea that you would be called upon to account for every minute of your time with such precision. Let us agree that your judgments are approximate."

"Ballinger did not kill that wretched creature!" Harkness said tartly. "If you knew him as I do, you wouldn't even have entertained the idea. Look among Parfitt's own ghastly confederates, or some miserable victim of his disgusting trade."

"Your loyalty does you credit, sir," Winchester replied.

"It's not loyalty, you damn fool!" Harkness shouted at him. "It's simply the truth, man. If you can't see that, you should be occupied in some trade where you can do no harm."

Winchester smiled patiently and turned to Rathbone. "Your witness, Sir Oliver."

Rathbone considered for only a moment, weighing, judging, deciding. "Thank you, Mr. Winchester, but I believe Mr. Harkness has already told us exactly what happened." He drew in his breath and plunged on. "This witness of yours, Miss Benson, is apparently reluc-

tant to testify as to the theft of the cravat that Mr. Cardew was wearing that afternoon. You have conclusively proved it to be the
instrument with which Mr. Parfitt was strangled to death. Without
this witness's testimony, it seems to me, as it must to the jury, that
there is every reasonable doubt of Mr. Ballinger's involvement with
any part of this unhappy matter, let alone his guilt in Parfitt's death.
Surely the answer is exactly what it appears to be? The man was killed
by some victim of his revolting trade."

For once Winchester was genuinely startled. "My lord," he began,
"that . . . that is an unjust conclusion regarding Miss Benson's reluc-
tance—"

"Whether it is doubt, remorse, or fear that some punishment will
be visited on her for lying," Rathbone responded, now suddenly sure
that Winchester was hiding something, "that is surely irrelevant. She
is not here to tell us about the cravat, or to suggest that it ever left
Rupert Cardew's possession!"

Now Winchester was pale, the tension in him palpable. "Hattie
Benson is not here to testify because her dead body was carried out of
the Thames at Chiswick, three days before Mr. Ballinger was arrested," he said hoarsely. "Strangled exactly the same way as Mickey
Parfitt!"

A woman in the gallery screamed. Someone else muffled a cry,
and a man let out a gasp.

One of the jurors lurched forward as if to rise to his feet.

The judge banged his gavel and demanded order, and was ignored.

Rathbone felt himself go cold, as if there were ice water in the pit
of his stomach. His mind was numb, darkness at the edges of his vision. How in God's name had that happened? No wonder Monk
looked like a ghost. He must have known.

Suddenly Rathbone was overwhelmed with pity—and a profound
and terrible fear.

11

"I'm sorry," Monk said quietly as he and Hester sat in the parlor. "I wanted to have a better answer before I told you. I hoped I could find out enough to say that there was never anything you could have done."

Hester sat perfectly still, as though she were frozen. Tears prickled in her eyes, and she was furious with herself because they could be out of guilt and an sense of overwhelming failure as much as out of grief for Hattie. Was she too used to the death of street women, even young ones, long before their bloom was gone and they were riddled with disease? They came in injured, and she knew that patching them up was often only temporary.

But Hattie had trusted her. Monk himself had trusted her to keep Hattie safe.

"I'm sorry," she whispered. "I should have been able to protect her. I suppose it ruins the case too, and Ballinger will get off. Without Hattie's testimony, there has to be reasonable doubt, and Rupert's name will be shadowed again too. Oh, damn! Damn! Damn!" She wanted to cry properly, to let the sobs come, and to swear as she had heard soldiers do, words Monk had never heard, and she would rather he never knew that she had heard them, let alone remembered them.

But there was no time for that now, and there were far more urgent uses for her energy. One of the worst things she would have to do was tell Scuff, because he had been with her when they'd first met Hattie. It was after nine in the evening now, but there would be little time in the morning. She would have to stay with him tonight, judge very carefully how much comfort to offer. She had no idea how he would take it. He had grown up on the dockside and must have seen death many times before, possibly the deaths of people he knew. How she reacted would mark him, perhaps for all his life. She must not show fear, but neither must she ever let him think she did not care.

Monk was saying something. She looked up and saw the anxiety in his eyes.

"I'm sorry," she said very gently. "I didn't hear you. What did you say?"

"Do you want me to tell Scuff? He'll have to know."

"No." She shook her head. "You have enough to do. You need to sleep. I'll tell him, and stay with him. Besides, if he needs to cry, we can do it together." She smiled, and the tears slid down her cheeks. "He'll expect it of me, and it'll be all right." She stood up and turned to go.

"Hester!"

She looked back. "Yes?" She thought he was going to thank her, and she did not want to be thanked. It wasn't as if she'd given him a gift.

"I love you," he said quietly.

She drew in a shaky breath, using all her strength not to go back and cling to him and let the tears come. "I know. If I didn't, do you think I could do any of this?" Then, without waiting for him to answer, she went up to waken Scuff and tell him Hattie was dead.

She knocked on the door because she always did. He must have a place where no one else entered without his permission. As she had expected, there was no answer. She turned the handle and went in.

The night-light was still burning. He had to have enough to see by if he woke up. He must never have that first moment of terror not knowing where he was, of imagining the bilges of Jericho Phillips's boat, even for an instant.

"Scuff," she said quietly.

He did not move. She could see his head on the pillow, hair ruffled, still damp from his bath.

"Scuff," she repeated, more loudly.

He stirred, and when she spoke a third time, he opened his eyes and sat up, holding his nightshirt around himself with one hand.

She came and sat on the end of the bed, where he could see her face in the light.

"Wos wrong?" he asked, noticing the tears. "Wos 'appened?" His perception of her grief was instant, and it filled him with fear. She realized with a sharp stab how much of his world was bound up in her.

"Hattie's dead," she replied, so he would not be afraid that it was something to do with Monk. "She was killed—not an accident, though. William just told me. He wanted to wait until he could find out exactly how it happened, but it came out in court today."

He blinked. "Somebody killed 'er?" He gulped, then reached forward and put his small, thin hand over hers, so lightly, she saw it rather than felt it. "Don't cry for 'er," he whispered. "She were always gonna finish bad. This way it won't 'urt so much. Quick. Like yer should pull a tooth out, if yer've gotter, like."

She wanted to hug him, but it would be an intrusion too far. Not everyone liked to be hugged.

"You are quite right," she agreed, angry with herself because her voice trembled. "But I still feel that I need to know how she left the clinic, and who helped her. You understand?"

He nodded, his eyes never leaving hers, still full of fear. If she wavered even slightly, all his doubts would storm back, drowning his courage.

"D'yer reckon as someone took 'er?" he asked.

"No, I think they more likely tricked her, told her she'd be safe, or told her a lie of some sort. I want to know who, because I mustn't ever trust that person again." Did that sound too extreme? As if she never forgave a mistake? Would she make him fear that if he made a mistake he would forfeit love forever? "If they did it on purpose, I mean," she added.

" 'Ow'd they kill 'er?" he whispered. "Like Mickey Parfitt?"

"Yes, exactly like that. I expect she didn't even know what happened."

"Were it the same person wot done 'im?"

"Yes, I expect it was. She was found in the water, as he was, and pretty close to the same place."

"In't Mr. Ballinger in jail?" He pulled the bedclothes a little tighter round his body.

"He is now, but he wasn't when she was killed. But neither was Rupert Cardew."

His eyes opened wider. "Yer think as 'e done 'er?"

"No, I don't. But they might try to make it look that way, to get Mr. Ballinger off."

"Yer like Mr. Cardew, don't yer?"

"Yes. But that doesn't have anything to do with it. At least, it shouldn't."

He looked puzzled. "You wouldn't like 'im anymore if 'e done it?"

His hand was still lying on top of hers, as if he had forgotten it. She was careful not to move. "I might still like him. You don't stop liking people, or even loving them, because they've done something horrible. I suppose first you try to understand why. And it makes a difference if they're sorry—really sorry. But it doesn't mean they don't have to pay for it, or put as much of it right as they can. You have to have right and wrong the same for everybody, or it isn't fair."

He nodded. "So wot are we gonna do?"

"Find out what happened."

"Termorrer?"

"Yes. I'm sorry I woke you up to tell you, but there might not be time in the morning . . . and . . ."

He waited, eyes shadowed.

"I just wanted to tell you now."

His mouth tightened. "You thought I were gonna cry." He was on the very edge of it, and angry with himself.

"No," she told him. "I thought I was. I still might!"

He smiled at her widely, as if it were funny, and two large tears spilled over and rolled down his cheeks.

This time she did put her arms around him and hug him. At first he merely let her, then quite suddenly he hugged her back, hard, hanging on to her and burying his face in her shoulder, where the hair that had slipped out of its pins was loose.

IN THE MORNING MONK went back to the court, and Hester and Scuff went to the clinic.

"You don't have to be here," Squeaky said as soon as she was through the door and into the room where he was working at a table spread with receipts. "Nor you neither," he added to Scuff.

"Yes, I do," Hester responded. "And Scuff can help me." There was no allowance for argument in her voice, and no prevarication. "I want to find out exactly what happened to Hattie Benson, why she left here and who said something to her that prompted her to go."

Squeaky regarded her dismally. "Won't do no good. Maybe she lied to you. Have you thought of that?"

"Yes, and I don't believe it. It came out in court yesterday, Squeaky. She was murdered, exactly the same way as Mickey Parfitt—strangled and put in the river, up at Chiswick."

"Gawd Almighty, woman!" Squeaky exploded. "What d'you want to go and say that for, in front of the boy? Sometimes you're a cold-hearted mare, and that's the truth!"

Scuff charged forward, fists clenched, glaring at Squeaky across the table. "Don't yer dare talk to 'er like that, yer bleedin' worm! Yer in't fit ter clean 'er boots . . ."

Hester thought of pulling him back, and then decided not to. She could not rob him of the right to defend them both, but she had to bite her lip to hide a weak smile.

Squeaky backed off a little, only a matter of leaning away while still in his chair.

"Y'in't fit ter . . ." Scuff went on. Then he drew in his breath and regarded Squeaky with disgust. "D'yer think I'm some kind o' baby, then, that you can't tell me the truth? Yer gotta pretend, as if yer think I can 'ear yer?"

Squeaky considered for a moment. "I grant that, pound for pound, you're worse than a wild cat," he opined. "Never mind defending you, I should be looking after myself from the pair of you." He turned to Hester, his eyes bright with a strange, almost embarrassed amusement, as if he were pleased but did not want them to know. "And how are you going to find out who took poor Hattie to the door and pushed her out, then?"

"I'm going to ask," Hester replied. "We will begin with a full account of who was here, when they arrived, and what they did, exactly."

"Like the bleeding police," Squeaky said with disgust.

Hester caught Scuff just as he was about to launch forward at Squeaky again, his fists clenched.

"Yes," she agreed. "What did you expect? That I would first ask everyone nicely if they'd set Hattie up to be murdered?"

"I s'pose you want me to write it all down?" he said accusingly. "Don't blame me if they all walk out in a huff."

Hester thought of several retorts, and bit them all off before she said them. She needed his help.

"Who was in that day?"

"You think I can remember?" he countered.

"I think you will know exactly who was here, what they did that was useful, and how much they ate," she replied. "I shall be disappointed in my judgment of your skills if you don't."

He considered that a moment or two, weighing up her precise meaning. Then he decided to take it as a compliment, and dug his books out of the desk drawer, finding the appropriate pages for the day of Hattie's disappearance.

Scuff watched him, fascinated.

"Does 'e 'ave it all there, in them little squiggles o' writing?" Scuff whispered to her.

"Yes. Marvelous, isn't it?" she replied.

Scuff gave her a sideways look. She had not yet persuaded him of the necessity of learning to read. He could count. He considered that to be enough.

Squeaky read out who was resident and who had arrived that morning and at what time. He also listed what duties they had performed, and if, in his opinion, they had been requisitely appreciated for their efforts.

Hester made a couple of notes on a piece of paper, borrowing his pencil for the task, then set out to question each person in turn.

To begin with the people were defensive, imagining their work was under attack, and frightened of losing the safety of food and a place to sleep.

Scuff followed Hester most of the time, as if he were protecting her, although he had no idea from what.

"She's lyin'," he said casually as they left one young woman in the laundry, her sleeves rolled up, her hands red from hot water and the caustic soap necessary to clean sheets that had been soiled by body waste from the sick and injured.

"We'll check with Claudine," Hester replied. "Mrs. Burroughs to you. She'll know if Kitty was there or not."

"She weren't," Scuff told her. "I'll bet she were at the back door, doin' summink as she shouldn't. Are yer gonna throw 'er out?"

"No," Hester said immediately. "Not unless she did something to Hattie."

"Oh."

She glanced at him and saw the smile on his face.

She questioned two more women—patients not well enough to leave yet but able to be of assistance in cooking and cleaning. Their accounts contradicted Kitty's, and one of the other women's.

They found Claudine in the pantry checking rations. There seemed to be plenty of the staples such as flour and beans of several sorts, barley, oatmeal, and salt. Other things such as prunes and brown sugar were in considerably shorter supply.

Claudine smiled when she saw Hester's eye on the half-empty pot of plum jam, and then Scuff's, wide with amazement at what to him was a lifetime's supply of luxury.

"I'll give you a slice of toast and jam later, if you're good," she told him.

Hester nudged him.

"Thank yer," he said quickly.

"Unless you would rather have a piece of cake?" Claudine added. Her eyes were bright, as if she were laughing inside.

"Yes," he said instantly. Then he glanced at Hester. "Yes, I would—please."

Hester told Claudine of the discrepancy between the accounts of who was working where on the morning Hattie disappeared.

Claudine had already judged that it was important.

"That can't be right," she agreed. She turned to Scuff. "If you go to the kitchen, you'll find Bessie there. Tell her that I said you could have a piece of the plum cake in the third jar along. Don't forget, the third jar. Then she'll know that you are telling the truth. No one else knows it is there."

Scuff drew in his breath, and then let it out again. "I'll 'ave it later," he replied, taking a step closer to Hester. "Ye're gonna tell 'er who opened the door an' let 'Attie out ter get killed. I gotta be 'ere. Thank yer."

Claudine looked at him, then at Hester. "Is he right?"

Hester nodded. "Yes, I'm afraid so. She had strict instructions not to go out for any reason at all, not even to go into the main rooms where other people come and go. She knew she was in danger, and she was scared stiff that they would kill her."

Claudine's face filled with misery. "And did they?"

"Yes. Claudine, I have to know who persuaded her to go out."

"What good will it do now?" Claudine asked. "The poor girl is beyond help."

"It seems it was just a piece of stupid behavior. But if she was lured out on purpose, then I need to tie it together. The trial is going badly. It looks as if nothing will be proved, and Ballinger will get off on reasonable doubt. We will be back where we started." She did not add that the trade in pornography would begin again exactly as before, as soon as the man behind it had replaced Mickey Parfitt. Although, she feared that leaving this unsaid would not deceive Scuff for long.

Claudine looked at her, and her eyes were suddenly tired and bit-

terly unhappy. "Then you had better ask Lady Rathbone. She was
here that morning, working in the laundry and the medicine room,
just checking on supplies. She will know who is lying."

Hester was stunned. "Margaret was here?"

Claudine's face was unreadable. "Yes."

"How long?"

"About an hour, that I know of." Claudine watched her steadily.

"In the laundry?"

"Yes. Hester . . . I don't believe any of the women here would lie
to you. In addition to their gratitude, and perhaps fear for their future
chances of treatment, why would they? They'd lie to anyone else to
protect you, as easily as breathing, but not this. They all knew you
wanted Hattie protected."

Hester knew that was true. It was Margaret who'd had every reason to fear Hattie's testimony. It had just never occurred to Hester
that she would do this. In fact, for Hattie to have gone back to Chiswick and ended in the river, Margaret must have done far more than
simply getting Hattie to leave.

"She done it?" Scuff asked, looking from Hester to Claudine and
back again.

"Not killed her," Hester said quickly. "But, yes, it does look as if
she took her away from here."

"Then, who killed 'er?" he said, his eyes full of disbelief.

"I don't know. I don't know exactly what she did, or what she
meant to happen. But I'm going to find out." She turned to Claudine.
"Thank you. I think it's best if you don't say anything more to people
here, even if they ask you. Please?"

"Of course I won't."

Claudine seemed about to add something more, then changed
her mind. Hester guessed that it was some kind of warning, and from
the troubled gentleness of her face, a sympathy. She smiled back, not
needing words.

AFTER A SHORT, VERY firm discussion in which she told Scuff he
was definitely not coming with her, Hester put him in a hansom and

paid the driver to take him to the Wapping police station. She gave him fare for the ferry home, and she went on to the court.

Even the pavement outside was bustling with people, all eager to catch any word about what was going on inside. It was only with the help of an usher who knew her that Hester managed to get in at all. He escorted her through the hallway, and with some use of his authority, into the very back of the courtroom.

She had not long to wait—just a few minutes of Winchester's argument—and then the judge adjourned the court for luncheon. Hester was buffeted by the crowd pouring out, first from the back of the gallery, and then at last from the front. She saw Lord Cardew, pale-faced, looking a decade older than he had just a few weeks ago. She was ashamed of being so relieved that he did not see her. What could she say to him that would even touch the pain he must be feeling? How much courage did it cost just to come out of the house, let alone to sit here and listen as the horror grew deeper, and the doubt ate into all that had once been so bright and safe?

Then she saw Margaret and her mother, side by side, just behind two other couples, pale-faced and tense. They also looked neither to right nor left, as if they could see no one. The resemblance in the women—something in the angle of the head, a shape of eyebrow—made Hester believe that they were Margaret's sisters and their respective husbands.

But it was Margaret she needed to speak to, and alone.

She stepped forward, blocking Mrs. Ballinger's way. It was discourteous, to say the least, but she had no better alternative.

Mrs. Ballinger stopped abruptly, her face filled with alarm. But Margaret hesitated only an instant, then, grasping the elements of the situation, turned to her mother.

"Mama, it seems Mrs. Monk needs to speak to me. Something must have occurred at the clinic."

"Then, it can wait!" Mrs. Ballinger said between her teeth. "It is not even imaginable that anything there could be of importance to us now."

"Mama—"

"Margaret, I do not care if the place has burned to the ground!

Does she expect us to pass buckets of water?" She swiveled away from Margaret to glare at Hester.

"It is regarding evidence, Mrs. Ballinger," Hester replied, needing a considerable effort to keep her voice level and polite. "I would prefer not to take it to Mr. Winchester, but that is my alternative."

The last vestiges of color drained from Mrs. Ballinger's face. "Are you threatening me, Mrs. Monk?"

Hester felt the anger brew inside her. "I am trying to gain your attention, Mrs. Ballinger. Or to be more accurate, Margaret's attention. The matter in hand is more important than our personal feelings."

Margaret took her mother's arm briefly. "I shall find you when court resumes, Mama. Go with Gwen and Celia." And without waiting for her mother's reply, she let go of her and faced Hester. "We had better go to Oliver's rooms. Whatever you have to say need not be made a spectacle of out here. Come." Then, walking as briskly as possible through the last few people still in the corridors, she led the way to the room where Rathbone was permitted, for the duration of the trial, to keep his papers and to speak with anyone he might need to. The clerk recognized Margaret and, without question, allowed her in, and Hester because they were clearly together.

Margaret swung round as soon as the door was closed.

"Well, what is it? After your husband's accusations against my father, you can hardly expect me to be pleased to see you, or to imagine you have my welfare in mind."

It was not so long since they had been close friends, sharing laughter, dreams, even the excitement of Margaret's courtship with Rathbone, and her anxieties that he would never actually propose to her. She had not said so in as many words, but there had been a time when Margaret had feared that he would always love Hester, and had secretly imagined that Hester would have made him happier. It had been some time before she had realized that was not true.

Now they faced each other, several feet apart in the small room with its table, chairs, and bookcases, a world apart in emotion.

There was no time to waste in prevarication, or in an attempt to smooth the way to any kind of understanding.

"You were at the clinic the morning Hattie Benson left," Hester stated.

Margaret was stiff, her shoulders high and straight, a very faint color in her cheeks.

"You came here to tell me that?" she said with surprise. "You've lost your evidence. I know that. She won't testify to save your friend. Although how you can be a friend to Rupert Cardew is beyond my imagination. But, then, you have not been in court, and perhaps that is some excuse. I assure you, your loyalty is misplaced."

All kinds of bitter retorts rose to Hester's lips, especially as Margaret herself had not been in court the previous day, but Hester did not speak them. It would break the frail thread of contact between them, and she needed to know the truth.

"I want to know what happened to Hattie, Margaret; that's all I'm concerned with at the moment. I promised to look after her. I want to know why I failed, regardless of what she might have said on the stand."

"What she might have said is that she lied to you," Margaret answered. "You were kind to her, and she wanted to please you. I imagine she also had a very good idea of where her best future interests lay, should she ever be sick or injured, or need your help for any kind of problem. And she wouldn't be the first who lied to please the police, out of fear, or for revenge, or simply because it's easier than keeping up a resistance. You know as well as I do that street women survive by pleasing others, frequently those they are afraid of." She made a slight gesture, half pity, half disgust. "They know what people want, and they give it to them. It's their trade."

Hester shook her head fractionally, as if to rid herself of something. "Is that how you think of her, as someone who lies to please, that's all?"

"Oh, for heaven's sake, Hester, don't be so self-righteous. This is the time for truth. Yes, that is what I think of girls like Hattie. Maybe if I had had the misfortune of being born into her lot in life, I would be the same. I wasn't. I had fine parents, good health, good examples to follow, and I married a fine man. I show my gratitude for it in service to those less fortunate, but I'm not blinded by sentimentality regarding their nature, or their weaknesses. Sometimes I think you are."

Hester was overtaken by an anger that astounded her. She stood for a moment, trembling a little.

"I imagine we both have thoughts about others that are less than flattering," she said almost between her teeth. "Or even downright unkind. I want to know why you took Hattie at least as far as the door, and watched her go outside, when you knew that I had her in the clinic to keep her safe so she could testify at the trial. Why did you?"

"You sound like a policeman," Margaret said with a slight curl of her lip. "You are giving yourself airs to which you have no right. I gave my time to help at the clinic because I believe in the work you do there. I am not your servant to answer your questions."

"Either I ask you or William does," Hester said grimly.

"Then, William may try," Margaret snapped back. "I do not have to account to you for where Hattie went, even did I know."

"You don't have to tell me," Hester began, furious with herself because her voice was shaking.

"That is what I just said," Margaret told her.

"Because I already know!" Hester snapped. "She went back to Chiswick, where she was strangled and her body thrown into the river!"

Now it was Margaret's turn to blanch, and to find herself gasping for breath.

"Now perhaps you can see my concern," Hester added tartly. "Also why William may very well ask you where she went, and why you took her to the door."

Margaret regained her control with difficulty. "Obviously Rupert killed her! So she would not be called to the stand and say that she'd lied before, and she'd no more taken his cravat than I had. He kept it, as everyone supposes, and later strangled Mickey Parfitt with it, because he could not go on paying him blackmail. If you were a little less blinded by your own crusades, you would have seen that in the first place. I'm sorry Hattie had to die for you to face reality."

Hester could feel her fingernails dig into the palms of her hands. "The reality throughout is that Hattie was the one person who could have cleared Rupert," she answered. "And you took her to the door and let her out into the street, out of the place where she was safe, and someone killed her. It might have been Rupert Cardew. It might just as easily have been your father. He was the one her testimony would have hurt. And you were the one who sent her out."

Margaret stared at her, her face white to the lips, her eyes glittering. "Are you likening my father—my father—to Rupert Cardew? Rupert is dissolute, weak, and perverted . . . a . . . a vile man, who, for some unknown reason, in your own morality, your memory, or your need, you don't seem able to see for what he is."

"Of course I can see he's weak!" Hester's voice was rising in spite of her efforts to keep it level. "I don't know how dissolute he is, and neither do you. But your loyalty to your father blinds you from seeing that he too could be just as greedy, as cruel, and in his own way as dissolute. He may not watch little boys being raped and abused, but is he any better if he imprisons them and causes it to happen, so he can blackmail the wretched men who do it? Is corrupting others any better, any nobler than being corrupt yourself? I think it's worse!"

"My loyalty makes me know it could not be true," Margaret said between her teeth. "But you wouldn't understand that. You were in the Crimea being noble, saving strangers when your own father needed you. He died alone in despair while you were off glory-hunting. And if that weren't enough, who supported your mother in her grief? Not you! You didn't even come home for his funeral."

Hester was speechless. She could not catch her breath. Her whole body hurt as if she had been beaten.

"You don't know what loyalty is," Margaret went on, seeing her advantage and forcing it home. "I used to be sorry for you that you don't have any children of your own, only that little urchin you've picked up from the dockside to fill your emptiness. When it comes down to it, you don't understand what family is. You're too selfish, too absorbed with the image of love to know what the reality is." She took a gulp of air, then pushed past Hester and went out into the hallway again, leaving the door swinging on its hinges.

Was it true? Only part of it! Hester had had no idea of her father's despair, no idea he had been cheated, lied to, and betrayed. She heard of his suicide only after it had happened. Letters to and from the Crimea took weeks, and often she was away from Scutari when the ships from England landed.

Could she have known? Should she have? Her brother James had kept it from her. Her younger brother had already been killed in action. Was there something else she should have done? Should she have stayed at home in the first place?

No! She had followed not only her heart but her beliefs, in joining the nurses in the hellhole of Scutari, and even on the blood-soaked battlefields. She had eased pain, saved lives. And she had loved her father more than Margaret could ever know.

And she loved Monk. She would have wanted children to please him, to give him everything love can ever give, but she did not ache for them for herself. Yes, she loved Scuff. Why should she deny that? But for who he was, not to ease an emptiness within herself. Monk alone was sufficient—companion, ally, lover, and friend.

Had she made mistakes, perhaps even profound ones? Yes, of course. But never through indifference.

She stood still, dizzy, the room blurring in her vision, and waited until she was sufficiently composed to return to the courtroom and observe the afternoon's trial.

RATHBONE WAS FIGHTING FOR the defense as Hester had known he must do. He had no choice, legally or emotionally.

He called witnesses who, one by one, painted a picture of the trade Parfitt had run, and its patrons among the rich and dissolute, including, most pointedly, Rupert Cardew.

"Only the rich?" He pressed the witness, an oily, devious-looking man who stood very straight in the witness box, his hands by his sides.

"Course," the man replied. "No point in blackmailin' the poor!"

There was a faint snicker around the gallery, which died immediately.

"And the fashionable?" Rathbone continued. "The socially prominent?"

The witness regarded him witheringly. "In't no need ter pay if yer got no position to lose. If yer nobody, yer tell 'im ter sod off an' sell the pictures to whoever 'e wants."

"Quite," Rathbone agreed succinctly. "Thank you, Mr. Loftus." He turned to Winchester. "Your witness, sir."

Winchester rose to his feet. He moved just as elegantly as before, but Hester noticed the pallor of his face, and that the hand resting at his side was clenched.

"Mr. Loftus, you seem to be very well informed about this whole business. Far more, for example, than I am, even though I have had to learn as much about it as I can, for this trial. How is that, sir?"

"Oh, I know all sorts." Loftus tapped the side of his nose, as if to suggest some extraordinary sensory awareness.

"I accept that you do, sir, but how?" Winchester pressed. He smiled very slightly. "For example, how much are you involved in it yourself?"

Loftus drew in his breath, then caught Winchester's eye and apparently changed his mind. "Well . . . I see things."

" 'See things,' " Winchester repeated dubiously. "What things, Mr. Loftus? Well-dressed men coming from and going to a boat moored on the river, would you say?"

"That's right. Late at night, an' believe me, they in't there ter fish."

There was another titter of laughter around the gallery. A juror raised his hand to hide a smile.

"Late at night?" Winchester said gently. "In the dark, then?"

"O' course," Loftus sneered. "You don't think they're gonna be about when folks can recognize 'em, do yer? Yer in't bin listenin', sir." He exaggerated the "sir" slightly. "They in't there for any good."

"Too dark to be recognized. And yet you know who they were?" Winchester smiled back at him, eyebrows raised inquiringly.

Loftus knew he had been trapped. "All right!" he said angrily. "I 'elped now an' then. On the outside only! I never done nothing to those boys!"

"You helped on the outside," Winchester echoed him. "Out of the goodness of your heart? Or you were paid in kind, perhaps? A few pictures to sell on to others? After you'd had a good look at them yourself? Perhaps to sell back to the miserable wretches in them, caught in acts that would ruin them if their friends knew? Is that how you were so sure that Rupert Cardew was involved?"

Rathbone rose to his feet. "Might we have no more than two questions at a time, my lord? I am going to have trouble working out which answer fits which question."

There was another nervous ripple of laughter around the room.

"I'm sorry," Winchester apologized. "My confusion must be contagious." He looked back at Loftus. "Your reward for this help, sir? What nature did it take?"

"Money!" Loftus said indignantly. "Pure money, like you own, sir."

"You have none of my money, Mr. Loftus," Winchester responded with a smile. "But since you know Mr. Cardew was there, you must surely know the names of others. Who else attended those . . . parties?"

Loftus made a movement across his mouth. "Code o' silence, sir. You understand? All kinds o' gents like their excitement a bit on the spicy side. Ruin 'alf o' London if I were to speak out o' turn, I could."

"Not to mention your own future income, and that of the man behind the business, who will have to find another manager, now that Parfitt is dead. Could that be you, Mr. Loftus?"

Suddenly the courtroom was silent. All the small rustles of movement stopped. One could almost hear the rasp of breathing.

Rathbone rose to his feet. "My lord, Mr. Winchester is assuming facts that no one has proved. He keeps making suggestions as to this gray presence behind Parfitt, but no one has shown that he exists, let alone is going to pay Mr. Loftus for anything."

"My lord, someone sent the letter of instruction to Mickey Parfitt, so that he was alone on his boat the night he was killed," Winchester pointed out. "Someone put forward the money to buy and to furnish the boat. Someone found, watched, and then tempted the men susceptible to this kind of indulgence. Someone blackmailed them and drove at least one to suicide, and it appears, one to murder. And since Mr. Loftus has sworn that Rupert Cardew was a victim of this trade, and other witnesses have told us very graphically of his descent from bystander and gullible friend to witness of degraded and revolting scenes, it cannot have been him. One does not blackmail oneself."

The judge considered for a moment, then lifted one heavy shoulder in a gesture of resignation.

"Mr. Winchester appears to be right, Sir Oliver. You cannot have it both ways with Mr. Cardew. Either he was the blackmailer or he was the victim who struck back."

"My lord," Rathbone bowed. "It seems to me beyond a reasonable doubt that Mickey Parfitt was a vile man who provided a ready path to total degradation, a depravity that must disgust all decent people. He charged his victims for it twice over: once to purchase it, and then a second time to keep themselves from the disgrace of having it known to their friends and to society in general. How he was able to target those vulnerable to such weakness we do not know. Many answers are imaginable. If there was indeed a mastermind behind it, we do not know who that is. Personally, I should like to see him hang, as I dare say so would you. But it is repulsive to me that in our disgust we should vent our anger by hanging the wrong man!"

There were smiles of approval in the gallery. One voice even cried out in agreement.

The judge looked around, but did not reprove him.

Rathbone allowed a moment for them to settle down again. Then he resumed. "We are here to try Arthur Ballinger on the charge of murdering Mickey Parfitt. I put it to you that for all Mr. Winchester's elegance and his masterly exposure of the deeply vile nature of Mickey Parfitt's trade, he has not shown us that Mr. Ballinger had anything to do with it, either as investor or as victim."

He looked specifically at the jury.

"I propose in the next day or so to demonstrate to you the violent and deceitful nature of others involved on the edges of this trade, and how easy it would have been for any of them to have killed Parfitt. I shall show you a score of reasons why they might have, primarily involving greed. As has been amply demonstrated, there is a great deal of money to be made and lost in blackmail. Men's reputations are destroyed, fortunes ruined, and lives ended. Such circumstances breed murder."

Hester did not stay to listen. Rathbone would carefully lay all kinds of suggestions that would make the issue even less certain. He would probably not try to prove specifically that Rupert Cardew was guilty, but it might not be difficult to create at least sufficient belief that it was possible, so no jury would convict Ballinger. Then it would all begin again, perhaps only to end in more doubt.

She walked out into the late afternoon, the noise of the street, the traffic, almost another world. She tried not to think what it would mean for Monk if the trial ended in acquittal. Margaret would not forgive him. What would the River Police think? That he had charged the wrong man, or that he had been right and had failed to produce the evidence? Either way he had lost.

She forced herself to remember that it was being right that mattered, not looking right. She needed to know what had happened to Hattie. If Margaret had taken her to the door and suggested she leave, why had Hattie obeyed her? Where had she gone? To whom? Who had known where to find her, and had killed her to keep her from testifying? What would she have said? That Rupert was innocent? Or that he was guilty?

Now they would never know to whom Hattie had given the cravat, if indeed she had ever actually stolen it. Was it possible that Rupert had killed Parfitt after all? Why did that thought hurt? Simply the pain of disillusion? Or the humiliation of being wrong? Or the wrenching pity for his father?

THE FOLLOWING MORNING HESTER was at the clinic early, again asking questions, ascertaining as closely as possible what time Hattie had left. It was a still, heavy day, with rain threatening as she stood outside the door on the street and looked right and left. People were passing, as always. Which of them would do so every morning? Who had regular errands, trips to the baker or the laundry, jobs to go to?

It was too late for the Reid Brewery workers; they would have started hours ago. Factories or shops had been open for a couple of hours at least. Was there a peddler? None that she could see.

She tightened her shawl around her and walked down to Leather Lane and then turned north. A hundred yards away there was a running patterer telling the news in his singsong voice. She interrupted him, to his displeasure, and asked him if he had seen Hattie, describing her as accurately as possible. He knew nothing.

She retraced her steps and went south, almost as far as High Holborn, but no one had seen a young woman answering Hattie's description.

Discouraged that it was now too many days ago, she went back up to Leather Lane, along Portpool Lane again into the shadow of the brewery and all the way along to Gray's Inn Road at the other end. She walked north and was almost level with St. Bartholomew's Church when she saw a peddler selling sandwiches. She stopped and bought one, not because she was hungry but in order to engage him in conversation. It must have been desperately boring standing all day, virtually alone, just exchanging a word or two with strangers, hoping to sell them something, needing to.

She ate the sandwich with pleasure. It was actually very good, and she told him so.

He smiled, gap-toothed, and thanked her.

"I work just down the road." She indicated with her hand, still clutching the last of the sandwich. "Portpool Lane."

"I know who you are," he replied.

She was surprised. "Do you?" She was half convinced he had mistaken her for someone else.

"Yeah! Yer takes in street women wot are sick, or beat up."

She had no idea from his expression whether he thought that was good or bad. But there was no point in denying it.

"That's right. I'm looking for one now who left Tuesday of last week and is now missing. She's still pretty sick, and I'm worried about her." Hester was not sure how much of the truth she should tell. Panic was rising inside her, and she had to force it down, refuse to follow the fears of what would happen if she failed. Perhaps she was almost as afraid of what knowledge success would bring, things she would not be able to ignore.

"I wouldn't worry about it, love," the sandwich man said kindly. "She'll come back fast enough, if she needs ter."

Hester was momentarily at a loss. She fished out two threepenny pieces. "May I have another sandwich, please? That ham's extremely good." Actually, she did not want it; she had eaten enough.

He gave her one with pleasure, and tuppence change.

"I don't think she knows how ill she is," she improvised. "Some of those things are catching. I think she wasn't alone. She could give it to others." The story was getting wilder as she tried to interest him. "Maybe someone with children. Children get sick so quickly."

He shook his head. "Well, I dunno 'ow yer gonna find 'er. The street is full o' girls."

"This one was unusual-looking. She had very fair hair, almost white, and a lovely skin. She wasn't terribly pretty, but sort of . . . innocent-looking. Very clean, if you know what I mean." She looked at him hopefully.

"Tuesday last week, yer said?"

"Yes. Did you see her? About this time of day, or a little earlier."

"Who did yer say she were with?"

"I don't know. Another woman, maybe . . ."

"Older, eh? Sort o' respectable-lookin'. Bit dumpy. Brown 'air."

"Yes! Yes, that could be right." She had no idea who it could have been, but she had nothing else to follow. "You saw them? Where did they go?"

" 'Ow do I know? Up that way?" He pointed north again, past the church.

"To the church? To St. Bartholomew's?"

He rolled his eyes. "No, sweet 'eart, to the cabbies wot usually wait around there. Best place ter get one."

"Oh." She felt the heat rush up her face. "Yes, of course. What did the other woman look like, did you say? Can you remember? What was she wearing?"

"Wot d'yer think I am? Course I can't remember. It weren't nothing special, I can tell yer that. 'Cept 'er gloves. She 'ad real good gloves on. Leather. 'And-stitched, wi' a little piece o' toolin' on the cuff, about 'ere." He pointed to his wrist. "Must a lifted 'em, or 'ad a customer wi' a lot o' money."

"Can you describe her a bit more? What was her skin like? Her teeth?"

"Wot?"

"Her skin? Her teeth?" Hester repeated.

"'Ow do I know?" the peddler said indignantly. "'Er teeth were just like . . . teeth! Kind o' good, come ter think of it."

Hester felt her heart racing. "Little bit crooked at the front, but nice?"

"Yeah. That's right. Yer know 'er? She one o' yours, then?"

"Perhaps." Was he right, or had she put the idea into his mind and he was simply trying to please her, and get rid of her questions? "Thank you." She finished the sandwich and thanked him again, then walked quickly toward the place he had pointed to for the hansom cabs.

The description he had given fitted one of the women who had been in the courtroom with Margaret and her mother. Or any other woman in London with pretty and slightly crooked teeth, and enough money to buy good gloves. But Margaret's sister was the one who would help her, and her father, by taking Hattie Benson away to—where? Had Margaret's sister known it was to her death, or had she imagined it would be simply a house where Hattie could be kept until it was too late to testify?

It took Hester the rest of the day—and more money than she could really spare in cab fares, sandwiches, cups of tea, and petty bribes—before she found as many of the answers as she was going to so long after the event. Two women, answering the descriptions of Hattie and Gwen, or Celia, had taken a hansom from near St. Bartholomew's to Avonhill Street in Fulham, just short of Chiswick, almost half an hour after Margaret had shown Hattie out of the door of the clinic in Portpool Lane.

Another hour of tedious questions and invented excuses, and by the time it was growing dark, Hester had found the house where Hattie had been for a few hours.

"Yeah," the woman said grudgingly after Hester questioned her. She wiped her wet hands on her skirt. "Wot's it ter you, then? This is a respectable 'ouse, an' there ain't no 'oring goes on 'ere. It were a right lady as brought 'er 'ere an' said as she'd be stayin' fer a few days."

"But she didn't stay for a few days, did she?" Hester pressed. "She was gone in a matter of hours."

"So she changed 'er mind. She still were paid fer, so why should I care?"

"Who did she go with?" Hester felt her throat tight, her hands clammy.

"Said 'is name were Cardew. Didn't see 'is face, but real nice-spoken, 'e were."

Hester thanked her and turned to leave, stumbling against the doorpost but barely feeling the bruise to her hand.

"THAT DOESN'T MAKE SENSE," Monk said gently as they sat in front of the fire late that evening, the clock nearing midnight. Hester was exhausted, and still cold in spite of the warmth of the room. "Why would Margaret help Rupert Cardew in anything?"

"I don't know," she said miserably. "Maybe he lied to her?" She knew as soon as she had said it that it didn't make sense. She looked up and saw it in Monk's eyes. "Maybe Hattie lied, and she didn't steal the cravat at all. Perhaps Rupert paid her to say she did. Then she lost her nerve and wasn't going to go through with it."

"That explains why he would kill her, if he killed Parfitt in the first place," he agreed. "But why would Margaret take her to the door? Wouldn't Margaret want to keep her there, and have her take back her story?"

"Perhaps Hattie was afraid to do that. Maybe she just wanted to escape, and say nothing at all."

Monk nodded slowly. "That's possible. She couldn't face you—or me—so she ran away. As far as defending Ballinger is concerned, her failure to appear comes to much the same result. Her first story would be disbelieved. So Margaret helps her, and then probably her sister Gwen. It sounds more like her than like Celia. Hattie goes to a house where she believes she'll be safe. But Rupert finds her anyway. How?"

"Perhaps she's been there before." Hester buried her head in her hands. "William, what have we done?"

12

Rathbone rode home in a hansom sometime after Margaret had left the courtroom with her mother. It had been another good day. When Winchester had first presented his case, Rathbone had feared that there would be no effective defense. Now he was more than hopeful; he knew there was a real and very considerable likelihood that the jury would have a reasonable doubt as to Ballinger's guilt.

Although, the irony of it was that the picture that emerged of Parfitt was so repellent that the jury would be reluctant to hang the man who had killed him. In fact, Rathbone judged that several of them would want to shake the killer's hand and turn a blind eye to the law.

And there was a level at which this entire trial was not so much about who had killed Parfitt, quickly and more mercifully than he deserved, but about who had staked him, used him, and reaped the lion's share of his profit. Rathbone had seen the anger in Monk's face that drove him to pursue the deeper levels of the affair, and the guilt that his instinct had been too powerful to simply abandon the murder case in the beginning. There must have been moments when he would gladly have marked it "unsolved" and shelved it.

Now Monk was going to fail anyway, because no one would hang for the crime—either the lesser crime of strangling Parfitt or the greater crime of having created his opportunity in the first place, and then fed him with money and skill until he became a monster.

He understood Monk and wished that his failure were avoidable, particularly that Rathbone himself did not have to be such a powerful instrument in bringing it about. But he had no choice. The hansom pulled up outside his house. It was dark, and the streetlamps were shedding yellow light in the misty evening. Branches swayed, the leaves drifting in the wind. The air smelled of earth and rain.

The butler opened the door. Margaret was waiting for him in the withdrawing room. She was standing in the middle of the floor, as if she had heard him come and had risen to her feet. She looked tired. There were signs of strain in her face, and she was definitely pale, but her eyes were bright. As soon as he had closed the door behind him, she came to him quickly, putting her arms around him and kissing him on the cheek, and then the mouth.

Then she pulled away quickly. "We're going to win, aren't we? I can see it in the jurors' faces. They'll acquit him." She closed her eyes. "Thank God for that."

He held her tightly. "We're not there yet, but yes, I think they'll acquit."

She opened her eyes again.

"They have to know that he didn't kill that wretched man, not just that Monk can't prove it."

"It isn't Monk, Margaret. It's—"

"Yes, it is!" she responded vehemently. "Monk is the one who arrested him and brought the charge. I know he doesn't run the prosecution in court because he isn't a lawyer, but he's behind it, and everyone knows that. Don't quibble! You have to have them know it was somebody else, probably Rupert Cardew. They aren't bringing that girl to say she stole his cravat, are they!"

"No, of course not. They can't. She's dead." He watched her face, afraid of what he would see in it.

"I'm sorry to hear that," she said quietly. "But I'm afraid prostitutes come to a bad end quite often. And she lied. I don't know why. Maybe he threatened her. But it doesn't matter now. You have to make sure the jury understands that she was killed, almost certainly by Rupert Cardew. That's a good thing, for the case. Then they'll really know Papa was innocent."

"Do you hear what you are saying, Margaret?" he asked, pushing her a little farther from him, looking into her face. He saw the fear there, tightly controlled, the fierce protection, the urgency. There was no awareness at all that she had said anything to cast a shadow over her integrity.

"That justice will be done, and we'll be safe again," she replied.

Should he argue? Was there any point, or would she only be angry, and then push a further wedge between them? He knew he should not say it, and yet the words slipped out of his mouth: "Don't you care that she's dead, perhaps murdered?"

"Of course I'm sorry! I'm not heartless," she retorted with a touch of anger. "But she had a life that was always going to end badly." She shook her head. "There's nothing we can do about it. We have to fight for complete justice—exoneration for Papa. And then perhaps Monk will put it right by charging Rupert Cardew again. He can, can't he? I mean, there's no double jeopardy or anything like that, because he didn't stand trial. He might even have killed Hattie as well. Then if you can't prove he killed Mickey Parfitt, you could always hang him for killing her."

"You said it as if you would like that," he observed. Why was he provoking a quarrel, pushing her away? All she wanted was for her father to be free from all taint or suggestion of wrongdoing. Was that not natural? Wouldn't he do exactly the same if it were his father? Wouldn't Lord Cardew fight just as hard and as ruthlessly for Rupert, when that time came? Would he ask Rathbone again to defend him? Would Rathbone accept?

Would Monk even be in command of the River Police anymore to pursue it? Or by then would it be some new man?

Hester would not have found this loyalty so cut and dried. She was far more complex, more torn by conflicting passions and convictions. And yet at this moment, at least, she was easier for him to understand. She would weep for Hattie; she would not accept that it had been inevitable; and she would weep for Rupert Cardew, and his father. What about for Monk? He was her own. She would fight for him, blindly, without care for injury, weariness, even temporary defeat, just as Margaret fought for her father. But would Hester be sure that Monk was right? He thought not. It would not lessen her love for him, but she would consider the possibility that he had been mistaken, even that the error had been moral as well as factual.

Was that good, or bad?

Margaret was staring at him, her eyes puzzled and angry. "If he's guilty, then he deserves it," she replied. "I don't like it, but I accept it. Don't you?"

"I don't know. I don't find the difference between right and wrong so simple."

"He murdered Parfitt, and probably Hattie as well, and he was looking to see my father hang for it. What is complicated about that?" There was challenge in her face, a stiffness, nothing anymore that he could reach out and touch.

"Proving it," he said coolly. "But I will go to see your father tomorrow and ask how hard he wishes me to press the issue. He has until Monday morning to decide. As it is now, I think we have a good chance of reasonable doubt. I could call him to testify, and he can swear his innocence, but that will allow Winchester the opportunity to cross-question him. He may prefer not to do that. It is his choice, not yours or mine." He put a finality into his voice, closing the subject from any further discussion. He sounded cold, and he knew it, but he felt cold inside, as if a door had been shut, and he did not know how to open it again.

IN THE MORNING HE went to see Arthur Ballinger in Newgate Prison. He had to wait some little time before at last Ballinger was brought to see him. In the gray light he looked tired, and for the first time Rathbone was acutely aware of how afraid he was. Pity twisted inside Rathbone for Margaret, and he wished he had been gentler with her, but he did not know now how to retrace his steps.

"Oliver!" Ballinger said sharply. "Why are you here? I thought it was going well?"

"It is," Rathbone replied. Why did this man make him feel so uncomfortable? He had spoken to scores of clients in circumstances like these, both the guilty and the innocent. He cleared his throat. "I need to know if you wish to testify yourself or not. You don't need to make up your mind until Monday morning, but you must give it very serious consideration."

"Why wouldn't I?"

"Because it will give Winchester the opportunity to cross-question you, and I can't protect you from anything he says, nor can I foresee what it might be. Don't underestimate him. As it is, I believe we have a very good chance of a verdict of not guilty, because there is more than reasonable doubt."

"Doubt?" Ballinger said unhappily. "Reasonable doubt is the same as saying they believe I am guilty but they can't prove it. I need 'not guilty,' Oliver, with certainty." He took a breath. "I need them to believe that someone else killed that wretched creature."

"They will say 'not guilty,' " Rathbone assured him. "And you cannot be charged again. It is finished."

"In court, perhaps, but not in the public mind. There I am still ruined. For God's sake, man, can't you see that?" Ballinger controlled the panic rising in his voice with obvious difficulty. "Saying that the case was inadequate is not enough." He fixed Rathbone with an intense gaze. "I need them to know that they had the wrong man, Oliver. I need that! There is another man out there that the police should be pursuing. I imagine it is Rupert Cardew. They must go after him as diligently as they did after me. I don't give a damn if his father is a decent man that everyone admires, or how sorry for him they might feel. My family is decent too."

He hesitated for several seconds, and Rathbone was about to speak again when Ballinger seemed to reach some decision, and continued. "And you have no idea what good I've done that I don't boast about, or seek reward for. But that won't stay anyone's hand, or their tongues."

Rathbone looked at him and felt profoundly sorry for him. He was right. The talk, the suspicion, would remain, the belief that somehow he had escaped justice. He would be saved from the punishment of the law, but not of society.

"Are you sure you want to, Arthur?" he said gently. "This case is still very lightly balanced. Emotions are high. Don't ever mistake Winchester for a fool because he occasionally makes people laugh. He will go for your throat if he has the chance."

"Then, I won't give him the chance," Ballinger said bitterly. "Rupert Cardew is a dissolute and violent young man, and he should answer to the law like anyone else. Parfitt was a scab on the backside of humanity, but Hattie Benson was simply an ignorant young woman who made her living in the only way she could imagine. She had little alternative but the match factory, or a sweatshop somewhere. Whoever killed her should hang for it, and I can see that in the jurors' faces, even if you can't."

Rathbone knew that he was right, but he was still afraid of the risk. It seemed brutal to warn Ballinger, but it would be a betrayal of Rathbone's duty not to.

"You would be safer to leave it as it is," he said gently. "I have to tell you that. The risk is considerable."

"What does 'considerable' mean?" Ballinger said sharply.

"The balance is with us now, but not heavily. That could alter. They could hear something, the mood could change on an attitude, an answer they don't understand, a witness saying something . . ."

"I'll take that chance. I will not leave that courtroom with the world believing I am guilty but I escaped because I had a good lawyer."

"There is a chance you could be found guilty." Rathbone said it, and the words all but choked him. "Sometimes it depends on a thing as trivial as a like or dislike. It's skill and chance as well as justice. For heaven's sake, Arthur, you know that!"

"Are you advising me against trying to clear myself?"

Rathbone hesitated. He was not sure. If it were he and he knew himself innocent, the practicality of not seeking more than to escape the noose might not be enough for him. He might believe more deeply than at an intellectual level that truth would prevail. Would he insist on fighting, or would he be cautious, careful, willing to settle for the lesser prize?

Perhaps he would. Monk would not. Hester wouldn't even consider it. She would always fight for the best, the ultimate—win, lose, or draw—he had no doubt of it. But was she wise?

More to the point, would she do that when giving medical treatment to someone unable to make their own decision, lacking the strength or the knowledge and depending upon her? No. He knew the answer without even considering. She would not take the risk with someone else's life.

But she would cut off a gangrened limb rather than let the patient's whole body become infected and die.

"Oliver!" Ballinger said sharply.

"I think you should find another way of clearing yourself. Perhaps do all you can to help Monk, or anyone else, to prove who it was and bring them to trial. It will be slower, but—"

"No," Ballinger said firmly. "I will do it now. I won't subject my family to this horror any longer. And for God's sake, you can't expect me to leave my fate in the hands of William Monk!"

"But—"

"Are you refusing to take my instructions, Oliver?"

"No. I am advising you, but in the end I will do as you wish." He felt like a coward saying it, as if in some oblique way he had betrayed Ballinger, but he had no choice.

They spoke only a little longer, and he left. Outside, a fine rain soaked him thoroughly before he was able to get a hansom, and it perfectly suited his mood.

He was unable to let the matter go. He went straight to Portpool Lane, to the clinic, on the chance that—in spite of the fact that it was Saturday—Hester might be there. He might learn more about exactly what had happened to Hattie Benson. He felt guilty as he walked in through the familiar, shabby entrance. One of the girls who had seen him before greeted him cheerfully.

He was guilty because he wished to see Hester, even if she was abrasive, unsympathetic, or told him things he would prefer not to know. There was something clean, even astringent, about her beliefs. He could not remember a time in all their friendship when she had tried to manipulate him. Heaven knows there had been some uncomfortable times, some quarrels, many differences of opinion. He had thought her outrageous, and he had said so. She had thought him pompous, and had said that too. But they had been honest, not only in word but in intent. Just at the moment, he would welcome that.

He realized, as he spoke to Squeaky Robinson—who lived here and so was always around—that he also felt a different guilt. This one was edged with acute discomfort; he was afraid of what he might learn here.

"Upstairs," Squeaky said, pointing a finger over his shoulder. "Can't leave it alone. Should be at home, that one. But the boy's off with Monk, boating or some such."

"Thank you," Rathbone said quickly, and walked on past him before he could be ensnared in conversation. He went up the stairs two at a time, in spite of their narrowness. He knew every turn and creak, every unevenness, and did not miss his step.

He found Hester making beds in one of the larger rooms, which was unoccupied. She heard the creak of the door as he pushed it wider, and turned to see him, surprise widening her eyes.

"Oliver?" She dropped the sheet, and it fell on the bed in white folds, and he smelled the pleasant cleanliness of fresh cotton. "Is something wrong?" She looked at him more closely. "What is it?"

There was no point in trying to approach it obliquely, with her, of all people. "I need to know more about how Hattie Benson left here, and anything else you can tell me about her."

She studied his face. "Why?"

That was the one response he had not foreseen. "What do you mean, why? She was going to testify. Then she left here and was found later that day floating in the river. She was unquestionably murdered, and almost as certainly by whoever murdered Parfitt. You know all this."

"If I knew who killed her, Oliver, I would say so, whoever it was," she replied. "I have the confidences of no one, and no loyalties other than to pursue the truth. I had a duty to protect her, and I failed. I have no duty to protect whoever killed her. You might have." She did not fill in the rest of the thought; it was unnecessary.

It made him hesitate for a moment. "I . . . I believe the only way I can best serve my client is by knowing as much of the truth as I can," he said slowly. "You may find it hard to believe it was Rupert Cardew who killed her, but if it was—and it is possible—it would not only gain an acquittal for Arthur Ballinger, but it would restore his reputation, without which he is ruined." He hesitated again, seeking a way of saying what he had to more gently. There was none. "And I appreciate that an acquittal for Ballinger means that Monk was wrong, and you cannot separate your emotions from that. I wouldn't ask you to."

"It's loyalties again," she said with a twist of irony in her smile. "Yours is to Ballinger, because he is Margaret's father. Mine is against him, because that would make William wrong. But it's hardly the same depth of importance, is it?" It was not a question so much as a reproof. "Do you think I would see an innocent man hanged rather than have my husband shown up in a mistake? What would that make me? Or him?"

"Nor would I see a guilty man go free because he is my father-in-law," he responded.

"He is your client," she corrected him. "That binds you to give him the best defense you can, unless you actually know that he is guilty. Then you would have a problem with which I could not help you. But you don't know that, or you wouldn't be here asking me about Hattie."

"Don't chop logic with me, Hester," he pleaded. "You don't know who is guilty either, or you would have told Monk and it would be all finished, except for the sentencing."

A sudden, deep compassion filled her face. He did not immediately understand it. Then he realized what his own words had been— "all finished, except for the sentencing," not "except for the trial." Some part of him feared that Ballinger was guilty, and she had seen that.

"I have to know, Hester," he said, his throat dry. "He wants to testify. I need to know what to prepare for. Can't you understand that?"

"Oh." There was a finality in her voice, an intensity of emotion that made him suddenly afraid.

"What is it?" he said. "You know how she went. You would have insisted on finding out. Tell me."

Her face was pale, her eyes terribly, blazingly direct. He knew that whatever the truth was, it was going to hurt one of them. The only question was which one, and how much.

"Margaret took her to the door," Hester said quietly. "There she met another woman, who was well spoken and wore ordinary clothes, at least an ordinary shawl, but had excellent-quality and most unusual leather gloves, hand-tooled with a little design above the wrist."

Rathbone felt as if he had been punched. The shock left him without breath. "It can't be," he said after a moment regaining his voice. "You must be wrong. Who said Margaret took her to the door? Someone is lying."

"It was Margaret herself, Oliver. She doesn't deny it. She was afraid Rupert Cardew had paid Hattie to lie for him, and she wanted to prevent her from doing that."

He shook his head, refusing to believe it. "But Hattie was strangled and put in the river!" He was almost shouting. "You can't imagine that Margaret had any hand in that. It isn't possible."

Hester touched him, just gently, a hand on his arm. He could feel the slight warmth of her through the fabric of his jacket. "Of course I don't think she had any willing or knowing part in it," she agreed. "She took Hattie to the door and persuaded her to leave. Someone else met her there. I would guess it was Gwen, but I can't be certain. That second woman took her to a house in Avonhill Street in Fulham, less than a mile from Chiswick."

"Somewhere she would be safe," he said quickly. "She must have left it herself, and run into one of Parfitt's men. Margaret couldn't know that would happen."

"Of course not," Hester agreed, but there was no light in her face, no relief from the sadness. "And the landlady said a man was with her. He called himself Cardew."

"And you weren't going to tell me?" he said incredulously. "You just said you have no duty of loyalty to anyone, only to the truth." That was definitely an accusation. It was hard to believe Hester, of all people, to be such a hypocrite. And she hadn't had to tell him of her loyalties: she had just proved where they lay by keeping the information about Cardew quiet. He felt more deeply betrayed than he had thought possible. He realized with a jolt of surprise how profoundly he had still cared for Hester, perhaps idealized her. It brought a sting to his eyes and his throat. Too much that he loved was melting under his hand, and slipping away.

"Do you really believe that Margaret and Gwen were working in cooperation with Rupert Cardew to murder the one witness who could have saved him, and thus condemned their father?" she asked.

"No, of course not! They . . ." He stopped.

"Yes? They what?" She waited.

"Perhaps she wasn't going to save him?" he replied. "Maybe Cardew paid her to lie, and she wouldn't go through with it. He realized that, and that's why he killed her."

"With Margaret's help?" Hester's eyebrows rose in disbelief, but there was no triumph in her face. "And Gwen's? Can you imagine what Winchester will make of that idea on the stand?"

She was right. It was unbelievable.

"Did you really want to know that, Oliver?" Her voice broke into his nightmare. "If you did, then I apologize for not telling you. I made a wrong judgment, and I'm sorry. I know that you have to act honestly. I thought it would be impossible for you if you knew that."

He felt dizzy, as though the room were whirling around him. She was right—of course she was right. But he did know now. The terrible thing was that he could believe it. He remembered Margaret's face as she looked at her father. She obeyed him without thought, without judgment. He was part of the life she had always known, the fabric of her beliefs, the order in everything.

That was natural. Perhaps Henry Rathbone was the cornerstone of Rathbone's own life. He could not think of any values, any thought or idea that they had not shared with each other over the years. Their trust was so deep, it had never needed expressing. It was as sure as sunrise; it was the safety that reassured all other doubts, so he never feared an endless fall.

"Oliver?"

He heard her voice, but it was a moment before he could recall himself to the present, the small room in the clinic, the bed with the clean sheet on it, and Hester looking at him.

"What are you going to do?" she asked anxiously.

"I don't know. I really don't know. I suppose you are certain of all this?"

"Yes." Her voice was gentle. "Margaret told me herself, when I faced her with it. She didn't evade it. She didn't say it was Gwen, though. That I deduced by going out and asking people in the streets. I found a peddler who saw Hattie with another woman, and described her. I found the hansom they took to Fulham, right to the house. I took the same cab to the same house, and spoke to the woman who owns it. There might be one chance in a hundred that I'm wrong. It was another woman who looked just like Hattie, at the same time on the same day. And another Mr. Cardew rented the place for her. And our Hattie turned up dead later that day, in the river just a mile away."

"One chance in a hundred?" he said bitterly. "Perhaps in a million."

"I'm sorry."

"Did this landlady see Cardew's face?" It was a desperate last throw. Rathbone knew how he sounded even asking.

"No. He stood well back in the shadows, and he had a heavy coat on, and a hat. He could have been anyone."

He could think of nothing to say, nothing that eased the increasing pain inside him.

"Thank you . . . I . . ."

Hester shook her head. "I know. Winchester won't call me, and you shouldn't. I can't testify to anything firsthand. Do whatever you feel is the right thing."

"The right thing!" The words escaped with a wild bitterness. "For God's sake, what is that?"

"Do you believe Ballinger is guilty?" she asked.

"I don't know. I honestly don't know. I suppose I fear it. It will be a kind of hell if he is." He meant it: he was not exaggerating the horror he saw in his own imagination.

She looked at him steadily. "Would you have Rupert Cardew hanged to save him, because he is your family and Rupert isn't? If you would, Oliver, then what is the law worth? What if Lord Cardew felt the same way, and would have anyone else hanged, guilty or innocent, as long as his own son didn't have to face himself and his deeds? Would you accept that? Is that really what you believe—one law for your family, another for anyone else?"

"What about loyalty, what about love?" he asked.

"What have you left to give, if you have already given away yourself?"

"Hester . . ."

"I'm sorry. I don't always like it, but I can't believe anything different. It doesn't mean you stop loving. If you could care only for those who are good all the time, we would none of us be loved. I'm sorry."

He nodded. Then he touched her hand briefly and turned to go.

HE REACHED HOME AT lunchtime; Margaret was waiting for him.

"Where have you been?" she asked, her voice sharp-edged. "You didn't say you were going out."

"I left before you were up." He found himself defensive. "I went to see your father. He wants to take the stand. I think he shouldn't, but I couldn't persuade him."

"Why shouldn't he take the stand?" she demanded. She was wearing pale blue, her hair pulled back a little severely, and she looked angry. "He must defend himself. The jury has to hear him deny all the charges and explain that he is a solicitor. He acts on behalf of all sorts of people. Even men like Parfitt are entitled to legal advice, and to a defense, if they are wrongly accused."

"They are entitled to it even if they are rightly accused," he pointed out.

"Don't quibble!" she snapped. "Why don't you wish him to testify? You haven't explained that to the jury—I don't know why not."

"Because I don't want to say it more than once," he replied tartly. "It sounds like an excuse if I push it too hard, like protesting too much. I am keeping it for my final address to them."

"Well, Papa should still testify. He'll look guilty if he doesn't. You've said that often to me. It seems to them like running away. If they hear him, see him, they'll know what kind of a man he is, and that the whole charge is ridiculous. It's Monk trying to make a name for himself. He probably knows he's wrong by now, but he daren't back out of it or he'll look a fool."

Rathbone felt as if a nightmare were tightening its coils around him. "Margaret, did you go to Hattie Benson in the clinic, take her to the street door, and persuade her to leave?"

There were two spots of color in Margaret's face. She lifted her chin a little higher. "She was going to lie about Rupert Cardew, and Hester would have seen that she went through with it. If you think I could allow my father to be hanged for something he didn't do, then you have no idea of either love or loyalty."

"Love doesn't mean betraying what you believe in, Margaret, and no one who truly loved you would ask it," he replied, his voice trembling.

She closed her eyes. "You pompous fool!" she said between her teeth. "Love means caring, passionately. It means sacrificing yourself for another person because they are more important to you than your career or your ambition, or the way other people admire you, or your money, or even your own life!" Her voice was shaking. "But you wouldn't understand that. You like, you want, perhaps at times you can need, but you don't love! You're a cold, pious, self-righteous man. You don't want a wife; you want someone to hold on your arm at parties, and organize your household for you."

Rathbone felt as if she had struck him. He tried to think clearly, find the reason, the balance, but all that filled his mind was crippling emotion. Hester's words rang in his ears, but he knew even trying to repeat them to Margaret would be useless. And they would sound like Hester, which would make matters even worse.

He should leave, now before he said something that he could never take back.

But as he stood on the outside step again, he was at a loss to know of anything that could have made it worse.

HE TOOK A HANSOM and rode in it all the way to Primrose Hill, not even considering the possibility that his father might be out. Only as the cab set him down on the pavement and he fished in his pocket for the money to pay the driver did he think of it. It was a mild Saturday afternoon. Why should Henry Rathbone be at home when there were a hundred other things to do, friends to visit?

"Wait a moment," he told the cabby. "He may be out. I'll be right back to tell you." He turned and strode up the path, now in a hurry as if every second counted. He banged on the door, and thirty seconds later banged again.

There was no answer. His heart sank with a ridiculous, overwhelming disappointment. He was angry with himself for behaving like a child. He stepped back, and the door opened. Henry Rathbone looked grubby and disheveled, a gardening fork in his hand. He was taller than Oliver, lean and just a trifle stooped. His gray hair was sparse and windblown, his blue eyes mild.

"You look terrible," he observed, looking Oliver up and down. "You'd better come in. But pay the cabby first."

Oliver had already forgotten the cab. He strode back, paid the man, and thanked him, then went back to the door and into the house.

"Where's whatshisname?" he asked. He could never remember his father's manservant's name.

"Saturday afternoon," Henry Rathbone replied. "Poor man has to have some time to himself. He's got a grandson somewhere. Go and put the kettle on the cooktop while I wash my hands and put my tools away. Then you can tell me what's happened. I presume it is something to do with your father-in-law's case? Quarter of London is talking about it." He rarely exaggerated.

Oliver obeyed. Ten minutes later, they were sitting in the large, old armchairs on either side of the fire in the familiar sitting room with its watercolors on the wall and its shelves upon shelves of books.

The tea was poured, but still too hot to drink, although its steamy fragrance filled the air. There were also several slices of fruitcake on a plate. It was rich and inviting, even if Oliver had thought he might never feel hungry again.

"What is your dilemma?" Henry asked.

"I don't know that I have one," Oliver replied. "I can see only one acceptable choice, but I hate it. I suppose . . ." He stopped, uncertain what it was he wanted to say.

Henry took one of the slices of cake and began to eat it, waiting.

Oliver started to sip his tea, trying not to scald himself.

Several minutes passed in silence, comfortable but still needing to be filled with words to frame the burden.

"You are required to do something repugnant to you," Henry said at last. "If you are certain Ballinger is innocent, then probably you need to show some evidence that someone else is guilty. Rupert Cardew? Is it Lord Cardew you are so loath to see suffer?"

"I can't do that," Oliver replied. "The evidence is flawed, very badly flawed. Winchester would demolish it, and leave Ballinger looking even worse."

"And you are afraid that Ballinger is guilty? If not of killing Parfitt, then at least of something, presumably of financing this boat—or worse, of using Parfitt for the blackmail?"

There it was: simple and astonishingly painful, the truth, in his father's mild, exact voice. Oliver had no need to answer—it must have been clear in his face. Nevertheless he did so. They had always been frank with each other. His father had never asked for trust, or said how much he cared—at least not that Oliver could remember— but it would have been totally unnecessary, even absurd, a stating of something as obvious as breathing.

"Yes. Worse than that. I'm afraid that Hester is right and he killed the girl who would have testified that she stole Rupert Cardew's cravat and gave it to one of the men who worked for Parfitt, or even to Ballinger himself."

Henry straightened up a little in his chair, his face even graver.

"You haven't told me about this. I think perhaps you had better do so now."

Quietly, with simple words, Oliver told him all he knew, including his conversation with Hester that morning. His quarrel with Margaret was still too painful, and he brushed over it, more by implication
than detail.

"I see," Henry said at last. "I'm afraid you are in for a great deal of
distress. I wish I could remove it for you, but I can't. There is no honorable way except forward, and eventually anything else would hurt
even more. I'm sorry." The pain in his face, the sharp note of helplessness in his voice, made further expression redundant.

It was growing late, and outside the light was failing. At this time
of the year, sunset came early, and the long twilight slowly drained
the color from the land. The wind was gusty and warm, sending the
yellow leaves flying.

Henry stood up. "Let's walk a little," he suggested. "There are still
some good apples left on the trees. I really should have picked them
by now."

Oliver followed him, and they went out of the French doors onto
the grass and down the garden. The hedge was full of bright berries,
scarlet hips from the dog roses, darker bloodred haws from the may
blossom. There was a rich, sweet smell of rotting leaves and damp
earth, and the sharper tingling aroma of wood smoke. A few purple
asters were in bloom, shaggy and vivid, and the tawny bronze and
gold chrysanthemums.

Beyond the poplars in the distance, a cloud of starlings swirled up
into the darkening sky, making for home.

The scene was all so familiar, so deep in his heart and mind, that
it was woven through every memory and dream he could imagine. It
would be absurd—embarrassing, even—to say so, but his love for his
father was so intense he could not bear to think of life without his
friendship. Would he place his father's safety, his happiness before
Margaret's? He did not really have to ask himself; he knew the answer
before the question formed. Yes, he would. To betray him would be
unbearable.

But at the same moment he also knew that Henry Rathbone
would never do the things that Arthur Ballinger had. He made mistakes, had flaws in his character; of course he did, everyone did. Oli-

ver did not wish to think of them, but he knew they were there. He could have named them, if forced to.

But he also knew that Henry would never have asked someone else to pay the price, or take the blame for him.

Perhaps Margaret believed the same of Ballinger? Were her memories just as deep, as woven into her own life, her beliefs? Was he being unfair to her?

But his withdrawal from her had nothing to do with ambition, or even with love. It had to do with Rathbone's own identity. She was asking him to destroy himself, but if he did that, there would be nothing left for either of them. What she was asking of him was not a case of personal sacrifice; that might have been a more difficult decision. It was an issue of doing something he believed—no, something he knew—to be wrong.

He looked up at the sky as the starlings wheeled back again into the wind, still flying as if to some understood pattern, all going home to roost for the night.

Henry seemed to know he had reached a conclusion. He did not raise the subject again. They turned and walked together back through the apple trees toward the house.

At home Rathbone and Margaret passed the weekend in bitter silence. The politeness between them was like walking on broken glass.

At dawn on Monday morning, Rathbone went again to see Arthur Ballinger to try to persuade him not to testify. As it was, he had a good chance of acquittal. He could prove his actual innocence later, if someone else were charged.

But Ballinger was obdurate. He would not leave the courtroom with this accusation still hanging over his existence, crippling his life, shadowing and tainting the lives of his family. Even the possibility of a guilty verdict did not deter him. He simply did not believe it could happen.

Was that supreme hubris, or was he actually innocent and Rathbone had badly misjudged him? He entered the courtroom still uncertain.

As soon as he called Ballinger to the stand, there was a rustle of excitement, a movement, a stiffening of attention.

Ballinger mounted the witness stand. He looked pale but composed, as grave as an accused man should, and with appropriate humility. He was clearly taking all the advice that Rathbone had given him. He looked the model of a good man unjustly afflicted by circumstance.

Nevertheless, Rathbone was as nervous as if he were on trial himself. His mouth was dry and his muscles ached with the built-up tension of going over and over every possibility in his mind. He was afraid his voice was going to betray him by cracking. He did not even glance at Margaret, who was sitting with her mother and sisters in the gallery. He could not bear to see the coldness in her face, nor to wonder where their lives were going after this, whatever the outcome.

He dared not fail.

Ballinger was sworn in and faced Rathbone expectantly.

"Mr. Ballinger," Rathbone began. He cleared his throat. He was unaccustomed to being so nervous. "Did you know Mickey Parfitt?"

"I met him once, several years ago, very briefly," Ballinger replied. "I don't remember him. I know only because of the transaction concerned."

"Indeed. And what was that, Mr. Ballinger?" Rathbone knew that he had to draw this out now, because it was a matter of record, and if he did not, then Winchester would make more of it.

"It was the sale to Mr. Parfitt of a boat, by a client I represented," Ballinger replied levelly.

"Was this boat the same one we have heard about, used for pornographic performances and the imprisonment of children?" Rathbone kept all expression from his face.

"I don't know. I only advised my client in the sale of the boat."

"And was this client whom you represented Mr. Jericho Phillips, the same Jericho Phillips you later represented when he was tried for murder earlier this year?"

There was a rustle of movement, a sigh of indrawn breath around the gallery.

The jury sat motionless, faces pale.

"It was," Ballinger answered quietly. "I believe that every man is entitled to the protection of the law, and a fair and just trial."

"So do we all, Mr. Ballinger." Rathbone nodded gravely. "That is why we are here."

Neither of them even glanced at the jury. They could have been alone in Rathbone's office.

"Have you ever visited this boat, Mr. Ballinger?" he continued.

"Once, at the time of its sale. It looked a very ordinary sort of craft. I was merely assuring myself that it was described correctly in the papers concerning it, which it was."

"Did you ask Mr. Parfitt how he intended to use it?"

"No. It was none of my business." A slight flicker crossed Ballinger's face. "But if indeed he used it as has been described, it is hardly likely that he would have told me."

"Quite." Rathbone allowed himself the ghost of a smile. "Were you, to your knowledge, acquainted with any of the men who frequented either boat, after they were turned to the use of pornography?"

"Certainly not. But of course men who practice this kind of behavior do not tell people, other than those who share their vices. From what I have heard during this trial, it seems they indulge in them together. Therefore, they would know each other."

"Quite." Rathbone found that the fullness of Ballinger's answer made him uneasy. He had advised Ballinger to be extremely careful, to say only yes and no, but Ballinger was either too nervous to obey or too sure of himself to heed advice. Rathbone should leave that subject.

"Mr. Ballinger, where were you on the evening that Mickey Parfitt was killed?"

Ballinger carefully repeated the exact story he had told before, and which had been borne out by the witnesses.

Rathbone smiled. "Inspector Monk has testified that he followed your route, to the minute, and discovered that he could find a small craft and row down to Parfitt's boat at its moorings, spend the time on board that it would take to kill Parfitt, and then row back to Mortlake again. He took a cab back to the crossing opposite Chiswick Eyot, and still was there at the time you said you were. Did you do that?"

Ballinger smiled back. "Mr. Monk is the best part of a generation younger than I am, and leads a very physical life. He is a river policeman. He probably rows a boat every day. I wish I were as young and as fit as he is, but, unquestionably, I am afraid I am not. I did not do it, nor had any desire to. But even had I wished, it would have been beyond my ability."

"You did not?"

"I did not. It is my misfortune that I happened to spend that particular evening visiting an old friend in Mortlake, instead of at home with my wife, or out to dine in a public place. It is my additional misfortune that Inspector Monk has never forgiven me for acting for Jericho Phillips, insofar as I obtained your services to defend him when he faced trial. Monk appears not to believe that a man accused of evil acts is not guilty until he is proved so in law, and he is entitled to a lawyer to defend him of as high a quality as the one who accuses him. It is the very foundation of justice."

There was a murmur of approval from the gallery. Ballinger eased a little where he stood in the witness box, and met Rathbone's eyes across the distance between them.

Rathbone felt a sense of warmth himself, as if he had achieved what duty required of him.

"Thank you, Mr. Ballinger. Please wait there in case Mr. Winchester has any questions to ask you." He returned to his seat.

Winchester stood up and walked forward. "Oh, I have. I most certainly have." He looked up at Ballinger.

Rathbone had been very careful. Hattie Benson's name had not even been mentioned. Winchester was bluffing, putting off the acknowledgment of defeat, lengthening out the tension.

"A most moving testimony, Mr. Ballinger," Winchester observed. "And interesting. I notice that Sir Oliver very wisely did not ask you if you were acquainted with the prostitute Hattie Benson, who was so sadly murdered in the exact manner that Mickey Parfitt was. Even to the use of the knotted rag to strangle her, leaving bruises at intervals around her throat."

"Because he knows that I have no knowledge of it," Ballinger replied levelly. "I may speculate, of course, as we all may, because we know with whom she was involved, by his own admission."

"Ah, yes." Winchester nodded. "Mr. Rupert Cardew. But of course since she is dead, her testimony remains unspoken."

"It might have remained unspoken even if she were alive," Ballinger pointed out. "It is possible she repented of it, and told him that she could not go through with it."

Rathbone's sense of ease was slipping away from him. He rose to his feet. "My lord, this is a piece of speculation that has no place here. We cannot know what Miss Benson would have said, nor can we question her to prove its truth, or otherwise. If my learned friend has something to ask Mr. Ballinger, please instruct him to do so. Otherwise, he is wasting the court's time."

The judge leaned forward, but before he could speak, Winchester apologized.

"I'm sorry, my lord. I shall proceed. Mr. Ballinger, you said that you had no direct knowledge of the trade that was carried on by Mr. Parfitt in the boat you helped him purchase?"

"That's right. None at all," Ballinger replied coolly.

"And to the best of your knowledge, you were not acquainted with any of the men who patronized it and indulged in these acts, and, as a result, were blackmailed?"

Rathbone stood up again. "My lord, Mr. Winchester is merely repeating evidence we have already been through."

The judge sighed. "Mr. Winchester, is there some point to all of this?"

"Yes, my lord. I intend to call Mr. Ballinger's honesty into very grave doubt—in particular, with regard to this last issue."

"To what purpose?" Rathbone demanded. "He has said that he does not know any of these men, as far as he is aware. None of us knows what weaknesses or vices people may have, and thank God, for the most part, it is none of our business. They may be men you know! Or any of us knows." He spread his arms in a wide gesture, to include the whole room, the jurors, the gallery, even the judge. "And since the court does not know who they are, this is futile."

"Sir Oliver is right," the judge agreed. "Move on, Mr. Winchester, if you have anything else upon which to cross-examine Mr. Ballinger. Otherwise, let us put the matter to the jury."

"But we do know who these men are, my lord," Winchester said clearly. "At least I do."

Suddenly there was total silence in the room. No one stirred. No one even coughed.

"I beg your pardon?" the judge said at last.

"I know who they are," Winchester repeated.

Rathbone felt the sweat break out on his skin and a prickle of fear sharp inside him, although he did not even know why. He stared at Winchester.

"Were you aware of this, Sir Oliver?" the judge asked.

"No, my lord. I would question its veracity, and why Mr. Winchester has not referred to it before."

"I came by it only this weekend, my lord," Winchester replied to the judge.

"From whom?" the judge demanded.

Rathbone knew the answer the moment before it was spoken.

"From Mr. Rupert Cardew, my lord," Winchester said. "In the interests of justice, he provided it—"

Rathbone lurched to his feet. "How can that possibly be in the interests of justice?" he demanded. "It has nothing to do with the case, except possibly to prove that there were a large number of men who may well have had motive to wish Parfitt dead. And who is to say that this list is accurate? It could be the complete fabrication of a man who has an intense interest in seeing Mr. Ballinger convicted, in order to remove all suspicion from himself!"

"He will testify to the names, if necessary," Winchester replied. "And with diligence, it should be possible to prove that all of them have visited the boat, at some time or other, most of them fairly regularly."

"A long and tedious job," Rathbone rejoined. "And irrelevant to this case, my lord!"

"Not irrelevant, my lord," Winchester said. "I mention it to throw extreme doubt on Mr. Ballinger's innocence in this matter. Sir Oliver paved the way for me in his own examination by asking the witness about his knowledge of the boat, and Mr. Ballinger replied that he did not know its business, nor was he aware of knowing any of the men who patronized it. I have the list of names, my lord. I regret to say that I myself am acquainted with two of them—"

The judge was rapidly losing patience. "Mr. Winchester, you appear to be behaving in the worst possible taste, titillating the most vulgar aspect of public curiosity, in a matter that is repellent and does not further your case in the least."

"My lord, every one of the men on this list is personally acquainted with Mr. Ballinger! Every one of them, without exception. Why would he lie about it to this court, under oath, if it were not something he wished to—indeed, needed to—conceal?"

There was a gasp, a rustle of movement right around the room, then a terrible stillness.

Rathbone felt his muscles clench like a vise. He would like to have believed that it was Rupert Cardew making a desperate move to save himself from the suspicion that would inevitably follow Ballinger's acquittal. He turned and looked at the gallery, and saw Rupert immediately, ashen-faced and perfectly steady. This would ruin him. Society would never forgive him for betraying the names of those who had soiled the honor most of them aspired to but had not the courage to defend.

Winchester broke the silence. "I will call Mr. Cardew to the stand to name them. Should anyone doubt him, Sir Oliver can, naturally, question him on the issue, and require him to prove what he says. But I shall not do it unless your lordship insists. This knowledge would ruin many families, and call into question legal decisions, possibly even Acts of Parliament. The possibilities for blackmail are so momentous that the damage would affect . . ." He stopped, leaving their imaginations to fill in the rest.

"Sir Oliver?" the judge said a little huskily.

It was defeat, and Rathbone knew it. He would not bring down the whole order of society to save Ballinger, even would such a thing have done so. And it would not. He could see in the jury's faces that the balance had tipped irrevocably against him. They knew Ballinger had lied, possibly about everything. And strangely enough, even if Rupert had turned on his own social class, for which he would never be forgiven, the jury believed him, possibly even admired him. He had chosen the honorable thing to do, at a terrible price to himself.

"I . . . I have nothing to add, my lord," Rathbone answered. Only as he sat down again did he even consider that perhaps he should have demanded that the names be made public. Then in the instant afterward, he knew he should not. Winchester had them. If there was anything to be done, he would do it. He would investigate, examine, and if necessary prosecute any corruption. It did not occur to Rathbone, even as a fleeting thought, that Winchester was bluffing. Cardew's face and Ballinger's denied that.

He made a desperate final summation, but he knew he could not succeed. The tide was against him, and he had no more strength to turn it.

The jury was out for an hour, which seemed like eternity. When they came back, their faces told the verdict even before they were asked.

"Guilty." Simple. Final.

Rathbone was in a daze as the black cap was brought to the judge. He put it on his head and pronounced sentence of death.

Mrs. Ballinger cried out in horror.

Margaret slipped to the ground in a faint.

Without thinking, Rathbone scrambled from his seat and went to her just as she was stirring. Gwen was with her, holding her. Celia and George were trying to support Mrs. Ballinger.

"Margaret! Margaret," Rathbone said urgently. "Margaret?" He wanted to say something, anything to comfort her, but there were only empty promises, things that were meaningless.

She stirred and opened her eyes, looking at him with utter loathing. Then she turned her face away toward Gwen.

He had never felt so completely alone. He rose to his feet, trembling, and walked back to his table. The court was in an uproar, but he neither saw nor heard it.

13

WHEN A PERSON WAS sentenced to hang, it was the law that three Sundays should pass before the execution was carried out. It was both the longest and the shortest period of time in the sentenced person's experience. Unquestionably it was the most painful.

Toward the end of the first week, Rathbone was alone in his room in chambers when his clerk entered and told him that Hester wished to speak with him.

At first Rathbone was not sure if he wanted to see her. Pity would only add to his hurt, especially from her, and there was nothing she could say that would help. There was no help. And yet he had never had a better friend, except for his father.

"I have a few minutes," he told the clerk. "Come back after about ten minutes and say there is a client wishing to speak with me."

"Yes, sir." The clerk withdrew, and a moment later Hester came in. She looked calm and composed, but still very pale. She was dressed in the same blue-gray she often wore, and it still suited her just as well.

Rathbone stood up. "What can I do for you?" he asked quietly.

She sat down in the chair opposite the desk, as if she meant to remain.

He sat also; not to would have been discourteous.

"Probably nothing," she said with a tiny smile. "I wanted to know if there was anything I could do to help you. William told me there was nothing, and that you might even prefer not to see me. I would understand that. But I would rather come and be asked to leave than not come and then afterward learn that there was something I could have done, or said."

"How like you," he replied. "Always do, never hesitate, and never abdicate."

A shadow crossed her face, a moment of hurt.

"That was a compliment," he said wryly. "I have spent too much of my life weighing and judging, and in the end doing nothing."

"Not this time," she answered. "There was nothing more you could have done. If Rupert hadn't come forward, you would have won. I'm not sure that would have been a good thing, even for Margaret, not in the end."

"It would have been a bad thing for Monk," he said frankly. "Everyone would have said he had made a second mistake, gone after the wrong man because he had a personal vendetta against Ballinger over the Phillips affair. He might even have lost his job. I'm glad that didn't happen." Surprisingly, he meant that. He had not thought he would; the void inside himself was too big to allow much thought for anyone else.

Hester gave a slight shrug. "That's true, and I thank you for it. But it's past now. What about you?"

"I doubt I'll lose any clients over it. No one wins every case."

"For heaven's sake, I know that!" she said impulsively. "Most people know perfectly well you only took the case because he was family and you had no choice! No one else would have managed a defense at all. And you nearly won."

He looked at her steadily. "Did Monk persuade Rupert Cardew to speak?"

"No." She did not evade his gaze. "I did. Not for William—at least, not only for him. It was for Scuff, and all the boys like him."

"That won't put an end to the trade, Hester." The moment the words were out of his mouth, he regretted saying them.

"I know," she conceded softly. "But it will stop some of it. Maybe quite a lot, at least for a while. People will know that we're prepared to fight, and those who get caught will pay for it. Above all, Scuff will know."

For a moment he could not speak, his throat was so tight, so choked and aching.

She put out her hand across the desk. She did not touch him, but she left it where, if he moved even a few inches, he could reach her.

"I'm sorry, Oliver. I really am sorry."

"I know."

She said nothing more for several moments.

There was a knock on the door.

"Come!" Rathbone answered.

The clerk came in. "Sir Oliver—"

"Ah, yes," Rathbone said quickly. "Please bring some tea, and a few cookies, if you can find some."

"Yes, sir." The clerk withdrew obediently, his face calm with understanding, perhaps even a touch of relief.

Hester smiled. "Thank you. I'd like tea."

He had asked for tea without thinking, but now he realized how much he wanted her to stay. He did not know how to begin, but the confusion inside him was an almost overwhelming pain. In a matter of months all the certainties he had begun to take for granted had gone.

"How is Margaret?" she said quietly. "I thought of going to see her, even though I have no idea what to say. Sometimes just being there is worth something. But I don't think she would receive me. We . . . parted on bad terms."

"She wouldn't," he agreed. "She blames you, at least in part. She blames everyone except her father. Most of all she blames me." He knew there was bitterness in his voice, but he could not control it. His anger and pain came welling up, and it was a relief to let it flow. "She is convinced Ballinger is innocent and that it's all a monstrous conspiracy of vengeance, cowardice, misplaced loyalty, and error. And on my part, professional ambition over love of family." He needed Hester to deny it, to tell him he was right and that it was not true.

She looked stricken. "I'm sorry." Her voice was so low, he could barely hear her.

"There was nothing else I could do!" he protested.

"I know that," she answered quickly. "But disillusion is one of the worst pains we experience. Nobody can let go of their dreams without tearing themselves apart too. It's like killing pieces of yourself. She'd blame everybody who sees what she can't bear to see, because we won't let her pretend anymore. Whether we mean to or not, we are the ones forcing reality on her."

"What good would it do if I were to lie to her?" he protested. "Any hope now would be false."

"Hope of what?" she asked. "That he is innocent, or of saving him from the gallows?"

He shrugged helplessly. "I don't know. Of saving him, I suppose. I don't think she has even faced the possibility that he is guilty of any of it. Not of Parfitt's murder, certainly not of Hattie's, and not of blackmailing the wretched men who used the boat. If she believed any of it, I imagine the rest would have to follow. I don't know what to do, even what to say. She's treating me as if it were my fault."

Hester shook her head fractionally. "That's because you're the only one who isn't to blame. And you're the one who won't support her illusions."

"I can't!" he said desperately. "Lying is no good now. It won't stop it from happening. It doesn't affect the truth, or that everyone else can see it. Sooner or later she's going to have to face the fact that her father's guilty—not just of corrupting other people, finding and feeding on their weaknesses, but of blackmailing them for exactly what he has helped them to do. He profited from the torture and humiliation of children, and he murdered Parfitt. I still don't know why. That seems to have been a pointless piece of violence, and completely un-necessary. And he murdered Hattie Benson because she would have testified that it wasn't Rupert Cardew, the only other obvious sus-pect."

He took a shaky breath, and went on. "If Margaret doesn't even acknowledge that, then she's going to spend her whole life angry, and bitter because her father was unjustly hanged. That's a kind of terrible madness. It will destroy her."

Hester put out her hand and touched him very gently. "Give her time, Oliver. Some things we can't face immediately. As long as he protests his innocence she can't turn her back on him, whatever the evidence. Could you, if it were your father?"

"My father would . . ." He stopped. What he had been going to say only supported Hester's point. His father would never do such a thing? No, he wouldn't. But, then, perhaps Margaret believed just as passionately in her father, regardless of evidence. Hester was right; she would not be released from it until Ballinger admitted his guilt. Perhaps she couldn't be, without betraying herself, and the guilt for that would destroy her also.

How terribly wide the damage spread.

Hester smiled. "I know. I love your father, and I don't believe he would ever even think of anything like this. But, then, Margaret would feel the same. Sometimes we only know one side of a person we love so intensely."

He could think of nothing to say.

"Parents especially are part of who we are," she went on. She looked down, away from meeting his eyes. "I still can't tell myself that my father failed because he took his own life. I wonder if I fight so hard over the things I believe in, to prove I'm not like that. I don't give in." She looked up again, and her eyes were full of tears. "I iden-tify with the soldiers I nursed in the Crimea, and delude myself I'm like them, because I saw how they suffered and I loved their courage so much."

Rathbone realized that he too was suffering a disillusion, not in Ballinger, because he had never cared for him, but in Margaret her-self. Perhaps he had expected her to be more like Hester—more able to face the unbearable, more foolishly, passionately brave. And yet it was those very qualities in Hester that had frightened him, and had made her such an unsuitable wife for him. He had wanted Hester's virtues, but without the danger. He loved Margaret, but not with the reckless fervor that counts no risk and no price too high.

Was he disillusioned in her, or in himself?

"She wants me to mount an appeal," he said, remembering the scene vividly, although it had been a couple of days ago.

They had been standing in the withdrawing room, the dusk heavy outside, the gas lamps burning but the curtains still open onto the garden. She was dressed in dark gray, as if ready for mourning, and her face was colorless. She was so angry she trembled.

"Are you?" Hester asked, interrupting his thoughts. "Do you have any grounds? Did Winchester make some mistake?"

"No," he said simply.

She swallowed and cleared her throat. "Did you?"

"Not so far as I know. Tactical, perhaps. Maybe if I had tried harder, I could have persuaded him not to take the stand himself, but he was adamant. I don't think you can refuse to let a man speak in his own defense, if you have warned him of the danger and he still insists. But perhaps I should have thought of something."

"You can't go on retrying a case every different way until you get the verdict you want," she pointed out.

He looked down at the desktop. He knew he shouldn't say what he was going to, and yet the words spilled out.

"Margaret says I should have built in some error, so that I could have appealed afterward. She believes I have put my own career before her father's life, because I am ambitious and essentially selfish." He met her eyes. "Is that true? If I really loved her, more than I loved myself, would I have?"

"Have you ever made a deliberate mistake?" she asked, as if turning the thought over in her mind.

"No." He smiled bitterly. "Not deliberate. Many accidental. Would an appeal court know the difference?"

"Possibly," she granted. "But unless you were totally incompetent, it wouldn't make them grant a new trial, would it? Anyway, what good would a new trial do? They'd only come to the same decision, except that someone else would be representing Ballinger, probably less well, and certainly with less dedication. It isn't reasonable, Oliver. Don't try arguing with her. You won't win, because she isn't listening. She is terrified. Everything she is and believes is slipping out of her grasp."

"I'm still here," he said simply. "She just doesn't want me. I've done everything I can to save Ballinger. I failed. But I think I failed because he's guilty."

"She'll realize that in time."

He knew in that moment, with an overwhelming grief, that he was not sure he would ever see Margaret with the same tenderness and trust, even if eventually she did accept the truth.

"She has made it a condition," he said aloud.

"A condition? For what?" Hester looked puzzled.

"If I do not manage to appeal for her father, Margaret will leave me, go back to comfort and care for her mother." Now that he'd said it, it was real, not just a nightmare hovering around him like a covering darkness. And yet the house was unbearable. They walked around each other, icily polite. He came to bed late. She was either asleep or pretending to be. He did not speak. It was over a week since they had touched each other, even in the smallest gesture. It was infinitely worse than being alone.

Hester was looking at him, her face a little pinched with anxiety. "And if you could manage to think of some way of bringing about an appeal, which you would still lose, because the evidence is the same, then she would forgive you?" she asked.

He started to answer, and then realized that he did not know.

"She is grieving, Oliver." Hester answered her own question. "She is in too much pain and confusion to listen to reason. She wants a way out of the truth. At least part of her knows she will have to accept it one day, but now she can't face it. She wants you to rescue her from it, and she blames you because you can't."

"She's not a child!" he said with a flare of his own confusion and loss. "The truth of it is that she has to choose between her father and me, and she chooses him, guilty or not." Saying it was like cutting his own flesh. "You wouldn't have done that. You would always choose Monk."

"I don't know what I would choose," she said honestly. "I haven't had to. There's part of all of us that chooses the most vulnerable, the one who needs us most, because we can't live with the guilt of turning our backs on them."

"Are you thinking of Scuff?"

"I don't think so. He would never expect me to sacrifice anything for him. I'm not sure he would even understand the idea, although he would do it himself, without thinking."

"That's what Margaret wants from me, loyalty without thinking."

"If you love someone, you do not ask them to destroy the best in themselves," she answered. "Love also means the freedom to follow your own conscience. If you can't be true to yourself, you don't have much left to give anyone else." Again she touched his arm through the cloth of his jacket. "Don't give in to temptation because it would be more comfortable for you, in the short term. She needs you to be the best in yourself. In time she will be glad of it."

"Do you think so?" Rathbone was asking for the answer he wanted to hear.

"I hope so," was all she could say.

He looked at her steadily, thinking that she possessed a kind of beauty he had not really appreciated before. Her face was too angular, but there was an intense gentleness in it he saw only now. She was awkward at times, too quick; far too clever; her honesty was sometimes painful to receive; but there was a generosity of spirit he needed; and always, always there was courage.

She blushed very slightly and stood up.

"Give her time," she said again. "And perhaps it would be better not to tell her I called." She hesitated, then decided not to add any more.

She passed close to him on her way out, but only smiled briefly as she reached the door. "Thank you for the tea." And she was gone, and the silence washed in again, surrounding him with loneliness.

THE FOLLOWING MORNING THE message came from Newgate
Prison that Arthur Ballinger wanted to see him, urgently. Rathbone
had no choice but to go. He was duty-bound as Ballinger's lawyer,
apart from the fact that Ballinger was Margaret's father, and a man
condemned in a matter of days to be hanged. Less than two weeks
were left. Rathbone could not even imagine how that would feel.

He dreaded finding the previously bluff and rather arrogant Ballinger now a pathetic ghost of himself. Would he be frightened of
death now? Surely a priest was the only one who could help him?

Would he plead for Rathbone to find some way, any way at all, to
save him from the rope? That would be embarrassing, even repulsive,
and Rathbone would wish for any form of escape from that. He might
even feel nauseated. His throat was tight and his stomach was churning already.

The hansom ride was all too brief. The prison gates opened and
clanged shut behind him. He made all the usual civil remarks, and
followed the prison guard down the narrow corridors to Ballinger's
cell. Did the place smell of human fear and despair, or was it his imagination?

The huge iron key turned in the lock. The door opened with a
faint squeak of hinges, and Rathbone was facing Arthur Ballinger.
The floor was black, draining the light from the room. The white-
washed walls made everything ghostly, giving back a dead reflection
of the air and the glimpse of sky outside.

Behind him the door was shut and locked.

After everything that had happened, what on earth was there to
say? How could they speak as normal? It would be absurd.

"What can I do for you?" Rathbone said simply. To ask Ballinger
how he was would be farcical.

"Appeal, of course," Ballinger replied.

He did not look as crushed as Rathbone had expected. Rathbone
should have been relieved. He would avoid the revulsion of weeping,
begging, the sight of a man robbed of every dignity. And yet looking

at Ballinger's face—his bright, angry eyes—he wondered if it was madness he was seeing. But perhaps insanity was the only refuge left to him. How should he answer?

Ballinger was waiting.

"On what grounds?" Rathbone played for time. Had the verdict really snapped Ballinger's hold on reality? He looked afraid, but not panicky, not wild-eyed, and certainly not confused. "I've reviewed the case—of course I have—but I can see no legal errors, and there is certainly no new evidence."

"I don't care on what grounds," Ballinger answered, coming a step closer to him.

Rathbone was aware of a sense of physical fear. Ballinger was a big man, broad and heavy. He was going to be hanged in two weeks anyhow—what had he to lose? Did he also blame Rathbone for his conviction? Sweat broke out on Rathbone's body, and his stomach knotted. His mind raced.

"Can you tell me something with which to plead for clemency?" he said, surprised how steady his voice sounded. "So far you have claimed that you are not guilty, but if Parfitt attacked you, there might be some way of making his death a matter of self-defense."

"And say I'm guilty?" Ballinger responded angrily. "Haven't you got any bloody sense at all? If I killed Parfitt, then obviously I killed Hattie Benson as well. What excuse do I give for that?"

Rathbone felt the heat burn up his face. Ballinger was right; it had been a stupid suggestion, given without thought.

"I need the verdict reversed, not some pathetic plea for clemency," Ballinger went on. "Prove Rupert Cardew killed Parfitt, because he was blackmailing him and he couldn't pay anymore."

Rathbone was cold. The room could have been walled with ice. The man he saw in front of him was a stranger.

"Did you kill Parfitt?" he asked.

"Of course I did!" Ballinger snapped. "But the verdict was only on balance of probability. You could still make it look like Cardew. Clearly the same person killed the girl as well, so I'd be free of both charges."

Now Rathbone was shivering. It was a nightmare. He must be at home, asleep uncomfortably, and he would wake up. All this would disappear.

Ballinger took another step toward him.

"I can't," Rathbone said grimly, refusing to move backward. "There are no grounds for appeal."

"Then make some, Oliver."

Rathbone said nothing. This was ridiculous. He could understand desperation. He had seen it many times before, even refusal to acknowledge the fact of one's own death. But it was usually an insane hope, not a demand for something of which there was no possibility. And Ballinger had seemed anything but a weak man.

"Don't stand there in self-righteous horror," Ballinger said sharply. "You know nothing about it. Parfitt was filth, a parasite on human depravity."

"I know that," Rathbone replied. "And if I could have mitigated your killing him, I would have. But I will not blame someone else for it."

"You think Rupert Cardew is so worth saving?" Now Ballinger's voice was a snarl, his face ugly with contempt. "He's another kind of parasite—useless, worthless, utterly selfish. Not even an honest passion of vice. Just bled his father dry, then when he was in trouble, turned on his friends."

"His friends being the other men who used those wretched children, and were blackmailed for it?" Rathbone asked.

"Weak, cruel cowards of men," Ballinger said with contempt. "Bored with the ease of their lives and looking for a little danger to sharpen the appetite. I've seen it all before. I didn't create their vice, I merely fed it, and profited—and for a damned good reason."

In spite of his revulsion, Rathbone was curious.

"A good reason?" His voice grated as he said it.

Ballinger's face twisted. "Sometimes your stupidity astounds me! You live in your safe, prudish little world, posturing as if you fight evil, and letting it pass by under your nose because you won't break the rules and risk your own neck. You don't look because you don't want to see—"

Rathbone tried to interrupt, but Ballinger ignored him, his voice harsh. He was sweating in spite of the cold, and his physical presence dominated the room.

"I told you I stopped pollution of the river by that damn factory. How the hell do you think I got Garslake to reverse the judgment on appeal? He's Master of the Rolls, head of the entire civil appeal system, and half his friends own factories like that."

Suddenly Rathbone was horribly afraid. Sickening thoughts swirled in his mind.

"At last . . ." Ballinger breathed out slowly. "How would you influence men like that, Oliver? They have all the money they can imagine, all the power, all the deference, the respect, the glory. You can't bribe them, and they don't need to listen to reason, or mercy. But by God in heaven, they need to listen to the threat of exposure! I have pictures of Lord Justice Garslake that would make your stomach heave. And he'll make the right damn decisions, or I'll ruin him, and he knows it."

Rathbone could think of nothing to say. Words fell over themselves in his mind, and all were inadequate for the understanding and the horror that filled him.

"Think!" Ballinger shouted at him. "Think of a way to appeal, Oliver. Because I have very vivid and explicit photographs, far more than the few you saw in court, of a large number of gentlemen performing acts that are not only obscene, but are with children. Some of these gentlemen are of excellent family, and hold high offices in law and government. One or two are even close to the queen. If something unfortunate should happen to me, such as my death, other than of disease or old age, these photographs will fall into someone else's hands, and you do not know who they are or what they would do with them. You would not like that, because they may not use them as judiciously as I have. They are very, very sharp weapons indeed. So regardless of what you feel about me, you will see to it that I remain alive and in good spirits."

Rathbone was so appalled, he could not speak. He started at Ballinger as if he had risen out of the ground like some hellish apparition, and yet was so horribly, passionately human. It all made sense, the temptation, the logic, the rage, and the success.

"And don't bother to look for them," Ballinger went on. "You will not find them—not in two years, let alone two weeks." He smiled. "The judiciary, in particular, would suffer. So you had better find some way to see that my conviction is overturned, whatever you have to do to bring that about. I don't think I have to explain it for you, but if necessary, I can, and I will. There will be more than just me asking you for rescue, or blaming you, should you fail."

Rathbone had thought the nightmare could get no worse, and now it had doubled, tripled.

"Why did you kill Parfitt?" he asked. It hardly mattered; he was just curious. "Was he growing greedy? Or threatening to bring the whole thing down himself?"

"No, there was nothing wrong with Parfitt," Ballinger said quite casually, almost as if it were by the way, no more than incidental. Then suddenly his voice filled with intense emotion and he stared at Rathbone unblinkingly. "But I have to keep this power. There is so much still to be done, not just about pollution, but slum clearances, child labor . . ." His eyes were brilliant, feverish, watching Rathbone's every flicker of expression. "What can you do, Oliver, with all your brilliant arguments in court? Can you move those men one inch from their comfort and their power?"

Rathbone did not bother to reply—the question was rhetorical. They both knew he could do nothing.

"I can," Ballinger went on. "But I knew that Monk would never let it go. He believed I was behind Jericho Phillips, and he was determined to get me hanged. Parfitt's death, in the same trade, would draw him like a magnet. If he hanged Rupert Cardew for it, wrongly, it would finish him in the police forever."

"God almighty!" Rathbone swore incredulously. "It was to get Monk?"

"No, you fool!" Ballinger snarled with sudden savagery. "It was to save me. Monk is like a rat: he would never let go. I don't intend to spend the rest of my life looking backwards over my shoulder to see what new plan he has to ruin me."

"And poor Hattie was going to testify that she stole Cardew's cravat and gave it to . . . whom? Someone of yours?"

"Tosh Wilkin, if it matters."

"No, not really." Rathbone knew the moment he said it that Tosh would not have the photographs.

"Find a way, Rathbone," Ballinger said between his teeth. "You have too much to lose if you don't."

Rathbone did not move. His limbs felt heavy, his chest as if there were a tight band around it.

"Don't stand there like a damn footman," Ballinger said with a sudden blaze of fury. "You haven't got time to waste!"

Wordlessly Rathbone turned and banged on the door to be released.

HESTER HAD COME HOME from the clinic a little earlier than usual, but Monk was barely through the door when Rathbone arrived at Paradise Place. He looked so ashen, Hester was frightened for him. His hollow eyes and the dragging lines of his face made it clear that he was almost at the end of his strength. She offered him tea immediately, and went to put the kettle on without waiting for his answer. Also without asking him, she put in a stiff dash of brandy.

When she returned with it already poured out in a large kitchen mug, Rathbone was sitting next to the fire in Monk's usual seat, and he was still shivering. Monk sat on a hard-backed chair.

Hester put the tray down on the table between them, with Rathbone's mug nearest to him, and then she looked at Monk. His face was pale too, and the lines in it were more than those of tiredness.

Monk gestured to her chair, opposite Rathbone, and she sat obediently.

"Ballinger has photographs," Monk said simply. "They're with somebody who'll make them public if Ballinger is hanged. We don't know who's in them, but what they're doing is obvious. Ballinger said they're all kinds of people: in government, judiciary, business, even the royal household. He blackmails them, not for money but for power, to bring about the reforms he believes are just. At least that's what he told Rathbone. Any of that might be true, or might be lies, but we can't afford to take the risk."

"He wants me to mount an appeal." Rathbone looked at her. "That's the condition for his silence. But I can't. There are no grounds."

For a moment Hester was stunned. It was monstrous. Then the more she thought of it, the more it made sense. It might all be true. It would be a passionate and almost understandable reason for all he had done. She could see the temptation. If she had had such power to use in the reform of nursing, she would have played with the idea, and please God, discarded it, but perhaps not? But, then, it could also be a brilliant way of defending himself, because they could not afford to ignore him.

"I'm surprised he trusted someone else with the pictures. How do you know they are all together, with one person?" Hester asked.

Rathbone stared at her, horror in his face.

"I'm sorry," she said quietly. "But I wouldn't give everything to one person, would you?"

"Oh, God!" he said in utter wretchedness. There was no hope in his voice.

"You are certain that Ballinger killed Parfitt? It was not one of Parfitt's other victims who did it?" Monk asked.

"Oh, yes. He told me as much." A painfully bitter smile touched Rathbone's lips. "Actually, he did it to ruin you, get you off his trail forever. He meant you to go after Rupert Cardew, and then he would have proved him innocent, at the last moment, carried Lord Cardew's everlasting gratitude, and seen you off the force with your reputation shattered. Nothing you said about him after that would have been listened to. Even evidence would have been disregarded."

Monk looked startled.

"He knew you suspected his part in Phillips's boat and it would be only a matter of time before you came after him," Rathbone went on. "With your care for Scuff, you wouldn't have let it go."

Hester looked across at Monk and felt a sense of warmth fill her, as if even in this ghastly situation she still wanted to smile, still trusted in a goodness, an inner beauty that would survive.

"I'm sorry," Monk said with a little shake of his head. "What can we do? If we could think of any way of appealing, would you?"

"I don't know," Rathbone admitted. "But there isn't. There's no new evidence, and no legal grounds. I suppose the only thing I can think of is to find the photographs and destroy them. But I have no idea where to look. Who would he trust with such things? There can't be so many people."

"Are we sure he was telling the truth?" Monk looked from one to the other of them.

Rathbone pushed his hand through his hair. "I believe him. He still wants to go on forcing through the reforms he cares about. But I can't think of any way of proving it, and can we afford to take the risk?"

Hester spoke slowly, weighing her words, uncertain of her own feelings. "Even if we could find these photographs and destroy them, and we were certain they were the only ones, do we want to? It is a sin and a crime to abuse children in such a way. Why do we want to protect men who are doing such things? I'm not sure that I do. And I'm not sure that I want to have that kind of power over people in anyone's hands, even my own. How do you decide what to use it for, when to stop, how many people's lives you can destroy along with the guilty?" She shook her head minutely, her shoulders rigid, aching, with the muscles knotted. "No one—"

"I see! I see," Rathbone said sharply, his voice raw-edged. He pushed his hand through his hair again. "I should have seen it. But whatever he could do, I still don't have grounds for an appeal."

"Then, we have to look for the photographs," Monk replied. "At least it will tell us who is vulnerable, even if we have no guarantee that they are the only copies."

"God, what a nightmare!" Rathbone said softly. He seemed about to add something more, and then changed his mind.

"We'll need help," Hester said practically. "We can't possibly do it all by ourselves. We don't even know where to look, or how to make the right people listen to us."

Rathbone raised his hand. "Who else could we trust?"

"The people at the clinic," she replied, thinking as she answered. "Squeaky Robinson, perhaps Claudine?"

"What on earth could she do?" Rathbone said incredulously.

"Make inquiries in society," Hester replied. "I don't mix with the sort of people who would be worth blackmailing for power, and you can hardly ask."

Rathbone blushed very faintly, and she knew he was thinking that at any other time they would have asked Margaret to help, but now it was impossible. But Hester would not say so, or even that he himself would hardly be wishing to move in his usual social circle. He had not even considered how life would be after his father-in-law was hanged. There would be no waking up from this nightmare.

"And Crow," Monk added. "I'll ask Orme. His knowledge of the river is better than mine."

"I'll ask Rupert Cardew," Hester said, looking at Monk, then at Rathbone. She expected them to argue, and she had her rebuttal ready.

"He could be putting his life at risk, after what he's already done," Monk warned her.

"I know. And I'll remind him of it. But I have to ask. It's a long path back from where he was, and I believe he means to take it."

"If he stays in London, he's ruined," Rathbone said grimly. "Doesn't he understand that? He'll never be forgiven for what will be seen as betraying his own."

"He knows," she assured him, remembering Rupert's ashen face when she had asked him to testify. "He's ruined anywhere in England. I expect he'll go to Australia, or somewhere like that. Start again."

"What hell for his father," Rathbone murmured. "Poor man."

"Better he go having made amends than stay here as he was." Hester shook her head a little. "He hasn't left himself such a lot of choices. This is the bravest thing, the cleanest. But he can do this one thing more before he leaves. He may be the only one who knows some of the people Ballinger knew. And Ballinger probably gave the pictures to someone who was in them himself. It would be the best way to make sure he obeyed."

Monk swore under his breath, but he did not argue. He stood up. "Then we'd better start. Where's Scuff?"

She was horrified. "You're not taking him?"

He raised his eyebrows. "Of course I am. You think he'd be better off staying here alone? You think he would stay? At least if he's with me, I'll know where he is."

She let out her breath slowly. He was right, but it was not good enough, not safe enough. But, then, probably it never would be. Life wasn't safe.

THEY WORKED FOR SIX days, starting before dawn and stopping only late at night. Monk and Orme went up and down the river. Rathbone went through every social acquaintance and business connection of Ballinger's that he could trace. Claudine listened to society gossip and asked inquisitive and even intrusive questions. Squeaky Robinson put out inquiries among all the brothel-keepers, prostitutes, and petty criminals that he knew. Crow sought all the dubious medical sources, procurers, and abortionists. Rupert Cardew risked his safety, and even his life, asking questions. Once he was beaten, and was lucky to escape with no more than severe bruising and a cracked rib.

Every lead fizzled out, and they were left with no more than fears and guesses as to who had the photographs, or even if they were real.

Rathbone decided to try one more time to plead with Arthur Ballinger, for the sake of his family, if nothing else, to tell them where the photographs were, and allow them to be destroyed.

He would go in the morning. At midnight he stood in the drawing room of his silent house and stared out through the French windows into the autumn garden. The smell of rain and damp earth was sweet, but he was barely aware of it. The wind had parted the clouds, and the soft moonlight bathed the air, making the sky milky pale, the black branches of trees elaborate lace against it.

The room was not cold, but he was chilled inside.

There was nothing else left but to go back to Ballinger, and he must do it in the morning.

He finally closed the curtains and went upstairs, creeping soundlessly, as if he were in a strange house and did not wish to disturb the owners. He changed into his nightclothes in the dressing room and walked barefoot to the bedroom. The lights were out. He could not hear Margaret move, or even breathe. It was a curiously sharp feeling of isolation, because he knew she was there.

H E WOKE AT SIX and rose immediately, washing, shaving, and dressing silently, and going downstairs in a house still chilly from the night. The maid had lit the fires, but they had not burned up sufficiently to warm the air.

The maid boiled the kettle for him and made a cup of tea and two slices of toast. He had to force himself to eat it, standing at the kitchen table, making the girl uncomfortable. The master had no business alone and miserable in her territory. It was not the way houses were supposed to be run.

He thanked her and left, catching a hansom a block away from the house, and finding himself all too quickly outside the cold gray walls of the prison. It was only twenty minutes before eight, and the sky was so overcast it seemed still shadowed by the retreating night.

As the lawyer of a condemned man he was admitted immediately.

"Mornin', sir," the jailer said cheerfully. He was a large, square-shouldered man with a ready smile and a gap between his front teeth. "Don't often get folks 'ere this time o' the day. Mr. Ballinger, is it? Not long for 'im now. Best it's over, I say. Longest three weeks in the world."

Rathbone did not argue. The man could not know Ballinger was Rathbone's father-in-law, or anything of the bitter and complicated relationship between them. Rathbone followed obediently along the stone corridors. He could hear no voices, no footfalls, because he walked carefully. Yet the silence seemed restless, as if there were always something just beyond his hearing. It was cold, and the air smelled stale. No one had let wind or light inside to disturb the centuries of despair that had settled here.

This was no place for a man to end his days. Remembering Mickey Parfitt did not help. Rathbone forced himself to think of the children, like Scuff, small, thin, humiliated, and forever afraid. Then he found he could straighten his shoulders and accept the necessity of the situation. Nothing on earth could make him like it.

The jailer stopped at the cell door, and the sudden jangle of his keys was the first loud noise. He poked one into the lock, turned it, and pushed the door. It swung open inward, with a slight squeak of hinges.

"There y'are, sir," he invited.

Rathbone took a deep breath. This was loathsome. He would not have wished to walk into Ballinger's bedroom and find him in his nightshirt, half-asleep, expecting privacy, even at the best of times. This was a loss of dignity that was degrading to both of them.

He stepped in. The light was faint from the single small, barred window high in the opposite wall. It was a moment before he realized that what looked like a heap of bedclothes on the floor was Arthur Ballinger's body.

Without even knowing he did it, he let out a cry and stumbled forward onto his knees, grabbing for the flung-out hand. His fingers closed over the flesh, feeling the bones. It was cold.

"Sweet Jesus!" the jailer said from behind him, his voice shaking. He held the lantern up, whether it was for Rathbone to see, or himself, was unclear.

The light showed Ballinger in his prison nightshirt, sprawled awkwardly, one leg bent. The back of his head was matted with blood, but from his staring eyes and protruding tongue, it was hideously clear that he had been strangled to death. The bruise marks from hands were darkening on his throat.

" 'Ere," the jailer said. "Yer'd better get up, sir. In't nothing we can do fer 'im. Best get out of 'ere an' tell the chief warden. 'E in't gonna like this."

Rathbone was frozen; his legs would not obey him.

" 'Ere," the jailer repeated, suddenly his voice gentle. "Up yer get, sir. Come on, sir, this way."

Rathbone felt the man haul at him, taking his weight, and he rose to his feet, trembling.

"How could this happen?" he asked, still staring at Ballinger.

"I dunno, sir. There'll 'ave ter be an inquiry. In't fer us ter say. We'd better get out of 'ere an' tell someone. Yer didn't touch nothin', did yer?"

"His . . . his hand. It's cold," Rathbone stammered.

"Yeah. Must a bin done last night. Come on, sir. We gotta get out of 'ere."

Rathbone allowed himself to be led away, stumbling a little, hardly aware of passing through the corridors, crossing a hallway, and being ushered into a warm office. The chair he was put in was soft, and someone brought him a cup of tea. It was hot and too strong, but he was glad of it. He heard footsteps outside, hurrying, anxious voices, but he could catch no words, and for a moment he hardly cared.

How had this happened? Ballinger was due to be hanged in less than a week. Why would anyone kill him? And how? A jailer had to have helped, colluded. Someone had paid, perhaps a great deal. Surely that was proof that the photographs were real, and all that Ballinger had said of them was true? What fearful irony that all his care to keep his power had actually ended in his own death. Were his secrets dead with him, or simply waiting to be laid bare, one by one? Most likely they would only be guessed at when a trust was betrayed, an inexplicable judgment made, a suicide, a law passed against all expectations.

How was he going to tell Margaret? How much? He winced as he thought how she would blame him for this too. If he had gained an acquittal, Ballinger would have been at home with his family, safe, and with all the power still in his hands.

Or perhaps he would have been murdered anyway, just not here?

And if there had been no danger of an appeal, would he have been left to hang?

No. If he'd been hanged, then someone had had the instructions to make it all public. He must have been killed by someone who intended either to destroy all the pictures or to use them himself. God, what an unimaginable horror!

It was worse even than Rathbone had expected. When he told her, she stood in the center of the morning room, her face sheet-white, swaying a little on her feet.

Afraid she was going to faint, he took a step toward her. She backed away sharply, almost as if she feared he was going to strike her.

"Margaret!" he said hoarsely.

"No!" She shook her head and put her hands up to ward him off. "No. You're lying."

"I'm sorry—," he began.

"Sorry! You're not sorry. You made this happen," she accused. "If you hadn't put your career before your family—"

"I couldn't defend him." He was burning with a sense of the injustice of her charge. "He was guilty, Margaret. He killed Mickey Parfitt."

"Parfitt was vermin," she retorted. "He should have been killed."

"And Hattie Benson?"

"She was a prostitute, a whore who was going to lie to protect Rupert Cardew."

"Protect him from what? He didn't kill Parfitt. And you've just said Parfitt needed killing. You can't have it both ways."

The tears were running down her cheeks, and she was gasping for breath. "My father's been murdered, and you're standing there justifying yourself! You're disgusting. I used to love you so much, because I thought you were brave and loyal and you fought for the truth. Now I see you're just ambitious. You don't even know what love is!"

He felt as if he had been slapped so hard that his flesh was bruised. He stood without moving as she turned away and walked to the door. When she was in the hall she looked back at him. "I'm going home to look after my mother. She will need me. I will send for my belongings." With a rustle of silk and the sound of her footsteps on the floor, she was gone.

Rathbone could not measure how grieved he was or how deep the wound, or how, and if ever, it would heal.

THE OVERCAST WAS SO heavy that it was dusk before five in the afternoon. Monk came home to find a fire, bright and warm in the parlor, and Hester and Scuff sitting beside it. There was a pot of tea on the table between them, and they were eating hot crumpets with butter. Scuff had crumbs on his chest. He was sitting in Monk's chair and looked a little guilty when Monk opened the door, but he did not move. He was waiting to see what would happen, maybe how much he belonged here.

Hester stood up and walked over to Monk. She kissed him on the cheek, gently, then on the mouth. He slid his arms around her and held her until she pulled back.

"I know," she said softly. "Crow came and told us. Someone murdered Ballinger in his cell."

Monk looked past her at Scuff. The boy was watching him, waiting, the crumpet held in his hand, dripping butter onto his clothes. His eyes were wide.

"It isn't the way I would have chosen," Monk replied. "But maybe that's an end of it. It's hideous for Rathbone, and for Margaret, but there was never anything we could have done to change that."

Scuff was still watching Monk.

Monk smiled at him. "No more river trade on those boats," he said.

"What about them pictures yer was lookin' fer?" Scuff asked.

"I don't know. Maybe they're destroyed, maybe not. But they're only pictures. If the people in them get blackmailed, we'll worry about that if we ever get to know. Finish your crumpet before it's cold."

Scuff grinned and took a big bite of it, scattering crumbs onto the floor, and onto Monk's chair.

"Next time the chair's mine," Monk said with a nod.

Scuff hitched himself a little farther back against the cushions and continued smiling.

Codicil to the last will and testament of Arthur Hall Ballinger.

To my son-in-law Oliver Rathbone I leave all my photographic equipment: cameras, tripods, lighting, and such photographic plates and negatives as have already been exposed.

They are to be found in my bank, in my private safety deposit.

I trust there is some heaven or hell from which I may observe what he does with them.

Arthur Hall Ballinger

ABOUT THE AUTHOR

ANNE PERRY is the bestselling author of two acclaimed series set in Victorian England: the Charlotte and Thomas Pitt novels, most recently *Treason at Lisson Grove* and *Buckingham Palace Gardens,* and the William Monk novels, including *Acceptable Loss* and *Execution Dock.* She is also the author of the World War I novels *No Graves As Yet, Shoulder the Sky, Angels in the Gloom, At Some Disputed Barricade,* and *We Shall Not Sleep,* as well as ten Christmas novels, most recently *A Christmas Odyssey.* Her standalone novel *The Sheen on the Silk,* set in the Byzantine Empire, was a *New York Times* bestseller. Anne Perry lives in Scotland.

www.anneperry.net

ABOUT THE TYPE

This book was set in Goudy, a typeface designed by Frederic William Goudy (1865–1947). Goudy began his career as a bookkeeper, but devoted the rest of his life to the pursuit of "recognized quality" in a printing type.

Goudy was produced in 1914 and was an instant bestseller for the foundry. It has generous curves and smooth, even color. It is regarded as one of Goudy's finest achievements.